FOR MY WONDERFUL, LOVING, AND SUPPORTIVE MOTHER,
ANN MARIE BROWN. I LOVE YOU INFINITY AND MORE THAN THAT.

HODDER CHILDREN'S BOOKS

First published in Great Britain in 2022 by Hodder & Stoughton

1 3 5 7 9 10 8 6 4 2

Text copyright © Erik J. Brown, 2022
Cover illustration © Luke Martin, 2022

The moral right of the author has been asserted.

A CIP catalogue record for this book
is available from the British Library.

ISBN 978 1 444 96878 1 (WTS exclusive)
ISBN 978 1 444 96016 7 (trade paperback)

Typeset in Dante MT Regular by
Palimpsest Book Production Ltd, Falkirk, Stirlingshire
Printed and bound in Great Britain by Clays Ltd, Elcograf S.p.A.

The paper and board used in this book
are made from wood from responsible sources.

Hodder Children's Books
An imprint of
Hachette Children's Group
Part of Hodder & Stoughton Limited
Carmelite House
50 Victoria Embankment
London EC4Y 0DZ

An Hachette UK Company
www.hachette.co.uk

www.hachettechildrens.co.uk

ANDREW

I hope the afterlife has a little movie theatre where you can sit in silence and watch the sequence of events that led to the watershed moments of your life. Take me, for instance: a tasteful long shot of the patient-zero bird that first got the bug – set to a Philip Glass score, something foreboding and moody – and then it jumps over the pandemic and all the stuff with my family and friends dying and focuses on some survivalist nutcase out in the woods setting a bear trap eleven months ago.

Time lapse of the trap, bears walking past, a thick branch falling on it and somehow not setting it off, leaves covering it.

And then while I'm sitting there, munching on afterlife Sour Patch Kids and butter-flavoured popcorn, thinking to myself *where the hell is this going?*, my dumb ass saunters on-screen and I step in the bear trap.

Oh, that's right.

I remember I spent almost three hours screaming and crying, trying to figure out how to open the trap. Finally I ended up tying down the metal catches with T-shirts from my pack, and used the branch the universe

1

foreshadowed – the one that kept the trap from cutting my leg clean off – to pry the rusted jaws open.

Now I'm just hopping around the forest with a yellow T-shirt tied over my wounded leg. At least watching this in the afterlife I'll have the tongue-burning delights of Sour Patch Kids.

Unlike now, where all I have to eat in my pack is the canned food I grabbed in Jersey before I had the silly idea to get off the main roads.

I shift my weight on the crutch beneath my armpit, wincing. It's actually just a big tree branch I found. Last night I wrapped a sweater around the Y-shaped fork to pad it, but it's not working and now it feels like my armpit is just a massive bruise.

The pain in my leg is worse. Every step I take with my good leg creates a pull in the bad one that shoots fire up my calf. I tried resting last night after I found the crutch branch, shivering while my leg went numb with damp cold. I nodded off a few times, half expecting to die like that, but when the sun came up this morning, my eyes still opened.

Now here I am, hobbling through the woods with absolutely no idea where the closest road is. I just hope that if I keep walking straight it will lead me to *something*. A road, a town, a stream to clean my wounds. Anything before infection sets in. And of course now I'm on the lookout for more bear traps, so that slows me down, too.

Because of the low cloud cover I have no idea what time it is when I stumble upon not a road but a cabin. It's cute. Modest. From what I can tell from the outside, it's maybe two bedrooms. There's a small front porch with two chairs under a wide picture window. The shades are drawn and leaves litter the front gravel drive and pile against the stairs.

No car in the driveway. Maybe it's empty. Abandoned – the owner dead in their condo in some city or in a mass grave.

Or shot dead on the side of the road by another survivor.

I take a few tentative steps out of the woods on to the gravel.

It doesn't look like anyone has been here in a while. A small, chunky garden gnome sits at the bottom of the steps, a fluffy sheep in her lap. She sits on a toadstool, smiling at the drive as if she's waiting for someone.

Kinda creepy.

Especially since the leaves aren't covering her. Like she just shook them off herself.

But I don't think too much about that – garden gnomes that come alive when you aren't looking are the least of my troubles. There are four steps up to the front porch. Maybe I can just hop up them, see if the door is unlocked.

Of course it won't be – that would be too perfect. A nice little cabin open and free for the taking? Maybe even something to eat. I let my mind have a short food fantasy moment, as a treat, then crunch across the gravel to the steps.

JAMISON

The house is too quiet. I should have put on some music, something to distract me from the absolute silence. But now I can't be bothered to stop and put a record on.

Seventeen. That's how many cans of black beans I have left. I write it down on the yellow legal pad on my knee, crossing out the number nineteen from last week. I do this every Monday morning: count the food I have and watch the numbers slowly dwindle. It was maddening at first, but now it's almost meditative.

Eight cans of corn. I cross out the number nine on the sheet and write the new number to the right of it. There are maybe two more weeks before I run out of space and need to start a new sheet. And this time it will all be in my handwriting, not my mom's.

Pasta sauce. It's written in her barely decipherable scrawl. And then her perfect numbers – zeros slashed and sevens with a line through the middle so there's no misunderstanding – before her writing stops and mine takes over.

I don't need to count the jars of pasta sauce because I didn't make any pasta last week, so I leave the number eleven there and continue on down.

UNITED STATES
EAST COAST

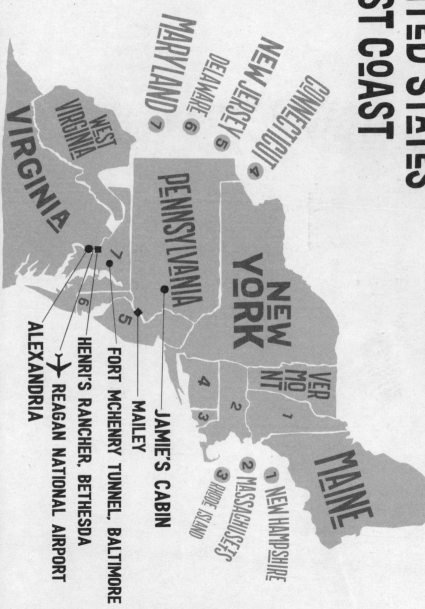

CONNECTICUT ❹

NEW JERSEY ❺

DELAWARE ❻

MARYLAND ❼

WEST VIRGINIA

VIRGINIA

PENNSYLVANIA

NEW YORK

VERMONT

MAINE

❶ NEW HAMPSHIRE
❷ MASSACHUSETTS
❸ RHODE ISLAND

7 — JAMIE'S CABIN

— MAILEY

5 — FORT McHENRY TUNNEL, BALTIMORE

6 — HENRI'S RANCHER, BETHESDA

✈ REAGAN NATIONAL AIRPORT

ALEXANDRIA

ERIK J. BROWN

Hodder
Children's
Books

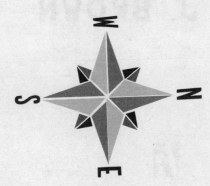

KEY WEST

FLORIDA

GEORGIA

SOUTH CAROLINA

NORTH CAROLINA

YULEE
JACKSONVILLE

DARIEN

FORT CAROLINE

HARDEEVILLE

COOSAWHATCHIE

RALEIGH

JUPITER
DELRAY BEACH

ISLAMORADA

KEY LARGO

HOMESTEAD

N

S

W

E

But something stops me. A sound outside, like leaves crunching.

I jump up and look out the kitchen window. The world outside is grey and cold, while the wood-burning stove behind me keeps the kitchen nice and warm. The back deck is covered in leaves, but there aren't any animals or people to be seen. The trees are still bare, the spring buds not ready to come back from the harsh winter just yet.

'You're hearing things again,' I tell the silence of the kitchen. I talk to myself a lot now. It used to make me think I was going insane, but now it might be the only thing *keeping me* from going insane.

Last week I swore I heard someone walking across the gravel drive out front, but by the time I psyched myself up to look, no one was there.

Just the thought of the crunching gravel creates the sound in my mind, this time unmistakably coming from the front of the house. But it's not real – I'm making it up again. Or it's an animal, but it's way too much rustling to be a squirrel or a fox.

Usually all it takes is a quick reminder that, yes, I am alone and there's no one out here before the sound goes away, but this time it doesn't. It sounds strange, though. There's no one-two pattern of footsteps; instead it's a lopsided crunch of gravel and a short, quiet click.

Then the first step on the front porch creaks.

My heart leaps and sweat gathers at the nape of my neck. I hold my breath and my body burns with fear, but I can't move. There's a grunt and a thump from outside. The second step.

It's definitely a person out there.

Finally, I break free of my paralysis, running for the living room. I have no idea when the last time I even went out the front door was; probably a few weeks back. Before I heard the noises the last time.

Outside, there's another thump as whoever is there loudly reaches the third step. The rifle leans up against the wall by the front coat closet. I grab it and put my back to the wall across from the front door. The rifle might not even be loaded, but I don't have the time to check. It *should* be. I haven't used it, after all.

The front door.

Shit.

I have no clue if it's locked, or if it would matter. Maybe that loud thumping is a battering ram or something.

This isn't made up. It's not me jumping at shadows and silence.

The doorknob turns. It's not locked.

There's someone out there, and now they're coming in here.

The door swings open and I take aim.

ANDREW

He has the gun on me before I even realise he's there. I'm not unobservant; I'm just distracted by the throbbing pain in my leg. But once I'm looking down the barrel of some kind of rifle, everything goes numb.

'Wait,' I say, throwing up my arms. I put all my weight on my good leg and drop the makeshift crutch.

The boy in front of me must be around my age. Maybe sixteen, seventeen. He has that look, though. I saw it happening to me when people I knew started dying – with every glance in the mirror it got worse. I was young, but I began to look haggard. Tired. Beaten down. He has that same broken stare.

That's how I know he won't hesitate to shoot me.

'Wait,' I say again. 'I just came here looking for supplies. I didn't know anyone was here.'

'Well, I am,' he says. He isn't looking me in the eye; instead he's focused on my chest, aiming the rifle at my heart.

This is becoming a theme for me, and I'm not a fan. I flash back to the last time I had a gun pointed at me, on the side of the road in New Jersey. To the rash, senseless violence that could have been easily avoided.

My stomach lurches. I don't want things to go bad like that again.

'I'm sorry,' I say. 'I can leave.'

But I'm not so sure I can. I've been hobbling through the woods for the past day and a half looking for some shelter and a way to clean my wounds. Finding some medical supplies, a pantry full of food and Tom Holland wouldn't hurt either.

Instead, here we are. And not a Tom Holland in sight.

'Then turn – slowly,' is all he says.

I try to bend over, reaching for the crutch, but he lets out a warning that sounds like 'eh,' then adds, 'Leave it.'

'I need it to walk,' I tell him. 'I'm hurt.'

He glances down at my bad leg, looking at the torn denim for some time. His gaze drifts up, finally meeting my eyes.

He has nice eyes. Dark blue. Clear but frightening. Like he's prepared to pull that trigger if he has to. I know the feeling.

'Turn as best you can,' he says. 'I'll pick it up and throw it to you when you're out there.'

I want more than anything to let out a frustrated sigh, to tell him he's a jerk-off.

But the jerk-off's got a gun, so I don't. The world has ended, but jerk-offs still have a leg up.

Ha. Leg up.

Christ, even after the apocalypse I can't resist a pun.

I turn my foot like I'm doing some fucked-up version of the hokey-pokey. You put your right foot in, you put your right foot out, you put your right foot in and get a bullet to the chest.

I finally have my back to him when it hits me – he could have been lying all along. Maybe he doesn't want to look me in the eye when he shoots me.

'Please,' I say, glancing back. 'I need help. I can't make it much further out there. Please just help me and then I'll leave. I need to clean this wound and wrap it with a bandage that isn't a shitty Walmart T-shirt before it gets infected.'

'I don't have any supplies.' His voice breaks as he speaks. Is that his tell? Is he lying?

'Bullshit. You're telling me you're out here, alone, with no first aid supplies?'

'I am. Now step forward.'

'How?'

'Hop.'

'Christ.' I let out the annoyed sigh I've been holding in. Finally, I put my back against his wall and slowly, carefully, slide down.

'What are you doing?' he asks. I use my hands to brace myself as I scoot down the wall, being careful to keep my right leg up until my butt hits the floor. Then I lower it slowly.

'Shoot me if you want,' I say. The pain's excruciating, and at this stage of the game, what the hell's the point any more? I survived the bug when better people didn't. Better people like my little sister.

Now all that's left is people like me. I focus again on the gun pointed at my chest, and the boy who's holding it.

People like *us*, I guess.

'But remember,' I say. 'If you do, you're the one who has to carry me out of here.'

'Get up.' He points the gun right in my face.

Good. Then it'll be over quickly.

'I'd make a *Dreamgirls* reference and tell you I'm not going, but this doesn't seem like the right audience for that.' His silence and confused look prove my point. I let out a joyless laugh. 'Just do it, dude.'

The idea of a quick death is actually starting to sound appealing. It lets me off the hook. No more guilt. Who knows what comes next – maybe a movie theatre that will show me all the watershed moments in *this* guy's life that led to him shooting me – but even if what comes next is just darkness, it's better than the pain. Better than being aware of how truly fucked everything is.

Still he doesn't pull the trigger. I watch his face change from anger to fear.

He isn't going to do it.

'Get up.' But his voice is wavering.

Wait. What's that feeling in my gut? Is that . . . hope? Maybe I was wrong before about his eyes. They were frightened, not frightening.

'I. Need. Help.' All confrontation and fight have left him. I can see he doesn't want to shoot me just as much as I don't want him to. He'll help me if I can convince him. 'I'm alone,' I say. 'I have been for over five months. Please.'

He's lowering the gun now.

'Please,' I beg him. 'My name's Andrew. I'm not infected and my last family member died five months ago. My sister. She was twelve years old. You're the first person I've talked to since.'

The last part is a lie, but I don't want to think about the Fosters. I look away from him as my eyes burn with tears.

'Dammit,' he says under his breath. He sets the gun against the back of the sofa and holds out a hand to me. 'Come on.'

I take his hand and he helps me stand. My muscles tense; I take a breath so as not to cry out. As we pass the cabin door he slams it shut with his foot.

My mystery boy is strong and manages to do most of the work himself. We make our way over to a dining room off the living area. There's a large wooden table with six chairs around it.

With his free hand, he flicks the switch by the doorway and the chandelier hanging above the table lights up.

He has electricity?

'Hop up,' he says, turning me around. I do as he says and push myself back on to the table. 'I'll be right back, wait here.'

'Oh, OK, because I was thinking of making myself a sandwich.' He looks back at me on his way out of the dining room, as though he doesn't realise I'm joking. I open my mouth to apologise, but he speaks first.

'Sucks for you, I'm all out of bread.' As he leaves I swear I can see a smirk pulling at his cheeks.

Excuse me, new kid, having a post-apocalyptic sense of humour is *my* thing. But his joke manages to put me a little more at ease.

I throw my coat to the floor and look around at the cabin for the first time. A gun to the face, I've learned, tends to shut down one's attention to detail. The fireplace is cold and empty. I would expect to see animal heads on the wall, a mounted big-mouth bass, a crocheted rug under the couch in the living room. Instead, the living room rug is white shag and the sofa is an oversized and expensive-looking grey leather number. There are two other leather chairs in the living area, and mounted above the fireplace is a sixty-inch TV covered in dust.

The dining room has no china cabinet or sideboard. Instead there are framed pictures on the walls, scattered in a way that makes it seem like whoever did it spent a lot of effort making it look effortless.

I look closer at the picture of a child and his mother at the beach. They're both white, but the mother's tan hints that they've been in the sun for a while. Lucky. Any time I tried to tan I just burned. It looks like the son is similar, as his skin is still fair and there's an unabsorbed glob of sunscreen on his shoulder.

The mother has brown hair. She's wearing red sunglasses and a white-and-navy striped bathing suit, and is holding a sun hat on her head, the brim pushed up by the wind.

The boy is no more than seven; his smile is wide and gapped with missing baby teeth. Freckles dust his nose and cheeks. He's closing one of his eyes against the glare of the sun; the other is bright blue.

I recognise this boy, only ten years older.

The now-older boy enters the dining room with a small plastic box in his hands. He sets it down on the dining room table and looks over at the picture he caught me examining.

'Is that your mom?' I ask him.

He frowns and doesn't answer.

'Sorry,' I say. 'I'm nosy. I'll shut up.'

He pulls the lid off the white container and sets it on one of the chairs as he digs through medical supplies. My eyes go wide.

He doesn't just have gauze and alcohol and antibacterial ointment. He has a small jar of burn gel, individually wrapped sterile syringes, cotton balls, peroxide, a few sterile scalpels, and instruments that I recognise from medical dramas that used to run on repeat before the bug.

Shit, maybe Tom Holland *is* here!

He unties the brown – formerly yellow – T-shirt from around my leg, then reaches down to the cuff of my jeans. He tries to pull it up, but the blood and damp weather have made the denim shrink and the jeans go no further. I breathe in deeply as pain shoots up my leg.

'Don't think jeans were a good choice today,' he tells me.

'This happened yesterday.'

'Take them off.'

'Shouldn't you buy me dinner first?' I ask. I don't realise I'm going to say the joke until it's already out. My face warms, but my embarrassment is short-lived as he finally lets his smirk grow into a smile.

I unbuckle my belt and pull my pants down to my knees, taking my left leg out first. He helps me with the right leg as we both pull at opposite sides so the denim doesn't rub against my wound.

'Jesus!' His eyes go wide at what's left of my calf. It's the first time I've seen it without the jeans obstructing the view, and my stomach churns. He leaves the room, running to the kitchen, but I can't pull my eyes away from my leg. My chest tightens and my arms and legs tingle with fear.

Things are worse than I thought.

It looks like raw meat. The back of my leg from just below my knee to the cuts from the trap is swollen and a beautiful shade of horrific purple. My left leg is dirty but about half the size of the right one.

The boy comes back with a small glass vial and a bottle of pills in one hand. In the other is a small leather-bound notebook, the pages of which are well-worn and yellowed. He sets the vial and pill bottle down on the table along with the book. I pick up the vial; it's cold and filled with a clear liquid. The word *bupivacaine* is printed on the label. Whatever that means.

'Where did you get this?' I ask him, reaching for the bottle of pills.

The *-illin* suffix on the label tells me it's antibiotics. Even post-apocalypse, those SAT prep courses weren't such a waste after all.

He unwraps a sterile syringe and sticks it into the vial, filling the plastic tube and setting it on the table before getting up and heading back to the kitchen. 'You aren't allergic to penicillin or any antibiotics, are you?' he calls out. I hear the sound of water pouring into a glass.

'I don't think so. How do I know?' I ask.

He returns and hands me the glass and two pills. 'I

14

guess take it and find out.'

'This won't kill me, will it?'

'If you're allergic, yeah, probably.'

Great bedside manner, dude.

His eyes drift down to my leg. 'But you said this happened yesterday, so if you don't take them, the infection will definitely kill you. And it'll be worse.'

He's probably right. If it's infected already and I do nothing, I'm dead. Do I have a choice? Yeah, I guess I just risk it, but . . . that hasn't worked out so far. And amputation without anaesthesia – well, I hope even I don't deserve that. I swallow the pills and drink all the water.

He picks up the syringe filled with the liquid from the vial he brought out.

'What's that do?' I ask, still nervous. Why am I taking pills and medicine from a strange boy in the woods?

'You'll see.' Before I can stop him, he sticks it in my leg and I howl out in pain. He pulls it out and sticks it in again, further down.

'What are you doing?' I scream.

'Just a little more.' He sticks me several more times, holding down my leg just above my knee while he does so. Tears are streaming down my face and I can hear my heart throbbing in my ears. I curse and scream until he finally stops.

He returns to the kitchen with the vial and used syringe. The burning in my leg begins to subside, but the memory still aches. The shriek of a tea-kettle comes from the kitchen and I glance to the doorway, my vision blurred by my tears.

He soon emerges with a large ceramic bowl, moving

slowly and setting it down on the table.

'You have a stove, too?' I ask him.

'I'll show you later. How does your leg feel now?'

Numb. The leg pain is almost gone. My brain has gone back to focusing on the pain in my armpit from leaning on the crutch.

'Fine,' I say.

'I wouldn't say "fine",' he says, pulling a chair out and sitting down. He pulls the medical container over. 'But at least you won't have to bite a stick to deal with the pain while I stitch you up.'

He sets a few needles and black thread on the table and takes out the bottle of rubbing alcohol. He dips a washcloth in the hot water, wringing it out with one hand at a time, then sets it down on the table and waits in silence.

'Still hot,' he says, looking up at me.

'Who are you? Some kind of kid doctor?'

He smiles his sad smile; it's nothing like the grin he has in the pictures hanging on the wall. 'Sorry.' He holds out his hand, red from the hot water. 'I'm Jamison.'

'Andrew. Nice to meet you.' We shake. His hands are warm and I'm jealous – it feels like I won't ever be able to shake the cold from my bones. When he lets go, he pours alcohol into a cupped hand and then rubs them together.

Jamison picks up the hot towel and begins to clean the area around my wound. I flinch, expecting pain. But there is none.

Watching him clean my wounds, I'm immediately thankful that Jamison, Kid MD, gave me some kind of local anaesthetic. The white washcloth turns red-brown, but as he cleans the wounds, things don't look so scary. Gross, but not scary.

'So what happened?' he asks. 'A dog attack you?'

'No.' I shake my head and let out a groan. 'It was a damn bear trap.'

Jamison shoots a look up at me as he continues cleaning. 'You're kidding.'

'I'm not.'

His smirk returns. 'It's the apocalypse and you decide to make enemies with Wile E. Coyote.'

'Seriously.' I let out a sigh. 'I had no idea people even used those things any more. I'm sure it was set up before the bug but, honestly, who sets a damn bear trap?'

'How did it not cut your leg off?' he asks, looking at the gashes.

'Dumb luck?' I tell him. 'It didn't snap all the way shut.' I still don't understand how the branch landed between the jaws of the trap and didn't set it off. I barely even stepped on the trigger myself.

Jamison threads the needle. He douses it with alcohol and puts the needle to one of the wounds in my leg. 'Any feeling coming back yet?' he asks.

I shake my head and he slides the needle into my skin. I tense up at the sight but feel no pain.

'It's gonna be a pretty rough stitch job since the needle's flat,' he says, not looking away. 'But it should help you heal faster.'

I watch as he pulls the thread tight on the first puncture. 'Seriously, how do you know how to do this? Were you pre-med or something before the bug?' Maybe he's older and just looks young?

17

'No,' he says. 'My mom taught me how to sew buttons on my shirts or fix a seam that busted. Same principle, right?'

I look back at the pictures on the wall. Out of the corner of my eye, I see Jamison glance up at me, follow my gaze to the picture, then look back down at my leg. I don't press the matter further.

'Why'd you decide not to shoot me?' I finally ask after he's sewn up three of the six wounds in my leg. How is he so good when none of the rest of us survivors are?

He lets out a sigh. 'I guess because . . . I don't know.' He shakes his head. 'Probably because I'm too stupid to realise when I need to look out for myself.'

'If that makes you stupid, it means I'm a hundred and fifty per cent dipshit.'

'I figured out that part when you said you stepped in a damn bear trap.'

I laugh, and it feels like it's the first time in months. Maybe it is.

He ties off the final stitch and wipes away the blood. Then he throws the wet towel back in the bowl of bloody water and holds out his hand to me.

'Think you can walk? You can take a shower if you want.'

I stare at him. 'Shower?'

'Yeah. W— I have well water.'

I caught that almost-'we'. So he's alone. 'Running water *and* electricity?'

'And a hot water heater that runs on that electricity.'

My stomach does a flip with excitement. This place

sounds amazing. I let myself think, just for a second, whether I could take it from him. After he didn't shoot me, after he helped me, could I take this place? But that second is enough to make me feel sick.

'You OK?' Jamison asks.

'Yeah. And yes, I would love to shower.' Only the shower, then I'm gone.

I straighten my leg out in front of me and set the heel on the floor. The pain increases a touch, but it's bearable.

I put a little more weight down. A little more pain.

A little more weight . . . and . . . not a little more pain. That's good, right?

I put the rest of my weight down and make the second biggest mistake of my life.

JAMISON

As soon as Andrew screams, it's like time means nothing again. When he burst in, I flinched and almost shot him right there. But I couldn't. My finger wouldn't move. It was right on the trigger but it was like my hand was numb. Even when he told me he wasn't leaving and I'd have to kill him, I couldn't. Just like the deer I could never shoot when my mom tried to show me how to hunt. Like the animal traps that sit in the garage, unused. And it's like the purple face of my mother. The burst blood vessels in her horrified eyes and the raspy breath. The sick and the smell and . . .

Andrew is screaming in agony on the floor. Maybe I did something wrong. He could be allergic to the antibiotics or the local anaesthetic and he's having a cardiac episode . . . or whatever happens when people are allergic to those things. That's not in my mom's notebook.

Oh God. I just killed someone.

Or it could be a trick. He could be faking it, calling out to whoever is outside waiting for him. Waiting to take this place from us.

No, from me.

Because I'm all that's left.

But this doesn't sound like a trick. He sounds like he's in pure agony. I drop down to the floor next to him.

'What hurts?' I shout over him. 'Can you tell me what's wrong?'

Tears stream down his red face. He's pulled his leg up, holding it by his thigh. There's no more blood on his wounds but . . . oh no. I move around his leg and put my hands on his knee. He flinches and grabs one of my wrists, managing to grunt out, 'No, don't!'

'OK, OK.' I put my hands up. 'But let's try to get you on the couch. Just hold your leg out straight and don't let it hit anything.'

He does as I say and I slip my arms under his to lift him up. The smell of dirt, sweat and body odour stab at my nostrils. I manage to carry him to the couch in the living room, and he lowers his right leg carefully, letting out several quick breaths.

'You OK?' I ask, but it sounds stupid. Of course he's not.

He opens his eyes and gives a fake smile. 'Stunning.' Though he still looks like he's in pain, he's making jokes again. That's gotta be good.

I dart back to the dining room to grab my mom's notebook. The pages look like nonsense because my mind won't quiet itself. I can't do this. It's all way too much.

'What is that?' Andrew's voice snaps me from my thoughts.

'A book.'

He sounds fascinated. 'Oh! We don't have these . . . what do you call them? Boops? Up north.'

I give him a frown because there's no way I'm letting

him have a smile off that awful joke.

'Right,' he says. 'I'm the one with the busted leg. 'K, I'll shut up now.'

'It's a notebook. My mom was a doctor and this is the notebook she started writing after everything . . . When things got bad.'

'She wrote it for you,' he says. His eyes are focused on me and they look sad. Because he knows that she wrote it thinking she wouldn't survive the superflu. Which she was right about.

'Yes.' I bring my attention back to the book. 'When it got bad in the city, when the hospital became overwhelmed and the shipments of medicine stopped and they realised no one was surviving the flu, she started grabbing supplies. Everyone did . . . the doctors, nurses, custodial staff. And it wasn't long before . . .'

I trail off because he knows what happened. The refrigerated trucks for the bodies, the mass unmarked graves that couldn't be dug or filled fast enough. And no one in power doing anything to help or stop it. They just kept trying to force everyone to go about life as usual. To get back to the idea of normal.

It was as if no one learned anything from the other viruses that came before. Spanish flu, Hong Kong flu, Ebola, HIV and AIDS, swine flu, and more recently Covid. All the diseases the news used to compare this virus to when *nothing* was like this. They thought civilisation would be fine because it was before. The world gave us warnings but they went unheeded. At the cost of everything.

Here, we didn't even try a mandatory quarantine like

the Netherlands or a lockdown like in France and Spain. Everyone was full-on Live Free or Die in America. And so they did.

I decide to change the subject. 'I think your leg might be broken. But . . .'

'But what?'

I broke my arm when I was ten. It was bent at a weird angle and his leg doesn't look like that. Swollen, yes. Bruised, absolutely. But I didn't notice any bumps that would indicate the bone snapped. Though he did step in a bear trap. I flip to the front of the book, where my mother wrote the acronym RICE: rest, ice, compression, elevation. Rest, ice and elevation he could do. But the ACE bandages are out in the shed with some other supplies, so compression might have to wait.

'The sun's going down. You OK to stay put until tomorrow?'

No, Jamie, shut up! He can't stay here; he's a stranger who could kill me and take everything.

Andrew's face lights up. 'On this comfy couch? Hell yeah.' Then his smile drops. 'Why are you helping me, Jamison?'

Do no harm. It was my mother's catch-all for 'be nice to people'. And now I can picture her giving me that Jamison-what-did-I-tell-you? look. I'm helping him because it's the right thing to do. Although the world's different now. The *right* thing to do might change from person to person. Andrew's right thing might be to kill me while my back is turned.

'I guess I just hope you'd do the same for me.'

His eyes drop away from mine, so maybe he wouldn't.

23

Then something comes to me.

'Oh! Hold on.'

Andrew jumps, his attention returning to me, but I'm already out of the room, heading down the hall towards the linen closet. I move the sheets so I can see the safe I hid on the back of the top shelf – where even my five-foot-eight mother couldn't reach it – and enter the code. The first thing I see when the door swings open is the dark outline of the handgun that makes me so nervous. I push it aside and take out the large orange pill bottle.

Back in the living room, I shake out two pills and hold them out to Andrew.

'What are these?' he asks, taking them from me and holding them in his palm.

'Painkillers. The good ones.'

Andrew looks back to the hallway. 'Why weren't they with your other supplies?'

Because my mom tore the house apart looking for them when the vomiting started. She knew what was coming. It's usually the fever that kills, but everything before that is pure agony.

My mom was trying to avoid all that pain, so she told me what we would do if we got sick. Take as many of the painkillers as we could stomach and drift off to sleep. But I kept thinking what would happen if we were different from the other victims of the superflu; immune or just lucky. They were saying a virus this deadly could mutate to become less lethal as infection went on.

I didn't want her to give up, and I didn't want to be alone. So I hid them. In the tank of the toilet, first. It was a sick kind of irony that she was throwing up so close to them for so long, all the way up until she couldn't get out of bed. Then I put them in the safe.

I tell Andrew a lie, because he doesn't need to know everything that happened before he came here. 'My mom kept them there. Probably doctor training or something. I'll get you some water and ice for your leg.'

I head into the kitchen – cutting through the dining room and picking up the empty glass I gave him – but he calls out, 'It's OK, Jamison! I can dry swallow them.'

Great, so he can choke to death on the horse pills and I'll have to carry another dead body out to the firepit. The thought threatens to rain sadness on whatever brightness Andrew's presence brings. Having him here is giving me something to do other than count my food and worry about hunting.

When I get to the living room the pills are gone, but I still hand him the glass and a towel and a two-gallon-size ziplock bag of ice. He looks at the water, then places it on the coffee table. I tell him to wrap the bag in the towel and lay his leg on top. He winces as he does so, but doesn't howl in pain.

'I should probably make some dinner. You're supposed to take those with food. I'll get you some sweats to put on, too.'

'Jamison, wait.'

I turn back and he is leaning up on his elbows. He motions his head towards the door.

'Can you grab my pack for me?'

I pick up the backpack and bring it over to him, letting

him search through it. He pulls out some dirty clothes and sets them in his lap, along with a pack of Band-Aids, a dirty toothbrush, toothpaste, a small Nalgene of water and a lighter.

'Here we go.' He takes out three cans one by one and hands them over to me. Garbanzo beans, olives and vegetable soup.

'No, this is your food, you keep it.'

'You help me, I help you. And since I don't have medical training, this is what you get. Oh . . . and these.'

He reaches back in and I realise that must be where his gun is. My heart leaps into my throat, but my hands are full. He handed over the cans to distract me so I couldn't fight back.

Instead he pulls out three books and holds them out to me. I set the cans on the back of the couch and look at the books. The first cover is worn and has an old cruise ship on the front. It's called *The Voyage Out* and it's by Virginia Woolf. I've heard of her but not the book.

The next book in the stack is *The Shining* by Stephen King. This one I've heard of. Saw the movie, never read the book. And finally there's a worn, spiral-bound road atlas.

'Food and stories,' I say.

'Isn't that all you need?'

I finish making dinner – just a soup with canned vegetables – and bring it out to him. We sit in silence as we eat. As *I* eat. Andrew hasn't taken a bite yet. He locks eyes with me.

26

'Hot,' he says, blowing on the bowl.

'Sorry.'

'Don't be,' he says. 'This will be the first hot meal I've had in a while.' But he's looking at the soup like it's a bowl full of spiders. 'How is everything still working?'

I swallow a mouthful of soup. 'You mean the electric?'

'I meant the water park down the street – it's winter, what the eff, guys?' I'm starting to think Andrew will never not make a joke. 'But yes, that, too. You said it's well water, but aren't hot water heaters natural gas?'

'There's no gas lines out here. Everything's electric. We used to come out for holidays. A bad thunderstorm in the summer could knock out the power for days. A snowstorm in the winter might do the same. Driving three hours here a few times only to discover we didn't have power was enough to give my mom a personal vendetta against nature.'

Andrew laughs and blows on a spoonful of soup.

'So she spent a shitload to change the roof tiles to solar, and there's a battery backup that stores excess power.'

The last time we drove out here, I started wondering if my mom had sensed all this coming. Like she had some intuition that the world would eventually be wiped out by a plague and we'd have to survive out here on our own. That's why she taught me how to hunt. Or *tried* to teach me how to hunt.

Before the superflu, coming out here felt like another home, an annexe of what we had in Philly. Coming out here this final time felt different, as if, because we were leaving our home in Philly for ever, it severed the connection to this place. And now this place is just that. A place. It feels wrong.

'Three hours?' Andrew says, and eats a spoonful of soup. 'Where was that from?'

'Philadelphia. Where were you from?'

'Connecticut.'

'You walked all the way down here from Connecticut?'

He nods and looks back at the soup as if he isn't sure he wants to eat any more. But then he does and says, 'Winter was really bad up there. So the first nice day in January, I left.'

'You said you were alone for five months.' It's March.

'I did, you are correct.' There's something in his voice that makes it sound as if there's more to the story, but I let him leave it there.

We finish dinner in silence. He still looks uncomfortable, so I ask how his leg is as I take the bowl from him. He looks at it, bites his lip, then looks up at me.

'I'm going to be honest with you, Jamison. I . . .' He pauses and reaches under the cushions of the sofa.

Shit. Did he hide a gun while I was in the kitchen?

He holds out two pills. '. . . didn't take the pills you gave me.'

'You . . . Why not?'

'Because I thought you were trying to kill me?'

I glance down at the bowls in my hands. 'Is that why you wouldn't eat the soup at first?'

He scrunches up his face like a kid who just got caught in a lie. 'Kinda, yeah.'

I can't help but smile. I almost laugh. Almost. Apparently, we both think the other is trying to kill us at all times.

'You do remember that time, about two hours ago, when I held a gun on you, right? I could have killed you then.' Even though that's a lie. He doesn't know I couldn't do it. Or that as long as I've had that gun on the other side of the room, I've never been able to pull the trigger when it's facing a living creature. Paper targets are fine, but anything with a heartbeat . . . 'I promise not to kill you if you promise not to kill me,' I offer.

Andrew picks up the glass of water. 'Best deal I've made all apocalypse.' Then he downs the pills. I smile and head into the kitchen to clean the dishes.

When I get back to the living room, the sun has gone down. I light two candles and set them out on the side tables next to the couch and chair.

Andrew's barely awake. When I ask if he's OK, he gives me a grunt. Maybe the pain meds were a good idea. He'll be knocked out long enough for me to sleep without worrying about him getting up to murder me. I think he's being honest, but I can't be complacent. Who knows if his promises are worth anything.

Andrew's soft snores fill the silence. I call out to him quietly but he's fully passed out now. I reach for the Virginia Woolf book and am flipping through it when something falls out on to my lap.

It's a thin piece of paper ripped from what looks like a handwritten address book. It reads: *Marc and Diane Foster. 4322 Leiper Street, Alexandria, VA, 22314.* Their phone number's listed as well, but that isn't much use now.

I watch Andrew sleep, wondering why he would have something from an address book. My mother had one, but she never even used it. Most people used their phones to store that info.

I put the piece of paper on the table, closer to him, so he'll see it when he wakes. I open the book one more time and begin to read.

ANDREW

When I wake, sun is flooding the living room. There's a fire roaring in the fireplace. I stretch out on the couch and a burst of pain from my leg makes me gasp.

There's a blanket on me.

Jamison gave me a blanket while I was passed out. My face warms, but I notice he isn't in the living room with me.

I sit up and something on the coffee table catches my eye. The address I've been carrying around for weeks is there, next to my books. It must have fallen out when I was going through my bag. I grab it and stuff it quickly into the pockets of the sweatpants Jamison gave me last night.

'Jamison?' I call out.

'You can call me Jamie.'

I startle at his disembodied voice and wince again at the pain in my leg. I sit up a little more and see him sitting on the floor near the front door. There's a new, bigger tub of what looks like medical supplies that was absolutely not here last night. Jamie is tying a large piece of foam rubber to the top of the branch I had been using as a crutch.

Seriously, where is he getting this shit? Is there a Joann Fabrics in his backyard? You know what? I'm not even going to ask. He's got electricity, water and a fridge – *of course* he has foam rubber, too. He probably got it from his neighbour, Tom Holland. At least his padding is better than a T-shirt. I want to make a drag queen joke about padding but I know it will go over his head.

All my good material is wasted on this kid.

'Why are you *lurking* behind the couch?'

He stops tying and turns his attention to me. 'Oh, I'm sorry. You were saying you enjoyed having hard wood dig into your armpit?'

Does he not hear himself? Are straight boys immune to innuendo?

Like I said. Good material. Wasted.

'Looks great. As you were.'

Jamie goes back to the foam and I can't help but smile as I watch him work. The muscles in my cheeks ache at being used so often for the first time in months.

Wake up, smile: the apocalypse has provided a cute boy to nurse us back to health.

Jamie has a look about him that just doesn't match his personality. He's big, both tall and wide. I watch his hands as they move; they're large but somehow delicate. He doesn't look up at me once while he works, so I stare at him freely. Even with his face turned down, I can see his handsome features.

He shouldn't be helping me. He's like so many guys I've known from school who picked on people like me.

But that isn't him. There isn't that defensiveness about him that there was with other guys our age. The ones who worry that if they get too close they might catch the gay. One guy told me that once and I looked him up and down, pointed at myself and said, 'You couldn't catch this gay if you had tickets to *Hamilton*.'

He kneed me in the balls and pushed me into the mud. But then I got the satisfaction of telling everyone his knees touched gay balls – through two layers of clothes, and everyone knows the gay spreads even *faster* through natural fabrics.

'OK,' Jamie finally says, shaking me from my thoughts. He stands and leans the crutch against the wall. 'So, about your leg.'

'We should just cut it off, right?'

He gives a lopsided grin and takes the notebook his mother wrote for him and flips through it. 'We could try something less drastic first?'

Jamie holds out the open book and I take it. There's a horrible drawing of a person with a bent arm – Jamison's mom was *not* an artist – and the acronym RICE next to it. Rest, ice, compression, elevation.

I gasp. '*Rest*, Jamie? Seems a little extreme, doesn't it?' But it sounds amazing. Rest. I feel like I haven't rested since . . .

Jamie nods. 'You're right, I'll go get the hacksaw.'

I give him a polite chuckle and start flipping through the notebook. At the front are several journal entries from early last June. That was when everyone kept saying, 'It's just a summer flu! People die from the flu all the time!' Apparently, Jamison's mom knew something was up. At the end of one entry on June 29, underlined in her barely legible handwriting, it says: *107 dead in one day!*

I assume that's just at her hospital. Because by August they weren't able to keep up with the number of dead. By the time the internet went down, there were estimates that almost 178 million people were dead in the US alone. Over half the country. Less than seven months from the first reports of mass bird deaths in Croatia, Nepal and Guyana in mid-May to the bug wiping out any semblance of civilisation in November.

Who knew it would take longer to gestate a tiny human than to destroy the world?

I flip through further, the entries getting increasingly worse before they end abruptly in August. After that it's just medical texts and notes addressed to Jamie. There's a table of calculations for medicine, giving the correct dosage per pound; diagrams of splints for arms, legs, fingers and toes. I come to a stop in the last quarter of the book. Brown speckles litter the pages and some of the handwriting is smeared with it.

Blood.

Jamison's mom was still writing when the bug got her. I flip a few more pages and the blood spatters get larger. The handwriting gets more difficult to read. Then the pages go abruptly blank.

'This is pretty incredible,' I say, flipping back to a less morbid page – small diagrams of an appendectomy? Christ, Dr Jamison's mom had a lot of faith in her boy, didn't she?

'I wish my parents were doctors. My dad didn't leave *any* "accounting for the end of the world" books behind and all my mother left me was a sense of humour.'

I try to smile, to show off that sense of humour, as I hand the book back to Jamie.

'I think your leg might be broken, which would make sense, it being caught in a bear trap and everything. But we can't exactly be sure without an X-ray, which my mom did not take from the hospital.'

'Very short-sighted on her part, if I may say.'

Jamie holds a hand out to me. 'Here, we should do this on the floor.'

I bite back another innuendo – See? Wasted – and let him help me off the couch. This time his hands are cold and mine are warm.

He helps me over to the floor, where, less than twenty-four hours ago, I sat down and decided to let him shoot me. Insert Paul-Rudd-Look-at-Us GIF.

Oh man, I hope Paul Rudd survived the bug.

There's a pile of clean clothes and a large bowl of soapy water on the floor next to a small pile of bandages. At my look, Jamie blushes.

'Right, so since you didn't get to shower last night, I thought you might want to wash up before we wrap your leg. Also, that's probably how you'll need to clean yourself for the next few weeks until you can put weight on it.'

I groan. 'That's right, you have a hot water heater.' The idea of a shower sounds delightful right now.

He motions to the bowl. 'I guess this is the next best thing? Anyway, I'll wait outside for you. Just call out when you're finished.'

After he leaves me – taking the tub of supplies back out to the shed with him – I take way too long to undress, and by the time I do, the soapy water is cool. I work quickly, scrubbing away at my skin until the water is cloudy and I smell less like an apocalyptic dumpster. Then I pull on the clothes Jamie set out and call him.

He returns and takes my dirty clothes and the bowl into the kitchen. When he gets back he crouches next to me and asks me to lift my leg up. I do as he says and he pulls the leg of the sweatpants up to my knee.

'OK, you can lower it again.' His eyes are on the stitch job he did last night. My leg is still swollen. He places a gentle hand on my knee and warmth explodes across my body. My cheeks burn and I swallow hard.

He's the first person who's touched me in . . . I have no idea how long. The bug ruined hugging and all touching in general. This feels so . . . not weird but . . . wrong. And also right.

'Are you OK?' he asks.

Absolutely not. 'Yeah.'

'I'm going to touch your leg, but I promise I won't press down. Just tell me if anything hurts.'

'Uh-huh.'

He puts his hands on either side of my leg and my body heats up. His hands move down from my knee to my shin, slowly, his fingers gliding over the hairs of my legs – which are very clearly standing on end. He raises his hands away when he gets near the stitches and my skin feels like it's trying to reach back out for him. Begging for that touch again. I almost gasp when his fingertips return.

My hands tremble and I clench my fists in an attempt to hide it.

I glance at Jamie, his full attention on my leg. Thank God. At least he doesn't notice my reaction.

He makes a 'hmmph' sound.

'What?' I ask.

'Most of the swelling is at your calf, not your shin.' He takes his hand away and grabs the notebook. I shiver as my body immediately cools and I wish he was touching me again.

'What does that mean?' I ask.

He finds whatever page he's looking for in the book. 'Your . . . fibula might be broken.' I give him a confused look. 'The thinner bone next to the big one that makes up your shin.' He spins the notebook, where there's a very clearly traced skeleton form with the major bones labelled in Jamie's mom's handwriting.

'What does that mean for me?'

'It hopefully won't need to be reset, because if it does . . .' He stops and shakes his head. 'Let's just worry about that later. For now, rest, ice, compression.'

Shit. A broken bone and no hospitals to help.

'How long does it take a bone to heal?' I don't want to know the answer. I've never had a broken bone in my life. When I was four, my thirteen-year-old next-door neighbour accidentally hit me in the chin with a baseball bat, and even that didn't break anything. I do have a gnarly scar on the underside of my chin, though.

And don't think I haven't heard all the jokes about taking it to the face! I actually haven't, and it's disappointing. Like, it's *right* there, everyone.

Jamie shrugs and says, 'I broke my arm when I was ten . . .'

Ah, I knew he was one of those kids. I try not to smile as I picture the kid from the beach photo in the dining room jumping fences and climbing trees like he's invincible.

'It took me a little over two months to heal. Maybe six weeks or so for you.'

'Six weeks?'

'It could be less?' he offers. 'But, then again, it could be more.'

'Dammit.' I sit back. But what's this other feeling? Is that relief? It means six more weeks to delay the inevitable. I squeeze the piece of paper in my pocket. Six more weeks to pretend I'm someone else. 'What's today's date?'

He consults another page of his book, the one a silk ribbon attached to the spine is tucked into. 'March . . . twenty-third.'

I do the math in my head. Six weeks would bring me to the beginning of May. Even mid-May might be safe. My deadline – the last day I know I'll find the Fosters still in Alexandria – is June 10.

But then I can't avoid highways. I have to get back on the roads again, the *main* roads. No more wandering through small towns and woods. I mean, the plus side of that is no more bear traps.

Yay.

And then there's the risk of running into other people again.

'What's wrong?' Jamie asks, shaking me from my thoughts. I look up at him, and his face is kind and concerned.

38

It makes my stomach flip and my chest ache. This kid had been out here by himself for months before I broke in. And now he's helping me. He's a better person than I am. Somehow the apocalypse hasn't changed him like it did me. And everyone else out there, for that matter.

How did he escape unscathed? Maybe it's this place. And if that's true, I don't even deserve six weeks of respite. Six weeks is too long. No more delays. I have to get better and get going. Alexandria awaits.

'Nothing,' I say. But already there's a sinkhole in my gut that I know will become a pit when I have to say goodbye to Jamie.

JAMISON

Once Andrew's leg is freshly wrapped, I help him up on to his good leg and hold the crutch out to him. 'I'll try to find you a real crutch when I go into town on a supply run. But for now, this will help you get around a bit.'

'Fabulous. I'm thrilled to be serving you Tiny Tim realness.' He says it with what sounds like a hint of frustration, and my eyebrows jump up.

'I'm sorry,' he says. 'It's great. I mean, I really appreciate you helping me.'

It hasn't even been a full day, but having him here gives me something to do. Something to distract me from the silence and the memories and the fear.

It also doesn't hurt to have someone to talk to.

Just by being here, Andrew helps me in a way I didn't think I needed.

'Come on,' I say. 'Let's get some breakfast going.'

I help him to the kitchen and sit him down at one of the tall bistro chairs in the corner. He sits on the edge and his leg sticks out towards the stove, which is still hot from the logs I threw on earlier this morning.

Andrew picks up one of the old newspapers I use as kindling to start the fire. He won't find much in there.

It's from early August, before my mom and I came out here, and it's filled with shortened obits and rumours about the NIH creating a possible vaccine.

Andrew gives the paper a long look, humming. 'Yes, I'll have the scrambled eggs topped with cheese and Heinz ketchup, turkey bacon and a side of wholewheat toast with the house-made almond butter. And a glass of orange juice, please.'

Smiling, he hands the newspaper back to me. I hide my own smile and throw the newspaper back on the pile.

'Canned baked beans and a Pop-Tart it is.'

'You have Pop-Tarts?'

I open a cabinet and pull down one of the boxes I nabbed from a store in town several months back.

'Skip the beans, I'll eat the whole box.' He holds out his hands, grasping for it like a toddler.

'You need to up your protein intake to help you heal.'

'It's a little hard to find good protein sources in the apocalypse, Jamie.'

I open the freezer and show him the stores of meat from the fall.

'What is that?' Andrew asks me.

'Deer.' I take one of the small packages and move it to the fridge. I'll make a chilli with it tonight for dinner.

'You can hunt?'

'My mom taught me.' Technically it's not a lie because she did teach me. There's enough meat left to sustain us for a little over eight weeks. Any longer than that and I'll *have* to go hunting. The idea gives me anxiety deep in my gut. But if it's between starving to death and killing an animal, I'll kill the animal. I wasn't a vegetarian before the apocalypse, so it shouldn't be a problem now.

That's a lie; ending a life yourself is different from buying a pound of meat wrapped in plastic from Whole Foods. Perhaps on another supply run I'll find a restaurant with solar panels that powers a walk-in freezer stocked with meat for years.

Yeah, we're gonna starve to death.

The anxiety in my stomach constricts like a snake. Maybe I could show Andrew how to hunt when he gets better. Tell him what to do and he can be the one to pull that trigger.

I throw some beans in a pot on the stove and place a pack of Pop-Tarts on the counter. It's gone quiet and I don't like the silence that much, so I make small talk while I stir.

'You left Connecticut, and where were you going?' I remember the address in Alexandria that fell out of his book. Out of the corner of my eye I see him bristle slightly.

'You haven't heard?' he asks.

Heard? 'I got here in late August, so if it happened after that, then no?'

'You know about the Netherlands' and the UK's quarantine, right?'

I nod. Full-on, closed-borders, violators-shot-on-sight quarantine. Italy picked up after – using their experience with Covid to try to get ahead of the superflu – and Germany followed suit.

'Apparently it worked. Their numbers dropped off and

word is they're sending help. I figured I'd head south and see if help actually comes.'

'Who did you hear this from?'

He's silent for a moment. 'Just some people on the road. And there's graffiti everywhere. It says "DCA-6/10".'

'What's that mean?'

'I didn't know at first, but apparently it's the airport code for Reagan National Airport outside DC. And 6/10 is June tenth, the date the new EU is supposed to arrive.'

So Alexandria must be a stop along the way, or just a random bookmark and it means nothing.

'If it's the EU coming, wouldn't it mean October sixth?'

He sighs loudly behind me. 'It's *Americans* spraying the graffiti, Jamie.'

I turn to look at him, trying to figure out if this is all a joke. 'You really think someone's coming?'

He shrugs, and when he finally speaks again he sounds defensive. 'Better than doing nothing. It's the end of the world, do *you* have another place to be?'

'Is that why you decided to walk through the wilderness and get caught in a bear trap?' I meant it as a joke but it still sounds like I'm scolding him.

For a moment he looks like he's about to yell at me. But when he speaks, his voice is even, calm. 'I got off the main road because there *is* nothing better out there. *Nothing* has gotten better. You've been here for how long? You don't know what it's like out there.'

'I'm sorry, that's not what I meant.'

'People out there aren't like you, and maybe I tried to get off the road so I didn't have to keep . . .' He lets out a frustrated sigh and looks away. 'Can we change the subject?'

'Yeah. Sorry.' I stir the beans. 'Do you want any more pain meds?'

He doesn't answer at first, then says, 'Yes.' As I leave the kitchen he adds quietly, 'Please.'

I don't know what happened to him to make him leave the road, but whatever it was, he doesn't seem to want to talk about it, so I'll leave it at that. It's none of my business. He's stuck here till he heals, and then he's gone, back on the road. Then I can come up with other ways to distract myself from the memories and nightmares.

I return to the kitchen and pass the pills to Andrew – adding in two antibiotics – and hand him a glass of water. He downs them and remains quiet while I continue to reheat the beans. Out of the corner of my eye I see the wood piled in the bucket next to the stove is low. Only three more split logs left.

The silence in the room is awkward, and this is the perfect excuse to leave.

'I have to get some more wood.' As soon as I say it, I expect him to make a dirty joke.

But all he says is, 'OK.'

I'd be lying if I said I wasn't a little disappointed.

When I step outside on to the small deck off the dining room, the air is thick with fog. The deck shines with dampness, which means the wood will be damp, too. I'm glad I came out for it now; this way it has some time to dry off in the house.

I make my way across the wet grass to the shed. The

wood is still piled high and in two rows along the entire length of the eleven-foot-long shed. I undo one of the bungee cords that keeps the blue tarp across the wood. We didn't chop trees down for it; this was all a mistake purchase from over a year ago. The winter before the superflu, my mom ordered four cords of wood, not realising a cord was 128 cubic feet of wood. It used to surround the entire shed, but now I'm down to this final couple of rows.

I pull up part of the tarp to grab a few split logs. When I reach down to grab the bungee cord from the grass to re-secure the tarp, I stop.

There, in the grass next to the bungee cord, are four cigarette butts. I swallow hard and look up at the trees surrounding our yard. The fog is still and lifeless. I listen, trying to ignore the thump of blood in my ears, trying to hear a twig snap or shuffling feet or even the rough exhale of smoky breath. But there's nothing. No birds – all of them probably dead from the superflu – no insects, no people.

My gaze drops back to the cigarette butts. Whoever left them must be long gone, but they were here long enough to smoke four. And they knew enough to hide behind the shed.

Maybe they saw me through the kitchen window and decided to leave. My chest tightens.

Maybe Andrew was lying and he wasn't alone after all.

I gather the wood and head for the back door again, watching for movement from the trees or the side of the house. My senses are on high alert. I push the sliding glass door open with the back of my hand and use my back to slide it shut behind me.

Andrew is perched on his good leg, stirring the beans, his other leg out to the side and just barely resting on the ground. He turns and gives me an arched eyebrow.

'I thought you'd gotten lost in the fog and I'd have to eat this whole box of Pop-Tarts by myself.'

His joking eases a bit of the tension in my chest. If he were with someone, I would think he'd be more worried about them and less making jokes about Pop-Tarts. And they wouldn't let him go into a strange house by himself while he was injured.

'Poor you,' I say, dropping the wood into the metal pail by the stove. 'You can sit back down. I'll take over from here.'

He hops, carefully, back to his seat. The beans are bubbling, so I put two Pop-Tarts in the toaster and continue to stir, thinking about the cigarette butts out in the yard.

And the fact that someone might have been watching this house.

ANDREW

After our brunch of Pop-Tarts and beans – I know, ew – Jamie takes our plates and begins washing them, making me feel useless.

'Can I help?' I ask, desperate for him to give me something to do. Even if I can't, I'm damn sure going to try.

'No, I told you to go lie down and prop your foot up,' he says, looking over at me as he scrubs. 'If you break your other leg, I'm gonna be pissed.'

'Stop making everything about you, Jamie!' I shout. 'I'm the victim here.' It's a risky joke considering he may not get my humour yet.

Thankfully his smile tells me he understands. 'I'm the one who'll have to listen to your girly screams of pain. *I'm* the victim.'

'It's not OK to call it girly any more. That implies girls are weak.'

'My single mother raised me alone for sixteen years. Then, when the world was burning down around us, she taught me how to administer your medication, dress your wounds and wrap your leg. *Then*, for a good thirty pages of the notebook she wrote all this in, she was sick and

47

dying. And not once did she make the sounds you made yesterday.' His smile is forced now.

We all lost people, so I know how he feels. I want to give him a hug more than anything in the world. I want to run across the room and pull him against me and squeeze him and thank him. I want to thank his mother for everything she did to prepare Jamie for this life. I want to tell him about my family as well and share our pain.

I'm probably silent for too long because he speaks next. 'Sorry. It sounded a lot less dark in my head.'

'No, I want to know more about her, actually.'

'My mom?' He sounds surprised.

'She sounds like she was a smart lady. Plus, maybe you can share some of her survival tips with me. I'm not doing too well myself.' I want to know more about the woman who made this kind, sweet boy and hi, wow, these pills work fast.

'Maybe when you can actually walk.' He dries off his hands and comes to help me up and into the living room to lie on the couch.

'How long until I wear out my welcome here, do you think?' I ask.

'If I had to guess, I'd say twelve hours ago.' He shoots me a smirk and I narrow my eyes at him, trying to hold in my own smile. 'I'm not gonna kick you out while you're hopping around on a tree branch. What kind of monster do you think I am?'

He isn't a monster. He proved that much when he didn't shoot me. That moment alone was enough to prove he isn't like the others I've met. Isn't like me. But he went beyond that. He's still helping me.

'Thanks, Jamie.' I don't know how else to say it. There's more to be said, but my brain isn't functioning. I'm too happy. And stoned. Because again – thank you, Jamie's mom – she got the good stuff.

'You don't have to thank me. Anyone would do it.'

That's not true. He knows that, though, and he's trying to play it off like he doesn't. Like he's not the only one to help me since the world went dark and the bug killed everyone we've ever loved.

He throws more wood on the fire, then heads back into the kitchen to finish cleaning, and I shut my eyes for a bit.

My belly is full – ish – I'm warm in front of the fire, the pills are creating a nice swimmyness in my head, and while the throb of my leg hasn't gone away, at least now I don't care about it. I smile, and for the first time in a very long time I'm thankful to be alive. Thankful I'm not alone.

I open my eyes as Jamie comes in. There's still the goofy smile on my face.

'You good?' he asks. He's smiling, too.

'I'm good.' I nod.

He looks like he's trying not to laugh as he sits down across from me in the chair. It's his chair. All the chairs in this house are his chair, but that one is *his* chair. I have my couch and he has his chair.

Oh my God, change the subject.

'What the hell were you doing every day before I

49

showed up?' I ask him, imagining him sitting in *his* chair, alone.

He thinks for a moment. 'Um, hunting? I spent a lot of time looking over my mom's notebook.'

'Always be prepared. Such a Boy Scout.' Are my words slurring?

'And that's about it.'

'That can't be it. You described, like . . . an hour of stuff. Nine a.m., wake up, shoot Bambi, gut Bambi, freeze Bambi, take a dump, knit a sweater, read notebook; ten a.m., twiddle thumbs.'

His smile widens, showing off his teeth. They're nice and straight and I want to ask if he had braces as a kid. I imagine he did. Dark blue ones, to match his eyes.

He smacks his forehead and says, 'I forgot about my nine forty-five knitting time.'

'Seriously. You've been hanging out here, all alone, doing nothing but hunting deer? What about in the winter when it was too cold to go outside?'

He pauses, pursing his lips. 'Exactly how stoned are you?'

'I'm floating in orbit with the International Space Station, don't change the subject.' I pause, *changing the subject* and letting my eyes go wide. 'Do you think they're still up there? Alone in space and they can't get back here? No idea what happened to their families?'

Their families. My mind always comes back to the families spread out across the world, not knowing who is still alive and who died. Or how they died. All the warmth and comfort I was feeling is gone because I'm focused on my leg again. The only thing keeping me from moving on from this place and letting another family know who died.

And how.

Jamie's thick eyebrows go up. 'I hadn't even thought about them before this moment, honestly. But yeah, I guess they are.'

'Shit.'

'They have to know at least a little of what's going on. Maybe they got them back before NASA's people called in sick.'

'Maybe.' I can't stop thinking about it now. What about the people in subs underwater that don't come up for months at a time? What about the people in an Antarctic research facility? I remember reading about a protected island off the coast of India that was home to the most isolated community in the world. What about them? Do any of them even know what happened?

'Wait, here's something I would do.' Jamie stands and walks over to a console under the window looking out to the front porch. I sit up on my elbows and watch him as he opens the centre cabinets and lifts the plastic top of a record player. I notice for the first time the speakers on the top of the console.

'Vinyl, very Brooklyn hipster of you. Wait, what's the Brooklyn of Philly?'

His shoulders go up and he spins, his nostrils flaring. 'How dare you!'

I laugh because even Jamie's attempts at being offended come off as playful. He smiles and returns to thumbing through records. 'Do you have a preference?'

'What's your favourite?'

He takes out a record. Without showing me, he puts it on the turntable, starts it up and places the needle on to the spinning vinyl. His large, delicate hands move slowly and with great care. Like he's disarming a bomb that could explode at any moment.

He places the record sleeve on top of the console, then goes back to his chair. The silence before the music sounds messy, crackling and popping. Like it's been played often. The deep voice of a woman arrives first, then the sound of a bass, piano and harmonica kick in.

I lie on the couch, listening to the words and music. It's slow and soothing. I look over at Jamie. He has his eyes closed, his lips moving softly.

I smile as I watch him mouth the words. He doesn't open his eyes until the singer lets out the final long note. When he does, he turns red and smiles, looking quickly away from me. The next song opens with bass and harmonica and is a little faster.

'Sorry, she was my mom's favourite so I grew up listening to her.'

'Who is it?' I ask.

'Nina Simone. I love her voice. She was supposed to go to this music school in Philly in the fifties but they wouldn't let her in because she was Black. She kicked ass in the audition but they didn't want a *jazz* singer to be the first Black student they accepted.' He says *jazz* like it's a filthy word.

'Racist pricks.'

'She showed them, though. She got a job performing

in a bar and eventually became one of the biggest names in music. You've heard her songs. Even if this is the first time you've heard her voice.'

We stop talking and listen. Every once in a while, he slips into the music and nods along or moves his lips during a favourite part. He tells me about her songs and her performances. As he speaks, I know this must have been how his mother spoke of her as well. Sharing this knowledge with her son.

'If I was a girl, my mom said my name was gonna be Nina after her.'

'So can I call you Nina?'

'If you feel you have to.'

The music cuts to scratches and vinyl pops and he gets up to flip the record. When he sits back down, I ask him, 'So, Nina, what were you like before you had to go all off-the-grid survivalist?'

He smiles. 'A C-plus, maybe B student with a part-time job at an ice cream shop. You?'

'An artsy-fartsy student with a rebellious streak and a significant lack of parental supervision.'

'Sounds fun.'

I pause, then say, 'At the time, I guess it was. My mom died first. It was still pretty early on. They knew of the bug, but by the time they knew how bad it was, she was practically dead.' Nina Simone continues singing as I speak. 'After that we were pretty good. We did everything we were supposed to, wiped down our groceries, stayed away from people. But then, after a while, my dad got sick and he left. We aren't sure where he went. I heard him coughing in the middle of the night. You know that cough?'

He nods. Of course he does. It's a stupid question.

'Anyway, at one point the cough stopped and I figured he fell asleep. When I woke up the house smelled like bleach and there was a note on the kitchen table. It said he was sick and coughing up blood. He told us not to come looking for him and to stay in the house. That was . . . August, maybe September? I don't know, time was kind of nebulous at that point. My little sister got sick in November.' I remember that because it was after the internet went down.

Looking back, it may not have been a great idea to leave my only shelter in the middle of winter. I'll own that. I stayed as long as I could, but being alone in that house . . . I couldn't bury her because the ground was frozen solid, and I couldn't leave her outside to the elements and animals.

So when I couldn't take it any more, I left her in her bedroom, under her covers. I said my goodbyes, and I left.

'So . . . you haven't seen anyone since November?' he asks. There's a hesitation in his voice I can't quite figure out.

'Yep.' It feels rude to lie – and so poorly! – but we want to stick with happy thoughts.

'What was her name?'

His question catches me off guard.

'My sister?' He nods. Most people would leave it, afraid they'd drag out an awkward, uncomfortable conversation. Not him – he asks me point blank.

54

I'm happy to say her name. 'Elizabeth.'

'What was she like?'

I smile. This is even better. 'Really smart. And *funny*. My parents . . .' I'm talking too much and bite my tongue. Tears add swimmy vision to match my pill-popped mind. 'Lizzie got me. She wasn't like them.'

'I'm sorry.'

I shrug. 'It happened. We can't do anything about it now. I was next to her the entire time she was sick. I cleaned up her blood, shit and vomit, and I'm still here. If I'm not immune . . . I don't know what else it could be.'

He nods. I don't want to keep talking about this. The meds dull the physical pain but do nothing for the emotional. In fact, it feels worse. Everything feels heavier.

'Happy thoughts,' I say. 'I'm not flying any more and I need happy thoughts to get back up there before my leg starts hurting again.'

He smiles. 'Favourite movie?'

'You first.'

He shrugs. 'I don't know . . . *Avengers: Endgame*?'

'Ugh.' I shake my head. 'Such a typical straight-guy movie. Pssh . . . *Endgame*.'

And just like that it's out. Out of the closet and into the world. My heart lurches and I'm scared. What if he kicks me out? Shit, what if he kills me? You can't have civil rights laws when there is no law. But he doesn't even flinch. Maybe he missed it?

'Go on, then,' he says. 'What's yours?'

'*Vertigo*.'

He shakes his head. 'Never seen it.'

Of course not.

'I'm not surprised. I'm a weirdo. I only know it because my dad was a big movie nerd. He used to make us watch these old classics as a family on Saturday nights. We would each get a week where we picked the movie, but my dad's only rule when it was my sister's or my turn was that it had to be more than ten years old.'

'Why ten years?'

I shrug. 'We started it when I was ten and he wanted to expose me to movies made before I was born. It just became a rule.'

'So you didn't get to watch any new movies?' He narrows his eyes. 'Did you even see *Endgame*?'

'New movies I could go see with friends. For family movie night it was only older ones unless he or my mom picked it. *Vertigo* was one of the few my dad picked that I actually liked. It's Hitchcock, 1958. Everyone loves *Psycho* or *North by Northwest*, but *Vertigo* is all about toxic masculinity from the Master of Toxic Masculinity himself.'

'I saw the *Psycho* remake on Netflix.'

I make a face. 'You disgust me.'

He smiles. 'Favourite food?'

'Lasagne. You?'

'Ice cream.'

'Ice cream doesn't count, *Jamie*, it's dessert.'

'Doesn't mean it isn't food.'

'Again, you disgust me.' He still hasn't brought up my slip. 'Favourite date.'

'Movie, then dinner.'

'Inspired, really. You must have been a huge hit with the ladies.' Is this me sussing him out? Am I trying to see if Jamie has any possible interest in me? What an adorable meet-cute that would be to tell our post-apocalyptically adopted grandchildren! *Pop-Pop pulled a gun on Grandpa after he stepped in a bear trap!*

But no, that would be silly, because what are the odds that I step in a bear trap *and* meet another gay guy in the middle of the Pennsylvania woods after a viral apocalypse? Before the TV went dark – because the internet went first – most of the estimates said over two billion in the world were dead. I'm way too stoned to do the math, but with those numbers, how many queer people my age could be left?

'All right, smartass,' he says, shaking me from the downward spiral of queer existential dread. 'What's your big date?'

'April twenty-fifth.'

He stares at me like he doesn't understand. 'Christ. Jamie, you'd get these references if you watched a movie outside the Marvel Cinematic Universe.'

'Is it a movie? I don't get it.'

I groan and sit up on my elbows once more. 'Picnic under the stars in a park.'

'Oh right, you're from Connecticut. We don't see stars in Philly.'

The pain meds have fully encapsulated my brain in a wave of numbness, so I speak before I realise what I'm doing. 'Did you have a girlfriend before all this happened?'

He pauses. 'I did.'

'Is she dead?'

'She is.'

'Sorry.'

'How about you?'

I watch his face. Is he really asking me if I was dating a girl? Did he totally miss the 'straight guy' comment? 'I was single, fortunately . . . or unfortunately. However you choose to look at it.'

'Fortunately.'

'Should I ask about her?' I know the answer is probably no, but he speaks anyway.

'Her name was Heather. We started dating last April. She died the first week of June. It was still early enough that they released her body for a funeral. A week later and they probably would have dumped her in a mass grave like the rest.' He pauses as Nina continues to sing. 'No one else came. It was just her parents and me. Everyone else was either sick or scared of getting sick.'

The image of Jamie sitting alone at this poor girl's funeral, wearing an ill-fitting suit, breaks my heart.

'I felt bad for them, but afterwards I didn't know what to do so I just didn't talk to them. They could still be alive. I should have checked on them before I came out here with my mom.'

I know how he feels. Checking in on people because you feel you owe them something. I think of the address in Alexandria, and guilt washes over me like a tsunami. Maybe I'm getting too comfortable here.

'Sorry,' he says, looking up at me. 'Happy thoughts.'

The muddled fog of painkillers helps me hide the guilt.

No, not hide. It's still there, but I can ignore it a bit more. It feels easier to pretend like nothing's wrong.

'Yes, happy.' I pause and smile as an idea pops into my head. 'All right. You're going to get a crash course in movies that aren't Marvel.'

'I've *seen* other movies.'

'Not *Miss Congeniality*.'

'Is that the title of the movie?'

Oh my fucking God. He's hopeless. He is so lucky to have my broke-legged ass right now. 'Yes, Jamie. That's the title. And you have to picture Sandra Bullock when . . . you do know who Sandra Bullock is, right?'

'The blindfold movie.'

My jaw drops. *That's* his Sandra Bullock movie?

'So anyway! *Miss Congeniality* . . . Sandra Bullock is in a Russian restaurant, undercover. No, no, wait, there's totally a flashback with some major character development I have to hit first.'

'This movie is great.'

'Shut up, you're gonna love it.'

So I tell him the entire movie, from beginning to end. He doesn't interrupt me once to tell me it's stupid or he's bored, not even when the drugs muddle my memory a bit and I flub the set-up for a joke or I have to think a little longer to remember what happens next.

The only issue is, he doesn't laugh. He smiles or lets out an exhale-chuckle through his nose, but not once does he laugh.

It's like he can't do it any more.

JAMISON

Having Andrew in my house is odd, but in a good way. He's been here a little over a week and we've kind of just slipped into this strange domesticity. It's like he's been here far longer.

Honestly, I think it's because he reminds me of my friend Wes. Not that they're similar in any way. They especially have different senses of humour – Andrew is sarcastic and deadpan while Wes loves telling the corniest jokes. Though when Andrew does make a corny joke, it's fun to react the same way I did with Wes.

There's still something about Andrew that feels familiar, like we've been friends since we were kids. Because that's what we are now. Friends.

At least I hope we are, considering I'm in a looted Home Depot looking for a gift for him. That's not the main reason I'm here – it's getting warmer and I wanted to find seeds to plant in the backyard – but thought I'd look around while I was here.

I feel a little bad having to leave him alone back at the cabin, but I figured it would be nice to give him some alone time.

The swelling in his leg has gone down, but I can see

the winces and pained faces he makes. He never slows down. It's like he's refusing to let himself rest. I might be wrong, but it seems like he's eager to leave and trying to learn to deal with the pain so he can get out sooner. I tried to give him some pills before I left but he refused because they were making him constipated last week.

And now I know why it seems like we've been friends for ever. Because Andrew can't help but say *everything* on his mind. Even the TMI stuff.

I smirk as an idea comes to me. I leave the indoor garden area – the seeds rustling against their paper pouches in my backpack – and head for the plumbing aisle. Halfway down the aisle I find the plungers and my smile grows. He'll definitely feign offence while thinking it's the dumbest, funniest thing. A combo of Andrew's humour and Wes's. Sarcastic and corny.

Now I just have to decide if I go for the cheapest one, $2.99 in pre-pandemic prices, or the most expensive, $17.99.

But before I can even begin to weigh the humorous pros and cons, the sound of crunching glass shakes me from my thoughts.

Then voices, hushed but clear.

I get low and run in the opposite direction down the aisle and around a dishevelled endcap. The new people's voices echo through the store, but I can't hear what they're saying. My heart pounds in my chest and I drop my backpack slowly, and quietly, to the ground. I unzip it and take out the handgun.

Andrew has the rifle back at the cabin; I double-checked

that it was loaded and explained how to shoot it, but at the time he looked like he was barely paying attention. I should have told him about the cigarette butts, that there was someone nearby. But every day when I went out for more firewood, I would count the butts. Always four.

I assumed whoever it was had been there and left long ago. Maybe they wanted an empty house and left when they realised it wasn't.

But now I'm starting to think there are more survivors in the area than I originally thought.

There are at least two people talking. I can't count their footsteps, but two is already outnumbering me, and that's enough to make my hands tremble as I pull on the backpack.

'Hey, Howie!' The voice makes me jump because it's not one of the two whispering. This one is just a few aisles over from me. 'Over here.'

The voices shift and begin to sound closer. I raise the gun slightly, ready to shoot if I have to. My chest tightens and it becomes hard to breathe. The pounding in my ears blocks out the sound of their footsteps.

I scan the empty, dark aisles. The paint section is to my left, behind me is lumber – but all the wood is gone and the aisles are bare.

There's a brief shuffling sound of plastic and the clang of metal against the floor that makes me almost jump out of my skin. They're in the next aisle.

I catch the tail end of a conversation from further away. It's a woman. '. . . more on fortifying than this.'

'We can't do both?' a man asks.

'Apparently not.' She sounds annoyed. And closer. They're a couple of aisles down.

And they're heading towards me.

Their flashlight beams flit across the floor, growing larger. I spin and duck into the next aisle as light washes over the floor where I was just standing.

'I mean,' the woman continues. Her voice is lower, like the closer she gets to the plumbing aisle, the less she wants the first guy to hear. 'We need to do something. The winter probably kept people in, but they might start out searching now that the weather's warming up.'

'But Chad also says we have a small window to get the irrigation set up if we want to get the crops we need. We can't have a hundred people walking around with watering cans all day.'

A *hundred* people.

Her voice holds a warning. 'Howie.'

Howie replies in the same tone. 'Raven.' They stop walking just feet away from me, about to turn up the plumbing aisle. 'Yes, there's more people out there, but we need food.'

Raven jumps in. 'I'm not saying we don't, but we need to be able to *protect* what we have.'

'Or we get our numbers up, have people join us. But they won't if we can't feed them. Or ourselves.'

Raven sighs like she's not convinced.

'Besides,' Howie says, with what sounds like teasing in his voice. 'We already voted. You were the one who wanted everyone's input.'

Raven chuckles. 'Yeah, and look how that bit me in the ass.'

'Today would be cool, folks!' the first guy calls from down the aisle. It sounds like he's straining, plastic clacking together.

'Cool it, Jack, we're coming,' Howie says, turning up the aisle.

'Trying to throw your back out?' Raven asks.

'I'm not trying to be on the trench-digging team,' Jack says. 'Besides, you were the one who left the kid out at the truck.'

'He's a better shot than Raven,' Howie says as he grunts and picks something up.

'He got lucky *once*.' Raven and Howie argue about one of their crew being a better marksman while they lift what sounds like PVC pipes. When they take the first load out to their truck and their voices are barely audible, I make a run for the back of the store.

I don't want to wait for them to get back and decide on what else they might need to grab. Especially when two of them are apparently ready to shoot anyone who comes by.

A small crack of daylight filters through the jamb of the back door. I reach out in the dark and feel for the handle, expecting it to be locked. But the door opens easily, squealing on rusty hinges.

I flinch as my eyes adjust to the bright sunlight. The lock looks like it's been pried off with a crowbar, the door bent and broken from the outside. I pull over a broken cinder block and prop it up against the door so it doesn't close, then take one last look inside the darkened hardware store.

For a moment I think about the people in there. They must live close by. They're growing food, too. They have plans and votes and, from the sounds of things, leaders.

But they also have guns, and they expect to have to use them. They even have a 'kid' at the front of the Home Depot guarding their truck because he's a better shot than the others. The idea makes me nauseous.

I can hear Raven and Jack talking from the front of the store, so I turn and duck into the trees behind the shopping centre, glancing around quickly and watching for movement. Even once I reach the highway on the other side, I stay low.

It's a two-hour walk back to the cabin – it would have been faster if I took one of the bikes from the shed, but I wanted to be able to hide on the highway if I saw anyone. Still, it gives me time to think about what it could mean if we joined up with another settlement.

Maybe Andrew and I would be welcome, but then I picture the both of us stationed outside another Home Depot or a grocery store that hasn't been completely ransacked. We have guns and we have to shoot anyone else who might come by.

Even in the warm sunlight, the thought gives me chills.

I'd never be able to join up with a settlement who were so willing to end other people's lives. After everything we've all been through with the superflu. If the news was even close to correct on the death toll estimates, then there's very few people left. Maybe Andrew would be able to join up with them. He was heading for Reagan National, after all.

So maybe I would just stay on my own.

Chills return, and something else. It feels like grief. The idea of Andrew leaving and me being alone again creates a pit in my chest like all my vital organs have gone missing.

I have to tell him, to give him the option to leave and join up with them if he wants to. Because of course he'd want to.

I won't tell him. Not yet, at least. I don't want to worry him – that there might be other survivors around us – but, even more, I don't want him to leave.

ANDREW

Jamie is late. I get up from the chair on the front porch and hobble inside to check the time on the clock hanging on the kitchen wall. It's almost 3:30. He was supposed to be back an hour ago.

I go back to the front porch and sit on the top of the front steps so my leg is going straight down towards the little garden gnome. I flex the muscles in my bad leg and there's that familiar throb of pain. But it's only a dull ache now. I bend my knee and put a tiny bit of weight on the heel of my foot. The pain increases a bit, but it's bearable.

I think about standing and trying to walk on it. If it wasn't really broken, maybe it was just some muscle tearing and walking will be better. I can leave now . . . or tomorrow, and get back on the road. But if it *is* broken like Jamie thinks, and isn't fully healed, I might ruin any progress I've already made.

And I can't risk that. Especially since Jamie is late.

'He's fine, right?' I ask the gnome. She doesn't answer because she probably has a gnome-like sixth sense and knows he's been shot and left in a ditch on the side of the road. Maybe the little sheep in her lap told her.

My stomach burbles with a combination of fear and

hunger. I skipped lunch because it felt rude to eat Jamie's food without him. But I was also anxious as hell. He took the handgun and left the rifle – which I probably suck at shooting anyway – for me, but I'm still worried about him.

I shouldn't be, though. What does it matter if he gets killed by someone and I'm left to heal in his house all alone until I can go find the Fosters in Alexandria? But the worry in my gut tells me it absolutely does matter.

It matters because Jamie helped me when he didn't need to and because he's kind and sweet and has an adorable smile and . . . And sometimes when he puts his arm around me to help me up, I get that fluttery feeling in my chest that makes it hard to breathe.

And then sometimes when I can't sleep I imagine staying here for ever and just skipping my quest to Alexandria. Why should I travel so far just to give a family bad news? We've all had bad news. Bad news is, like, the *only* news post-bug.

Hey, guys, sorry your parents are dead but just wanted to let you know! Guilt makes my stomach burble even more. But staying here, with Jamie, is a nice fantasy. The guilt gets replaced by those flutters again and that's not so bad . . .

No. That's a silly fantasy. I scoot down the stairs and put my foot on the gravel at the bottom of the first step. I'll just test it. Use the handrail to balance myself and put a tiny bit of weight on the leg. If it goes even close to that first day of pain I'll sit back down.

Gravel crunches at the end of the driveway and I tense

up. My body burns with a blend of excitement and fear. Jamie is home, or . . .

But it's Jamie's eyes I see when he rounds the turn in the drive. Then his smile that, yes, does bring those flutters again.

He gives me a quick wave and his gaze drops down to my leg.

'You're late.' I cross my arms.

'Sorry.'

'I burned dinner.'

'Well, that's just because you're a shitty cook.'

I snort and he gives me a lopsided grin.

'Seriously,' I say. 'Everything all right?'

He opens his mouth like he's going to say something but stops himself. Then he takes off his backpack and sets it down at the bottom of the steps. He crouches and unzips it, taking out a handful of paperback books with library stickers on them.

'I stopped at the library in town on my way back,' he says, handing the books to me and hopefully not noticing how red I'm turning. 'I wasn't sure what you wanted so I just kind of judged by the cover.'

'You know you're not supposed to do that, right?' I give him a smug look and he shrugs. This cute boy saved my life, gave me food and now stories. All you need, indeed. 'Thank you.' I point one of the books at him. 'But this doesn't mean you get to skimp out on your film education. You're disgustingly lacking on the pop culture front.'

He reaches for the books and nods. 'Yeah, yeah. Then

let's go make something to eat and you can poorly explain another movie to me.'

''Scuse your mouth!'

He tries and fails to hide another grin and holds out a hand to help me up. And right on time, it's the hard-to-breathe express train. He lets me go up the stairs first, holding his hands out to catch me if I fall.

'Was the rest of your trip *fruitful*?' I ask.

'What? What do you mean?'

I turn back to look at him because he sounds thrown off, and yes, even his face seems to be confused. Unsure if he should be smiling or concerned or fearful.

'The seeds?' I say. '*Fruit*ful. Like veggies and fruits?'

'Oh. Yeah.'

He should have made fun of me for that joke. Rolled his eyes or pretended to fake retch like he usually does. 'You OK?'

Jamie nods and smiles politely. 'Yeah, just beat. And hungry.'

'Then you relax and I'll make dinner.'

'Didn't I just say you're a shitty cook?'

'Oh my God, you're such a bitch when you're hangry, Jamie.'

He chuckles – just a light laugh through his nose – and leaves the backpack by the door.

'Hey,' he says as I reach the doorway to the kitchen. 'Why didn't you bring the gun outside with you?'

I look at it, propped up against the wall by the front door, and shrug. Because I really didn't want to have to use it. And if I brought it out and someone else came up that driveway, I would have.

'We're out in the middle of nowhere. Who was going to stop by?'

Jamie just stares at the rifle. 'I don't like . . .' He stops and shakes his head. 'Never mind.'

'You don't like what?'

He opens his mouth and looks at me. His cheeks turn a light pink and he shakes his head. 'Nothing. I just worry is all.'

He worries? About me? My mouth goes dry and I duck into the kitchen to hide my burning cheeks.

'Sit down,' Jamie shouts, hanging his coat on a hook behind the door. Then he follows me into the kitchen. 'You make me nervous walking around all the time. You can't heal if you aren't resting.'

So he *does* worry about me.

'You're a very stubborn patient,' he says, throwing a log into the stove. 'Why do you keep pushing yourself?'

Because deep down I know the truth. That I can't stay here for ever. As wonderful as it is to have a cute, nice boy taking care of me, I have to go. The longer I stay, the smaller my window gets to arrive in Alexandria by June 10. And I've already had so many setbacks.

I obsess over all the possibilities once I leave here and head to Alexandria. I could arrive and find the house empty; maybe the Fosters already left to find their parents. And this new option I've been pondering where I go right to Reagan National instead and try to live a life on the lam. But then I imagine running into the Fosters in whatever settlement the EU helps set up and trying to

71

ignore the guilt. Trying to pretend like my life is fine while they grieve, never understanding what happened.

Another possibility is I get there and they're alive and I have to tell them what happened in New Jersey. How their parents died.

Or I arrive in Alexandria and the Fosters are dead and have been since before I ever met their parents.

But I can't tell Jamie about any of that because he'll either kick me out, be scared of me or try to make me feel better. I just don't know which one of those would be worse.

'Because I feel like enough of a burden as it is,' I say.

'Well, you need to own that and get over it.' His tone is joking, but maybe he's right? I take a seat at the kitchen table while he digs through the cabinets. 'What movie will you be telling me while I prepare our food?'

'Why don't you tell me one?' I say. 'You can even just tell me *Endgame* if you want.'

He finally cracks a smile. 'I can't tell them like you. All I remember is the big scenes like when everyone who died comes back at the end.'

And wouldn't it be nice if that could happen in real life?

'Fine,' I say. 'But you have to help me. I only saw it, like . . . thirty times so I don't remember all of it.'

He glanced over his shoulder. 'As opposed to the eighty times you watch every other movie to memorise them?'

'Exactly. So start me off. Captain America's in his Snapper's Anonymous meeting, right?'

'Nope.' He glances at me and shakes his head. 'Iron Man is trapped in space with Nebula.'

'See? You're a natural!'

And we talk through most of the movie together. I'm surprised when Jamie actually chimes in with a scene I forgot – specifically the taco scene with Banner and Ant Man. About halfway through the time heist, and after our lunch, Jamie starts to look a little bored.

'What's wrong?' I ask.

He shakes his head. 'Tired, sorry.'

'Go lie down then, I can clean up here.' I reach for his plate but he gently grabs my wrist.

'I'll clean it up later, don't worry about it.'

He lets go, but my skin still feels like it's on fire where he touched me. When I look into his eyes, he does seem tired, and now I'm the one worrying about him. And worrying about what happens if I leave.

He stands up and puts our plates in the sink, then holds out a hand to help me up. I take it.

And I'm worrying about what happens if I stay.

JAMISON

Packs of seeds are spread across the outdoor table, organised based on when they are supposed to be planted – and a stack that were to be sown indoors in early spring that I'll have to save for next year. I write each type on to a tablet and put a note of when they need to go in the ground.

Andrew looks over the top of the library book I brought him on the seed supply run I did a few weeks ago. It's some novelisation of a movie that was never released because of the superflu. I told him he needs to read it and tell me what happens.

He's been here for about six weeks and we've spent most of our evenings with Andrew retelling movies to me, scene by scene.

'You're so organised,' he says now. 'I would have just thrown them all in the dirt and waited to see what popped up.'

'And then you would have starved.' We aren't starving yet, but the food in town is getting scarce. I did end up planting a whole bunch of the seeds I nabbed from the Home Depot, and vegetables are already starting to sprout. And the weather has been good to us – we should have a first crop ready by June. These seeds are the leftovers that need to be planned further out, including some winter cabbages.

'Or gotten scurvy.'

He turns back to his book and I glance at his leg propped up on the chair across from him. He's been able to move a little better. The swelling is gone and the bruising is yellowed and faded. Another week might be all he needs.

I turn back to the tablet and write down that the mustard greens should go in the ground at the end of July.

'Jamie.' His voice is cold and scared.

I hear a twig snap and see movement out of the corner of my eye. I jump, reaching for the rifle and aim it at the man at the treeline. The man has long, coarse black-and-grey hair with a matching beard. The skin on his face is slightly reddened by the sun. I can see his smile beneath the beard. There's a rifle, too. He holds it low, but still pointing at us.

'Stop there.' I'm trying my hardest to make my voice sound intimidating, to make it sound like I can pull this trigger. But the gun is shaking and my palms are already sweaty.

'No need to start shootin',' the bearded man says. 'How many of youse are there?' He takes a step forward.

'I said stop.' My voice breaks and I sound like a child.

Andrew whispers, 'Jamie.'

He doesn't have to say any more because the movement catches my eye. There are more people emerging from the treeline. A Black woman in her thirties with a vest and short hair, an older white woman with grey hair pulled back into a ponytail. There are three more men; two are older white men, maybe forties, while the third is a tall, stocky kid with brown skin who looks like he's the same age as Andrew and me.

All of them have guns. Three rifles, three handguns.

'You're outnumbered,' the man with the beard says. 'So how 'bout we lower our guns and talk?'

Talking sounds fine.

I turn to Andrew, trying to see his reaction to this. He looks sceptical, and if I'm not mistaken it looks like he doesn't want me to lower the gun. But I don't have a choice. There's more of them than there are of us. I don't know if those guns are even loaded, but if they are, we're screwed.

And I still don't think I can shoot them. My stomach is in knots and I can't psych myself up to think about it, let alone do it.

I lean the rifle against the deck railing, and the rest of the interlopers lower their own weapons. I let out a soft breath of relief as the bearded man hands his rifle to the woman with the grey ponytail and comes towards us.

When he reaches the bottom step of the deck, he holds out a dirty hand. 'Howard.'

Howie. Now I have a face to the name. I look back to the people at the treeline, wondering if one is Jack or Raven. My eyes fall on the kid and I wonder if he's the one who's a better shot with the rifle in his hands than the others.

'Jamison.' I take Howard's hand firmly and give it a

shake, locking eyes with him.

Howard looks to Andrew, who gives his name, then Howard asks, 'Mind if I sit?'

I do mind that, sir. I would like for all of you to leave and never look back and also, feel free to step on a few bear traps out there.

I turn to Andrew, who still looks at me like he's ready to set the world on fire. I step aside, trying to be diplomatic, but I grab the rifle anyway and carry it over to the other side of the deck. Out of the corner of my eye I can see the others in Howard's group move their weapons up, then lower them once I set the rifle down and sit between Andrew and Howard.

Howard takes his seat.

'Nice place,' he says.

'Thanks,' I say. You can't have it, Howard.

As if reading my mind, he says, 'Don't worry, we're all set up, we're not going to take your house.' He reaches into his front pocket and I see Andrew flinch, but Howard only withdraws a pack of cigarettes.

The cigarette butts. They must have been his, or someone from their settlement's. I wonder how long they've been watching us.

Howard smiles at Andrew, probably seeing the same flinch I did, then holds out the pack, his eyebrows rising.

'No thanks,' I say.

'Those'll kill you.' Subtle, Andrew, very subtle.

Howard chuckles but proceeds to light up. 'Not much these days don't.' He lets the smoke out through his nostrils, like a dragon warning us that he can breathe fire. He tucks the pack and lighter into his pocket and leans back, relaxing.

'What can we do for you, Howard?'

'The town nearby – I assume you frequent it?' he asks.

'Not so much, now that the tourism industry's kaput,' Andrew answers.

'Stop it,' I say to him. He's poking the bear – or the dragon, to maintain the metaphor.

Howard smirks and continues, his eyes falling on the seed packets scattered on the table. 'Well, there *was* plenty there to be had. But not so much any more.' He takes another puff on his cigarette and says, 'There's more of us.' He motions to the people along the trees. 'Quite a few more.'

I want to call his bluff, but there's no point. We're already outnumbered, so he's got no reason to lie to us. The six of them are enough to intimidate Andrew and me.

Howard continues. 'That's a lot of mouths to feed and not much in the way of food delivery any more. So we started out to see who might have been in the area, just poking around. Going door to door to collect.'

This isn't door to door, it's an ambush.

'Collect?' Andrew asks.

'Taxes. We claim these lands for our settlement and you're living on it. You've been living in the house, so we're not looking to take that from you. But this is America, and if you live on our land you need to pay taxes.'

'You want *money*?' Andrew asks.

'Money's not worth the paper it's printed on any more. We're looking for food.'

'We don't have any food.'

Howard holds up a hand. 'Stop there. You don't need to start our relationship off on the wrong foot by lying. We know you raided the town nearby and left the scraps. Plenty of people did. The scraps that we then took. But again, there's more of us than there are of you, and I think we can come to some kind of mutual agreement. Maybe you'll need medicine or protection in the future. So you've gotta pay up now. You help us, we help you.'

'And if we say no?' Andrew says. I haven't spoken a word. I'm frozen with fear and I can't help but look back at the line of people at the edge of the yard.

'I think you know what happens if you say no.'

I do – they'll kill us. It might not be now, but they'll kill us all the same. They'll come back with more people and it'll be worse.

'Do you know what the term "no taxation without representation" means, Howard?' Andrew asks. I want to elbow him and tell him to shut up and just let them take some of our food, but I can't move.

Howard chuckles and takes another long drag of his cigarette. 'I *am* your representation.'

'I didn't vote for you.'

'Andrew, stop,' I finally say, but I don't look at him. I'm still watching the others with the guns. They're gonna take what they want and we can't stop them; they have the people and the weapons.

Howard looks between us, back and forth, then takes one final drag on his cigarette before rubbing the amber tip of it against the deck railing. He flicks the butt into the yard and reaches back for another—

But pulls out a handgun instead.

It's trained on Andrew. Steady, unwavering. Everyone else along the backyard raises their weapons, too. My heartbeat quickens and I put up my hands, leaning towards Andrew – putting *myself* in front of Andrew – but Andrew still doesn't move and I wonder if he saw this coming.

'We're taking your food,' Howard says. All pretence of politeness is gone, along with his smile. He whistles and three of his group come forward. 'You can come after it if you want, but believe me when I say we'll fight for it. We've fought for it before.'

When he says this, there's a strange look in his eyes – I'm not sure if it's sadness or anger. Maybe Raven was right and they should have focused more on security than crops. Someone else might have shown up at their settlement and done what they're doing to us. Now they're low on food. The three moving up the stairs pull bags from the packs on their shoulders. The Black woman hands Howard one of the bags and she takes a few steps back; her gun is at the ready, but not pointed at us.

Howard says, 'Keep an eye on them, Rave.' She nods, and Howard joins the others in the house.

So this is Raven.

I hear them opening cabinets, ransacking, taking what's

ours. Just don't let them go searching the rest of the house. Don't let them take the medical supplies. Don't let them try the lights or the water. Don't let them find the safe and make me open it and take the handgun and ammo. They can't leave us with nothing.

'What are we supposed to do?' I ask Raven.

She shrugs. 'What all of us do now – do what you have to, to survive.'

'And you have to do this?' I ask.

She takes a deep, steady breath, then says, 'We do. But . . .'

Raven takes her eyes off us long enough to look towards the house, then she takes a short step forward. She lowers her voice.

'This is more . . . performance than anything else.'

'Performance?' Andrew asks, not bothering to keep his voice down. Raven looks annoyed but continues anyway.

'*Do* you think you'd survive out here alone? Just the two of you?'

'How do you know it's only the two of us?' Andrew asks.

'Because they've been watching us,' I say. 'That's right, isn't it?'

Raven nods. So all this is to leave us desperate enough to come find them, because they need people. They need numbers and security, and maybe even people to work their crop fields in return for food and protection. And they want us to think we need them as much as they need us.

Their work is fast, and when they emerge, all three of

them hold bags filled with our food. Raven goes back to the treeline and Howard turns his attention to us.

'We left some of it. Enough to keep you going for a few days.'

A few days. That's not counting the deer in the freezer that was supposed to last us longer than it will now. And they've already taken the rest of the food from town.

'Remember what I said. Don't come after us. Don't throw your life away for nothing. Now, if you want to come out and *join* us, no weapons, you're more than welcome. We'll find a way for you to help out and a way for you to get paid.'

Raven was telling the truth. This *is* just a performance. I wonder if they even need that food.

'If we begin to starve, what do you think we'll be forced to do to you?' Andrew asks.

Howard shrugs again. 'I suggest you come up with another plan before that happens. Because you'll lose.'

He turns and heads towards the others. Andrew whispers to me.

'Grab the gun.'

'No.'

'Jamie—'

'No, Andrew. Just . . . no.' Only one of the men still has his gun on us; the others have turned back into the woods, disappearing in the foliage. If I were someone else, I could do what Andrew is asking. If I were stronger.

I can't do any of that. And now we're going to starve to death. I'm sure all of them would do it in a heartbeat. In fact, I know it. Howard's eyes told me everything.

I turn back to Andrew and I'm surprised to see he's glassy-eyed. He looks frustrated and I can see the muscles in his jaw clench and unclench. He's probably pissed at me. Maybe now he sees how weak I am and he's embarrassed that he was ever scared of me.

He pushes himself up, grabbing his crutch, and I watch as he hobbles into the house to take stock of what's left and figure out how long until we starve.

We skip dinner that night, and Andrew goes to bed early. I follow shortly after, lying in my bed, thinking about the food we have. There's enough canned food for a week. More if we can keep the venison going. And the seeds in the garden are starting to germinate, so maybe we can take vitamins until they produce crops.

I'll hunt in the morning. I'll do what I need to now, because I don't have any other choice.

But more than that, there's something else distracting me. I keep trying to come back to the food, to focus on what's important, but my mind wanders to Andrew. My gut reaction when Howard pulled the gun.

I tried to get in front of it. It didn't matter because the others by the trees had their guns on both of us, but my focus was only on Howard's gun, pointed at Andrew. Most of my night is spent imagining what would have happened if Andrew got hurt, if they killed him. And if I survived.

I spiral, thinking about every possibility that could have happened. Mainly, though, I can't figure out why the whole incident is affecting me so much. Andrew, who I met six weeks ago, is someone I was willing to jump in front of a gun for.

Spiralling again. Howard didn't shoot, so it doesn't matter. I tell myself that over and over. We're fine, it didn't happen, we'll survive this. I'll do what I have to in the morning.

When I wake, the sun isn't up yet, but blue pre-dawn light peeks through the curtains.

I get up, shower, dress and sneak out the back door. Heading for the field I've been trying – and failing – to hunt in. I lie on the ground and pull a brown tarp over my back, looking through the scope of the rifle at shadows cast by the trees. Waiting for the sun to rise.

As the morning goes on, I keep telling myself I don't need to be out here. We still have *some* food after what Howard left us.

But we're still gonna need some protein, and that means waiting here, for *something*.

Then I hear it – the crack of twigs, the rustle of dead leaves. There's a flash of brown and white as a large doe prances into the field from the treeline. My heart leaps.

My finger floats against the trigger as I line up the black lines in the rifle sight where the doe's heart is. She looks around, her ears twitching atop her head.

I can do this. I have to do this. I have to, *I have to*. My finger applies more pressure. The trees behind the doe rustle and a small fawn hops from the woods; white spots speckle its brown fur. My finger flicks away from the trigger.

The fawn frolics around its mother with abandon, springing up and down on its spindly legs. It has no idea of the metal projectile moments away from taking its mother's life.

C'mon, this changes nothing. I put my finger back on the trigger as the doe bends her long neck down and nibbles at the grass. The fawn stops hopping and bends down as well, sniffing. Its tail twitches with excitement at all the new smells and sensations. I move the sight over to it, following it as it explores the new world it was only just born into.

I see my mother's face again. This time her eyes are open and pleading with me, and I can barely hear her as she asks me, again, to end the pain.

I can't do it. I can't kill a mother deer in front of her baby. Not this one. I'll get another one. Maybe tomorrow or . . . I don't know.

'Goddammit,' I whisper under my breath. The doe and the fawn look up from the ground, their ears twitching. I let out a sigh and stand up, throwing the tarp off my back. 'Yeah, I said "goddammit"!' I shout at them across the field. Neither of them moves.

'Go,' I say, waving my hand again. They remain where they are, staring at me. 'Move it!' I point the gun at them and they don't even flinch.

I hold the rifle steady. If they're so keen to die, we might as well eat. Only this time I can't even bring my finger up to the trigger. As the deer watch me and I watch them, I drop the rifle and crouch down, holding out my hand to the fawn.

The fawn looks back at its mother as if asking for permission, but the doe is already scanning the rest of the field. The fawn takes a tentative step forward, lowering its head.

It approaches me slowly. When it reaches my hand it stays back but stretches its neck forward, breathing in my scent. I smile as its wet nose touches the tips of my fingers.

I reach out with my other hand and touch the fawn's fur. It's soft and hasn't grown coarse yet. I look up at the mother, who is watching me like a hawk. She trusts me, but only so much. Her eyes tell me, 'Hurt my baby, I hurt you.'

'It's all right. I won't hurt it.' I pet the fawn from its head down its back, and it shakes its little tail. It's like they intuitively know something happened to the human population. Like the silence of the roads and the significant lack of human-animals walking on two feet means things have changed for them. Like their world is less dangerous.

'All right, I think your mom wants you to head back now.' I take my hand away and its wide eyes look like they're wondering a million things at once.

The spring breeze has cooled the sweat on my back. I fold the tarp and tuck it under my arm and lift the rifle, slinging it over my shoulder. The fawn tenses, ready to run.

'It's OK, kid, I'm done for the day.'

The fawn turns and begins walking back to its mother, stopping every few feet to sniff at the ground.

'Be careful,' I tell the doe.

I smile and head back to the house.

*

There's a book on the coffee table. It's the first thing I see when I walk into the living room and my mouth goes dry.

It's *The Voyage Out*. I call out to Andrew but there's no answer. There's a piece of lined yellow paper sticking out of the top. I know it's from Andrew and I'm terrified to take it out, but I can't leave it there. I can't ignore it. He wasn't on the back deck waiting for me as usual and he's not the kind of person to sleep in.

Slowly, I pull it out and unfold it.

Seeing his handwriting hurts like a knife.

Jamie, it says. *I'm sorry. I hope you don't find this until you come back from hunting. I didn't want to be here when you got back. This is a trope you wouldn't know anything about because it's only in shitty movies you've never seen. It's the coward's way out.*

I am a coward.

Hi, my name is Andrew and I am a coward.

(Hi, Andrew.)

I had to leave. This is your food, and your home, and I've been enough of a burden. But I want you to know how much I appreciate everything you've done for me. I NEED you to know how grateful I am. You're a really good person.

He wrote something else after this but spent a lot of time scribbling it out so I couldn't see it.

I took some food. Just a few cans . . . I hope you managed to get a deer so I don't feel so guilty. I think you did.

I'm going to miss you so much, Jamie. And again, I'm really sorry. I'm more than sorry. I think there's no word for what I am right now.

87

Stay safe.
Love, Andrew.
I read it over and over, hearing his voice in my head.

I'm unable to move from the couch or even think. He's gone. He's gone and I'm alone again.

ANDREW

This is karma. Point taken, universe! But you didn't have to be such a bitch about it. I got way too comfortable here. Just days ago, I was sitting in the living room with Jamie, going through the movie *Best in Show* – almost got him to laugh with 'Harlan Pepper, if you don't stop namin' nuts!' – when I realised, maybe I didn't need to go down to Alexandria after all. Maybe I could stay here with Jamie, let my deadline pass and pretend the Fosters have gone on to live their lives elsewhere. And Jamie and I could just be best friends and I could deal with the shit I did in my own way.

But no. I like it here too much and now the universe is all, 'Ah, you think you deserve happiness?' and throws a wrench in our life.

But it's a wrench in Jamie's life. And it's all because I decided I could stay. That I didn't need to get right with the world.

I feel awful. But I have to go. I've overstayed my karmic welcome. If I hadn't been here when Howard and his people showed up, Jamie could have gone with them. Or he might have even gone out in search of them before then. Instead he was taking care of me. Giving me his food. Hunting for me.

And when Howard showed up, Jamie remained calm. He stayed quiet and didn't let his anger or fear get the better of him. He didn't lash out and do something reckless.

Like I did.

I told Jamie to shoot Howard and his group. If I were to stay here with Jamie, as much as I *so* want to, I feel like it would change him. I'm like a toxic contaminant trying to corrupt his good nature.

I'm also scared if I don't leave now, I never will. There's some not-so-new feelings popping up. The feelings that have been growing over the last few weeks of us trapped together. The feelings that are bound to hurt so much more and bring on the inevitable the longer I drag it out. At some point I'm going to have to either tell Jamie I like him or keep it a dark secret for ever.

And one secret is enough.

This delay was always supposed to be temporary, and the longer I stay, the less temporary it feels. The more at home I feel. There's a terrible pull between continuing south and staying put.

I could say I'm torn and don't know what to do, but that's not true. I know I have to leave simply because I really don't want to. It would be so much easier to just be selfish and stay put. Attempt to move on with whatever semblance of life I have after the apocalypse, but I know I could never. A part of it has to be Jamie. The kindness he showed me – reminding me that kindness existed in the world.

If I'd found this house empty, I'd be staying here

indefinitely. Hell, I'd probably join up with Howard when they came knocking. But sometimes I catch myself thinking about what Jamie would do if he were me. And now, more than ever, it's clear he would go to Alexandria.

Maybe . . . I want to be that kind of person, too.

I lie in the darkness, waiting to hear the soft snores from his bedroom. Every once in a while, it's just a sigh or grunt. I listen for it sometimes when I wake from a nightmare, to make sure he's still there.

It's not creepy, shut up.

Once he's asleep I slip out of bed and grab my bag and crutch. I've packed my clothes . . . and also some of the clothes Jamie has given me. The ones that are too big for me but still smell of the detergent he nabbed in bulk sometime before I came into his life. I sneak into the kitchen and take three cans of food, including two of mushrooms, which I know he hates.

He'll thank me for that.

Water, clothes, food. I've got almost everything I need.

I put out the book my aunt gave me for my fifteenth birthday, my favourite book, and leave it and the note on the coffee table. After taking one more look around the living room, remembering the first time I saw it and all the time Jamie and I spent in here together – sans gunplay of course. Listening to Nina Simone or talking about movies or our lives.

Maybe it's a moment of self-sabotage, a way to keep me here longer, but I slowly put my foot fully on the ground. There's a little soreness, but that's it. Enough that I'll need the crutch sometimes, but not enough to stop me.

So I limp, quietly, to the front door and leave the cabin.

I expect Jamie to come running out after me. To hear me making noise and come out with a gun.

But he doesn't wake up. I look back at the dark cabin, lit only by moonlight. It looks peaceful. Very peaceful. Except for that garden gnome by the stairs lurking in the shadows.

'Bye, Jamie,' I whisper. 'Thank you.' My eyes drift back to the garden gnome. 'See ya, gnome.'

And early on the morning of May 2, I leave.

Late on the morning of May 2, I'm regretting all my life choices. Classic Andrew! I'm sitting on a metal guardrail, for the seventh time this morning, trying to rest my leg. Walking around the house in short bursts was fine. It turns out walking several miles on a crutch is no fun at all.

Shocker.

I'm in pain and moving so much slower than I thought, but I have to keep going no matter how much pain or frustration I feel. Have to get out of here before I lose my courage. Before all this logic I've built up during the witching hour turns into vampire dust in the harsh light of day. If I get far enough, I'll realise it's too far to turn back now.

It worked before. Of course, then I had the convenience of a blizzard that snowed me into a shopping centre in Norwalk.

Pushing off the guardrail, I realise I've only thought about Jamie ninety-eight times so far today. That has to be a good sign, right?

I'm barely back to the centre of the road when I hear something echoing through the stillness of the highway. It's a low thump, thump.

My breath catches in my chest. Maybe I was hearing things. Could it have been my own step echoing? My bag banging against my back? Water sloshing in the pack?

Thump.

No, there it is again. It's erratic but it's not coming from me. I limp to an abandoned car, ducking beneath and looking back the way I came. There's someone in the distance, obscured by the heat haze from the cracked asphalt.

I slip off my bag and toss it beneath the car before I climb under after it. Whoever it is can't see me from where they are. They probably aren't even looking for anyone.

I stay still in the shadow of the car as they approach.

From where I am it looks like a white male, and he's on a bike. Something hanging off the sides makes the low thump sound as he steers around the potholes and cracks in the road. The brim of his baseball hat casts a shadow over his face.

He's fifteen feet away now and . . .

It's Jamie.

My face betrays me, pulling into a smile. I want to laugh. I want to shout and scream and cry and hug him. He came all the way out here. He came after me.

But then the excitement dies in my throat.

He came after me. He shouldn't have done that. He should have stayed where he was; it was his home.

I remain silent beneath the car, watching him pedal slowly past. There are two packs tied to the back of his bike. Two of them. One for him, one for me. I smile again, laying my head against the road. He gets further and further away as he pedals. Tears burn my eyes.

He pedals past a car and then he's gone from my sight.

My stomach clenches. He's gone.

No.

'No.' It's a whimper at first, like my body isn't letting me talk any louder than that. It knows I shouldn't, that it's not safe for Jamie. But I don't care. I need to see him again.

'No!' Louder, better.

I scramble out from under the car.

'Jamie!' I'm screaming it now. I repeat it over and over and over, yelling after him. He has to turn around. I try to run, the wooden crutch digging hard into my armpit. I leave my bag beneath the car.

He rides around in a circle, turning back to me. I can't see his face beneath the shadow of his baseball cap, I can't see if he's smiling or not, but I am.

I shout his name again, trying to move faster. I'll probably fall and break my leg all over again but I don't care.

He puts on the kickstand and gets off the bike, walking towards me. There he is. The only person in the world left to even care about me. And all at once I realise it was a mistake to run off. Leaving him was easier than trying to convince him not to come. But seeing him here, now, gives me full-on heart-eyed butterflies in my gut. They're stupid and, like Jamie, they shouldn't be here. But they are.

And so is he. My Jamie. My stupid, stupid Jamie who left his home and followed me because he thinks I'm a good person. It's selfish and I *so clearly* have not learned my lesson because right now I want him here.

I come to a stop ten feet from him.

He isn't smiling. In fact, he looks downright pissed.

He stands there, his arms crossed. Maybe I should have stayed under the car after all. What if he wasn't looking for me? He could have decided he needed to find someone else and just happened to pass me. He didn't know my route so he wasn't tracing my steps; he was following his own route.

'I'm sorry,' I say. It looks like he's not going to say anything. But then . . .

'You're a real dickhead,' he says. 'You know that?'

He turns to his bike and unties one of the packs – a yoga mat and sleeping bag rolled up and tied to the top – and tosses it over to me.

'Transfer your stuff into this one, it holds more.' Then he cuts off the other pack, slings it over his shoulders, and turns back to me. 'Well, come on.'

'That's it?' I ask. His eyebrows furrow in confusion. 'I left without saying goodbye and all you want to say is "Well, come on"?'

He shrugs. 'I . . . I also called you a dickhead?'

I snort and limp over to him, pulling him into a hug.

'Should I have been meaner?' he asks, though I'm

squeezing him so tightly his voice is strained. 'I should have punched you in the arm or something, huh?'

'This is fine,' I say, still squeezing him.

Once I'm finished moving everything from my bag to the one he brought, I look up at him. 'Why did you come after me? Why not go find Howard and the others from yesterday?' He doesn't owe me a thing – if anything, I owe him more than I can pay, but what else is new, amirite? But why come looking for me instead of going to a larger group to survive? And he clearly didn't come here to convince me to go back to the cabin, otherwise why bring these bags?

He frowns and crosses his arms again. 'You mean the people who robbed us? The whole group that took literal peanuts from us?'

'They stole the honey-roasted peanuts?' I yell. Jamie tries not to smile and fails.

'They couldn't be doing that well for themselves if they'd take food from two people on their own.'

I hadn't thought of it that way. From what that girl Raven said, I figured it was just the group's way of showing dominance, and maybe trying to force us to join them. But maybe they needed us more than we needed them.

Just like I need Jamie more than he needs me.

Jamie holds out his hand to help me up. 'When my mom and I went out to the cabin, it was to leave the city. Everything was going kinda off the rails and we knew the cabin would be safe because we were secluded out there. Course, that didn't keep *you* from breaking in.'

I point a finger at him. 'I did not break in – you're a lunatic who left the door unlocked.'

He continues as if he didn't hear me. 'And now with Howard and Raven's crew there . . . It just doesn't feel safe any more.'

I frown and guilt returns. 'I don't know how to tell you this . . .' Without going into detail about the Fosters. 'But it's not so safe out here either.'

'I watch your back, you watch mine?'

I nod. 'Sounds good.'

We leave his bike since it would mean one of us pedalling slowly while the other tried to keep up by limping along on a crutch. After about five minutes he finally says, 'I told you why I came after you. But why did you leave? Why the rush to get away? We still had food, and we could have made it last until you were all healed.'

And here it is. This is where I should tell him the truth. About the family in Alexandria.

But seeing him again reinforces everything I was trying to suppress. The heart-eyed butterflies that would die if he finds out I'm a real-life, grade-A horrible person and decides to leave me. I can delay the inevitable just a bit longer. Keep telling him the half-truth.

'If there is some *real* civilisation out there, with a whole government and everything, I don't want to miss them. I know you don't believe me, but I do think someone might be coming. The quarantine worked in Germany and the Netherlands.'

'The news and the US government said the same about the UK and Italy. And people online said it was bullshit.

Which . . . My mom and I were out at the cabin alone and she still got it. This thing doesn't care about quarantines. It survived everything.'

'I know.' I heard that part, too. 'I know it's a rumour, but . . . what if it is true?' If it is true, the Fosters might be gone if I don't get there before June tenth. If it isn't true, then I rushed out for no reason.

Jamie thinks on it. I can see him running all the options in his head. Then finally he nods. 'Let's get to DC by June tenth, then. We have a month, plenty of time.'

Plenty of time to figure out how to tell him the rest of the truth.

Yay.

Walking south is significantly more difficult than I remembered. My leg injury isn't helping.

Two other things we didn't think about were the sun and the heat. The sun didn't burn in the winter, and walking quickly kept my body temperature up. Now, walking quickly does nothing but make us both sweaty and tired.

Lucky for us, few people cared about sunblock during the pandemic. They ransacked drugstores for medicine and food. The sunblock display is practically untouched, which almost makes it look like they're still open for business. We stop the first chance we get and take several high-SPF bottles, and Jamie hands me a dark red Phillies hat. 'You can be a bandwagon fan now,' he says, smiling.

'Go, Phils,' I say, putting it on my head.

He tosses his own baseball cap on to the floor and grabs

a straw panama hat with a strip of navy ribbon around the base. It makes him look like he's on a vacation in Cuba. When I say this to him, he puts a heavy glob of sunscreen on his nose and doesn't rub it in.

We're going through water faster than we're finding it, so we begin to ration it. Whenever we find a thick area of trees, we stop and rest in the shade for hours at a time, trying to keep up our strength.

I try to imagine staying back at the cabin, to see if my conscience would have kept quiet. The answer is always no. I want to tell Jamie that I'm sorry for leaving. But he doesn't complain and I'm thankful he's here. When I ask him to stop, he agrees without making me feel bad. When I ask if he's OK, he nods and smiles and asks if I am.

But I'm still lying to him every day. That part kinda sucks. It doesn't help that we don't see any of the graffiti I saw before. Nothing saying 'DCA 6/10 HELP COMING!', which makes me nervous. Maybe it was all disinformation.

But no, I don't want to believe that. There can still be a reason for Jamie to go to Reagan National while I go to Alexandria. We'll find other survivors on the road and he can continue with them and I'll find a way to get to Alexandria. I'll be able to do it on my own if I know someone else is there to protect Jamie.

On the fifth day I leave the crutch where we camped. Jamie says I'm probably fine as long as I take it easy. So no sprinting.

On the sixth day, it isn't as hot, but as noon approaches, the clouds filling the sky behind us begin to look ominous.

The pain returns to my leg as well. It's a fun new superpower that comes with an improperly healed leg – I can tell when rain is coming.

We've been walking along the highway. There are large stretches of empty road and a smattering of abandoned cars here and there. Some of the cars are filled with bodies, but we don't need to stop and look. We do check a few of the empty cars but they're either locked, don't have keys or don't start when we try the ignition. Not that it would matter if they did, because it seems like we'd just be stopping as soon as we reached another roadblock of cars in a half mile or so.

'We should probably get off the road and find shelter soon,' Jamie says, glancing at the clouds. 'The last thing we need is to get struck by lightning.'

'Aw, man. Now that the lottery's defunct that's the only gamble we really had left.'

'At least wait until we've been travelling for a month before you do it.'

We walk another mile and a half before we take an exit into a small town called Mailey. We pass a large wooden sign on the ground; the beams that held it were chopped away with what looks like an axe or a hatchet. The sign has similar marks across its typeface, large gouges of wood taken out. It's painted white with dark green lettering that reads 'Welcome to Mailey, PA! Our home is your home! Pop. 1,113.' The paint is peeling and cracking.

'Well, that looks fucking ominous,' I say, my hand dropping to the gun that Jamie gave me, just to make sure it's still there.

'Yeah.' Jamie unslings the rifle from his shoulder, checks to make sure it's loaded, and looks around us. 'Let's take it slow.'

Thunder rumbles to the north and west of us as the storm rolls in. The wind's picked up. I'm on edge. One look at Jamie and I can see he is as well. The wind gusts in our ears, making it harder to hear if someone's coming up on us. As we move into the centre of town, I dart my eyes around constantly.

It doesn't look like the other cities and towns I've seen. The streets are empty save for old leaves that blow in the wind. The pavement has cracked and split from the winter snow and now green weeds poke up, swaying back and forth.

No windows are broken; nothing has been set on fire. The stores don't even look as if they've been looted. In fact, they look more like they've been neatly packed up. As if the town was dead even before the bug wiped everyone out.

It's growing darker as the black clouds creep towards the sun like tendrils of smoke across the sky. A wind gust creates a miniature dust devil that dances across the road and dissipates as it hits the waving grass on the other side.

We turn a corner, and the street sign above it reads, 'Viking Lane'. My eyes are so focused on the sky that when Jamie puts his hand out to stop me, I jump and grab on to his arm, pulling it to my chest. He's looking down at the ground. I follow his gaze and let out a cry, but a rumble of thunder drowns it out.

Right at my feet is a decayed and decapitated body of a man. He's tall, even without his head, and his leather-like skin is tight against his bones. His frayed clothes hang loosely from his body. Seeing a dead body is nothing to me, but I'm still shocked.

'Where's his head?' I ask. His neck is a ragged tatter of broken bone and shredded flesh. The ground around his neck is dark and oily with the remains of washed and sun-baked blood. There are dried brown bloodstains on his shirt and pants and deep cuts in his arms and hands. 'He was still alive.'

I point to the cuts on his hands and arms – defensive wounds. At least, that's what the police procedurals on TV called them.

Law & Order: Avian Flu. Now isn't the time to make a joke. Why does all my best material pop up at serious moments? My therapist would call it a coping mechanism.

It feels like someone's watching us. Jamie must feel the same way, because when I look over at him his eyes are darting around Viking Lane as well.

Lightning turns the sky purple and a loud crack of thunder follows shortly after. Thick drops of rain begin to plop to the ground around us and the smell of petrichor is all at once a terrifying one.

Jamie nods to the right of us. 'Let's try over there.'

I follow his gaze to a storefront that looks like it used to be an ice cream shop – what's that old saying? You can take the boy out of the ice cream shop, but you can't take the cliché out of the other boy who's with him. Now the windows are dusty and the inside looks vacant. I step around the body and move towards it, looking around for the eyes I swear are following us. It could be my imagination; I *hope* it's my imagination.

I pull on the glass door of the shop and it swings out. The wind blows dust around until we shut the door behind us.

'Watch the front,' Jamie says. 'I'm gonna check the back. And take out your gun.'

The handgun Jamie insisted I be in charge of. I take it out and watch as the storm rolls in. The rain begins to pound against the glass storefront. Lightning illuminates Viking Lane in a bright purple flash and I see a face in the storefront across the street. I cry out but thunder cracks again.

The man is standing back from the window, but his shape is burned into my eyes. I know exactly where he's standing. I hold my breath, waiting, shaking in the darkness. The lightning flashes again and I get a brief look at him once more before I flinch and lose sight of him. He's standing there, naked, staring at me from across the street. There's an axe in his hand.

'All right, looks like the back door can only be opened from the inside.' Jamie's voice makes me jump and I drop the gun. I flinch, expecting it to go off. Instead it just clatters across the floor. Jamie stops it with his foot, widening his eyes at me like I'm a total dork. Which, all right, I'll give him.

'He's over there. He's got an axe.' The panic in my voice has him moving. He picks up the handgun and walks to the window in three quick strides. He holds out the gun to me and then points his rifle towards the shop, looking through the scope.

Lightning flashes again.

'There, see? He's just . . . staring.' I shiver.

He adjusts his sight. Pointing to where he saw the man standing. We wait in silence as the rain patters against the window. Thunder rumbles. Another flash of lightning and Jamie's eyes go wide.

'Did you see him?' I ask.

Jamie's look of shock turns into a smirk. He tries to hold in a laugh but it comes out as a snort.

'What? Is he still there?' The window is starting to fog. I wipe my hand across it and the moisture comes away dirty with dust.

Jamie doubles over, grabbing his stomach. Tears are streaming from his eyes.

'What?' I shout. 'What's so funny?'

Jamie just points and continues laughing. Another flash of lightning and I still see the man standing there, naked and staring. Is he seriously laughing because the guy's naked? Real mature, Jamie. I don't even think this would be the first time someone was attacked by a naked, axe-wielding madman.

Jamie takes deep gasps, still laughing, and holds out the rifle. 'Here,' he says between gasps. I holster the handgun and look through the scope at the man. I can see the outline of his still body through the darkness. Lightning flashes and I jump when I see his pale gaze. My jaw drops open, and now I know why Jamie's laughing so hard.

'It's a mannequin!' he shouts. Revealing the truth

unleashes another wave of giggles from deep within him and he has to sit down. He wipes at his cheeks but more tears quickly replace them.

I smile, redness sweeping over my face. I see through another flash of lightning that the axe I thought the naked mannequin was holding is, in fact, an umbrella wrapped around its wrist.

'All right,' I say.

'The Naked Axe Man Cometh.' Jamie is sent into another fit of howls.

'Oh, I feared for our lives, I'm funny, I get it.'

'The Axe-*Man*nequin!'

'All right, that's enough,' I say, chuckles breaking up my own words. Only it isn't enough. This is the first time – in the *entire* time I've known Jamie – I've ever heard him laugh. All my snarky remarks, my clever jokes, my anecdotes, retelling him movies, none of it made him laugh like this.

And it sounds wonderful.

I sit down on the floor and laugh with him, his laughter infectious. Within moments my stomach hurts from laughing so hard. When there's finally a lull, we both look at each other. The silent eye contact sends us both into another round of snorts and giggles.

The body outside is the furthest thing from our minds for just a little bit. After our laughter subsides, Jamie manages to realise that there's fresh water pouring from the sky. He searches the back room, bringing out several plastic buckets and bowls, and sets them outside. We sit down to watch as they fill up.

Every once in a while, Jamie lets out another chuckle. I smile and elbow him, and his laughter comes back. I could listen to his laugh until the day I die and never get sick of it.

JAMISON

I can't believe they actually made a movie called *Mannequin* in which *a mannequin* comes alive and runs amok in Philly. Andrew told me all about it in one of his movie summaries before he went to sleep.

And now here I am, thinking about *Mannequin*. It sounds like a Hallmark movie, which is a secret I haven't shared with Andrew yet.

I love Hallmark movies.

He thinks I haven't seen any movies because I don't like them. But that's not entirely true; I just only watched Hallmark Channel movies. And I've seen *way* too many of those. In fact, I've seen so many, there are some I've rewatched in their entirety thinking they were a new movie, only to realise at the end I had seen them before.

But that's what I like about them. They're safe and predictable.

Unlike the world now.

My eyes are dry and they burn. A long yawn makes my jaw ache and I glance down at my watch. It's only one in the morning. I told Andrew I would let him sleep until three, then I can sleep from three until nine or so. I remind myself to talk to him about going to sleep earlier and getting up earlier to try to cover as much ground as we can before the sun gets high.

The temperature is only gonna rise as we get further south. Maybe we should stay up all night and travel in darkness, so we can rest during the day. I remember hearing somewhere that's what you're supposed to do in the desert.

Andrew's leg is doing much better. I can only see his limp now when I *really* focus on it. I wait until he asks me if I want to stop and rest because it seems like he's worried we won't make it to Reagan National by June 10. When he asks how I am, I tell him I'm fine, when in reality I'm exhausted. The heat and the walking are taking their toll.

It's been a week since I left home to come after Andrew and I'm thinking about it again. Most nights while I'm up and Andrew is asleep, this is what I think about. He asked me why I came after him and the question haunts me.

Because I don't know the answer. No, I do know the answer, it's just that the answer doesn't make sense to me.

I told him it wasn't safe at the cabin any more, and that might have been true, but it wasn't the whole truth. After I found Andrew's note I couldn't stop picturing him getting hurt again. Falling and breaking his leg. Stepping in *another* bear trap. Meeting a group like Howard's, only this time they didn't bother talking first.

Eventually the worrying was too much. It was like the beginning of the superflu all over again – every night I would be up, pacing around the house, trying not to read posts online about the sick and dying, worrying about my mom while she was at the hospital.

'On the front lines', they kept calling it. As if she was a soldier and that made the fact that she was risking her life mean more.

It was the same worries I was having with Andrew. Picturing him out here on his own. Then finally I couldn't keep worrying about it any more and decided to do something about it.

I stifle another yawn and turn to look at Andrew, sleeping soundly, and I can't figure out what it is about him that makes me feel this way. Maybe it's the fact that we've spent the last several weeks around each other non-stop. Or maybe it's just that he's the only person I've been able to talk to since October.

I blink, but my eyes refuse to open. My body slips forward and I snap awake, sitting up straight. One look at my watch makes my stomach drop. It's 2:30 in the morning. I fell asleep for an hour and a half.

I stand up, looking around the store in the darkness. Outside, the clouds have cleared and Viking Lane is drenched in full-moon blue. The light filters through the dusty windows.

The back room is empty. I listen at the doorway for any sounds of someone shuffling around but hear nothing, so I walk back to Andrew. He lies spread out on the sleeping bag, arms and legs splayed wide. He breathes deep and heavy through his open mouth. I step into the light filtering through the window.

Andrew stirs, talking in his sleep. I look back at him and smile – only the talking sound isn't coming from him.

It's coming from outside.

My heart lurches in my chest, blood pounding in my ears. I turn back towards Viking Lane.

Footsteps scrape across the pavement, the deep voice of a man shouting. He's singing. Singing something familiar, too – I recognise the lyrics but can't quite place them.

I see his shadow first, cast across the weed-cracked asphalt by the full moon. I step back away from the window, moving into the shadows of the ice cream shop. I check my feet, making sure the moon isn't illuminating any part of me.

The moonlight exposes Andrew's arm. I reach down, the man's voice getting closer and louder. He's walking *towards* the ice cream shop. I reach for Andrew's wrist, my other hand hovering above his mouth, ready to clamp over it if he cries out. As the man's shadow falls across the floor, I pull Andrew's arm out of the moon's light and put his hand on his chest, then raise the rifle towards the window.

My eyes drop to the handgun on the floor next to Andrew, who remains asleep. The man leans against the store window, his back to us, and I breathe a quiet sigh of relief. But I still keep the gun on him because in one hand he has a half-empty bottle of whisky, and in the other he has a small hatchet.

The metal of the hatchet clangs loudly against the window as the man takes another swig. Andrew sleeps through the clanging as it reverberates in the empty shop.

'Everyone's Gone to the Movies.' The lyrics hit me as soon as he starts up again. It's Steely Dan. My mother had the album back at the cabin. Every time she played it and this song came on she would make a face and say, 'Oh, I hate this song.' For good reason, too.

Hearing the drunken singing by the man wielding the axe makes the lyrics even creepier.

Kids if you want some fun, Mr LaPage is your man, my brain sings the first two lines, sending goosebumps across my body. 'Mr LaPage' takes another swig of liquor and pushes himself off the window. He looks back at the window and stops, looking in at us.

I raise the gun again, my finger at the ready. This time I'll pull the trigger. It won't be like the deer. Andrew's next to me, asleep, and I'm not letting this guy anywhere near him.

I swallow hard but my mouth is dry.

I wait for him to smile at me, to say something, anything. Instead, he closes one eye and fixes his long dry hair. He's looking at his reflection in the moonlight. He pulls at the beard around his mouth and turns back on to Viking Lane.

I stand and walk towards the window, watching him go. He gets to the body in the middle of the road and stops, standing over it. He drops the hatchet on the ground with a loud metallic thud, then he takes another long swig of whisky before he reaches between his legs and unloads a stream of urine over the dead body in the street.

My teeth clench and I hold on to the gun tightly. I turn away from the window in disgust and walk back to where Andrew lies on the floor. Mr LaPage walks back in front of the window and down Viking Lane.

After I'm sure he's gone, I breathe out a heavy sigh and set the gun down. My palms, neck, and forehead are all sweaty. It has nothing to do with the proximity of Mr LaPage; it was the way my brain was working while he was close to us that makes me nervous. He was right there, with a hatchet – the same hatchet he no doubt used to chop the head off a man in the middle of the street.

Still, I didn't pull the trigger. I didn't *need* to, but even if he had seen us and come in, I don't know if I could have. In the moment I was so sure I would protect Andrew, but the more I thought about it, the more I realised I wouldn't even be able to shoot a drunk dude with an axe. I could have tried to reason with him first. I could have woken Andrew up and the two of us, guns drawn, could convince him to leave. Then we could run.

Instead, I was scared. Scared of what would happen if I pulled the trigger and killed him. Would I be just as bad as Mr LaPage at that point? I don't know why he killed the man in the street; perhaps he wandered into town. Maybe he held up Mr LaPage at gunpoint. Maybe Mr LaPage sneaked up behind him barefoot and buried the hatchet into the man's back. Mr LaPage had his back to me. If I shot him, it would be the same thing.

I'm wide awake now, my body coursing with adrenaline. I let Andrew sleep until four in the morning, when I finally begin to calm down. I shake him, hard, and he wakes. I decide not to tell him about Mr LaPage. The way the man was drinking, he must be passed out by now, and will still be passed out by the time we leave in the morning. There's no need to worry him. Andrew was already terrified seeing

112

the mannequin. This time, when I think of it, I don't smile or laugh.

I lie on the sleeping bag and close my eyes. I'm able to drift off into a twilight sleep, waking up every once in a while. Each time the sky outside is a brighter shade of blue. At seven in the morning, I sit up.

'Let's get an early start today,' I say when Andrew looks over to me.

'You sure?'

'Yeah, this place creeps me out.'

ANDREW

Our first day out of Mailey, we walk fifteen miles. Part of it is due to the storm cooling everything down; the other part is Jamie. It's like he's in a rush. It might have to do with the heat, or maybe he wants to get as far as we can as fast as we can while it isn't oppressive, not realising the further south we get, the more nervous I am.

On the second day I ask if he wants to stop in the next town to look around for bikes. He says no, he likes the walk and we're making good time. But he means to Reagan National.

Alexandria is about 182 miles from Jamie's cabin. Then the airport is only ten miles from Alexandria, so if we walk at the pace we went yesterday, we could make it in a little less than three weeks – which would be the beginning of June. We'd be cutting it close, but as long as we keep moving, we should make it by June 10.

We actually do manage to keep the pace. Jamie doesn't want to stop in most of the towns and we begin sleeping under trucks on the abandoned highway. We open one truck to discover it's half-full of a supermarket food delivery. Including bottled water!

'This must be one of those pirate trucks,' Jamie says.

I heard about them, too. People would rent trucks and either purchase or steal massive quantities of supplies to sell at a premium on the street. The truck is black and nondescript, but there's white paint splashed across the side in an almost perfect square, blocking out some kind of writing beneath it in red spray paint. But only three corners of the phrase are visible under the white splatter.

Supermarkets had more staples – dairy, bread, canned goods – than fresh vegetables or meat before the shipping chain started to break down link by link. When they shut down the borders, most of the veggies stopped coming and everyone switched to canned and frozen. Then slowly the frozen foods vanished, too.

The last time I went to the store with my dad, most of the shelves had been picked clean, and they didn't bother to restock them because they knew the shelves would be barren again as soon as the doors opened. Instead, boxes had been cut open and stacked on dollies for us to pick through. We waited in line with our masks and they let us in six at a time. And of course, the new policy was 'you touch, you buy'.

But Jamie and I touch whatever we want in the truck, checking expiration dates and looking for bulges in the cans. After we stock up on what we can carry, we close the door behind us, because Jamie's afraid rodents will somehow get in. Opening a box of Sharpies, he writes over the white paint: 'OPEN ME! FOOD INSIDE.'

'Yeah, because that doesn't look like a trap,' I say.

'Eh, the people who need it will risk it.'

I love how optimistic he is. It works for him, but maybe

that's because he's never had to deal with liberal parents who *still* manage to shock you when you come out and they say it's a phase. Or how about that time in sixth grade when it seemed like you were making fun friends who invited you to meet them at the movie theatre on Friday night and then never showed up. Or, no! Silly me, they *did* show up. They just went to the earlier showing of the movie so they could come out and find you waiting there after an hour. And then try to gaslight you into thinking you heard the time wrong.

Yeah, optimism isn't my thing.

Sometimes I wish I could think like Jamie. His logic is sound, but it's also so full of hope. That makes me smile, and we continue on our way.

It's our twenty-seventh day travelling and we can see Baltimore in the distance. What's left of it, at least. New York looked similar. Only the last time I saw New York, the fires were still burning. Baltimore is silent and clear. It's gotten hot again.

'Here's where things get interesting,' Jamie says, dropping his pack.

'Interesting how?'

'I was checking the map yesterday and I realised something.' He reaches into his pack and takes out the road atlas I nabbed from a Connecticut bookstore. 'All the major highways into or around Baltimore are tunnels. There's the Fort McHenry Tunnel, which follows 95.'

'All right, so what's the other one, and how far out of the way does it go?' We're getting close to Alexandria, but it's May 29. The first half of our trip was bogged down by my hobbling, so we only have eleven days to get to the Fosters or we risk them not even being there.

If they're still alive.

Jamie points at the atlas. 'It doesn't really take us out of the way. It's the Baltimore Harbor Tunnel. But I want to suggest getting off here, at Route 40.' His finger moves to the intersection of the highway and the tunnel. 'Then follow it over here to where it meets up with 695, and follow that back down to I-95.'

'But that's going right through Baltimore. We said we wanted to avoid the major cities.'

'Yeah, but I'm a little concerned about the tunnels. We don't know what kind of state they're in – they could have collapsed from disrepair, or they could be filled with bodies.'

My mind starts running. What if the city is a mess? What if there are people there? What if Jamie wants to stay with them for a while? So many possible delays. I'd have to leave him again.

The thought makes me nervous because he would probably try to come after me like he did before. Only this time I can move a bit faster and he might not be able to catch up. And this close to Alexandria I wouldn't be able to talk myself out of it.

I've come all this way. And yes, Jamie was never supposed to be here with me, but I couldn't have made it so far without him. But I do need to start thinking about how I get to Alexandria without him knowing.

The best way is to just keep on our path and hope that by the time he realises something is up, it's too late.

I say, 'Let's just take the route that stays on 95 and see how it is. If it's bad, we can go your way.'

'That's a lot of backtracking.'

It is, but this route is the most direct. And I have no intention of backtracking.

'It's better than going out of our way and through the city. I don't think Baltimore was super safe even before the bug.'

'If the tunnels have collapsed, we're still going out of our way.'

'We don't know that there's anything wrong with the tunnels.'

'There's also the Francis Scott Key Bridge down here.' He points further downstream of the Patapsco River to I-695. 'If you don't want to go through Baltimore, we can go back north to follow 695 down to where it meets up with 95 again.'

'Oh my God, you sound like my dad with all these different routes. And that's still out of our way.'

'I don't think the tunnels are a good idea, Andrew.'

'They're the most direct routes. We can take the McHenry and see how it is. Look.' I point up at a peeling highway sign. There's another one of those white boxes painted over the bottom corner of the sign – again, covering what looks like red spray paint – but it doesn't block the words 'Fort McHenry Tunnel, Toll Plaza 5 Miles'. 'We're almost there, we can check it out.'

'All right.' He folds up the map and avoids my eyes as he puts it away, clearly annoyed.

I don't want to go out of our way if we don't have

to. We've also gotten lucky, as we haven't run into anyone in over a hundred miles. Part of me believes that avoiding larger cities helps with that. The other part of me is starting to worry that maybe everyone else really *is* dead.

We reach the tunnel a little before noon, travelling mostly in silence since Jamie is, of course, now annoyed with me. But only my own footsteps echo against the asphalt and concrete. I look back and Jamie is gazing up at the mouth of the tunnel.

'You coming?'

'Yeah,' he says, still not looking at me. He takes off his pack and begins digging through it until he finds a small flashlight.

'It's a straight shot,' I say. There's legit one, and only one, way to go. It's not the catacombs in Paris, it's a tunnel.

He grunts and puts on his pack, then shines the light into the tunnel for me. I turn and we begin walking in, our footsteps echoing together now.

'You know, if you kill the battery in that thing, we're going to have to dig in the dark from now on.' The flashlight is mostly used when we have to go to the bathroom at night.

'I'll deal with it.' There's something in his voice. Is he scared?

I smile, still facing forward. 'Jamie, did you ever watch the show *Chernobyl*?'

'Shut up.'

'What if it dies while we are in *here*? What if right as we get to the halfway point we're engulfed in darkness?'

'Shut. Up.'

'You're scared of the dark,' I say, turning to him. We march into the tunnel, following the darkness.

His voice wavers slightly as his eyes dart around at the shadows. 'You're scared of mannequins, what's your point?'

'I can't believe this. Big, bad survivalist Jamie is scared of the dark. Did you have a night-light as a kid?'

'Yes, well into high school.'

Oh my fucking God, is that adorable or are my standards apocalyptically lowered?

'I'm not scared of the dark,' he says, clearly lying. 'I'm scared of the tunnel.'

'What's it going to do? Bite you?'

'Collapse.' He's pointing the light at the ceiling, looking for cracks.

'Right, because a flashlight is going to sto— AH!' I let out a cry as something cold and wet touches my ankle and floods my shoe.

'What?' Jamie jumps, and there's fear in his voice. The light moves over the tunnel quickly and I see the water. The tunnel's flooded up to my ankles.

'Great,' I say, lifting my foot out of the water, even though this accomplishes nothing. I set it back down and continue walking.

'Wait, stop.'

'Jamie, it's not collapsed.' I turn and take the flashlight from him, pointing it further ahead. It fades into the blackness as the tunnel curves ahead, but I can see the ceiling of the tunnel reflecting off the surface of the water below. 'It's probably just from the rain. This is a slope and the tunnel's wide open to the elements.'

Jamie doesn't answer, but when I turn to walk forward his feet slosh into the water as well. I hand him the flashlight and we continue.

It isn't until the light behind us has totally faded that I realise the water feels like it's rising against my legs. I chalk it up to us making small waves, but then Jamie speaks.

'The water's higher.'

'We're still sloping down.' But I'm not so sure that's the answer any more.

We keep moving in silence, but then the water passes my knees. It's getting harder to walk now. Then the water reaches my thighs and, yes, we may have made a mistake. Jamie doesn't speak, though. Either he's too pissed or he knows I've reached the same conclusion he has: we're already halfway through the tunnel and the mistake's been made.

The freezing water slips past my waist and my teeth are chattering. I turn to Jamie; he's still pointing the flashlight up at the tiled ceiling. He isn't mad, he's scared.

'Is it too late to say I'm sorry?' I ask.

'A little bit, but it's fine. We have to be close.'

We keep moving, but the water keeps rising. It's up to our chests and we lift our guns over our heads. But the packs are waterlogged and slow us down. There are a few cars that have rusted under all the water, the insides filled as well. Jamie flashes a light at one and we see the bloated body of someone floating against the window.

'I think it's the pumps,' he says. I don't ask for

clarification because my teeth are chattering but he gives it anyway. 'I think the tunnels have pumps that keep the river water out. There was a hurricane that hit New York and the subways flooded because the water couldn't be pumped out fast enough.'

'See? I told you it didn't collapse. And here you were, worried this would be more difficult for us.'

'Boy, is my face red.'

'Eh, looks a little blue.' I smile at him but then see that the flashlight is dimmer. 'Hey, Jamie. Remember that joke I said earlier about the flashlight running out of batteries?'

'Yeah. It wasn't funny.'

'It's even less funny while it's happening.'

Jamie looks into the flashlight. 'All right. Can we move a little faster?'

I nod and we keep moving. The water's almost to our necks. At this point we can practically swim.

'Don't let it get in your mouth or eyes,' Jamie says. The light is getting dimmer. What if the water gets higher? We can't swim because the canned food in our packs will weigh us down.

What do we do?

Jamie lets out a cry as the flashlight dies, and we're alone in the dark beneath a hundred feet of cold river water.

JAMISON

I cry out, grasping in the darkness for Andrew. I feel him jump away from me, startled, but then reach out and grab my hand.

'That's you, right?' I ask.

'Yes,' he says. 'I have you.' He links his fingers with mine and pulls me towards him. The water has stopped rising right at my neck, which means Andrew is barely above the surface. I wrap an arm around him and try to lift him up to my height.

'Thanks.' His voice wavers. He must be scared, too. We walk. I hold his hand and he's holding mine, tight. My arm is wrapped around his waist, holding him up.

I'm cold, I'm wet and I'm terrified. But with Andrew this close I feel safer, like whatever's in the dark can't hurt us. Not that there is anything in the dark. Not even whatever just brushed against my leg. I shiver and Andrew's grip tightens.

The water has gotten lower, but I don't notice it at first because my body's so cold.

We keep moving and when the water's down to our waists we move faster, splashing as we see light from the curve up ahead. We run until we escape the cold river water, the sun within our reach. Our packs are soaked and heavy but we're running full force.

Gasping for air, we burst into the warm sunlight, and I let out a loud scream of victory. I don't want to let go of Andrew's hand but I know I have to at some point, so I pull him into a wet hug and jump up and down. He joins me, squeezing me back and hollering as well. He's laughing again and I laugh, too. I let him go but I'm still smiling.

Andrew looks smug. 'I told you that was going to be our best option.'

'You're not allowed to make decisions any more.'

'Not even what we have for dinner?'

'Especially not what we have for dinner.' And now that we're on the subject, I remember the food we have in our packs. I set the rifle down and take mine off. It's still leaking dirty river water. Andrew takes off his as well and we unpack our clothes and canned food. The food labels are soaked, our books are soaked, the clothes are soaked, but worst of all, the road atlas is soaked.

'Have I said sorry yet?' Andrew asks. I open my mother's notebook, turning the pages gently so they don't rip. The writing is still there and the pages are intact.

'It's not bad. We can dry it out.' I set the book down in the sun, open to the middle, and Andrew gently unfolds some of the pages of the road atlas and puts it down next to the book in the middle of the road, placing four cans of food on top of the corners.

'Plus, look at the bright side.' I hold up a can, its label missing somewhere in the pack or in the wet piles of them on the ground. 'Every night is mystery dinner. I guess I'll let you choose a can every once in a while.'

We spread out our wet clothes and sleeping bags across the highway, turn our wet packs inside out, and lay out ourselves to dry in the sun. I take the last two batteries in my bag and swap out the dead ones in the flashlight. Andrew makes fun of me again for my claustrophobia and I make fun of him about the Axe-Mannequin while pretending it wasn't just claustrophobia. I think he thinks I was joking about the night-light. Keeping it well into high school was more out of habit than my fear of the dark. But that fear is real.

We go three more days without seeing another person. I'm surprised at how empty the roads are. Especially when we should at least be seeing other travellers on the way to Reagan National. Don't get me wrong, I'm more than happy to avoid as many people as possible until we get there, but still. It's eerily quiet on the roads.

In movies and TV shows about the apocalypse, the ones Andrew would be shocked that I've seen, the roads are always packed with abandoned cars – bumper-to-bumper traffic at the end of the world. But the reality of it is, when it got bad, no one wanted to go anywhere. We've come upon a few abandoned car or truck roadblocks on the highways, but mostly it's a few cars here and there, usually filled with bodies of people trying to get somewhere – to family maybe, or a favourite vacation spot. I can't help but feel sorry for them, never reaching their destinations.

We stop for a water break and Andrew takes out the

map, again. He's been looking at it every couple of hours the past two days but won't tell me why.

'What are you looking for?' I ask, tightening the cap of my water bottle.

'A different way around DC. But it's hard. Look.' Andrew points to the map and I crouch down to look. 'We could take 495, but it looks like it just runs in a circle around the city.'

'What's wrong with that?'

'Nothing, but look at Route 1.' He points out Route 1, running through Alexandria, Virginia. 'It basically starts to run parallel to 95 and if we take that to 495 and then cut through Bethesda, we can avoid taking 1 through DC.'

Alexandria. There's something about Alexandria, but I can't quite remember what it is.

'OK,' I say. 'So we go through Bethesda down here and . . .' I follow the road with my finger a bit, then look over at him. 'This still goes through Washington. Look, here's the Vietnam Memorial, the Lincoln Memorial, the Pentagon and finally Reagan National.'

He focuses on my finger as I point out each landmark. 'Huh, so it does.'

Something's up with him. 'Just to be clear, you want to cut through DC to avoid going through DC?'

'I thought it went around the city,' he says quietly.

I stare at him, trying to figure him out. Usually I can do this; at least it's been that way since I met him. It's not that I know everything he's thinking, but I can tell when he's annoyed – like when rain is coming and his leg aches. I can tell when he's thinking about something that happened before the apocalypse because he gets quiet, and when I ask him what's up, he smiles and says it's nothing or that he was thinking of a movie to tell me about.

Right now, I can tell he's hiding something. Then it hits me: the piece of paper in the book he gave me had an address in Alexandria written on it. So it *was* a stop he wanted to make. Alexandria is further south than Reagan National. But I don't know why he wouldn't tell me about it, or what's there.

I try to think of any number of reasons why he would hide this from me, but none of them seem right. He trusts me – he proved that when he let me torture him to help his leg heal. But I can't figure out why he doesn't trust me with this.

For the first time I wonder if I made a mistake in trusting Andrew. The thought makes my stomach hurt.

'Why do you really want to go there so bad? You can tell me, Andrew.' I'm hoping he'll just take the bait and tell me about Alexandria. I purposefully say 'there' instead of DC.

He still avoids my gaze. 'I just didn't look close enough at the map.'

I sit down next to him, tucking my legs under me. He's still not ready to tell me and I don't want to sit here making up possibilities. But I trust him, so I feel like I should let him know he can trust me. 'I know what this is about.'

He finally looks at me. It's not true. I know there's something specific he's looking for but doesn't want to tell me about; the most obvious thing it could be is that he wants to find someone. Andrew wants to be optimistic about something, but everything that's happened in his life doesn't let him. This is based on the limited understanding I have of his life, pre-apocalypse. His parents were strict and didn't necessarily approve of who he was. He didn't have someone like my mom, who was spiritual, not religious; who believed that what you put out into the universe you got back. Andrew wants hope, but he can't *let* himself hope.

'I understand that you want to find people,' I say. Something changes in his face and it looks like he's going to interrupt me, so I talk fast. 'If you want to go looking for someone, I think we should do it.'

My instincts – that ever-growing pit of fire in my stomach – tell me that going out of our way is wrong. But I do trust him, whether I should or not. So far Andrew has been so forthcoming about everything that he has to have a reason for this. I know it.

I try to give him a friendly smile but he doesn't smile back. I stand and hold out a hand to help him up. We'll take his way through Alexandria to find whoever he needs to find and I won't stand in his way. Maybe it's my own optimism taking advantage of me, but I think he'll tell me eventually.

We take 495 around DC and exit on to route 355 into Bethesda. The small town looks worse than Baltimore did from afar. The shops are looted, cars are burned, trash and leaves blow in the hot and humid breeze. The bodies littering the ground are much older than the decapitated one in Mailey. At least none of them outwardly look like they died from acts of violence. If they were flu victims, they were the walking dead kind, the ones who refused to rest and stay indoors, deliriously walking through the streets while fever cooked their brains and mucus drowned them.

The stay-at-home orders came too late – some time in early September after the vice president was sworn in. Most people didn't need the stay-at-home order; they had been staying in since July. But there were still a few, like the eight or so bodies in downtown Bethesda, who decided to press their luck. By the time the government tried to institute a full-on lockdown like a few European countries, the National Guard had already lost most of their ranks, so there was no one to uphold it.

Everything had happened either too slowly or too late.

Andrew's been quiet for too long, which always makes me nervous. I like it better when he talks, even if I just listen. I point to the broken front window of a Banana Republic. 'Should we replenish these rags?'

'Come on now, Jamie. You know the last fashions shipped out were for the fall line. Do you want to wear chinos and button-down plaid in a-hundred-and-three-degree heat?'

'Sounds hot. Eh? Get it?'

He rolls his eyes, but I see him smirk. 'I think it's my turn to retch at your bad joke.' He retches.

'Because your jokes are the height of humour.'

'Oh, I know. I mean, you should be paying me, my jokes are so good.' He nudges me and smiles, and something flutters in my chest. I don't have time to enjoy the fluttering, or even think about what it could mean, because someone speaks from behind us.

'If you two stopped joking around, you could hear an old lady sneak up on you.' We turn and there's a shotgun pointing at Andrew's face.

ANDREW

Jamie raises his gun and the shotgun barrel moves over to point at him. 'Don't,' the gruff voice says.

The woman holding the shotgun has to be in her late sixties or early seventies. She looks like she could be a cousin to Bea Arthur and sounds like she's smoked a pack a day since 1967. She's white and skinny, with short, curly white hair, and she's wearing a brown vest, a loose white button-down and jeans.

Jamie puts up his hand and places the rifle on the ground in front of her, and I follow his lead.

'Good boys,' she says, the wrinkles deepening around her eyes as she smiles. She lowers the gun, but not enough for me to stop worrying about where she might shoot us. 'Now let's start with what you're doing here. I haven't seen either of you two around town before.'

'We aren't from here,' Jamie says.

'I already know that part, if you were paying attention. I asked *what* you were doing here.'

'Just passing through,' I say.

'From where?'

'Philadelphia,' says Jamie.

'Connecticut,' I say.

'Which is it? Philly or Connecticut?'

'Both,' I say before Jamie speaks. 'I met him outside Philly on my way down from Connecticut.' I decide to be proactive and keep talking. 'We're heading to Reagan Airport. Have you heard?'

She nods. 'Help from Europe?'

'Have you been there?' Jamie asks.

'To Europe? Nah, never made it.' Jamie opens his mouth to correct her but she waves at him. 'I'm kidding. No, heard about it and seen the graffiti, but . . . all sounds like bullshit to me. Reagan's south-east, you're a little ways off. What made you come through here?' she asks.

'We wanted to pass through DC to see if there's anything left. In case Reagan was a bust,' Jamie says.

She frowns and lowers her gun further. We both slowly put our hands down. She lets out a low grunt that turns into a hacking cough. We flinch, and she holds up her hand to us and spits on the ground behind her.

'Don't worry, I've had this cough since 1982. It's not the superflu. It's the smoking. Which, sadly, I can't do any more. Unless you boys managed to find any cigarettes along the way for your new friend Henri?'

We shake our heads and I say, 'No, sorry.'

'Eh, just as well. Pick up your guns, come on. It's getting late anyway. You boys can stay the night.' She waves her hands at our weapons and starts walking away from us.

'Um, actually,' Jamie starts, but Henri interrupts him.

'It wasn't a question. Come on, it's not safe after sundown.' She turns to us, smiling. 'There's beasts roaming the streets at night.' She lets out a chuckle that turns into another coughing fit.

We follow her to a small boarded-up brick rancher with a five-foot-high iron fence around it. Brick pillars stand along the fence every five feet or so with concrete globes on top. The house is small, with a little front yard and a concrete driveway that's also gated off by the fence. An old brown Buick covered in dust and pollen is parked in the drive. A grease stain runs out from under it.

Henri unlocks the large padlock, pulls the chain and pushes open the front gate with a low squeal of rust. She holds it open for us and wraps the chain back around it as we scoot past her, locking us in.

Jamie shoots me a look of uncertainty, but for some reason, I don't fear her. It isn't because she's old. I know if she wanted to, she could have already shot us on the street. Instead she invites us back to her home?

Sorry, her *fortified bunker*.

She opens the door for us. It's musty and warm, but there's something comforting about it.

'Take off your shoes,' she says. The carpet is soft and I flex my toes against it, feeling something other than hard asphalt for the first time in over four weeks. The sunlight outside filters around the boards on the window.

On the walls hang still-life artwork and old photos. There's a wooden credenza with drawers against the wall in front of us. Gilt-edged frames of different people line the top of it. Including a young version of Henri, holding a smiling child in her arms. I don't want to ask her about it, as the rest of the house lies in silence.

'Drop your packs, get comfortable. Sit down.' She motions her arms to the living area to our right. 'Can I get you boys something to drink? I have water and canned juice.'

'Water will be fine, thank you,' Jamie says.

'For me too, thanks.' Look at us both still minding our manners after the apocalypse.

She goes into the kitchen area and I hear her take glasses down and set them on a counter. I think back on that first night with Jamie. How I was so worried about him poisoning me.

'What if she put something in the water?' I whisper.

'Why would she bring us back here to poison us when she could have just killed us in the street?'

'To save on ammo, most likely.' We turn to see Henri standing behind us, holding out two glasses of water.

Christ, she's quiet. That's twice now she's sneaked up on us.

We take the glasses and she turns around and walks back into the kitchen. 'Sit down, I said.'

We move over to the couch and sit. It's like sitting on a cloud. I let out a sigh as Henri comes back out from the kitchen with an empty glass. She takes Jamie's glass and pours a few drops from it into hers, then pours a little of mine in, too, and hands it back to me. She downs the water in a gulp and sets it on the coffee table in front of us.

She points to Jamie. 'If I wanted to kill you I wouldn't have spoken to you in the street. I would have shot you in the back.' Then she points to me. 'Then when you

134

turned around I would have taken you out, too. And yet here we are, sipping fresh sterilised rainwater and introducing ourselves.'

She sits down on the love seat across from us and puts her arms across the back of it.

'So I'm Henrietta, but call me Henri. Everyone did.'

'I'm Jamison.' He takes a drink of his water.

'Andrew. Nice to meet you.'

'You're both well met. Now, let's talk civics. You boys are cutting through Washington in hopes that the United States government got their act together enough to have their own little civilisation down here?'

'That was the idea. We figured everyone else who was following the signs would hole up there to wait until June tenth. And the government had to survive somehow,' Jamie says. I'm glad he's the one speaking; part of me fears that Henri comes with a well-tuned BS detector and will call me out on my half-truths as soon as the words leave my mouth.

She laughs. 'Oh, honey. Our government fell apart before anything else did. Congress took years to pass healthcare bills and then argued they were unconstitutional. Then when everyone started getting sick, all they cared about was their economy. What makes you think they could make decisions regarding the safety and continuance of our country? Those pricks were all just worried about themselves. No, Capitol Hill was the first town to reach population zero.'

She holds up her hand, shaping it into an O to emphasise her point.

'It's not just us, though. The foreign embassies didn't even bother to pull out their people. Which is why I'm not putting much credence in the Reagan rumours either.' She shakes her head, sadness in her eyes. 'Sorry, kids. It looks like it's everyone for themselves no matter where you go.'

Jamie nods. 'We figured, but no way of knowing without trying.'

'You're welcome to stay the night here. Longer if you need.' She pushes herself up from the couch with a groan. 'Best start working on dinner. Who wants to come outside and keep lookout?'

'Lookout for what?' I ask.

She looks at me, a knowing smile on her face. She reaches for her shotgun and tosses it over. 'I told you, there's monsters in the dark.' She turns, laughing and coughing as she makes her way to the back of the house. Jamie shoots me a look that says, *She's insane.* I shrug and stand up, following her out the back door into the yard.

There is a high wooden fence surrounding the yard. In the centre of it is a small firepit with a brick wood-fire oven and grill. Next to the house is a small wooden structure that has a moon carved into it. An outhouse. I assume she put it together after the water stopped running. I *hope* she put it together after the water stopped running.

'My late husband built this,' she says, hitting the brick oven with her hand as she passes it. She continues to a shed in the back of the yard, shouting to us as she opens the door. 'I thought it was a real eyesore at first. And we used it maybe twelve times in the twenty years from when he built it up till he died. But I tell you, it's been mighty useful since the gas stopped working on the inside stove.'

'My house had a wood-fire stove, too,' Jamie says.

'Good, then you can help me cook. Andrew, you keep watch. You see anything come over the fence, shoot it.'

'Yes, ma'am.' She *is* joking, right?

'And don't yes, ma'am me. The only people to call me ma'am were telemarketers and Jehovah's Witnesses.'

'So, Henri, what do these monsters look like?'

She looks at me with that same sly smile and hands Jamie four cans of food. 'You think I'm crazy, don't you?'

How do I say this delicately? 'You are talking about monsters that come out at night.'

Nailed it.

She shakes her head. 'Just because there're stories about monsters don't mean they don't exist in real life. Especially not nowadays.'

'Got it, metaphorical monsters.' I nod, looking over at the fence. She's talking about people. Howard's crew. Me. *We're* the monsters now.

'There, now you're using your head, kid. Just use your eyes along with it.'

I scan the fence as Henri and Jamie talk and cook dinner. The sun gets lower and Henri asks Jamie to start a fire in the pit for them so they can see. Under the gutters at both ends of the house are large black barrels collecting water from the downspouts.

At the back right corner of the yard are rows of fresh vegetables. Henri takes a pepper and a cucumber and fills a large bowl with water from the rain bucket using a spigot in the side. She washes the veggies and returns to Jamic.

Whatever they're making smells amazing. I look back at Jamie and Henri; they're smiling and talking as they cook. The sun has set and I can only see what the flames of the firepit light up, but Jamie looks like he's happy to be here.

A scratching sound comes from the other side of the fence to my right. I whirl around, pointing the shotgun. But almost as suddenly as it started, the noise stops. I hold my breath, listening for the scratch again and hearing only the sound of my racing heart. Maybe it was a tree, a branch blowing in the wind or something.

It isn't. There's a harder, louder scratch – several of them, like a creature pawing at the other side, and the fence shakes. I hear a growl from behind the fence, low to the ground. I point the shotgun where I think whatever could be making that sound is.

'The top of the fence, Andrew!' Henri's voice screams from behind me. 'Not there! The top!'

I raise the shotgun to the top of the fence. What could it be? What could jump up to the top of the fence? Henri's on the move. She runs to the side of the house.

'If you see it, shoot it and run to the house as fast as you can. Both of you. Don't wait to see if you hit it, just move.'

Henri grabs something. She runs to the fence and begins shaking whatever's in her hand, creating a piercing noise. She stops long enough for me to see it's a mason jar filled with pennies. She puts her ear to the fence, then shakes the pennies a final time, screaming.

She stops and we all wait in silence. A minute passes, but we hear nothing and Henri turns, smiling.

'There, all gone.' She puts the jar back and goes over to Jamie.

'What was that?' he asks.

She shrugs, unconcerned. 'Told you there's monsters.'

'Yeah, *metaphorical!*' I say.

'So there's real ones, too.'

Even with the monster scare, we eat outside. She's made us rabbit, which came from mason jars she canned herself, and grilled veggies. It's the first time since leaving Jamie's that I've had meat that wasn't stuffed into canned ravioli. It's absolutely amazing, and there's plenty of it.

We ask more about the 'monster', but all Henri tells us is she knows it's some hungry animal. A bigger one came over the fence one night after she had already gone inside to eat, but she never got a chance to see what it was, and never wanted to look. She took to calling it 'the monster' because that's how big it was.

'Plus I feel it adds a touch of whimsy to the apocalypse. It's probably a bear from the state park or mountain lion from out in the Alleghenies. Coulda swore I saw a boar one day back in the pre-superflu times.'

After dinner we go into the living room and light candles. We tell her about our lives, Jamie first, while she sips water and uses a small handheld fan. By the time I'm telling her about Jamie fixing my leg, he's snoring, passed out on his own shoulder. I look over at him and smile. Henri does, too.

I stand up and pull his torso over on to the couch so his neck isn't strained. I let him sleep as Henri moves over for me.

'He your boyfriend?'

I smile and shake my head. 'I'm not his type.'

She gives me a sceptical glance. 'He left home to follow you?'

'It was a vacation cabin, but yeah?' What did that matter?

'The vacation cabin with hot water and electricity.'

So? He was worried about Howard and his people. She doesn't get it – how bad everything is out there. She's been lucky. If she wants to make the trip up north for a hot shower, I'll give her the directions.

'Sounds like a nice place is all I'm saying.' She gives me another sceptical look, or maybe it's judgey. Maybe she thinks we were thoughtless for leaving.

I smile and nod, her eyes still on me. I look back at the pictures on the wall.

'Is one of these your husband?'

She chuckles, allowing the subject change, and points at a wedding portrait. 'That's us. Tommy and me. He passed in 2007. We had three great kids, though.' She points them out as she speaks. 'Tommy Jr, Kristy and Amy. Tommy and Kristy both have four little ones each with their spouses and Amy is . . . was pregnant with her first. Last I heard.'

Sadness clouds her glassy eyes.

'Is she . . . ?' I don't want to say it. It's horrible even thinking it.

She shrugs. 'Don't know. I stopped hearing from her when the phone went out. Little Tommy is. His wife, Maggie, called me last August to let me know. She called me again when their son William and daughter Anna died. That was the last I heard. Kristy lost her husband and three of her children. She called me every day until the phones died. I'm optimistic, so I like to think they're still alive.'

'Where were they?'

'Kristy was in Colorado. Tommy was in Maine.' She smiles a sad smile. 'Amy was in Florida.'

'Where in Florida?'

'Islamorada. It's right under Key Largo. She owned a bookshop down there. Called it Henri's Hideaway. There was a café and little reading nooks along the stacks, and hammocks out on a patio for people to relax and read.' Henri lets out what could barely pass as a chuckle before she coughs. 'I was always supposed to go down there. I was going to help her run it and . . .' Her voice trails off and her eyes get a little glassier. 'I kept putting it off. Putting off cleaning the house, getting it on the market.'

'Then the bug.'

A sad smile creeps across her face. 'You know, at the end of July – when we finally realised just how bad it would be – I started death cleaning.'

'Death cleaning?'

'I didn't want my kids to have to deal with all the shit Tommy Sr and I had accumulated. So I started cleaning. But here I am. The house is ready and no one's here to buy it.'

My heart breaks a little for Henri. I don't know what to say to her.

'Maybe you should leave with us. We can go down and look for her together if the Reagan National rumours aren't true.' It feels wrong lying to her, but she could help Jamie. She could stay with him if things don't work out in Alexandria. And then again if they don't work out at Reagan. It's the first time I think of those two things as a one-two punch for Jamie. Losing me, then finding out the rumours about a European convoy have been exaggerated.

She laughs and we both look to see if Jamie wakes up, but he doesn't. 'I don't want to slow you down.'

'Not like we'd be in a rush.' But knowing Jamie, he wouldn't mind at all.

'I also don't think I have a thousand some-odd mile walk in me, kid. Sorry, but I'm hunkered down here pretty nicely.'

But I can still see that sadness in her eyes. It looks like she *would* make the journey if she could. And I know I just met her – and I could be entirely wrong – but it sounds like she's thought about it before.

'I hope she's alive. But then I feel that guilt again. That I was being foolish before all this came and messed it up, thinking I had so much time. Mothers are supposed to be there for their daughters when they have a baby. And I'm not.'

'Maybe if there is help coming, they'll be able to find your daughter and bring her up here.'

'Maybe. If you're even heading for the airport, that is.'

I look up at her and she's giving me a knowing look, like she's accusing me of lying. 'How did you know?'

She scoffs, and if I'm not mistaken, she seems to be happy to move on to another subject. 'Honey, I raised three children and none of them were as bad at lying as you are. Every time Jamie said something about Reagan National, you had this little guilt face going. Tommy Jr used to pull that shit when he sneaked my smokes.'

I'm glad she kept this to herself until after Jamie was passed out.

'You're further out of the way than if you just went right through DC to the airport. And if you were hoping to be saved by the Spankin'-New EU, you'd have been there by now and not eating my food. Where are you really headed?'

'It's a long story.'

'But you haven't told him?' She points to Jamie. 'Otherwise he's the best damn liar I've ever seen.'

'No, he doesn't know.'

She shakes her head at me. 'He seems to trust you, to leave his whole life behind, so shouldn't you tell him before he finds out and it kills him? Again, I'm speaking metaphorically here. 'Cause after that happens . . .' She shakes her head.

'What if the truth kills him anyway?'

She shrugs. 'If you're really in a lose-lose situation, you need to figure out which option you can't live with.'

I look over at Jamie; he's still snoring.

'Well, I'm off to bed,' she says, patting me on the leg

and standing up. 'Do you want me to make up the spare bedroom for you?'

I shake my head. 'No, that's all right. I'll stay out here with him.'

'I thought you might. Good night, Andrew.'

'Good night. And thank you. For your hospitality, and your advice, too.'

She smiles and I hear her walk down the hallway into the back of the house. Her door shuts and locks. Not blindly trusting me. That's how she's survived so long.

She knows what I am. Just another one of her monsters.

JAMISON

Henri is up before me and I hear her walk outside to the backyard. I look over to Andrew, but he's still asleep on the couch across from me, so I get up and follow Henri outside.

'Good morning, James,' she says from beside the brick oven.

'You can call me Jamie. Can I help you with anything?'

She smiles and hands me the shotgun. 'I don't think they often go hunting in broad daylight, but just in case.'

She begins cooking – rabbit again, with sautéed peppers. It smells amazing and my stomach is already grumbling loudly.

'You should get a smoker,' I tell her.

'Should I?'

'You can preserve your meat with that instead of canning it.'

'Might not be a bad idea.'

We stand in silence while she cooks and I scan the fence line, listening for noises and hearing nothing but the end-of-the-world silence. No birds, no planes, no cars. Just wind and insects. I turn back to Henri.

'Why did you invite us in? You were behind us. You could have let us keep walking and we never would have met you or known where you live.'

'Yes, but then, like you said, we would've never met.' Her eyes crinkle with a wide smile. 'Do you believe in fate, kid? A higher purpose and God and all that?'

I let out a low grunt. 'I used to. Not any more.'

She nods. 'Same with me. It's hard to believe there's a greater purpose for everyone when ninety per cent of them have been wiped out. So I've been focusing more on luck than fate. If you met me before, you would've known I'm a gambling woman. I played the lottery twice a week, not for the money, just for the hope of winning. My kids were all set financially since Tommy had decent life insurance, and I had my pension, so I didn't need the money. Yet I still played.

'The most I ever won was five grand on a two-dollar ticket. Since the world went kaput I've been pushing my luck a bit more. I'm also a great judge of character, and I could tell you boys were on the up and up with just one look at you.'

'What if we weren't?'

She shrugs. 'Then my luck's run out and that's that.'

'So just like that you're ready to die?'

She looks at me as though I'm speaking in tongues. 'Are people running around killing each other with reckless abandon? Honey, if all that stops people from killing each other is the laws of men, then maybe we *deserved* to be wiped out by the flu. You have to trust people sometimes. The good in this world might surprise you. Look at me, look at the two of you. Here I am making you boys breakfast before you're off to retire to Europe. And your friend gave up the chance to sleep in a soft bed because he wanted to make sure you were safe in the middle of the night.'

I smile. She could be on to something.

'We're only the choices we make now. Press your luck, hon. People can surprise you sometimes.' She flips the rabbit in the pan and moves the veggies around. 'Now go wake up Andrew so you boys can line your bellies and be on your way.'

I move towards the house but stop to take a quick look back at her. I imagine her here alone, cooking for herself, fighting off strange beasts in the night. Every day she's been doing that. My life was like that before Andrew, too. Alone. Just the memory of it feels like a crushing weight on my chest.

After breakfast, Henri walks us outside, shotgun in hand. Andrew turns to her and smiles. 'Thank you again, for everything.'

Henri waves her hand, brushing the thought away. 'It was nothing.'

She reaches into her pocket and takes out a small tool. The metal is scuffed and it's rusted around a joint. She unfolds it. It's a multi-tool with a knife, pliers, screwdriver and several other implements.

'Here.' She holds the tool out to me. 'This used to be my husband's.'

'No, we can't accept—'

She cuts me off. 'I found it a few months back when I

was cleaning up. I thought we'd lost it but here it is. Take it. You might be able to use it on the road and I've got a whole toolbox in the garage.'

I'm not sure if I should take it. She's given us enough as it is. But then she sighs and grabs my hand, closing the multi-tool in it.

'Just take it.' I glance at it. It's engraved with the initials 'T.C.W.' 'If you boys are ever in the neighbourhood again, stop by. Only this time bring some food with you.' She winks as she opens her arms.

'Thank you, Henri.' I go in for the hug.

'You're welcome, sweetie.' She squeezes me goodbye and whispers in my ear. 'Remember what I said. People can surprise you.'

I nod. Then Andrew gets his Henri hug and we walk through the iron gate. Henri locks it behind us. We say goodbye again and she watches us go. When we turn the corner we wave to her one final time and she gives us a wave back.

Andrew tells me about her family and how she had a daughter named Amy who could still be alive in Florida. I think of Henri all alone up here and I want to go back for her. I'd walk her all the way down to Florida alone if I had to, but I don't think she'd come with us.

I come to a stop and point to a highway on-ramp sign. 'We could go that way. I checked on the map this morning and it said it meets up with 95.'

Andrew looks as though he's thinking about it for a moment but then shakes his head. 'No, I think we should keep heading this way.' He points straight, the direction we're going. Towards Alexandria.

I nod and we keep walking. But I still know there's something Andrew isn't telling me. And Henri's words resound in my head. *People can surprise you.* It could have been a warning, but only if she knew why Andrew was pointing us towards Alexandria. He wouldn't just tell a stranger something he wouldn't tell me.

He said he wanted to find other survivors. But Henri said there's no one left. It's only us out here so there's no logical reason for us to be passing through Capitol Hill and into Alexandria.

Then last night I remembered more about the sheet of paper that was in his paperback copy of *The Voyage Out*. I can't remember the name of the people, but I remember the street. Lieper Street.

It could be a family member. Or an old boyfriend. That would explain why he would leave and not expect me to follow; because then I'd be a third wheel. But he would tell me if that was it. Wouldn't he?

Whoever lives in Alexandria, he doesn't want me to know about them. He might be keeping quiet about it because he really wants to find whoever lives on Lieper Street and he's worried that speaking the hope aloud might ruin it all.

I'm curious what his endgame is. How does he expect to go looking through Alexandria without me asking him where he's going? How far do I let us go before I tell him I know something?

We turn down Massachusetts Avenue. There's a peeling orange sign warning about a construction zone in a mile and another that shows a lane closure graphic.

The city's silent, leaves and garbage blowing around in the gutters on the streets. The metal clang of a banner fastener blowing against a streetlight echoes around us. Most of the banners are faded and tattered from the weather.

I glance at one; through the tatters I can make out the printed picture of a panda bear. Something crunches under my foot. I look down; it's bones. Some small mammal, not human.

I scan the street. 'Do you notice anything?' I ask Andrew.

He looks around. 'What do you mean? It looks the same as everywhere else does.'

I grab his arm, stopping him. 'No, really look. What's missing?'

He shrugs. 'I see all the makings of an apocalypse. Abandoned cars, garbage, cracked asphalt with weeds overtaking the street. Mother Nature taking back what's rightfully hers.'

'There're no bodies.'

He doesn't speak as he looks around. Then says, dragging out the word, 'Yeah.'

'We've seen so many of them over the past few weeks I didn't even realise they weren't here until I stepped on those.' I point a few paces behind us at the animal bones. They're sun-bleached white, and completely dry. Unlike the people bones we've seen in differing states of decay.

'Maybe there's someone running around trying to clean up the bodies?' Andrew offers.

'But they decided to leave the garbage?' There are food wrappers and newspapers lining the gutters, faded and dried from the sun and weather.

Andrew shrugs. 'Are you really complaining about the cleaning habits of the apocalyptically inclined?'

I smile, shaking my head and shoving him. 'All right, keep moving.' Yet there's still something strange about all this that I can't quite put my finger on.

Clang. Clang.

Metal meets metal above my head.

I glance up. Another banner is waving in the breeze, the broken hook smacking the metal light post. Unlike the panda banner it's in one piece, and although it's faded, I can read what it says: 'Smithsonian National Zoological Park.'

Clang.

Right below the words is a picture of a lion. Its mane is large around its head, its mouth open in a ferocious roar. I stop breathing and my flesh crawls.

Henri's monsters.

She said they come out at night. The growling. The scratching at her fence. There are no bodies in the street because some*thing's* been cleaning up, not some*one*.

I scan the street again, my eyes wide in terror. The birds all died off because the virus transferred from them to us, but the other animals remained immune. The Smithsonian National Zoo is just a few blocks away. The animals could have escaped their enclosure, or someone let them out. If we believe Darwin, it means we're right in the middle of the fittest's hunting ground.

Clang. Clang.

Andrew realises he's twenty or thirty paces in front of

me and turns around. 'What's wrong?'

I take the rifle from my shoulder and put my finger to my lips. He mouths the word *what* as he scans the street. I close the distance between us in a few steps and pull him close, speaking quietly.

'The animals from the zoo – *those* are Henri's monsters. The one last night was probably small because she said the first one jumped over the fence – something like that.' I point up at the lion on the banner and Andrew's eyes go wide. 'Which means they're still around here. They're hunting as far as Bethesda, so maybe they've moved on from here, but we have to be quick and quiet.'

Andrew nods. I point ahead to continue down Massachusetts Avenue towards the points-of-interest signs for Dupont Circle and a few museums and monuments, the clanging of the banner hook following us like the sound of a dinner bell. Andrew takes the gun from his hip and we walk as quickly as we can, scanning the street around us as we move.

There's a small park to our left, trees line the street, and the grass on both sides of us has become overgrown.

My mind flashes back to nature documentaries, the leopards and cheetahs lying low in the high grass of the African savanna.

'We need to get off this road,' I say.

Then I see them – yellow eyes watching us from the treeline. I freeze. I lift the rifle scope to my eye and get a close-up look at the lion. He's crouched down low, ready to pounce at any moment.

As soon as we run.

'Andrew,' I call after him. He stops, turning to look at me and raising the gun.

'Oh God.' His voice is barely a whisper.

'He's watching us.' My mouth is dry and sweat soaks my shirt. 'When I say the word, run as fast as you can. Don't stop no matter what happens.'

'Jamie.' His voice is still low. I glance over at him but he isn't looking at the lion in the trees. He's looking behind me.

I turn my head slowly. I don't know how long she's been following us, but there she is. A large, muscular lioness walking towards us.

I turn back to the male lion in the trees. He isn't hunting; he's watching.

'Andrew,' I call out, not bothering to keep my voice quiet any more. 'Run!' I don't watch to see if he is listening. Instead I whirl around on the lioness that's just thirty feet from me. I see her through my scope and this time – for the first time – I have no trouble pulling the trigger.

The lioness charges at me as red explodes from her right shoulder. She howls in pain and probably anger.

I pull the bolt, dropping the rifle shell from the chamber and replacing it with a new one.

The trees rustle as the male charges from the treeline. I whirl around on him and pull the trigger on the rifle again. I miss him and hit the ground, but he jerks back.

Growing up in captivity, he knows what I am, and while he's probably never seen a rifle, he isn't dumb. He stops charging and his back arches, his hair standing on end as he lets out a roar that reverberates throughout my whole body.

I slowly move backwards. I pull the bolt on the rifle

again and hope there's another shell in there. The lioness is still limping forward, the male moving sideways towards her. Only fifty feet separate us now. I keep eye contact with the lion, but I want to look for Andrew. I can't hear him running any more, but that doesn't mean he's safe – there might be more of them ahead. Or something worse.

The two lions are still moving forward, side by side now. The lion leans over to the lioness and licks at her wound. They stop moving but watch as I continue to back away.

Maybe they're no longer seeing me as prey. Or they're waiting for one of the other lionesses hiding further ahead to pounce and take revenge for their injured pride.

'Andrew!' I scream out. I hear nothing in return as the lions continue to watch me. The lioness falls back as her leader steps forward, lowering his body close to the ground. He's going to charge me.

I raise my hands and step forward, shouting, trying to make myself look bigger. I think that's a thing; at least it is for bears. Undeterred, the lion steps forward again with his large paw. Maybe *only* for bears.

'Oh man.' Blood pumps loudly in my ears, sounding an awful lot like the low growl of a lion. I raise the rifle, making sure I get him in my sight before pulling the trigger again.

CLICK.

No! Out of ammo.

There's more in my pack but there's no time to get it. I wish I hadn't sent Andrew away. His gun could come in handy right about now.

I see a flash of yellow to my left – another lion – and my chest feels like it's going to explode. My body acts on instinct. I turn my empty gun on the lion, expecting to see it running at me from the embassy on the side of the road. This is how I'm gonna die – survived the apocalypse to be mauled by lions.

But it's not a lion. It's a yellow excavator left in a construction area. The orange barrels closing off the far-right lane have fallen over and rolled on to the grass separating the sidewalk from the road.

My eyes go back to the lion, which has moved several steps closer. He bares his teeth. The excavator has a cab. I think I can run to it – I can make it if it's unlocked, then wait in there and reload the rifle. I can do it. I just have to run.

But my legs won't let me. They continue to move slowly backwards away from the lion, as if they have a mind of their own. I'm almost past the excavator now.

GO! STOP WALKING BACKWARDS! I shout at my trembling legs, but they aren't listening. I sling the rifle over my shoulder and take a hard step to the side. The lion jumps, throwing its paw out to the side as well.

That's all my body needs to convince it and I'm running – but the lion's running, too. He isn't running towards me, though; he knows where I'm going and he's running towards the excavator, trying to cut me off at the pass.

My pack is weighing me down. I go around the back of the excavator. The door is right ahead of me. So is the lion, his claws out. I jump up on the excavator tracks and reach for the door handle. It doesn't turn.

I'm dead.

Somehow my brain forces me to pull the handle again and this time it turns – it isn't locked, just rusted. I yank it open as the lion reaches my side. I jump into the cab and pull the door shut behind me but it won't close all the way.

The lion bats at the glass door, prying at the gap between the door and the cab with his claws. He roars and gnashes his teeth at me.

There's tugging against my left. I turn, expecting to see another lion somehow reaching into the cab from the other side; but it's the rifle strap that's pulling at my shoulder.

My eyes follow the end of the rifle up to the top of the cab, where it's sticking out through the door, keeping it from closing. I take the strap off and turn in the cab, still pulling on the door as tight as I can, but it's clear that the lion's going to win.

With all my might, and hoping I don't break the glass, I kick out with both feet. The door swings open and hits the lion hard in the nose. Letting out a roar, he recoils and falls to the ground. I watch in slow motion as the rifle falls out of the cab.

I reach forward, my fingers grazing the weapon, which sends it away from me a little faster. I fumble, then manage to get it in my fingers and grasp as hard as I can. I pull it into the cab and reach for the door as the lion rears up. The door shuts with a metallic groan and I latch it just as the claws push against the window, scratching the plexiglass.

I let out a scream of celebration. The lion continues to scratch at the cab and roar at me. I'm breathing deeply. I feel like I haven't taken a breath since I told Andrew to run.

Andrew! I scan the road but don't see any sign of him, so that's good. He got away. I turn back to the lion. He's now pacing around the excavator, looking for another way to come at me.

I take my pack off and reach in for the bullets. My body tenses up. *No.* I move the clothes around, pulling them out along with the cans of food.

'No,' I say out loud. My voice is trembling. 'No, no, no, no, NO!' There are no bullets. I remember now, Andrew held on to them so he could take off his pack and hand them to me as needed. And I let him because I never thought I'd be able to use the damn thing.

I throw my empty pack against the front of the cab and sit back. The lion is still pacing. I hold my middle finger against the window.

'Keep pacing, Cujo.' Sweat's beading on my forehead. I pick up the bottle of water on the floor of the cab. It's full, thankfully. Henri saw to that before we left. I open it and take a sip. The sun's getting higher in the sky. By noon it's going to be over a hundred degrees in here.

I just have to hope the lion gives up before then.

ANDREW

I don't ask questions when Jamie tells me to run. I don't want to leave him but I'm hoping he has a plan.

'Run!' he screams. I turn and bolt. The rifle goes off behind me and I look back to see blood on the lioness prowling the street. I keep running. There's another rifle blast but I don't look this time.

He's still alive. He'll be fine. I keep telling myself this as I reach a bridge a half mile down the road. I run across it, looking down at the creek that flows beneath it. At the end of the bridge I turn around. I wait there, catching my breath.

Five minutes pass. I haven't heard a gunshot or a scream or even a roar.

'Come on, Jamie,' I say to myself. I sit down on the side the road, waiting to see Jamie come walking down the street. I picture the rifle slung over his shoulder, the smirk on his face. I imagine myself running towards him and hugging him tightly and him hugging me back.

I don't see his smirk, though. I don't see him at all. I stand up and pace back and forth on the road.

Maybe he's hurt? Maybe he's limping or the lion scratched him before he killed it and he had to clean the wound.

That option becomes less likely as the hours pass. I'm sitting at the side of the road now, my shadow getting long on the ground. Tears burn my eyes as every kind of horrible thought begins to run through my mind.

Jamie's dead. I break into sobs. He's dead and it's my fault. I wanted to go to Alexandria so I could ease my guilt and now my best friend – my only friend – is dead. I killed him.

I have to go back for him, but I can't. Not yet. I have to get to Alexandria first. If I find him dead now, I won't be able to go on. It becomes too real; I've learned that now. I've seen the bodies of my mother and sister – it isn't real until you see that life is gone from them. Until you see the corpse that looks nothing like the person they used to be.

I pick up my pack and turn away from the bridge. As I make my way to Alexandria, tears continue to stream down my face. I'm sobbing so hard I don't hear the thunder until the dark clouds are right over me, and when the rain starts to fall I let my sobs grow louder. I don't know what's tears and what's rain any more and it's better that way.

Lightning lights up the monuments as I pass by them. I cross another bridge over a larger river. I move under a tree and take out the road atlas, memorising the roads I have to travel to get to 4322 Lieper Street. The end of the line.

As soon as I do what I have to do, I'm going back for Jamie. If I can't find his body, if the lions have taken it, I'll go after them. I'll shoot them until I run out of bullets or they tear open my belly with their claws. But I'll save one bullet. Just in case.

The sky gets progressively darker as the afternoon grows late and the rain isn't letting up. Alexandria is just as empty and dead as DC, as the rest of the world. I know the animals that escaped from the Smithsonian haven't gotten this far because there are leathery bodies along the ground.

I stop at a house that has a front porch. Taking off my pack, I sit in a dusty chair and open one of the mystery cans of food. Stewed tomatoes. I put a forkful in my mouth and swallow without tasting it.

Then I look at the red pulp at the end of my fork and my mind immediately jumps to Jamie being ripped apart by lions. My stomach churns and, tasting the bile in my throat, I jump up and run to the edge of the porch, ready to throw up. But nothing comes. I put the can on the porch railing and sit back down, waiting for something to happen.

Anything.

I sit longer than I should. The rain begins to slow and the sun is setting somewhere behind the clouds. It's getting dark quickly now – I've completely lost track of time. I have to get up if I hope to see the street signs and house numbers, but my body won't let me move. I'm too weak. Worse than when I broke my leg.

I'm alone again. I don't want to feel like this any more. I wipe the tears from my eyes and put my pack on my shoulders.

Lieper Street is ahead. My hand goes for my gun instinctively as I round the corner. There's someone on the road ahead of me. It's hard to see in the dark, but it looks like a man and I can tell that he's armed. I take my hand away from the gun. Let him shoot me or kill me if he has to. I'm ready to give up. If after all of this, trying to do the right thing, I still lose Jamie? It's not fair.

Maybe it's Marc Foster. The universe is just bitchy enough that it's possible. I come all this way to tell him what happened to his parents and he shoots and kills me in the middle of the street before I can even do so. His parents' death remains a mystery.

The rain has stopped now; my teeth are chattering. I don't walk quietly – in fact, I make as much noise as I can walking down the street. The man turns and speaks.

'Why are you walking like an elephant?' he asks.

My heart leaps into my chest. I can't feel anything, but I'm moving. Running as fast as I can.

The closer I get the better I recognise him. His jawline, his arms, his legs, the way his chest is out, the way he stands with his shoulders back. I run into him and I pull him into a hug so tight it might kill us both.

Jamie lets out a low 'oof' and begins to laugh.

That laugh! The laugh that fills me with warmth and hope. I'm crying so hard I don't think he can hear what I'm saying.

'I thought you were dead. I waited so long and you didn't come and I thought you were dead.'

'I can't breathe,' he says, but he's laughing. His hands pat my sides and I realise I'm squeezing him around his arms. He's also wet from the rain. I loosen my grip and step back. I can see his smile in the darkening twilight and I can't stop myself.

He opens his arms as he sees me coming in for another hug. He laughs and I smile through my tears, resting my head against his wet chest. He may feel awkward but I don't care at this point. He's alive and he's here. I pull him close; I don't want to not feel him against me ever again. He doesn't even pull away. He's here. He's really here.

It's me who pulls away first, but I still have my arms around him when I ask, 'But how did you get here?'

'Did you see the construction site next to the road?' Vaguely? I remember an orange barrel or some yellow tape but that's it. I nod anyway. 'There was an excavator. I hid there while the lion waited for me. He paced around me with another lioness for a good four hours. Then the storm came, and I guess even big cats don't like getting wet.' He shrugs and I allow my hands to fall away from him.

'So they left you?'

'Reluctantly. They ran over to the treeline and watched me from there. Then they finally turned around – I guess they headed home or were going for reinforcements. So I ran. After a mile or so I hoped I was in the clear. Though now that I'm saying it, it's possible I led a pack of lions here, but at least you have bullets. Could I get some of them now?' He shakes the rifle back and forth at me.

I put the pack down and dig through it, taking out some rifle shells and handing them over to him. As he loads his weapon, something else crosses my mind.

'But how did you know to come *here*?' Why wouldn't he head for the airport? We're on Lieper Street. Looking at the mailbox to Jamie's right, I can see we're standing in front of 4314. Four houses down from the house I'm looking for.

He reaches into his pocket and hands me a torn road atlas.

'I found a souvenir shop with a stack of DC, Virginia and Maryland maps. I remembered something about Lieper Street – I couldn't remember the full number but I've been walking up and down this block for about thirty minutes. I figured if I kept walking I'd find you eventually.'

My body has finally gone numb. 'How did you know?'

'You had the address written down on a piece of paper. I found it in the book you brought to the cabin.' He shrugs and for some reason looks like *he's* the one who should feel guilty. 'I didn't think anything of it at first, but when you made us travel around DC I remembered the address.'

'So you knew I was coming here?'

'Yeah.' Again he sounds like he was the one who was caught in a lie.

'But you didn't say anything? You could have been killed by escaped zoo animals because I wanted to come here and you didn't even ask why?'

He shrugs. 'I figured if it was that important you would tell me when you were ready.'

Again, I feel I like I might throw up. He washes away in a blur of tears and I cover my face as I fall to my knees, sobbing. He drops and pulls me into a hug, rubbing my back as I cry. It's not an awkward patting; his touch is warm and comforting. He keeps telling me it's all right and asks what's wrong, but I can't form it into words yet.

I also like his hands rubbing against my back.

He stops asking me what's wrong and telling me it's all right and just lets me cry. My sobs taper off and he lets me go. I sit against the picket fence of number 4314 Lieper Street.

He's looking at me.

'Do you want to tell me what we're doing here?' he asks. He doesn't say it rudely or demand an answer. He wants to make sure I'm ready first. And I am. I finally am. He's come all this way and he's waited the whole time, knowing I was lying to him. He deserves to know.

'OK,' I say. Only how do you start a story that ends with you becoming a murderer?

JAMISON

'OK,' Andrew says. Then he pauses as if he doesn't know where the story starts.

'I wasn't alone the entire time I was out here. After my sister died, I mean. I left home in January but got stuck in Connecticut until the end of February. I was hoping to get as far south as I could before it got really hot.'

I nod. I know this part of the story already.

'I had just gotten past New York City when I ran into a couple. They were from Vermont. George and Joanne Foster. They were maybe in their fifties. We met at a supermarket in a small town in New Jersey I was passing through.

'I don't know if people didn't get around to looting it or what, but there was still a good amount of food on the shelves. We agreed we would each take whatever we needed and go on our way. I saw they had a gun, and I wasn't armed, so I let them do their thing and I took my stuff and that was that.'

I know this can't be the end of the story, though. My stomach is in knots, worried about what event would create the one thing Andrew would keep from me.

'They left before I did. A few miles down the road I

165

ran into them again. They had set up a fire and stopped to camp for the night. I was wearing layers and gloves but it was still so cold. I waved to them and I heard Joanne and George speaking, very low. Then they called after me.

'They invited me to share their fire, so I joined them. We ate our own food and we got to talking. They were heading south to . . . well, here. They were coming to meet their son, Marc, and his wife, Diane, and their two kids, Katie and Emily . . .'

He says these names like they're people he's always known. He doesn't have to pause to think or try to remember; he just says the names like he's always been on a first-name basis with the Fosters.

'George and Jo last spoke to them in October before all the cell signals started dropping. They had been travelling south since then.'

I swallow, despair filling my chest. I remember the sudden lack of graffiti Andrew claimed he had seen before the cabin, how we saw none of it along the way. And how we didn't run into anyone else on the road. Maybe there is no EU coming. He made it all up as an excuse, because he didn't want to tell me the truth. Whatever the truth is, I need to know this first.

'June tenth,' I say. 'There's nothing happening on June tenth, is there? You just needed to give me a reason why we were coming here.'

'Their daughter-in-law, Diane, she worked for a German pharmaceutical company. She's the one who told them the EU was sending help. Apparently viruses as deadly as the bug can mutate rapidly so they might become less lethal.

The EU were waiting until the virus burned itself out in America before they showed up. Last time Joanne talked to Marc and Diane, they said June tenth was the day.'

So he wasn't lying. But I still don't understand the secrecy. Maybe he knew the Fosters weren't going to let me come along. But that thought – that he would ditch me – threatens to rip a hole through my chest, so I push it aside.

'Anyway, they got stuck in Connecticut for a while, like me. As I said, the winter was bad. We got a *lot* of snow.

'I told them about my family and my plan to go south to avoid the winter again. I didn't tell them I was also looking for other people. I figured I would wait for that. Maybe see if they'd invite me to hang in Germany with them. I went to sleep that night and everything was fine. The fire was blazing and I was warm and comfortable in my sleeping bag.

'When I woke up it was dark and cold. At first I thought maybe they had left and the fire had gone out on its own. But then I heard them. They were whispering and I could hear the sound of their bags rustling. The moon wasn't full, but it was bright enough that I could see them. They were hunched over their packs. There were little piles of snow around them that hadn't quite melted. I stayed still, listening. If they were going to leave me, that was fine. I'd let them go. I didn't want to make a big deal out of it and I knew I could just go to Reagan alone if I had to.'

He's telling the story like one of his movies. I don't know which details are truly remembered and which he's embellishing. If he really does remember all this, it means he's been thinking about it non-stop. Torturing himself with every detail for months. My stomach clenches because I know the story can't possibly end well.

'Then I saw what they were doing,' Andrew continues. 'They had taken my pack and were rummaging through it. Taking the food I had brought with me. We were both in the *same market* and here they were, robbing me while I was asleep. I didn't get it. I still don't. Why would they do that?'

I know the question is rhetorical – after all this time it must be – but still I shrug.

'It was this one stupid thing they were doing and it . . .' His voice breaks and he swallows hard before continuing.

'I jumped up and started yelling at them. That's when George turned on me. I saw the gun in the light of the moon and I stopped moving. Joanne told him not to shoot me but he didn't put the gun down. He told me to turn around and walk straight into the woods at the edge of the road. I put my hands up but didn't move.'

Andrew stops talking, but I feel like I already know where this story is going. It's like watching a train chugging along to a broken part of track. I know it's going to derail, that the bad part's coming, but I can't do anything about it. It's already happened to him. He's already lived through this. I could ask him to stop, tell him he doesn't have to say any more, but he's kept this story to himself – held it in – for so long. He needs to let it out.

I reach for his hand and hold it, squeezing tightly. Andrew watches my hand like it's a strange creature sniffing at him. Then he finally squeezes back. When he continues, his voice has changed. His throat sounds tighter.

'I asked them to hand me my pack and I'd be on my way, but he said it was theirs now. It all happened so fast after that. Joanne said something, I don't even remember what, but it distracted George and I ran at him. I tackled him and slammed his hand down on the ground, but he wouldn't let the gun go. He hit me with his free hand, and I heard Joanne screaming at me, and then she was hitting me, too. My lip split open and my nose was bleeding. I don't even know which one was hitting me, maybe both. I reached out and grabbed the closest thing I could see in the moonlight and hit him with it.

'I don't know if that one blow killed him or created a bleed or what, but George stopped moving. He let up on the gun and it fell into the snow. When I got off him Joanne was screaming. She kept screaming his name and shaking him to wake him up. I still had it in my hand – the thing I hit him with. It was a can of soup. Not even one I had taken.

'I don't know when I picked up the gun, but I had it in my hand when Joanne turned and ran at me screaming. I shot her twice. I heard her . . .'

Andrew stops talking and tears fall from his eyes and he lets out a sob. I put my arm around him and pull him closer to me. The sounds he's making hurt my heart. His cries are exactly why I've been afraid to use the gun. Why even when my own mom asked me, I couldn't do it. She asked for the pills first, but I hid those, thinking she could get better. Then when the fever got really bad, she started begging me just to take her outside and shoot her. Screaming at me and my absent father and the other people she hallucinated while the superflu cooked her brain.

My own stomach churns with the same fear and anxiety, and I can't imagine how Andrew has dealt with this for so long.

I open my mouth to try to tell him it wasn't his fault, but I know he won't believe me. The guilt has weighed on him for too long. Instead I let him cry and don't say anything. When he composes himself, he continues. There's still more.

'I didn't sleep the rest of the night. I just sat there. I hoped I would freeze to death, but I don't think it ever got cold enough. When the sun came up I finally saw how they looked. They were both blue and dead. It was so much worse than the bug. Probably because *I* was the one who did it.

'The worst part is, I didn't take their food. They were trying to take mine. Food they didn't even need right in that moment. Food they'd had a chance to take twelve hours earlier. I can't understand why they didn't just take it from the store. Why take it from me? Then it happened again when Howard's people came to the cabin and I got so pissed at them. I could at least make sense of that because it was *your* food they were stealing. But with George and Joanne, why the hell did I care so much? Why didn't I walk into the woods like they told me to and wait for them to go?'

'You didn't know if he was going to shoot you when you turned around.'

He lets out a sad chuckle. 'He wasn't going to. I shot Joanne twice.' His face scrunches up in agony and he can't even look at me when he says, 'There were only two bullets in the gun. I think if they got down here and found their kids and grandkids dead . . .' His voice trails off. I want to make him feel better. I want to tell him about my mom and how she asked for a similar end and I couldn't even do that, but it's not helpful. It will just make things worse. I'll still be the coward I am and Andrew will still be a killer.

'So you came down here to find them,' I say. 'Before they left.' It's June 8. Two days until they would have been gone for good.

He nods. 'I looked through their stuff. Joanne still had an old address book, so I tore out the page and put it in the Virginia Woolf book. When I found it on the coffee table the morning after you let me in, I thought I'd dropped it.' He reaches into his pocket and takes out the wrinkled scrap of paper. 'Not that I needed it. I looked at it every day up until I met you.'

'Why didn't you tell me any of this before?'

'Because I needed you.' He locks eyes with me. 'Before, when I was hurt, I needed you. I was afraid that if you realised I was a murderer you wouldn't trust me and would kick me out. And then, when I got better, I thought I could come clean, but . . . I . . . realised even then that I still needed you.'

I knew he was hiding something, and I was afraid whatever it was would change everything. But it hasn't. I know who Andrew is and I know he's a good person.

And I know that I need him, too.

We sit in silence for a moment, then I stand up. 'All right, then.' I hold out my hand to him. 'Let's go.'

Andrew looks down the road towards the house in question, then back at his paper. It looks like he isn't so sure he wants to face them. I can't tell what scares him more: to find the family there, alive and well, or the other option.

Either way, I don't think it will help his guilt. I know it wouldn't do anything with mine. It's why I could never pull the trigger on that gun. No matter how much my mom screamed and cried. I didn't kill her; the flu did. I didn't cause her pain, so the guilt that came from her suffering could never be worse than the guilt that would come with killing her.

All I can do to help Andrew is hold his hand and be here with him. And tell him that I need him. Because I do. He puts the paper back in his bag and takes my hand. I pick up his pack and hand it to him, trying to psych myself up to just say the words: 'I need you, too.'

But the words stop in my throat like a ball of iron.

'Whatever happens,' I tell him, 'I'm here.' It's all I can get out.

He wipes the tears from his eyes and we head down Lieper Street. Heading for what might be Andrew's final stop. The idea fills me with a sudden dread.

I'm not going to let them hurt him. If they try to take vengeance for what he did – for protecting himself – I'll protect him.

Again, my body tenses with fear.

I told him whatever happens, and I mean it.

But the front of number 4322 does not bode well for us.

Dead leaves litter the front yard, the grass crushed beneath them. Weeds strong enough to burst through the leaf barrier are scattered throughout the lawn. There's a small pink Fisher-Price trike with wet brown leaves on its seat. A rubber ball is by the front porch, half-flat. The front gate is thick plastic that's cracked around stress points. I look at Andrew's face. He looks determined. I want to ask him what he's hoping for, but I'm also scared to know.

He opens the gate. Neither of us has our weapons out. My pack is over the rifle at my back. Andrew's gun is at his side, buckled into its holster. I want to find the family all alive. I want Emily and Katie to have blonde hair that they braid each night. I want Diane Foster to have a hunting rifle that she's used to defend her children from escaped zoo animals. I want Marc to be growing rows of vegetables in the backyard and collecting rainwater like Henri. I want Andrew to be able to tell them what happened with their parents and I want them to tell him that it's all right, that all is forgiven.

Even if it isn't.

'Hello?' Andrew calls out from the bottom of the front steps. 'We're here to see Marc and Diane Foster. I knew Marc's parents, George and Joanne.'

No one opens the door. Andrew walks up the steps to the front porch and knocks on the door. I flank him, looking into the windows. They aren't boarded up like Henri's. Andrew knocks again but no one answers; there isn't a sound inside the house.

Andrew turns the doorknob and the front door opens.

173

The house smells stale and musty. There's a thick layer of dust over everything, even the floor. I follow Andrew inside, taking the flashlight from his pack without him asking me to do so.

'Hello?' he calls out. 'We aren't here to hurt you. Marc, I knew your parents, George and Joanne. They sent me here to see you.'

I want to tell him that's not a good way of putting it, but I'm starting to think it doesn't matter. I run the flashlight over everything. None of it's been touched in months.

We search the first floor. Andrew doesn't call out again – either he thinks they aren't here or he's thinking what I'm thinking. I open the fridge, but it's empty. That's a good sign; they could have taken whatever they needed with them when they left. The backyard is overgrown. No veggies or barrels collecting rainwater.

I follow Andrew upstairs. He pushes open the bedroom door at the top of the stairs. Before I even point the flashlight inside, I see him slump against the door. It's a little girl's room. There are no toys on the floor but there is a stuffed animal on top of the bed, next to a long, thin lump. The blanket is pulled over what looks like a small body.

I reach for Andrew's arm, pulling him back, and we shut the door. The second bedroom is empty; there are toys on the ground. Maybe the rest of the family left. The bathroom is empty as well. We go to the front bedroom; the door is open. On the large king-size bed are two adults, their arms wrapped around a little girl. Their clothing is loose and moth-eaten, their skin tight against their bones, their lips pulled back over their teeth in mocking grimaces.

Andrew drops to his knees, sliding against the door jamb to the dusty floor. If he's crying, it's silent. I turn off the flashlight and lean down to him.

'Give me your hand,' I say. He doesn't move. I reach for him, pulling on his arm. 'Come on. There's nothing we can do. Let's go downstairs. We'll figure out our next move tomorrow.'

'They're dead.' I can't tell if he is relieved or devastated, and I don't want to ask.

'I know. Come on.' He still doesn't move. I bend over and use all my strength to get him on his feet. When he finally stands, we walk down the stairs together. Andrew sits on the couch and a puff of dust blows up around him. He drops his pack on the floor, kicks off his shoes and turns his back to me, pulling his legs up into the foetal position.

I put my hand on his back. I'm not even sure if it's helping him, but he doesn't try to buck me away, so I leave it.

I watch him and I wait for him to speak, but his breath deepens as he drifts to sleep. I am scared to sleep. I don't want him to wake up and do anything rash. I don't think he realises how important he is to me.

I didn't even realise how important he is to me. At least not until now. Not until he told me his story. I know why he didn't tell me the truth. His guilt, for one. But he was also worried I wouldn't trust him or I'd be afraid of him. I'm way past that, though. I was afraid when he first arrived at the cabin, but I know who he is now.

Even though he lied and kept the trip to Alexandria from me, it's not enough for me to be mad at him.

Because I know the real reason he was coming here. He was hoping the Fosters were still alive, and I think he was hoping they would want revenge. I honestly don't know what I would have done if that had been the case, but I'd make sure no one would ever hurt him.

What does that mean? At the time, walking up to this house, I was so sure, but in the darkness, next to Andrew, the idea is absurd. I don't know why this person is so damn important. Then it hits me.

It's because it feels like love.

The reason I moved in front of Howard's gun, and why I left my home to come after Andrew. What gave me the strength to finally shoot the rifle – though that may have also been to save my own ass.

I feel safe when he's with me and I want him to feel safe, too. Andrew's breath continues its steady rhythm across from me on the couch. I want to tell him but I don't know how. How do I explain it when I don't understand it myself?

The idea of kissing him isn't scary or strange – and I have thought about it. A few times. More so at night, before we go to sleep. When he says good night to me it feels like I should kiss him. The idea of holding him doesn't make me uncomfortable. Actually, it's the complete opposite.

I want to pull him close to me and hold him while he sleeps. It makes sense in my heart, though it doesn't make sense in my mind. Even the thought of more intimate things doesn't deter me.

But I'm scared. Disappointing Andrew is what scares me. There's a massive difference between thinking about things and doing them. What happens if I'm wrong and it's just friendship and loneliness and horniness all mixed up? And then we try something and it's awkward and weird and I suck, and then I've ruined the only relationship I have left.

It seems so trivial when I think of it like that because it feels like so much more than just 'the only relationship I have left'.

I keep my eyes open and my thoughts running as night turns into early morning. I don't know what time it is when I finally drift off to sleep.

I hear a gentle hum. In my mind I see an air conditioner. It's blowing on me and I'm lying under it in the afternoon sunlight.

My eyes open and the hum grows louder. As my mind clears, I realise it's not an air conditioner. The sun's up and the room is hot and stuffy. I look around, getting my bearings. I'm still in the Fosters' house, but Andrew isn't lying across from me any more. His shoes are gone as well.

I jump up, following the humming noise of a motor that grows louder as I reach the back of the house. There's movement in the backyard.

Andrew is pushing a gas-powered lawn mower through the tall grass. The backyard, which was overgrown last night, is half-cut. Clumps of wet, masticated grass are being spewed out of the side of the lawn mower. I push open the back door and stand on the deck, watching him. He's taken off his shirt and tied it around his head. His shoes and legs up to his knees are green with cut grass. Pink scars on the leg I sewed up stand out against the green.

I watch him, studying him like I've never done before. It's strange.

No, not strange.

Different.

He doesn't notice me until he loops around the back of the yard. He holds up his index finger, *one sec*. I nod and sit down on the steps, waiting for him to finish.

When he's done he cuts the motor and pushes it back towards an open shed next to the house.

'Sorry,' he says. 'It took me almost two hours of trying and the engine flooding before the damn thing finally started. I didn't want to risk turning it off and it not starting back up again.' He picks up a red gas can and puts it in the shed, too.

'You decided to do yard work.'

He looks up at the second storey of the house. 'I want to bury them. I want them to be able to rest together. I didn't like seeing them separated like that.'

'Did you bury George and Joanne?'

He lowers his eyes and shakes his head. 'The ground was frozen. I couldn't.'

I nod. 'All right. I'll help you.'

There are two shovels in the shed but only one pair of gardening gloves to share. It's almost eleven in the morning when we get started. By the time we finish digging four holes – two large, two small – the sun is low in the sky and our hands are covered in blisters despite swapping the gloves back and forth. For the last hour, Andrew declines all my offers for him to use the gloves.

We wrap each member of the Foster family in a different blanket and carry them down the stairs one by one. As the sky turns from orange to purple, we gently lower each of them into the ground. They aren't six feet down like they should be, but there isn't much of the Fosters left to dig up even if animals did try to get back here.

Andrew says a few words and tells them what happened to George and Joanne Foster. We cover the girls, then their parents. Andrew says one more time that he's sorry, and we put the shovels back in the shed.

We're in the house, tea lights flickering around us. We both smell like sweat and earth. We're low on water, which means our hands stay dirty. There's a river a quarter of a mile away, so we can wash up there first thing tomorrow morning.

'What do we do now?' I ask Andrew as he opens up a mystery can.

'Oh, Beefaroni.' But there's no joy in his voice. He doesn't even open the second can and digs in with his fork. He swallows three heaping forkfuls of the room-temperature pasta and hands the can over to me as he opens the second. 'I'm going to leave it up to you now,' he says. 'Do you still want to stick around with me?'

I choke on my food, looking up at him in surprise. 'Of course. Why wouldn't I?'

Something in my chest constricts. It never occurred to me that he might not feel the same way about me as I do him. It's not that I'm conceited; I didn't assume he would like me because of . . . I don't know, whatever reason he would like someone. But I thought he felt it, too.

He shrugs and stares down at the can he's opening. 'Wasn't sure if you were still interested in being friends with a murderer.'

'You're not a murderer.'

'Pretty sure that's what they call you when you *murder* someone. I think two might even make me a spree killer.'

'What happened to you was a mistake.'

He interrupts me. 'It didn't happen to me. It happened to the Fosters.'

'It was an accident. They didn't even *need* the food but they were willing to take it from you. Whatever it was that got into them, you didn't do it. What happened was bad. But that doesn't make you a bad person.'

He doesn't say anything, just finishes turning the can opener. The lid of the can sits on top of whatever the contents inside are.

'Henri said something to me,' I say. He looks up at me, interested. 'She said sometimes you have to give people a chance. Sometimes they can surprise you. I think that's true whether the surprise is good or bad.'

He looks like he thinks about this for a moment, then stares back down at the can in front of him. He uses his fork to pull the top off the can and smiles. 'Bad surprise,' he says. He turns it towards me so I can see the contents.

Canned mushrooms.

I scrunch up my face and shudder. 'Pass.'

'Come on, give me a good surprise for once.' He holds out the can to me, smiling through the dirt on his face. I notice for the first time there are two clear lines through the dirt on his skin, right under his eyes. I frown and I stick my fork into the can, grabbing a big rubbery forkful of mushrooms and putting them in my mouth.

I grimace, handing him back the can and chewing as fast as I can. He laughs as I swallow the mushrooms.

'All right, you finish the Beefaroni, I'll eat the mushrooms,' he says.

'That had better be our last can of those.'

He chuckles a few more times as we eat in silence.

His smile gives me a pang in my chest because I know he still doesn't feel better. Nothing I can say will ever make him feel better. I want to make him happy, but I don't know how.

I think about what it would be like to actually lean over and kiss him. I want to know if that would make him happy. If it would make me happy, too. Even seeing him eat a forkful of mushrooms doesn't gross me out.

I watch him chewing as he stares at a picture of the Fosters on the wall. In the photo, the Fosters are all smiling and wearing Mickey Mouse ears in front of Epcot.

Tomorrow morning we'll head for Reagan National. I can't stop thinking about it, all the people who might be there, waiting for us. Waiting for some European Union military outfit to show up and save us all.

The idea of leaving gets me homesick. *If* we were to leave. They might just be here to help get everyone back on their feet, or even just to run tests on us to try to find a cure. It's all been rumours so far, but if we believed it, other survivors would, too. And they wouldn't be a settlement, they'd be . . . nomads, I guess, like Andrew and me. Other survivors on their own might be a good thing.

I can't help but hope for that because the other option is just me. And I'm scared that after this, I might not be enough for Andrew to be happy.

ANDREW

From outside, Reagan National is one of the most nondescript airports I've ever seen. It's bigger than Bradley International in Connecticut, but isn't this named after the dude everyone had such a boner for in the eighties? Shouldn't the guy who killed thousands of gay people through inaction have gotten something a little more ostentatious from his right-wing fluffers?

Frankly I'm disappointed.

'Where should we go?' Jamie asks.

The economy parking garage to our right is blackened with soot from a fire on the second level that went out long ago. Concrete has cracked and fallen in chunks to the overgrown bushes below. Beyond it, at the far end of the terminals, is a tall control tower. I point at it.

'Maybe head that way? We can see if a higher vantage point can tell us where to go?'

He nods and we cut around the parking garage. The chain-link fence that should be blocking our way is cut open. Maybe we're going the right way after all.

As we walk around the terminals, each fence we come to has been cut open or broken for people to pass through. Jamie gives me a look that seems to say this must be correct.

But I don't like it. It's so quiet here.

Shouldn't there be someone on the road to greet people? Some kind of lookout on top of the parking garage? Maybe they're all in the ATC tower.

We round the corner to the main runways. They're cracked, weed-ridden and scorched with burnt rubber from before the bug.

'Holy shit,' Jamie whispers.

My heart leaps. There are a few dozen small planes – some only big enough to hold a couple of people, while others look like private jets. They're scattered around the runways like it's a parking lot. Their doors are open, but the planes are filthy, covered in caked-on dirt and pollen. They've been here a while.

But there's no one else around.

I scan the runway for movement. It's quiet and still.

'Shit,' I say. '*Did* they mean October sixth?'

Jamie must not find the joke funny because he doesn't say a word.

'Hello?' I call out. Only my own voice echoes back to me and it gives me chills. Jamie grabs my arm. He's pointing at a white American Airlines stair car parked by the terminal. And the body slumped up against it.

He pulls the rifle off his shoulder and I reach into the holster for the handgun. Its cool metal feels like fire against my skin. Like it's just itching to go off.

The body is old, its skin leathery and sun-dried. The white dress shirt is tattered and yellowing and hangs loose like a second skin falling off the bone. Dried blood cakes the side of the stair car like an arrow, pointing down to the hole at the back of the body's head.

'Andrew.'

I turn and follow Jamie's gaze. He's staring at the largest private jet on the tarmac.

'There's someone in there,' he says. 'I saw movement in one of the windows.'

I watch the small circles of darkness in the side of the plane. It could have just been a shadow. Or maybe it's a tiger den. That'd certainly be our luck.

But then I see movement, too. And a brief flash of a face. There's definitely a person in there. I turn to Jamie, asking with a look what we should do.

'Hello?' Jamie calls out. 'Is anyone there?'

There's no further answer or movement from the plane.

Behind us, I hear the rattling of the chain-link fence we climbed through moments ago. I spin, raising the gun. Jamie comes around me, rifle at the ready.

There's someone ducking under the cut fence, his backpack caught. He readjusts himself – still unaware we're here – and unhooks his pack from the chain link. Jamie has already lowered the rifle by the time the guy stands upright and sees us.

He's a Black kid, our age. His eyes go wide and then flash quickly to the jet we had been focused on. He puts his hands in the air and calls out.

'You here for the Europeans?'

Jamie and I share a glance and nod.

The kid frowns and opens his mouth to say something, but before he can . . .

'Chris!'

We turn back to the jet.

Two children – a boy and a girl – peek out from the doorway. The girl is about twelve, and her curly hair is pulled into a puff that sits at the back of her head, held back with a pink scarf. The boy is younger, maybe six, and clutches a stuffed green dog to his chest.

'Des!' the kid – Chris – shouts back. 'Get back inside until I tell you to come out.'

'It's OK,' Jamie says. He slings the rifle over his shoulder and shows Chris his hands. I follow his lead and holster my gun. 'We're not gonna hurt anyone.'

Chris looks unsure, and I already clocked the lack of gun on his part. I turn back to the kids and give a friendly wave. Neither of them returns it.

'Well,' Chris says. 'I got some bad news.' He motions for us to follow him as he heads for the jet.

Jamie and I follow, keeping our distance. Chris lunges up the stairs two at a time and hands his backpack to the girl, saying something to her that we can't hear. She disappears into the plane as Jamie and I come to a stop at the bottom of the stairs. I cast a quick glance at Jamie, gauging how he feels about this, but he seems calm.

'I'm Chris. My little sister's Desiree, and my brother's Keith.' He tugs at the stuffed dog Keith holds to his chest as Desiree emerges from the jet cabin, a massive navy-blue binder in her arms. We give him our names and he nods.

He takes the heavy binder from Desiree and comes halfway down the stairs.

'Assuming you two were expecting a bit more than . . .' Chris glances around the empty airport, then back at us. 'Us, I guess.'

'Kind of,' I say. 'I mean, it's nice to see other people . . .' Especially other people who aren't armed and seem friendly. It's also weirdly nice to see someone our age.

Chris holds out the binder to us. 'You should take a look at this.'

I take the binder and a laminated paper falls out. Jamie bends down to pick it up and I open the binder. The pages inside look like they're wrinkled from being out in the elements, but the computer printouts are still readable. The three rings holding them together are bent and scratched. I flip to the first page, which reads: *TOP SECRET CLASSIFIED – SUPPLEMENTAL MATL DECEMBER 16th INTELLIGENCE BRIEFING.*

Jamie shows me the laminated paper and hope slowly drains from my body like blood from an open wound. It's hope I didn't know existed until it was already on its way out.

The letterhead has the presidential seal at the top, and under it, it says *THE WHITE HOUSE, WASHINGTON.* The letter is dated December 17.

'Where did you get this?' Jamie asks.

Chris nods towards the dead body by the stair car. 'Him. He was Benjamin Wilson. Poor dude was in over his head. Well, guess we all kinda were, huh?'

Jamie glances over the letter. 'He was an intern?'

'That's a hard *was*,' Chris says pointedly. 'Things changed pretty quickly in the White House towards the end, so who knows what his official title was when he got sick. Anyway, he was the last one alive and knew people would come out here – people like us – hoping to find some help from the EU.'

'Who killed him?' I ask, nervous. Maybe it was this kid after all and he didn't like what Benjamin Wilson had to say.

'Killed himself. Got sick and decided to try to do something right before he died.'

I flip through the intelligence briefing in the binder. There's an official-looking Morse code printout on a US Navy letterhead, which I can't understand. But the page after translates it.

No aid available.
Quarantine failed.
Second wave worse.
Closing down.

Jamie sighs and reads a passage from the letter aloud for me. '"We got word from leaders in The Hague that there's been a resurgence of the virus. There is no help coming. Signals in Japan, Russia, India and Brazil have gone dead. South Africa stopped responding in October. UAE and Iran reached out in November, but nothing since. We're on our own."'

The rest of the pages in the binder are previous briefings, including all the things they hid from us. They knew in July how high the mortality rate was – 99.99 per cent, which, why not round it up to an even 100 per cent, guys? They didn't tell us that until August when we had all but figured it out for ourselves. There's a study on DNA and infection rate that's way over my head. And in the last briefing document in bold: *Estimated world casualties ~73-86% of pop.*

I close the binder. I don't need to see any more.

Jamie hands me the laminated letter and I read it quickly. The final paragraph confirms Chris's story. Benjamin Wilson was getting sick so he grabbed the documents he had and came here hoping to let people know what really happened. I tuck the letter back into the binder and hand it to Chris, who passes it to his sister. Desiree heads up the stairs past her little brother to the jet cabin.

'He wanted to make sure other people knew the truth,' Chris said. 'Poor sucker was probably the last government official left standing. Hell, if the whole line of succession was gone, he might have been the president. So he came all the way here with those documents . . .' He turns to look back at Benjamin Wilson's body. 'Sorry we don't have better news.'

Jamie runs his fingers through his hair, looking up at the sky.

I feel numb. Hopeless and numb. Jamie lets out a frustrated sigh and turns to me. His eyes ask me what we do next, but I don't have an answer for him, so I turn back to Chris.

'How long have you been here?' I ask.

Chris turns back to look at Desiree. ''Bout . . . four months?'

'Three months and two weeks,' Desiree corrects him.

'Have other people come through?' Jamie asks.

Chris nods. 'Plenty. Then when they heard no one was coming, they kind of went off on their own. Maybe back to their homes or to find someone else?'

Because what else is there?

'Why haven't you?' I ask.

He turns back to Desiree and says, 'Why don't you go get lunch started for you and Keith?'

Desiree frowns and starts to turn before saying, 'You gonna ask them?'

'Yeah, Des.' The subtle annoyance in his voice makes me smile because it reminds me of how my sister and I used to talk. This whole time he's been acting so much older than he probably is – he really couldn't be older than eighteen. But now that facade, that need to be the parent-slash-guardian, is slipping. Then all at once it's back up. 'Stop being a pain and get going.'

She rolls her eyes but does as her brother says, pulling Keith's arm as she goes back into the cabin. Keith finally gives us a quick wave, which I return before they head into the dark.

Once they're inside, Chris turns back to us. 'Our parents died back in September.' We don't need to say how sorry we are to hear it and he doesn't stop long enough for us to do so. 'It's just been me and them since. We're from North Carolina.'

Again, my eyes flick to his empty hands; to the belt around his waist with no holster. They travelled all this way without a weapon to protect themselves?

'A long way to travel for no reason,' he continues. 'By

the time we got here, all these planes were already parked and abandoned.' He motions around us. 'Guess they weren't able to refuel. Or they landed and lost hope or were never coming here for *them* anyway.' He nods in the direction of Benjamin Wilson's body.

'Where are you hoping to catch a flight to?' Jamie asks.

Chris turns back to the doorway; then his attention moves to two of the windows, where his siblings are watching. He flicks a hand at them and their faces disappear into the cabin.

'Our aunt is out in Chicago. It's a long way to travel on foot, especially . . .' His eyes flick over to Benjamin Wilson's body again. Especially if it's all for nothing. Then he nervously pats the side of the stairs. 'Don't suppose either of you know how to fly one of these suckers?'

I chuckle. So that's what Desiree wanted him to ask us. The smile on his face tells me he doesn't actually expect an answer. But wouldn't it be fun if we did know how to fly a plane?

'You might be waiting a while for someone who could fly this,' Jamie says.

Chris nods. 'Yeah. I figured we'd stay a few days past the tenth and do what we gotta do. What about you guys? Where you headed now?'

Jamie turns to me and I have no idea what to say. We could go back to the cabin, risk it with Howard's crew. Go back to Henri and help her fend off lions.

'I already took what supplies I could from the other planes,' Chris says. 'There wasn't much left. The airport didn't have a lot in the way of shelf-stable items either. I

191

was out looking for more this morning and didn't find much.'

I shake my head. 'We're good for now, thanks. We'll find something on the road.'

'Good luck,' Chris says. 'Sorry you had to come all this way for nothing.'

'Thanks,' I say. 'You too.' All the way to Alexandria for nothing and now Reagan was a bust as well. There was no reason for any part of this journey.

Chris heads up the stairs into the cabin of the plane. Desiree and Keith are back at the window, so I give them another wave before their heads disappear into the dark again.

'You hungry?' Jamie asks. We skipped breakfast, opting to wash quickly before heading here this morning. There's nothing here for us. And nothing left for us to do.

'Yeah.'

We leave Chris and his siblings, heading back towards the front of the airport. Leaving Benjamin Wilson where he took his final, sickened breaths before ending his own misery. Knowing there was no hope for himself or anyone else who came here.

I decide if I see any more graffiti, I'm crossing it out. But then I remember the lack of graffiti we saw around Baltimore. When I was alone, before Jamie, the 'DCA 6/10' graffiti was everywhere. But since heading here from the cabin I saw only three of those messages, max.

Then it hits me. The perfect square of white paint on the side of the truck and over a few road signs.

Someone else already crossed it out after coming here.

'You said Henri's daughter is in Florida?' Jamie asks. We're sitting by the parking garage, the empty cans of our sad brunch at our feet.

I nod. 'If she's alive. Islamorada.'

If. And it's a big if. Florida's pretty far, but we've already gone pretty far. Jamie reaches for the multi-tool hooked on to his belt. Henri's husband's. Henri gave the multi-tool to us, but it's not rightly ours. It belongs to their daughter Amy. And if Amy's still alive she deserves to have it, and to know her mother's up here, too.

Again, a big if.

'It's a long way to go just to return an old multi-tool,' I say.

'We'd be doing more than that.'

He has a point. And Henri did help us. We could go back to the cabin now, maybe ask if Henri wants to come – though I highly doubt it. And then there's what she said to me. Something that's haunted me since she said it. How helpless she felt, being up here, while her pregnant daughter was down there, alone.

It's entirely possible Amy is on her way up here, but . . . No, that's a long hike with a newborn baby – and dangerous, judging by our experience.

Then there's Chris and his siblings. They all have each other and they're hoping to go out to Chicago and find more of their family.

We already know what's behind us. It's more road and a group of survivors who decided the best way to force us to join them would be to intimidate us with guns and steal our food. We know there's nothing but the cabin. Is that enough? It would be for me. Jamie and me together in the cabin for the rest of our days sounds like a wonderful way to spend the apocalypse.

But would that be enough for Jamie?

Of course not. We've known each other for almost three months; he's bound to realise there's more out there for him than just nursing wayward gay boys back to health.

Maybe there's something more down south. More settlements and survivors. Maybe Henri's daughter. If I'm being honest, it's a terrible idea. But I want to hope. I have to hope.

No, it's not a want, it's a need. I need her to still be alive. I need there to be something left in this world that's worth hoping for.

Because before, I never thought I would survive after Alexandria. I expected Jamie to leave me because he only saw me as a murderer. I expected the Fosters to kill me out of revenge. I expected to be alone for ever.

Jamie hasn't left me, though.

And like Jamie did for me, Henri helped us when she didn't need to. I heard how upset she was when she said she couldn't be with Amy. She said mothers were supposed to be there for their daughters after they had a baby. But the world ended and she couldn't.

We need to help someone else. Jamie likes the Marvel movies; what was that thing Black Widow said about having red in her ledger in *The Avengers*? Because my ledger is redder than the end of Jamie's notebook.

So I say, 'Yeah. Let's go down there in search of one person like a needle in a Florida-size haystack, and if we don't find anything and civilisation really is only you, me, a seventy-year-old-woman in Bethesda, some tax-obsessed Pennsylvanians, Chris and his kids in Chicago, and an Axe-Mannequin, then so be it. Besides, we can always walk back up after the winter to let Henri know either way.'

Jamie smiles and he seems genuinely happy. For an instant I don't see the hesitation in his eyes that I've noticed so often. Then his smile drops slightly. No one else would have ever noticed. But I do. I know his face better than anyone else ever could and I know what his face says. He's apprehensive. Nervous about the entire prospect. Unsure.

I might be, too.

Halfway through Virginia the highway is completely clear. Every car we see is pulled over to the shoulder. Jamie points out the broken glass on the road and the broken driver's-side windows in some of the cars.

'Someone moved them,' he says, looking in and pointing at the shifter in neutral.

'Which means there're people around here who probably use this road.' Maybe on their way up to Reagan National. Or away from?

But we don't run into anyone. And we don't hear the sound of a single car while we follow 95 south. About ten days out of Alexandria, Jamie points to a Honda on the side of the road, a lopsided grin on his face. The windows aren't broken and a layer of dust covers every inch except the back windshield. There's a message scrawled in the dust and almost washed away by rain that makes me snort.

Apocalypse blowout sale!
FREE! Runs great!
1/4 tank of gas included!

Jamie opens the door and the car starts to ding. He reaches in and takes a pair of keys out of the ignition, and the dinging stops immediately. Jamie holds up the keys to me. A small foam sandal with the words 'Sea Isle City' hangs from them.

Jamie gives me a look. 'Should . . . we drive a bit?'

Oh my God, *yes*. My feet would sing. But none of this feels right. 'This doesn't seem like a trap to you?'

'How is it a trap?'

I thrust my hand at the message. 'The "free car" note is a dead giveaway! You probably turn the ignition and it explodes.'

He smirks. 'Remember when I left a message on the truck about the free food?'

Again with the optimism. Hasn't he learned his lesson yet?

'Do you really think someone would rig a car to explode on the side of the road? For what purpose?'

Yes, that's true. 'But why would they leave the car? If they were moving all those other cars out of the way, why leave this one here?'

Jamie looks further down the road. It's still empty, and right before it turns, there's another three vehicles pushed off to the shoulder. 'Maybe they found a better car?'

Before I can stop him, Jamie climbs into the driver's seat. He turns the keys in the ignition and for a moment it cranks and I think it's not going to turn over. Then the car roars to life – well, as much as a Honda Civic *can* roar – and Jamie gives me a wide, childlike grin that makes my stomach flip.

'Get in,' he says.

I roll my eyes. 'I'm going to set you up here and I *need* you to get this right.' I move around to the passenger seat and hop in. I stare at him as seriously as I can while looking at his goofy grin. 'You have to back up. I don't think you have enough road to get to eighty-eight.'

For just a second he looks concerned, and I'm so ready to punch him. Then his smirk returns. He shifts to drive and says, 'Roads? Where we're going, we don't need roads.'

'YES!' I shout and roll the window down. 'America! He knows *Back to the Future*!'

Jamie hits the gas pedal and the car lurches forward. He spins the wheel hard to the left and we get back on to the highway . . . just in time for him to hit the metal guardrail in the middle of the road.

'Oh,' I mumble, bracing my hands against the dashboard. 'But he doesn't know how to drive.'

'I'll figure it out.'

My eyes go wide. 'Wait, do you really not know how to drive?'

'I lived in a city! I took public transportation everywhere.' He reverses a little too fast and I grapple for the oh-shit handle above the window, because oh shit.

He hits the gas in drive and we speed forward for a moment before he slams on the brakes. Then we lurch again and he hits the brakes as though he isn't sure how to regulate our speed. I grab his arm.

'So hey! I'm going to say something to you that took my father three weeks of screaming and yelling to finally tell me.'

'What's that?'

'You're a shitty driver, now get out. I'm paying someone else to teach you.'

He frowns. 'You're lucky there's only a quarter tank of gas left.' He opens the door and hops out as the car starts to drift forward.

'Jamie, you have to put it in park!'

I scramble over to the driver's seat and stop the car. When I turn to look at him, he's wide-eyed and grimacing. 'Sorry.'

'You're a menace.' But I can't help laughing as I watch him walk around to the passenger side. Something in my chest loosens and I . . . feel better. Not great, obviously, but having Jamie here with me, making me laugh, making me feel normal – as normal as I can, given the multiple circumstances we find ourselves in.

It's nice.

I don't know what would have happened if I'd made it all the way down to Alexandria alone. Jamie coming after me was the best thing that could have happened. I like that he makes the world feel not so awful. And that he might be making me a better person.

Oh shit. I really just fell in love with a straight boy,

didn't I? I mean, it's clearly been there for a while and I only just noticed, but there it is.

'What?' he asks after I've been smiling at him for way too long.

I shake my head. 'Nothing.'

'Stop making fun of me, just drive.'

I'm not making fun of you, Jamie. I would never.

I've missed this – being able to just drive. We roll the windows down and keep the air off because my dad always said it used more gas – not sure if that's even true. Sadly for us, there's no radio. But even with the wind as our only soundtrack, it's nice.

Funny how little things can feel so big when you haven't done them in a while.

The car gets us just past Raleigh before the engine finally dies. When we unload our packs, I wipe the message off the back windshield and scrawl my own on top of the trunk. *Runs great! Just needs a little gas.*

From there, we're back on foot.

And foot travel takes so long! We even check a few cars along the way – all have been pulled off the highway – but none of the others have keys in them. We travelled almost a hundred and twenty miles in one day while in the car. On foot, in the summer heat and humidity, we only get about twenty. If we're lucky.

A couple of days are a wash because it rains so much we have to stop. About two weeks after we found the car we get sidetracked in a small town outside Coosawhatchie, South Carolina. We stop to check for food, but the

199

supermarket is completely bare. The two gas stations in town are empty as well.

We try the diners and the restaurants, but it looks like someone has taken all the food and supplies. Finally, Jamie says we should check a house. We've been trying not to break into homes while we're on the road, because it feels a little like grave robbing. I understand no one is going to be using what we take anyway, but it still feels wrong.

We find two houses that are open, their owners inside but still long gone. Whoever ransacked the grocery stores and gas stations hadn't gotten around to checking the houses yet, because we find plenty of canned and dry goods to fill our packs.

I say a quiet thank-you to the corpses on the couch and floor on our way out.

That night we stop just outside Hardeeville, South Carolina. It's night-time. We've eaten and we're by a stream so our bellies and water bottles are both full. It's a beautiful night, despite the stifling heat and humidity. Jamie is lying down, his hands folded on to his bare chest as he looks up at the sky. I'm sitting next to him, poking the small fire we heated our food on. We clearly don't need its heat, but it's nice to not sit in complete darkness.

'Do you think there'll ever be electricity again?' I ask.

Jamie shrugs. 'At some point. There's got to be an engineer somewhere in the world who knows how generating electricity works. They might even focus on wind power or something sustainable. Or maybe it will take decades for someone to invent something new.'

'So you're saying that no matter where we go, our days of hot showers are over.' There's a water heater back at the cabin. And solar tiles to power it. Sure, Howard and his crew might be a problem, but maybe there's something else we can give them to create peace between us.

'Unless you find a hot spring.'

Even in the heat I shiver at the thought of washing up in the cold stream tomorrow morning.

'No more internet,' I say.

'I'm actually OK with that.'

'Heathen!' I point an accusatory finger at him. He laughs and swats away my hand.

'The only thing it was good for was looking up stuff you didn't know. Other than that, it was all just people being assholes.'

He has a point, but I'm not giving in that easily. 'You know, if the internet was still around, someone could just look up how to make electricity again.'

'If the internet was still around and I'd looked up your broken leg symptoms online, it would say you were dying of total organ failure.'

'If the internet was still around, we could watch Netflix instead of me just giving you scene-by-scene summaries of movies.'

Though that's actually one of my favourite games.

Jamie has also told me his darkest secret: he loves Hallmark Channel original movies! Can't get enough of them. When he tells me those plots I like to interrupt with, 'Wait, let me guess. The guy and girl have a misunderstanding and don't speak to each other until a wise child intervenes.'

Nine times out of ten I'm right. The tenth time it's usually a wise old person who intervenes. But he does have a way of making movies like *October Kiss* sound good. There are also moments where he gets halfway through and I have to tell him, 'No, I think we've seen this one. She leaves her high-stress job to marry the widowed innkeeper, right?' But lately I've just let him continue.

I like listening to him.

Even if he does get to the part where the stepchild hops off a subway to interrupt an important presentation and this look of realisation dawns on his face and he says, 'Wait, have I told you this one before?'

'Well,' Jamie says now. 'Lucky for us *you're* a good storyteller. I like hearing your never-ending mind catalogue of movies.'

My lips are pulling into a smile I can't stop. 'You must be a shitty storyteller because I still don't understand the "plot" of *Mulholland Drive*.'

He sighs. 'Fade in, exterior, Mulholland Drive, night.'

'Stop! I don't want to hear it again.'

'All right, all right, I'll skip to the Winkie's Diner scene,' he says, sitting up.

'No!' I cover my ears as he goes into the scene.

'I had a dream about this place.' He has that evil smirk on his face. I tackle him and cover his mouth. He continues talking and laughing under my hand and pulls it away. 'It's the second one I've had . . .' I attempt to cover his mouth again as he struggles.

An explosion behind us lights up the night sky in red.

I jump off him and scramble over to our packs, picking up the gun from beside them. Jamie is there, his hand already lifting the rifle. My heart's racing. My lungs have stopped taking in air. We turn around, looking for the explosion, for the people, for the attack, but nothing's there.

'What was that?' he asks before I can.

We wait in silence, then a white light zips up from the ground a quarter mile away. Once in the sky, the light explodes into a shower of sparkling green. We lower the guns.

Fireworks.

There's another zip of white sparks followed by a purple explosion.

'Wait a second.' Jamie goes back to the packs and takes out his mother's notebook. He flips through the pages and smiles, turning it around to me. There are several tally marks, between twenty-eight and thirty-one, in eleven boxes. His mother's calendar system. It was too much wasted space to draw a full-box calendar so he keeps tallies and labels the boxes for the month. He points to the eleventh box – 'JL' written above it. There are four tally marks in it.

'It's July fourth.'

'I didn't even think about it.' Another yellow explosion lights up the sky.

'Neither did I, until now.' He tucks the book away and we sit down, our backs to the fire, and we watch the fireworks.

'I didn't expect to see fireworks ever again.'

'No.' Blue and red explosions at the same time.

'Maybe they have electricity and internet, too,' I say, joking. Our voices have a dazed tone to them as we watch the fireworks shoot up from the ground.

'Do you want to go find them?'

I do but I don't but I do.

I don't, but I think Jamie does. At least his voice sounds like he does. He's leaning up now, looking at me. And as another firework ignites the sky, he looks hopeful. He wants to find people. That's why Jamie left the cabin to begin with, because he thought I was looking for civilisation. And why we decided to keep going instead of turning back to the cabin, after all.

My heart aches as he smiles at me and I say, 'Sure. Let's go find them.' But even as the words leave my mouth, my stomach twists into a ball of nerves.

Jamie pulls on his shirt and my stomach knots. What if they're like Howard and the others back at the cabin? What if we're packing up and heading towards danger?

A purple firework explodes over us.

I pull the pack over my shoulders and it feels like it weighs more than it did a couple of hours ago. I don't say anything to Jamie as he dumps some of the water on the remains of our fire and we set off in the direction of the fireworks.

They're only a quarter of a mile away, but the walk there feels like millions. I hear them now. People talking. Laughing. Cheering.

There are a lot of them. The handgun is in my pack, the rifle over Jamie's shoulder. He looks back at me, orange lighting up his face as another firework explodes. His eyes ask for permission to continue. To walk out and see if these people with the explosive devices are safe.

And I can't tell him no.

He deserves to be happy. Not that I know this is what will make him happy, but it's a step in that direction. It's other people and not just me and my baggage. Maybe he can find a nice girl and I can go down to Florida on my own only to find out Henri's daughter is dead and there's nothing good left in the world.

Yikes. That just got real bleak. Hell, maybe we *both* need these people.

So I nod at him. And we step out into the clearing with our hands raised.

JAMISON

I count at least seven men with guns. The weapons are holstered, but when the men see us, their hands instinctively drop down to the butts of their handguns. I put my hands up higher.

A firework, the fuse already lit when we step into the open, shoots up into the sky and explodes, but no one looks at it. Everyone's eyes are on us.

My jaw hangs open. There's gotta be close to forty people here. A dozen are kids. It's more people in one place than I've seen in almost a year.

A large, white, barrel-chested man with thinning grey hair steps towards us. Four men flank him, two who look to be a little older than Andrew and me, the other two almost middle-aged.

'We saw your fireworks,' I say. 'We just wanted to come say hi and . . .'

And see if you were people we wanted to know, see if we could all be friends. They have fireworks, so they aren't worrying about food taxes.

I shrug. 'See if we can watch.'

The large man's face softens and he smiles. He puts a

big hand out to me and I lower my arms to shake it. He speaks with a slow South Carolina drawl.

'Danny Rosewood. Head selectman of Fort Caroline.'

'Fort?' Andrew asks. 'Are you military?'

Danny Rosewood turns and holds out his hand to Andrew, who shakes it. 'Naw, not military. Though some of us did have some experience in the armed forces.'

Danny Rosewood spins, looking around at the people behind him. He points to one of the men whose hands dropped to his gun.

'There he is. That over there's our sheriff, Grover Denton. What branch were you in, Grover? Army?'

'Air force,' Grover Denton answers. Denton isn't southern, but he has an accent I can't place. Midwest, maybe.

'Flyboy, that's right.' Rosewood nods and brings his attention back to us. 'And his second-in-command used to be a marine. A *girl* marine at that!'

He says this like it's supposed to be shocking and I can practically feel the dam of Andrew's self-control bursting as he remains quiet. I can't look at him because I know we'll start laughing.

'I didn't get your name,' Rosewood says.

'Andrew, sorry, sir.' The sound of his voice tells me I'm right – Andrew's barely keeping himself together. He doesn't say 'sir' sarcastically, but I know he means it that way, and I smile politely, trying not to laugh.

'Come on then . . .' Rosewood smiles broadly and steps

207

aside. 'By the grace of God, you're here, so let's keep the show going and you boys can make our acquaintance. Get to know some people.' His eyes flit briefly to the rifle on my shoulder but he doesn't say anything. Maybe because he's confident their people would end us before we could try anything.

Everyone behind Rosewood seems to settle as he pats Andrew and me on the shoulders. It's as if they were waiting for approval from their leader before lightening up. Another firework is lit and this time mostly everyone is back in the celebratory mood.

Andrew takes the explosion as a moment to whisper into my ear. 'Hear that? They got *lady* marines in these parts.'

I snort and whisper back, 'I hate you.'

'You love me.'

My stomach does a little flip and my mouth goes dry. Completely oblivious to the reaction he just got out of me, Andrew walks past to greet more people from Fort Caroline. I try to do the same. But I can't help glancing over at him through the crowd. Every time I do it's like he feels my eyes on him and he looks right at me, smiles and winks.

We pass through a toll booth where a woman with an AR15 waves to the driver – Grover Denton – and we continue our ride into Fort Caroline.

'No wonder it's called a fort,' Andrew whispers.

Grover looks back at us in the rear-view mirror, the dashboard lights casting his face in green. 'There was an old fort back in the 1500s, but it's not there any more. They just kept the name.'

'Who was Caroline?'

'The wife of one of the original settlers. Rosewood is related to them, actually.'

Andrew gives a condescending 'uh-huh' and I shoot him a warning glance. He shrugs and I look back into the rear-view mirror to see Grover Denton's furrowed brow relax. We're all quiet as we pull off the highway.

The streets are empty. The caravan of cars following us – and two school buses full of people – veer off as we drive through what looks like downtown Fort Caroline. The shops are all in one piece; no broken glass, no fires. There are lights at every intersection. They're the types of lights I used to see at night-time road work zones, two bright lamps atop a movable pole, pointed down at the road. Each light is powered by what looks like a gas generator, chugging along in the silent town.

'Was that everyone we saw back in the clearing?' I ask.

'No way.' Grover sounds happy about this. 'That's just the people who are on second shift tomorrow.'

I glance at Andrew to see if he knows what second shift means, but he gives me a quick shake of his head.

'You'll see,' Grover adds.

He pulls into the parking lot of an old two-storey motel. The whole building is dark except for the office on the first floor, which is lit only in candlelight.

Grover kills the truck and we step out, grabbing our packs from the bed and following him into the office.

There's no one there. The candle flickers alone on top of the desk.

'Cara?' Grover calls out.

A tall, pale young woman with long brown hair emerges from the dark back room. She looks like a ghost in this candlelight. She glances at Grover, but locks her eyes on Andrew and me like she's wary of us.

'We have new guests. Can you set them up?'

She nods and begins to look more comfortable as she reaches for two clipboards and puts them on the desk, facing us. Barely above a whisper, she says, 'I need you to fill this out, and you can go to room 2C.'

Her eyes dart up to me as she takes a metal key attached to an orange tag and slides it across the desk towards me. Not a plastic card, an honest-to-God metal key.

'It's on the second floor. Go right out this door and up the stairs, the second door on the right. It says 2C on it.'

I take the key and the clipboard, glancing at the form. It's a questionnaire, asking for our names, date of birth, place of birth. Normal at first, but then I notice at the bottom the questions change to ask who in your family survived the superflu, who died, how old they were. There are four pages in the questionnaire but I don't pay much attention to them because Cara's talking to Andrew now and sliding him a different key.

'And you can have 2D. It's on the second floor. Go right out this door and up the stairs, the third door on the right. It says 2D on it.'

I can't tell if she's trolling us or if she's serious, but Andrew smiles. 'Thanks, but we can share a room. I mean, he farts a lot in his sleep, but I'm used to it by now.' He nudges me playfully.

My face burns and I see Cara's turn red in the candlelight as well. Before I can scold Andrew, Grover speaks.

'Don't worry about it, there's no one else coming and I think there's only two other rooms taken right now. We have the space.'

The idea of Andrew being that far away makes me nervous. It was different in the cabin. He was in his own room, but it was still the same house. An adjacent hotel room somehow feels further. Maybe because we've slept right next to each other for two months now.

'I'll come check on you tomorrow,' Grover says. 'Be good, Cara.'

He waves and she glances up and gives him a silent nod, then stares down at her hands. She's frail and quiet and I find myself wondering how she even survived this long.

Andrew squeezes my elbow and nods to the exit and I follow. I glance back to see Cara turning back to the dark room behind the desk.

'Good night, thank you,' Andrew says. She stops and looks back at us but doesn't say anything.

Andrew and I walk up the stairs, to the second and third doors on the right. They say 2C and 2D, as promised.

'Well . . . this is me,' Andrew says, leaning against 2D and holding up his key. 'I had a great time. This is the best apocalypse conference I've ever been to. Seriously! I mean, the Zombie Zymposiums never have fireworks displays. Did you hear what I did there, Jamie? I changed the *s* in Symposium to a *z* to make it alliterative and clever.'

I laugh and open my own room. It's dark and when I flip the light switch nothing happens. I grab the flashlight out of my pack and flick it on.

The room has a king bed and there are candles strategically placed throughout. Andrew leans in the doorway.

'I believe you promised me lights *and* internet,' he says.

'Settle for a fort and a king-size bed?'

'Hmm.'

I look over at him. He has a sceptical look on his face and seems to be chewing the inside of his cheek.

'What's wrong?'

He shakes his head. 'It's nothing.'

'It's something. I know when you're hiding something from me, remember?'

That gets him to smile and he shakes his head again. 'Really. I don't think it's anything.'

'You'll tell me when it's something?'

'I will. Promise. And my promises *mean* something.' He unlocks his own door and narrows his eyes at me. 'Unlike yours and the internet's.'

'Good night, Andrew.'

'Night, Jamie.'

I find a matchbook by the bed and light a few of the candles. There's running water but it's all cold. I jump in the shower and clean myself off as fast as I can in the icy water, then change into fresh clothes to sleep in before blowing out the candles.

It's musty and hot in the room so I open the window, but it doesn't really help. I lie awake in the middle of the king-size bed, on top of the blankets. It's nice – comfortable, actually. But I can't fall asleep. It's too quiet. All I hear is my own breathing and the soft breeze outside, rustling the leaves on the trees.

Andrew is probably awake, too. He's probably lying there, listening to the same sounds I am and thinking about me. I would like him to be thinking about me. It makes me feel a little less strange if he thinks about me, too.

I'm suddenly overcome with panic. I can feel sweat beading at my forehead and lower back. My chest tightens and each breath feels shallow. The walls are closing in and I'm back in the Baltimore tunnel again, surrounded by bloated, waterlogged flu victims and stagnant water. But Andrew isn't here this time.

Without thinking I get up, grab the pillow and my room key, and open the door. Once out in the open air I feel a bit better, but my chest is still tight.

I knock on Andrew's door.

He opens it within seconds. Good, so he was awake. Just seeing him loosens my chest and I feel like I can breathe again.

'What's wrong?'

I shake my head. It feels ridiculous now, but seconds ago I thought I might die. 'I can't sleep over there. It feels . . .'

I don't know what it feels. Again, 'like dying' seems an overreaction, but Andrew nods like he understands anyway.

'I know, it's weird. That's what I didn't want to say before.'

'Um . . .' I hug the pillow to my chest. 'Can I sleep in here?'

'Yeah.' He steps aside and I go in.

ANDREW

Let's be clear on one thing. It's fucking torture having the boy you're in love with sleeping in the same bed as you. Like, right next to you.

But, like, a good kind of torture, I guess. If hell is real and I'm going there for being a murderer and I get to choose between the penis bees and sleeping in the same bed next to Jamie for eternity but never being able to touch him, I'm going with this comfy bed.

And Jamie's soft snores.

Penis bees be damned!

Jamie falls asleep instantly, but I can't help but watch him for a while in the darkness.

I said shut up, it's not creepy.

He's so kind and sensitive. I bet he knew how uncomfortable I was over here on my own. I almost knew he was going to come over so when I heard his knock I jumped right up.

It physically hurts to be this close. I know I shouldn't feel the way I do about him but I can't help it. He's not the first straight boy I've fallen in love with. No, that dubious honour goes to my best friend since elementary school, Clark Murphy, now a victim of the bug. Still, it doesn't hurt any less.

I don't even realise I've fallen asleep until the knocks come.

I jump up, reaching for the handgun, but it's not there. It's in my pack and my pack is on the other side of the room. It takes me a moment to remember we're in the hotel room in Fort Caroline.

It's morning and the sun glares against the venetian blinds hanging in front of the window. The knocks sound again.

But it's coming from next door. They're knocking on Jamie's door.

Jamie sits up. He rubs at his eyes. 'What time is it?'

'Shit. Go in the bathroom and stay quiet.'

He turns to me. 'Why?'

'Just . . . trust me. Go.'

He goes into the bathroom without asking anything else. Whoever is out there knocks again on Jamie's door. I glance around the room, looking for any sign that Jamie could have been in here last night.

I don't know who these people are, but they put us in different rooms on purpose. Sure, there are more than enough available, but they thought we'd want our own rooms. They didn't want two boys sharing a king bed if they didn't have to because that would mean something they probably weren't prepared to think about.

The knock finally comes to my door.

It's not Danny Rosewood or Grover Denton standing there. It's not even the motel night girl, Cara. It's a tall woman with her light hair pulled back into a tight bun. She wears a beige outfit that does nothing for her pale complexion and has a badge across her chest.

Oh, lookit, the Lady Marine.

'Where's your friend?' she asks.

I frown. 'Um, hi. Good morning, I'm Andrew.'

'Nadine Price. Your friend, where is he?'

'What time is it? He's a morning person so he probably went out to explore.'

She nods. 'Get dressed and meet me in the office when you're ready. I'm to give you a tour and you've got a meeting with Sheriff Denton at noon. We'll find your friend while we're out.'

She doesn't wait to answer and walks back in the direction of the stairs.

I shut the door and Jamie comes out of the bathroom. 'I met the Lady Marine! She's *nice*.'

'Sounded that way. Why didn't we just say I slept in here?'

Oh, Jamie. Sweet, innocent Jamie. 'Because I wanted to keep you my dirty little secret.' I shrug, pretending to play it off. 'Just force of habit. Any time there's a boy in my bed and someone comes a-knockin' . . .'

He smirks and turns a light shade of pink.

'Go back to your room before the Lady Marine does a room check again. And when you meet us in the office, pretend you were out for a walk.'

Jamie stands up straight and salutes me as he opens the door, looking both ways and dropping low, like he's trying to be stealthy.

Our plan works fine. When I reach the office, Nadine is sitting there in silence. Cara is there, too. Also quiet. The two of them probably get along famously.

As Nadine leads me out to the squad car in the parking lot, Jamie rounds the corner with his 'went for a walk' story. Nadine asks no follow-up questions and we hop in the back of the car and set off for our tour.

There are a lot more people living in Fort Caroline than we saw in the clearing last night. Hundreds, maybe. And they're all working. There's a group of people going through a drugstore and sorting products into large plastic bins. A crew of men with sledgehammers are gutting the inside of a storefront.

'What is all this?' I ask.

Nadine doesn't say anything at first, then quickly mumbles, 'Clean-up. Everyone has jobs to do.' She tells us there are three shifts. Eight a.m. to four p.m., four p.m. to midnight, midnight to eight a.m. The shifts change week to week so no one is fatigued working overnight, but everyone does their part to help clean up and start over.

That explains why none of the stores are looted. Why there's no trash or bodies in the streets. Why there are more parking spaces than there are cars. In fact, every road is empty of cars except for Nadine's.

'What did you do with the bodies of the flu victims?' I ask.

Nadine doesn't answer. I turn to Jamie but he's looking out the window, his eyes narrowed. His focus darts everywhere at once, trying to take it all in.

'Where did the flu victims go?' I try again.

'We cremate the dead. There's not enough space to bury them all.' The way she says it is curt and slightly rude. Like she finds my questions annoying, which, screw you, Lady Marine, I'm curious.

But she does have a gun. So I shut up and let her go on with this sad excuse for a tour. I smile at a young woman who dumps a load of books from a large brick library into a bin outside its doors.

She doesn't smile back.

I open my mouth to ask what they're doing with the library books but remember Nadine has the personality of a poisoned cornflake and shut it. I still turn to watch as someone else reaches into a wheelbarrow full of books and dumps them into a bin. There doesn't seem to be the same sorting going on with the books as there was at the drugstore. But at least they aren't burning them?

I hope they're not burning them.

Nadine comes to a stop at a large, windowless cinder-block building that says 'Fort Caroline Sheriff's Department' in silver letters across the top.

'This is the sheriff's department,' she says. You know, I bet she wasn't even a real marine before the bug. She probably gave tours at Disney World *pretending* to be a marine. 'You'll turn in your questionnaire here when you're finished with it. Sophie or Gloria work the front desk between nine a.m. and six p.m. And if you ever have a problem with one of the residents you can report it here, too. Other than that, we're mainly just here to help with smaller problems.'

'Like what?' Oh, Andrew, why do you ask things you

know she isn't going to answer?

But she surprises me. 'Theft, mainly. But even that's stopping. Everyone understands we're a community now and stealing from one person means stealing from everyone. Also, they understand the food ration rules. The food and supplies you came with will be added to the surplus and we'll give you ration certificates for those on top of your weekly allowance.'

Ration certificates?

But before I can ask, Jamie says, 'We have to turn in our supplies?'

'Just your food and anything deemed useful. You keep your clothes and water bottles.'

'What about books?' I ask.

She frowns and looks back at me in the rear-view. 'You're carrying around books?'

'Not a literature fan?'

'Not a fan of wasting space.'

Yikes. Maybe they *are* burning the books. Nadine pulls back out of the sheriff's lot and continues our tour through Sadville – I mean, Fort Caroline.

'What were those guys gutting the store back there for?' I ask. She seems to be in more of a habit of answering me.

'The selectmen have created a plan to condense the town so we have one drugstore, one convenience store, one grocery, and then there's the hospital. Any store deemed redundant is being emptied to the studs and when a need for something arises, they'll put it in there. Right now, it's just residential living. We have a few of the apartment buildings fully occupied and our scouting parties are travelling further out than they've ever been. Soon we're going to be even bigger and we'll need more space to put those people.'

I wonder if Fort Caroline realises they've invented socialism.

A group of five men surround an open manhole in the middle of the street. One waves Nadine around them and she continues.

'How far have you gone?' I ask.

'Virginia.'

Of course. That explains why it was harder for us to find food after leaving Alexandria. It also explains the cleared-out highway. I wonder if the people who left the car ran into a Fort Caroline motorcade.

Nadine adds, 'They're hoping to get to DC by the end of the year.'

'We passed through DC,' Jamie says. 'There's no one there.'

'Supplies, then.'

'Hope they bring their weapons,' I mutter to Jamie, and make a silent, growly lion face.

He doesn't smile. He doesn't laugh. He just keeps his eyes trained outside. His fingers move next to his leg, raising and lowering one at a time. Is he trying to speak in some code? Is this sign language? But when we pass another crew gutting a store, I realise he's counting people. Not all of them, though.

What is he counting?

Nadine takes us to the grocery store, which is an old

Aldi, and explains how the ration vouchers work. We'll receive our first vouchers once we turn in the questionnaire we've forgotten to fill out. Vouchers are delivered every Sunday morning. There's also a supply warehouse that processes what we came into the town with and we'll get vouchers from that as well.

She shows us the school next, informing us that children from five all the way up to fifteen are expected to be in school from eight a.m. until six p.m. I ask if after fifteen they have to move on to job placement. Nadine confirms this with a grunt.

She shows us where the hospital is, parking in the front and showing us into the emergency room, and the family medicine wing. There are a few people in the waiting room, but the most serious injury seems to be a big bald guy with a scrape over his left eye and an attractive blond dude with a cut on his leg that's already stopped bleeding. We pass a few hallways that are dark and the rooms on both sides look empty. Like most of the beds and equipment have been removed.

I make a joke about universal healthcare that lands like a dead fish and then we're off to the pharmacy. It looks busy. There are teams on both sides of it, reaching into plastic bins and filling boxes. They then hand the boxes off to other people who go into the pharmacy to empty them and return for another.

Stocking up.

'Where does all the extra stuff go?' I ask.

'The supply warehouse. It's just outside the main drag where almost everything is sorted and then sent here.'

It's methodical, and it's also kind of redundant – what with people emptying drugstores, taking the supplies to the warehouse for sorting, and then bringing them back here – but at least it's a system? And at least they're all working.

But as I watch everyone entering and exiting the pharmacy, I can't help but feel a little unsettled. There's something off about all this.

About everyone here.

Nadine drives us back to the sheriff's department, where Grover Denton is waiting outside for us. I thank Nadine for the tour as we get out of the car. And yes, it sounds a little sarcastic. But I try to smile so it looks like I'm being genuine.

Lady Marine probably knows I'm full of shit and doesn't respond.

Something is still bothering me about this place, and I don't know what it is. Maybe it's because it's *too* perfect? Everyone out and about is young and strong and working together to rebuild the world. There's a hospital. There's a school. There's a fucking Aldi, for Chrissake.

Grover's in the middle of his questionnaire spiel outside the sheriff's department – seriously, the Fort Caroliners have a real boner for this questionnaire – when he says something that actually surprises me.

'I assume the two of you have weapons.' We don't need to answer because he saw the rifle Jamie had last night. 'You can keep them – in fact, it's encouraged.'

Qué?

'Everyone who is able should have a weapon in case

outsiders try to raid the town. Since this is America, we do have the God-given right to a well-regulated militia.'

I'm torn here. One hand, yes, the world has changed and once again we need weapons. As much as I didn't want the handgun at first, I understand how important it is now. At least there doesn't seem to be a zoo in Fort Caroline.

On the other hand, I'm a little nervous about all these strangers with weapons.

Grover continues, 'You'll have to register your firearms here, though. And we also have ammo rations, which you can't stockpile. You need to account for every bullet you use. And of course it goes without saying, don't shoot anyone.'

I point to Grover and try to sound playful. 'But you still said it.'

'Oh good!' A booming southern voice makes me flinch as Danny Rosewood – flanked again by the same two young men who were with him last night – rounds the corner of the sheriff's station. He's wearing a full suit even in the hot July sun and large beads of sweat slide down his red forehead. 'I was hoping we wouldn't miss the end of the tour.'

'Right on time, Danny,' Grover says. 'I was just finishing up.'

'Y'all hand in your questionnaire yet?'

See? Boner City. And now I bet I have a contender for the creator of the questionnaire. How long do we think before he takes credit?

'Not yet,' I say. 'We were a little wiped after last night.'

'Not a problem.' He waves a swollen hand 'Not a

problem at all. Just make sure you get that in ASAP. The questionnaire was my idea—'

Eleven seconds.

'—one of my better ones, if I do say so myself. It's important to get it in so you can get your work placements. That's something we're *very* proud of here. Everyone's happy to pitch in and help get America back in business again.'

Back in business? Who is he kidding? There's no way any country is going to be the way it was before.

'Did you hear about Reagan Airport?' I ask, interrupting Rosewood's spiel. He turns to me, looks confused for a moment, so I help him along. 'The EU coming to help us.'

Realisation dawns on his face. 'Right! Back in June. We heard, but we also got word from a few of the newer folks that no help was coming.'

I nod. 'That's where we came from. It's going to be a while before anywhere is "back in business".'

Rosewood's grin widens and he claps a heavy hand on my shoulder. 'America first, son! We all built America from the ground up once, we can do it again!'

'Uh, actually America was *stol*—'

'What kind of job placements could the two of us expect?' Jamie interrupts me before I can remind Danny Rosewood that his ancestors killed the Indigenous people of America and then built everything lost to the bug on slave labour. Which, yes, maybe Jamie is right and I should keep my mouth shut right now. Danny Rosewood doesn't seem the type to change his mind easily and my knowledge bomb would only serve to make us less welcome.

Rosewood looks back and forth between us. 'How old are you boys? Seventeen? Eighteen?'

'Sixteen,' Jamie answers.

'He turns seventeen in November,' I say, hoping there's some clout to that. Danny Rosewood nods and continues speaking, but something happens with one of the guys behind him. The taller guy with the sad excuse for a moustache on his upper lip and a patchy beard lowers his eyebrows and looks between Jamie and me.

Shit. I know that look. When he sees me watching him, his eyebrows return to their normal position and he turns to face the pale boy to his left, who doesn't seem to be paying attention to anything.

'Oh, and this . . .' Danny Rosewood turns and claps Fuzzy Lip on the shoulder, 'is my youngest boy, Harvey.'

Harvey Rosewood nods at both of us, but when Danny Rosewood claps the pale boy on the shoulder – introducing him as Harvey's best friend, Walt Howser – Harvey gives me the same unfriendly look he gave me before. The look that said, *I see what you are, and we don't like it here.*

And then everything clicks and I feel light-headed. What's off about this place – it's the people. They're all relatively young, the oldest I've seen being either Danny Rosewood or one of the men by the manhole, who was in his early fifties. I haven't seen anyone on crutches or in a wheelchair. There were no sick people in the hospital. Nadine didn't point out the surgical wing. I didn't even think to ask what happens if someone gets sick. What if they have appendicitis? Do they have anyone to help?

226

Would they even help? Or would they think it's a drain on their stockpile of resources?

And then there's the look that Harvey Rosewood is giving me. The look that says, *You don't belong here.*

And he's right.

Rosewood bids us goodbye, his son looking back only once before he rounds the corner, and then Grover Denton drives us to the motel.

The entire ride I feel nauseous. I can't get out of here fast enough. But how do I convince Jamie? He isn't like me. I know he's sensitive and smart and I can probably persuade him, but how? He doesn't see the world the way I had to. He had a supportive, loving mother. Friends he didn't have to lie to for years. Jamie didn't have to spend his life constantly thinking ahead and trying not to say anything that might give away that dark secret that no one is allowed to have. He doesn't see the look Harvey Rosewood gave me or what it means.

For him, this is civilisation. It's what we've been looking for. For Jamie, this is his new home. He's never going to leave it.

He follows me into my room and I shut the door. I don't know how to say this. How do I get through to him?

But he speaks first: 'We have to get the fuck out of here.'

JAMISON

Andrew just stares at me. I was worried about this, that he'd be so excited at the idea of a settlement that he'd just want to stay – but we can't stay here.

'I'm sorry,' I say. 'I know it's all . . . probably great, but not for us.'

He shakes his head slowly. 'Can I just . . . fucking kiss you?'

My face burns and my stomach flips. 'W-what?'

'I'm kidding but not really. I hate this place.'

'It's fucking weird, right?'

'So weird!'

'I counted while we were driving. There were maybe thirty people over the age of fifty, total.'

Realisation dawns on his face. 'Yes! That's what you were counting?'

'I also counted how many women there are. A little over a hundred, but none of them looked under forty years old. The four doctors in the hospital were men. The one nurse we met was one of the few people I counted over fifty.'

'Lady Marine can't be over forty,' he points out. 'Cara downstairs is twenty, max.'

'OK, so that's two. And I wasn't counting at the time, but there were plenty of women in the clearing last night. Kids, too. But I didn't see them out there today.'

Andrew grimaces. 'All the women between sixteen and thirty-nine are, what? Playing daycare?'

'Thinking more along the lines of traditional gender roles. Also . . .' I'm worried he won't believe me, that he'll think I'm crazy or jumping to conclusions, but he does believe me so far. 'I didn't see one person of colour here.' Almost half Philly's population was Black – over half my school was – so walking through a new town where every person you see is white definitely sticks out.

It's something I noticed about the small town near the cabin when my mom first bought it. Then one summer we invited my friend Wes up for a week and he made a joke that he'd have to hide in our trunk if we went to town. Sure enough, as soon as we went to the supermarket someone called the cops on him. I'd never seen my mom so pissed.

Andrew keeps his voice low but he nods enthusiastically. 'It is *so* white. And I'm from Connecticut!'

That makes me laugh, but it's a nervous laugh. 'All right, so we need to get out of here.'

'Yes. Now.'

'No.' I hold up a hand. 'We should wait until night. It looks like they only have the tollbooth on lockdown, so we head through the woods and just get as far away as we can.'

'You think they won't let us go?' he asks.

I don't. It was the questionnaire that really got me.

They're so adamant about it, and not once during the tour did Nadine or Sheriff Denton say anything about leaving. I cross the room and take the clipboard Andrew put aside.

I flip to the second page. More questions about the superflu.

Who was the youngest in your family to be taken? 'Taken' like they just went somewhere and weren't the victims of a deadly virus.

Who was the oldest in your family to be taken?

There's an asterisk next to both of these that says to include extended family in this number. Then it takes a turn. That's probably why it's on the second page.

The questionnaire asks for religion, physical disabilities, mental disabilities and sexual orientation. At the bottom below all that is a section marked 'if female'.

Are you currently able to conceive?

Did you have children before the sickness? If so, how many?

Did you ever take birth control?

Have you ever had an abortion?

'Holy shit. Andrew.' He moves around and reads over my shoulder.

'Sexual orientation.' He doesn't sound surprised.

The next page is a full medical history, including another asterisk that reminds us to include extended family. There are more pages, but they're friendlier and ask about hobbies and skills, probably an attempt to make the whole thing look like something other than what it is: a registry.

'What happens if they don't like our answers?' Andrew asks.

'Let's not find out.'

I put the clipboard down and Andrew grabs my arm. I follow his gaze to the window looking out on to the balcony. 'What?' I ask.

'The blinds are open. They were shut when I left.'

But the bed isn't made, so Cara must not have come in. Or if she did, it wasn't to make the room up. Also, I doubt the Fort Caroline Motor Court has an active maid service.

'Oh no.' Andrew goes to the bathroom. Then he comes back out, looking in the closet and then under the bed. He opens the bedside table, our road atlas on top of it, and takes out the handgun I gave him. The holster is missing and the gun was just sitting in the drawer of the bedside table.

'What's wrong?'

'They took our bags, Jamie.' He pulls the slide and checks the barrel, like I showed him, then drops the clip out. He shows me it's empty.

I turn around, looking for his bag. It has to be here; they wouldn't take our stuff while we were out. They have no reason.

Only they do. They wanted the food and supplies. The ammo.

We can keep our weapons, of course, but they control the ammo. They control everything in Fort Caroline.

I fling open the door and go to my room, but I already know I'm going to find my own bag gone. But not my rifle, which is also empty.

Andrew stops in my doorway. 'They left the guns and clothes but they took our food and ammo.'

And *my mother's book.*

Andrew follows me down to the office. The door is open and Cara, the thin, weird girl from last night is there, writing in some kind of notebook.

'Hey!' She flinches and stands up, knocking over a coffee can full of pens and highlighters. Everyone else is out there working but she's in here doodling. I want to know what makes her special but don't care to ask right now.

'Our bags are gone. Where'd you put them?'

She hunches in on herself and backs up to the wall behind her. She doesn't answer me; she just watches as one of the highlighters slowly rolls off the desk.

'Where are our bags?' I ask again. Still, she doesn't answer.

'Jamie.' Andrew's voice is a quiet warning, telling me to calm down. They can take whatever food they want, but I want my books back. My mother's notebook is my main concern, but I also had the old book Andrew left me. I want them both and then we're getting the hell out of here.

'Where'd they take our shit?' My blood pumps in my ears and the muscles in my throat tighten.

'Jamie, stop it.' Andrew steps in front of me, putting his hand on my chest. It has almost an instant effect and my blood pressure lowers. 'Can you just . . .' He gives me a 'cut it' gesture with his hand and turns back to Cara.

He moves around the desk but stops himself.

'Do you mind if I come back here? I'll help you clean

up.' He points to the ground where the pens and highlighters are. Cara doesn't answer him and bends over to pick it up herself.

Andrew disappears behind the desk and I hear him talking quietly, only picking up a few words here and there. I pace the office slowly, trying to breathe calm into my mind while I formulate a plan. Wherever they took our stuff, it's gonna be guarded. And we already stand out because we're the strangers. They also took our ammo, which they said would be rationed out.

Andrew pops up with Cara and puts the coffee can back on the desk. 'Can you tell us how to get there?'

She glances at me as if I'm the asshole who stole *her* shit and reaches behind the desk to take a paper from a stack on the counter. It's a crudely drawn map of Fort Caroline. Cara circles a building in red marker she pulls from the coffee can.

'Supply warehouse is here.'

She puts the red marker back and picks up a pencil and circles the motel. 'This is where we are, and you make a left on Cherokee Avenue, a right here on Glower Road, then a right on Morgan Lane, another left on Magnolia Road, another right on Berks Street and it's ahead of you on the corner of Berks Street and Broad Avenue. You can also cut through the park here on Morgan.' She puts a graphite star at the corner of Morgan and Glower, then provides three different routes. 'But the first way is quickest. Unless you want to cut through the park.'

This explains why she's stationed at the motel. She might be shy and not a people person, but she knows her way around. Maybe she was in this motel even before the flu hit.

Andrew gives me a look that says he's got an idea. 'Wait here.' And he leaves us.

I take the map, gently, and look back over it, following her directions. There's a cross on a large square on the bottom corner. 'Is this the hospital?'

Cara glances. 'Pharmacy. The hospital has the caduceus.'

'The . . .' I don't even know what that word is. She points quickly. Oh, I've seen it before – it's two snakes wrapped around a winged staff. 'I didn't know that's what it was called.'

She's leaning away from me and doesn't even respond or look up when I speak. I feel bad for yelling at her and I'm trying to be friendly, but the damage is done. She doesn't like me, which is fine. She lives here so she can't be all that great herself. But there's still something about Cara that doesn't seem to fit this place. Everyone else seems happy to be here – or at least they're excited to pretend things are going back to what they saw as normal. Cara almost seems to be sleepwalking. Answering questions but only providing the information needed, nothing more.

Andrew is still gone and the silence is getting uncomfortable.

'Is this the sheriff's department?' I point to the building with the six-pointed star. Judging by the questionnaire, I don't think they'd mark the Fort Caroline synagogue, if it even exists.

'Yes.'

That's where they'll have taken our ammo. They wait for us to come register our weapons before we get the ammo rations. The battery-powered clock on the wall says it's almost one. The sun sets in a little more than eight hours. We have eight hours to get our ammo, and our food, without raising suspicion.

Andrew comes back with the road atlas in his hand. Cara watches with curiosity as he puts it down in front of her. She even seems to warm a bit to Andrew's presence. She seems less wary while he's in the room.

'We're trying to get here.' He points at the map. The page is turned to the southern half of Florida and his finger is on the Keys.

'Andrew.' He's telling her exactly where we're going when the entire point was for us to make a quick, quiet escape.

He holds a hand up to silence me.

'Could you map out a route for us from Fort Caroline to the Keys?'

Cara glances at me and then at Andrew, before falling back on the road atlas. She scans the map and then reaches for it but doesn't touch it. Her hands hover over it and she asks, 'Can I borrow this? I can have an answer for you in a few hours. I just have to know the scale, then measure out the distances and find the quickest route.'

Andrew looks at me and I shake my head. I try my best to communicate with a look that I don't like this idea, but he tells her yes.

She immediately takes the map and begins looking it

over, reaching for a ruler on the desk. Andrew joins me outside the office.

'Why did you tell her where we're going?'

'Because we need her. Maybe you think these people are going to *let us* steal food from them, but I don't. They will come after us, Jamie. And if they moved the cars on the road north to Virginia, who knows how far south they've cleared it? That means they'll be driving after us. We can't stop to check the map every few exits if we hope to outrun them. And at night it's going to be even harder.'

I sigh. He may have a point. We're going to have to get as far away as we can as fast as we can. 'And if she tells them where we're going?'

Andrew looks back at her. She's hunched over the map, writing quickly on a piece of scrap paper. 'I don't think she's going to tell anyone.'

'What makes you so sure?'

'I'm not. But she reminds me . . .' He pauses and shakes his head. 'I just trust her more than I do anyone else here. She's different from them. That's why they pushed her out here all alone. Everywhere else has shifts and she's the only one working this desk.'

And of course that makes me feel worse for being a dick to her. They have her working this motel to help orient the newcomers, and they probably have her map out their routes on scouting trips. And now I want to know what happens to her when she's outlived her usefulness. But that's Fort Caroline's problem. My only concern is what we're going to find once we get where we're going. And what we do after.

If Henri's daughter is dead, then we just pissed off the largest settlement we've seen for no reason. And we didn't go back to the cabin because we wanted to find more people, but maybe everyone is to an extreme like this now. Even if Henri's daughter is alive, she might be with a similar settlement.

'Come on,' Andrew says. 'We should see about getting our stuff back.'

'Hold on.' I go back into the office. 'Cara? Sorry to bother you.' Her shoulders go up but she doesn't look at us. 'I was hoping to give you another project to work on after that. If you think you can get it done by eight tonight.'

'What project?' She still doesn't look up.

'May I?' I point to the atlas and it looks like she's not going to give it up, but then she steps back from the desk. Andrew joins us, watching me with suspicion. I flip a few pages back and show her a page displaying the lower eastern portion of Pennsylvania. 'Can you plot a route to this area?' I point to an area north-west of Philadelphia.

'What town?'

'It doesn't matter. Just the area.' Her brow furrows as she scans the atlas page and doesn't answer.

'Any town?' She's still looking around the page, her eyes darting like she's trying to follow an annoying fly.

'Uh.' Andrew pushes past me and points at random. 'This one here.'

Her eyes focus on that one spot and she nods. 'From here or the Keys?'

'The Keys, please,' I say.

She nods.

'Thank you very much.' Andrew gives a lopsided smile when I glance at him. 'You OK with that?'

'I'm very OK with that.' He turns back to Cara, his smile disappearing. 'Oh, Cara? When you route from the Keys, can you . . . try to avoid this place as much as possible?'

I watch as she stops writing. At first, she doesn't say anything, then her eyes dart up and lock on to Andrew's, then mine. There's something in that look, but I don't know enough about her to know what it is. Maybe she's suspicious or maybe she's angry. Either way, it doesn't do much to comfort me. She turns her head away from us again.

'Yes.'

'Thank you, Cara.'

'You're welcome.'

ANDREW

We really shouldn't be splitting up. I mean, forgive Jamie, he's pop-culture blind, so he has no idea how when people split up in horror movies they always die. But I have no excuse. By the time we've got a plan formed it's almost three, which leaves us five hours to get everything together.

Barring any hiccups.

Jamie goes to the sheriff's station to register our weapons so he can hopefully get some of our ammo back. I already asked what happens if they don't give him any and he said we'll have to just check every sporting goods store along the route until we get some.

God bless America.

I'm heading for the supply warehouse using Cara's directions.

God bless Cara.

The supply warehouse isn't a warehouse at all. In fact, it's a strip mall of chain restaurants with a massive – empty – parking lot out front. There's a loud chugging sound happening behind the building, like a generator.

The signs have been pulled from the front but the architecture is unmistakable. I see you, Olive Garden. I see you, Cheesecake Factory. I see you . . . Red Lobster maybe? Or is it a Bob Evans?

They've made it easy for me by boarding up the Olive Garden and 'Bob Lobster' that bookend the Cheesecake Factory, whose doors are open. I walk in expecting someone to be standing at the host stand with a hundred-page menu of all the delicacies Fort Caroline has to offer. Oh, and how many ration coupons each one would be. But it looks nothing like I remember a Cheesecake Factory looking.

The entire restaurant is gutted and repainted white. The black tile floor is still there, but all the booths have been ripped out. There's electricity here. The dim lighting meant to hide all the calories you're consuming has been replaced with industrial-strength – daylight-white, God help us – bulbs. Even the ancient Egyptian-slash-Victorian pillars are gone. The walls on both sides of the restaurant have been cut open to pass into the Olive Garden and 'Red Evans' – which is now even less distinctive.

Instead of a host stand, there's a massive desk spanning the length of the restaurant, like a bank counter, blocking me from going any further. Metal shelves filled with everything from shampoo to Dinty Moore run in aisles throughout the restaurant and the ones next door. There are about twelve people walking through the aisles, stocking shelves from shopping carts.

I approach the desk. The woman closest to me stops stocking the shelf and comes over with a polite smile.

'Can I help you?' She's thirtyish, white and wears a name tag that says Jennette.

'Hi, Jennette, I'm Andrew. My friend Jamison and I are new in town and while we were on a tour someone swiped our bags from the motel.' She nods, looking unsurprised. 'I was hoping we might be able to get some food or supplies to replace what was taken?'

'Right. Hold on.' She puts up a finger and moves down to the far-right side of the desk. She reaches underneath and pulls up a small plastic box filled with hanging folders. She flips through quickly, scanning the tabs at the top. 'You said your name was Andrew?'

'Yes. We only just got here yesterday.'

She stops looking and sighs, squeezing her eyes shut. 'And of course it's the holiday and we're behind.'

'You guys get holidays off?'

'We get shift changes. They're doing fireworks on the third, fourth and fifth. But everyone's so wrapped up in celebrations that the work slows down a bit. It doesn't look like you've been processed yet.'

'Processed?' Their stupid questionnaire again.

'Yeah.' Jennette puts the box back and comes back over to me. 'Your property shouldn't have been taken from your room. Usually they just sort everything at the gates and then give you a voucher that lists your inventory. You bring it here, we double-check our records . . .' She waves a hand in the direction of the box. 'And give you your ration coupons to replace it. But your stuff hasn't been processed yet.'

'Gosh!' I'm trying to play dumb and nice. I lean forward on the counter. 'Any idea when they'll process us? I mean . . . I don't want to be rude, but we were hungry *before* finding you guys and now we don't have any food.'

'I know . . .' She bites her lips. I can see her trying to figure out a way to blend her pre-bug southern politeness with Fort Caroline authoritarianism. 'Let me see if I can find your bags. They should have been brought right here. What do they look like?'

I tell her and she excuses herself. I take the time to read the handwritten poster on the wall outlining the rules. Ration vouchers are handed out on Sundays, after church. What about the people who don't go to church? Oh, that's right, the questionnaire weeds them out.

Vouchers are coloured. Red, green and blue. On Sundays, red can use the Cheesecake Supply Warehouse between one p.m. and three p.m., green between three p.m. and five p.m., and blue between five p.m. and seven p.m. All other days the vouchers can be used at any time in the grocery store or pharmacy.

I scoff, imagining Danny Rosewood and the selectmen all sitting around a table coming up with as many rules as possible. Every time someone came up with a new one, they got a red voucher for themselves.

'Andrew?' Jennette is back and she's holding up Jamie's and my bags.

'Perfect! So what do we do now?'

'You can keep these.' She slides the yoga mats and sleeping bags over to me. 'But I don't think you'll be needing them any more.' She smiles brightly and I chuckle.

If you only knew, Jennette.

She unzips Jamie's bag and begins pulling out our things.

Jamie's mother's book, my old paperback of *The Voyage Out* my aunt Sara gave me, our food, first aid kit and water bottle. No ammo. They've already taken that.

Jennette takes out a clipboard and begins writing everything down, checking things off as she goes along and then setting them aside.

When she's done, she says, 'All right, so with all this food you get eight vouchers. The first aid kit you can keep or donate to the pharmacy. And do you want the books? I don't think the library needs any more.'

No. We saw them emptying it.

'The books are more sentimental. And I'll keep the first aid kit, too.'

'All right, then that's it!' She pulls the bags back but I reach out.

'Actually, can I keep the bags, too?'

She narrows her eyes at me. 'Why? We have shopping bags.' She was fine with me taking the yoga mats and sleeping bags but she's suspicious about the packs? Really?

'I'd rather use these. Easier to cart everything back and forth with.'

She gives me a shrug and lets me take them from her to fill them back up with everything Fort Caroline doesn't want.

'Do you want to trade the coupons for your food or swap?'

Swap? I look at the cans of food. It's nothing special but . . . maybe it can be. No. Jamie and I don't need to get greedy. Except . . . I reach up and spin the mushrooms around to face her.

'Any chance we can swap these bad boys?'

You're welcome, Jamie.

I refill our packs and head towards our rendezvous point – 'rendezvous point'? I've been in Fort Caroline too long. It's the park on the corner of Morgan and Glower that Cara said was a cut through to the sheriff's station. I'm turning on to Glower when someone calls out.

'Hey!'

I turn to see Harvey Rosewood marching towards me and my stomach drops. For some reason he's got his hand on the holster at his hip.

My stomach lurches and I immediately think of Jamie. Something happened. Something went wrong at the sheriff's station and they locked him up. And Harvey came looking for me.

He reaches me and smiles, his gums protruding like a great white's. That smile does nothing to calm my nerves.

'Andrew, right? How are you finding Fort Caroline?' His accent isn't as thick as his father's. Maybe a northern mother?

When I speak, I lower my voice a bit, slowing down. Butching it up, if you will. 'Finding it all right.'

'Good. Good. Where you boys from originally?'

'I'm from Connecticut.'

'Connecticut. I've never been to Connecticut.'

'I wouldn't go now.' I give him a fake laugh and his shark smile grows wider.

'How 'bout your . . . friend. Jamison?'

I swallow hard. I don't like the way he says *friend*. Like he means the *other* f-word. 'He's from Philadelphia.'

Harvey Rosewood nods, still goddamned smiling. 'I see you stopped by the supply warehouse. Get your rations all together?'

'I did. Jamie was supposed to register our weapons, too. I think he's at the sheriff's station.'

Harvey doesn't confirm or deny this.

'I should probably get going. That questionnaire of your dad's is pretty extensive.' I turn but he follows so I stop. I want to end this conversation. It feels like he's trying to trap me in some way. Like if he keeps asking innocuous questions he'll paint me into a corner of whatever he thinks we're doing. I know Jamie didn't say anything but . . . oh, shit.

Cara. Maybe I was wrong about her. Maybe she told Danny Rosewood everything. Maybe she's even Cara Rosewood. But she doesn't have an accent like them.

'You all right with the food there?' he asks. He knows we were taking it. I don't say anything. 'You don't have any special dietary needs, do you?'

Dietary needs?

'No. I'm good.'

'You sure? Nothing you'd rather . . . have more of. Or less of. Or not at all.'

I roll my eyes. 'I find the lack of caviar simply appalling. Is that what this is, dude? Making fun of the stuck-up Yankees? 'Cause post-apocalypse, it's a little gauche.'

His smile drops at that. 'How 'bout your *friend*?' There's that hidden f-word again. It's not Yankees he's making fun

245

of. And he's not talking about food. That look that he gave Jamie and me earlier. He knows. Or at least he's suspicious. And using the word *gauche* probably didn't help.

I can feel my knees start to shake. A bead of sweat slides down my spine and my mouth is dry. I glance around the road. There's no one else here. It's just me and Harvey Rosewood in the street. And he has a gun.

I try to speak slow and steady. 'Jamie doesn't like mushrooms. I love mushrooms but Jamie's not into them. That's the only *dietary* restrictions we would have. You cool with that?'

He stares at me for a full, silent ten seconds, his hand never moving away from the gun. Then finally his shark mouth returns and he claps me on the shoulder, turning around and heading back the other way. He shouts back, 'See you around, Connecticut.'

Not if I see you first, Harvey Rosewood.

When I get to the park, Jamie is waiting for me. Three steps away from Harvey Rosewood and I realised how scared I had been. I spent the last block or so trying to breathe and not cry. Seeing Jamie's face makes me feel safe again, but I can't hold it in any more.

I burst into tears and run to him. His smile drops and he lets the rifle fall to the ground as he pulls me into a hug.

'What's wrong?'

'Nothing.' But I'm still sobbing. I can't help it. Then I remember myself. I push away from Jamie, glancing around to make sure no one saw us. The park is empty and overgrown. The sidewalks are cracked and weeds grow knee-high through the fissures. Fort Caroline doesn't have a parks department yet.

'Andrew. What is it?'

'I was worried about you. Did you get our ammo back?'

He frowns and hands me the handgun he had tucked into his shorts. The holster is still missing. 'The handgun, yes. But they wouldn't register the rifle without you there. One gun per person, apparently. And they only let certain people carry the guns around town, so they won't give the holster back.'

'It's better than nothing. We'll find some on the road. I just want to get the hell out of here. Now.'

'We can't go now.'

I know. It's broad daylight. We'll have to wait for nightfall.

'I learned something,' I say. 'There's more fireworks tonight.'

'They have enough for a second show?'

'Third, actually. I think each shift gets one. So the people who will be on watch tonight are pulling double shift.'

Jamie smiles and I feel better already. 'So a third of them are going to be at the fireworks and everyone here is going to be distracted.'

'And no one will even notice we're gone until tomorrow morning.'

'Let's go pack.'

JAMISON

When we go to pick up the map, not only has Cara not ratted us out, she gives us an off-road route out of town. It's through the woods on the opposite side of the motel. She tells us to steer clear of the woods on the highway side because that's where they're going for the fireworks show.

She also tells us when the buses are heading out so we know when we need to leave.

It's just before sunset and the clouds are lit in vibrant pinks and purples, though Fort Caroline is dark. We head for the woods and listen as we walk, moving slowly. We agreed on this back in the motel. We'll move slowly until we get to the road Cara has highlighted for us. Andrew and I don't speak as we walk, listening to every sound around us. The cicadas are loud and drown out our footsteps.

We reach the road and turn right, just like Cara mapped it out.

I feel bad for leaving her. We should have at least said goodbye. Or maybe offered to let her come with us, if for no other reason than to not leave a loose end. Because that's what Cara is now, a loose end who knows exactly where we're going.

Henri's voice reminds me to trust people and I push the thought away.

We don't need to stop because we've both memorised our route. We spent our last two hours in Fort Caroline going over it until we could recite it. The less we need to stop, the better.

We travel through the night and into the morning, our legs aching and our shirts soaked in sweat. The sun is hot as it rises high in the sky; it has to be almost a hundred degrees and humid as well, but we both keep going. We don't stop to eat and we ration our water no matter how thirsty we get.

When the sun goes down, we finally stop to rest. We're somewhere in Georgia. Before we stopped I saw signs for Ludowici, South Newport and Darien. I check the road atlas while Andrew gathers sticks to start a fire. It will be a quick fire, just to boil the water from the nearby stream, then we'll put it out for the night. We don't want to draw attention to ourselves in the dark.

Cara has highlighted our suggested route in pink, with blue detours if parts of the road are blocked or if we need to get off the main highway. She also outlined the areas where Fort Caroline has already sent out scavenging parties to look for supplies. We're just past them. We've travelled almost forty miles in the twenty-four hours since we left.

And my feet definitely know it. I pull off my shoes, the blisters on the sides burning. Andrew sets down the sticks he's found and does the same as I start the fire.

'I think we're OK,' I say, nodding at the road atlas.

'We're out of their area.'

'Thank God.' He winces as he rubs at his foot. 'If we have to keep moving at that pace, I think my toes will fall off.' The shoe from his right foot – the leg that was injured – is more worn down than the left.

'Maybe we should try to find a car that runs again.' The roads have been clear, but that was part of Fort Caroline's clean-up along their scavenging routes.

'My life for air conditioning,' Andrew says, peeling off his sweat-soaked shirt.

I'm staring at him in the low light of the fire. My eyes are unwilling to move away and my stomach does that flipping thing it's been doing lately.

'What's wrong?' Andrew asks.

I shake myself from my stupor. 'Sorry. Nothing. Just tired.'

'Go to sleep,' he says. 'I'll finish this up and take first watch.'

'Not that tired, I'll be f—'

'Jamie. Go to sleep. It will be OK.'

He gives me a lopsided smile and I nod and lie back. He's only a small fire away but it still feels too far. My chest isn't tight like it was in Fort Caroline, but I still wish he were closer to me. Thankfully, I'm also too tired to worry about it. The last thing I see before I slip into a fitful sleep is Andrew's face.

And my stomach does the flip again.

We're slowing down, trying not to burn ourselves out. Before Fort Caroline, we were averaging between fifteen and eighteen miles per day, but now we're down to nine at most. We travel in near silence during the day, as if we're trying to conserve energy. Even *Andrew* has gone quiet. It gives me a chance to think about everything.

I don't know what these feelings are. Is it possible to be bisexual and not realise it? I ask myself that question all the time, but it's a stupid question, because the answer is, *Yes, dummy, no shit.* Then I think back – way back – and try to figure out if I knew at any other moments that this might be who I am. But I can't remember a time I felt like this before him.

Before Andrew, so many times, I was on the verge of just giving up. Scared to leave the cabin, horrified at the prospect of staying alone with all the memories that haunted me there.

Along came Andrew.

I wish my mom were still alive. As weird as it sounds, I could talk to her about this. I know she would be OK with whatever I am and she could help me talk it out so I can understand it myself. She'd just listen.

I don't have anyone to listen to me now and I don't want to tell Andrew. I could tell him anything but this. This would be a tease. Then again, that's me being optimistic. It would be a tease *if* he felt the same way about me, which I don't know if he does because I don't talk to him about it. I'm not going to assume that because I'm a guy and he's attracted to guys that it means he *must* be attracted to me. That's clearly not the case given that I'm attracted to Andrew but I've never felt an attraction to any other guys before.

Jesus Christ, this sucks. I don't know how Andrew even survived all this constant questioning and back-and-forth as a kid.

'And why is it so *fucking* hot?' I realise too late that I said the last thought aloud.

'Did . . . you just have a conversation in your head and say the last part aloud?' Andrew's grinning at me.

I sigh. 'Yes. I did.' Maybe my brain is having a meltdown. I want to empty my water bottle over my head, but relief will be short-lived. And then we'd have to boil more water over a hot fire. We pass a kudzu-covered sign on the side of the road welcoming us to Darien, Georgia.

'What was the first half of the conversation?'

I could tell him. This could be the moment when I say how I feel and ask what it means and if I'm being stupid or needy and it's all just temporary.

I've had three girlfriends in my life: Jessica Webley, Lori Hauck and Heather Brooks. Jessica hardly counts because it was the summer between seventh and eighth grade and when we went back to school in the fall, we ignored each other.

Lori Hauck was the first girl I ever said 'I love you' to. She was the first girl I went to a dance with freshman year, the first girl I took to an actual dinner date. It was Valentine's Day when we were fifteen and it was just the Mexican place down the street from my house – because nothing says romance like refried beans and melted cheese. Maybe that's why she was also the first girl to ever break up with me. I wasn't aware at the time that all those firsts might also be lasts.

Because of the apocalypse. Not because of Andrew.

But maybe because of Andrew, too?

With Lori I started creating daydreams about our future. Going to prom together, graduating together, going to the same college or being the couple who long distance actually works for. But then of course she broke up with me and started going out with Mike King, so all those daydreams went kaput.

That's where all this feels different. Things were still new with Heather when the superflu got her, and Jessica and I were kids practically pretending to be boyfriend/girlfriend. It felt temporary from the beginning.

With Andrew it doesn't feel temporary. If someone put a gun to my head and said 'Imagine your future without him', I don't think it would be possible. I open my mouth, hoping the words might come, but they don't.

'Look!' Andrew points ahead of us. 'Tell me that isn't a mirage.' I follow his finger across the blacktop, the edge of it looks wet and wobbles in the heat. I open my mouth to tell him, yes, it is a mirage, but stop.

Next to the road, the grass breaks and turns into water, then continues until it meets the horizon.

'Is that a river?' I ask.

'And it looks like a damn big one, too.'

'Go!'

Our walk turns into a sprint and I feel like our bodies are going to overheat, but we're so close. Sweat burns my eyes; it runs down my back and my legs. The pack on my shoulders hits my back, making a wet smacking sound. We reach the road that bridges the water and jump over the guardrail into the high grass.

I throw the unloaded rifle – we still haven't found a sporting goods store that hasn't been picked over – and the pack off my shoulders, and take off my shoes one at a time, hopping as I do so. Leaving a trail of sweaty clothes in my wake, I shed every piece of clothing on my body and run right into the water. My body shivers. The water isn't anywhere near freezing but it's a lot colder than the hot, thick air hanging above it. I dunk my head, letting the water cool me down, and feel rejuvenated.

Andrew and I swim around, then we move over to the muddy shore and sit up to our chests in the water. I realise it's the first time we've ever actually been fully naked in front of each other. I avert my eyes and I notice he does the same. It's like we're trying to be respectful to one another, but I don't know why.

I know why I do it; it kind of makes me nervous. But thinking about sex has always made me nervous. Maybe he's worried I'll feel weird.

'Have you ever seen *Stand by Me*?' Andrew asks me, the opening enquiry of our game.

So clearly he's not thinking much about sex right now. I have seen the movie, and I know where he's going with it.

'Don't ruin this for me,' I tell him, closing my eyes and letting my body move back into the cool mud.

'Do you regret coming down here yet?' Andrew asks.

'Not yet. But keep asking me and I will.'

He stops now, and we sit in silence. Then I hear it. It's quick and faint but I think it's there. I lift my head from the water, looking around. Andrew looks concerned.

'What is it?'

'Shh, listen.'

Silence; not even the trees are moving because the air is stagnant. Then I hear it again.

It's a bird chirping.

I thought the flu wiped them all out, but maybe they're like us. Maybe a couple of them were immune.

'No way.' Andrew stands up out of the water and I don't look.

But I do want to.

'Do you see it?' I ask.

'No. Let's go find it.'

I hold up my muddy hand. 'I'm drawing a line. I followed you to Alexandria, I'm on board for Florida—'

He interrupts, 'Florida was your idea!'

'But I am not going to follow you into the woods looking for a goddamn bird.'

'This is the first bird we've seen since the bug! This could mean the flu burned itself out. Since we're immune, there might be birds that were immune, too. The bug might be totally done.'

'That's all fantastic, but you're not an epidemiologist.'

'Oh, right.' He dunks his body into the water up to his neck. 'Still pretty cool, right?'

I grunt in the affirmative.

'So anyway, in *Stand by Me*, that scene with the swamp in the woods.'

I move to him. My chest tightens with nervous excitement even as I reach out for his shoulder and pull him close to me. I lock eyes with him and say, 'I had a dream about this place.'

'All right, I'll stop! No Winkie's Diner scenes.' He splashes me gently and his hand grazes my chest.

I smile but I don't let go of him or move away. My heart's fluttering and my stomach turns with anticipation. It's the closeness here. Everything hidden by water but still there. It's hard to breathe and I'm still staring into his eyes.

I watch as he swallows and tries to joke. His voice seems tentative. Like he isn't sure if he should be joking or not. That's new, especially for Andrew. It's like he feels as nervous as I do. He says, 'I swear even if they have electricity and DVD players in Florida, I am never watching that movie.'

I chuckle. The bird he was talking about has gone silent. The trees blow in a sudden light breeze, then something in the tall grass behind us shifts and I spin around.

There are two men walking towards us – two men I recognise.

If you asked me who were the two people I wanted to see least out of the surviving population of the world, it would be Harvey Rosewood and his friend Walt. Harvey has the rifle I dropped before I threw off my clothes.

It's not loaded, but the pistols in their hands are scary enough. We're way past their zone of influence, so Cara must have ratted us out. It's the only explanation.

'Andrew.' My voice is low and full of caution, but he doesn't catch it.

'Stop. I didn't talk about leeches, so you can skip the

creepy burnt homeless man behind the diner.'

'*Andrew*,' I say more sharply, and he finally realises something's wrong.

'What's this here?' Harvey asks. Andrew spins, his eyes wide with horror.

'Where's your gun?' I keep my voice low enough that they shouldn't be able to hear me, but if Andrew takes too long to answer, they might hear his reply.

'Pack.'

It's all he says, and I look down to see Walt carrying Andrew's pack. It's still zipped up. I got the handgun registered in Fort Caroline, so it's the only weapon that has bullets. Henri's multi-tool has a knife on it, but that's tucked in my pants somewhere in the high grass.

'Did we interrupt something, boys?' Harvey asks. There's a tone to his voice that sends a chill down my spine. I turn to Andrew and he looks pale.

'No,' I say, trying to remain calm. They haven't raised their weapons at us. There's no reason to panic yet.

'One of you dropped this, seems,' Walt says, holding up the bag. My heart's racing and the river water is very cold, or maybe that's just my blood.

'That's mine,' I say. 'Thanks, you can leave it on the bank.'

'I disagree, actually.' Harvey Rosewood smirks and the two of them share a look, but he doesn't drop the pack. 'But I think the most offensive thing is that you stole from us and then just decided to be this careless about our property?'

'It's not your property,' I say. 'It's ours – and was before we met you.'

They share another look.

They've stopped moving at the edge of the water. I've kept to the water for my own modesty, but an idea comes to me.

I stand up, stark naked, and walk towards them. It has the intended effect, as for a moment they're shocked at the nudity and look away. I approach Walt and hold out my hand.

'Mind if I put something on?'

He's so uncomfortable that what I said hasn't registered with him. He's trying hard to keep eye contact but hands over the pack.

'Hold on, now.' Harvey points the rifle right at me as I drop to a knee and unzip the pack.

I put my left hand into the air but my right one is still in the pack digging around.

Harvey doesn't move towards me but he also doesn't point the weapon away.

'Get your hand out of there,' he says. 'Now.'

I take out a T-shirt and slowly pull it over my head. 'Just trying to get decent, man,' I say. I hope they don't think it's strange I'm putting on new clothes instead of the ones scattered along our path from the road. My hand goes back into the pack, trying to find the gun, but it's probably all the way down at the bottom.

'Walt!' Harvey looks over to Walt as he points his gun at Andrew, and I freeze. There's cool gunmetal at my fingertips but I don't move. Andrew locks eyes with me, the water still up to his chest.

'Get your hand out of the pack,' Harvey says. Then he lowers his voice. 'Or my friend shoots your . . . *friend.*' He says *friend* like it's a dirty word, and I know exactly what's going to happen.

I don't need to imagine much longer because Harvey leans down to me and whispers something in my ear that proves my theory. He wears a disgusting yellow smile as he says it.

'I'll have him shoot your little *friend* in the leg. I won't kill him fast, but I'll kill him first. And you get to watch. How's that sound? *Friend?*'

Something in my stomach knots and all I can do is will my body not to shake with fear. I remember Andrew's screams of pain when he tried to stand on his broken leg. I never want to hear him make that sound again. I'll gladly die before that happens. I pull the gun and close my hand around it. I feel for the safety and flick it off.

'All right,' I say. 'I'm going to move slowly. There's no reason to do anything rash. You have the weapons.'

Andrew stands up from the water and raises his hands. I watch as Walt looks at the sky, away from Andrew's nakedness.

Now.

A lot happens at once. I stand and point the gun at Walt's belly and pull the trigger. The bang is loud on the silent riverbank. Not watching to see if it hit Walt, I turn on Harvey.

He raises the rifle to my chest and the trigger clicks on an empty chamber. Harvey has barely a second to realise his mistake before I put our gun to his yellow grin – which

259

drops slowly in surprise – and pull the trigger.

Blood spatters my face and the world speeds up again. Harvey is dead on the ground. Next to him Walt is screaming and clutching his side with both his hands. There's a weapon next to him and I kick it away.

Andrew.

I run to the water and he's still standing there, naked, his eyes wide with fear. 'Are you hit?' I ask, frantic. I can't be sure if Walt managed to pull the trigger before I shot him.

Andrew doesn't answer and I'm forced to scan his body for a bullet wound. It's the first time I actually look at his body – focusing my eyes on every inch of him – and I hate Harvey and Walt for this moment. This wasn't how it was supposed to be.

I reach for his shoulder. 'Andrew, are you OK?'

'Yes,' he says. He finally looks at me. 'Are you?'

'I'm fine.'

He motions to his face with a shaking hand. 'There's . . . blood.' I see it on my hands and they're shaking, too. I hand him the gun and dip my hands into the river, splashing my face.

I want Harvey's blood off me.

'Jamie, he's running.' Andrew points.

I turn and Walt is limping back the way he came, screaming and crying and leaving a trail of blood against the tall grass.

I take the gun from Andrew and aim. It feels so much heavier and my hands are still shaking.

I don't shoot. Walt disappears into the trees and he's gone. Then I look down at Harvey's mutilated face and see exactly what just happened.

I've killed someone. Walt had the gun on Andrew and I knew what they were planning to do.

They would have killed us. They would have killed Andrew.

Harvey's patchy beard isn't even part of his face any more.

I go find my own bag and my clothes and we get dressed in silence. I'm still wearing Andrew's shirt and it's way too tight for me. It also has Harvey's blood on it. I take it off and use it to cover Harvey's face, then pull on my own shirt.

'We should get moving,' I say. There's no need to stop and bury Harvey like we did the Fosters. There was a reason for that; Andrew did that all by mistake. This was the wrong place at the wrong time, but it wasn't a mistake.

'Hey.' Andrew takes my hand and pulls me towards him. 'Are you OK?'

'Yeah. We just need to . . .' My words die and I turn away from him to vomit into the grass. My breakfast mingles with Walt's blood trail and it makes me throw up again.

ANDREW

Once we're dressed and packed, we move quickly. I can see Walt's trail of blood moving one way in the forest, so we go the other direction. Jamie still doesn't talk once we reach the highway. It's hot and humid and taking breaths is difficult, but we don't stop.

We keep moving until the sun is a red blob in the western sky, then Jamie finally turns to me.

'Should we stop here for the night or keep going?'

'Stop.' I mean it more than 'stop here for the night'. 'Are you OK?'

'Yes.'

'Jamie, seriously, stop.' I reach out and take his hands. He squeezes mine tightly and I lock eyes with him. He looks like he's going to cry. 'Talk to me.'

'They were going to kill you.'

I want to tell him it's fine that he did what he had to, but I know it won't mean anything. It didn't to me. Instead I pull him close and for the first time he shrinks against me. For once, big, strong Jamie feels small in my arms.

Jamie continues, 'I had to do it. I'm sorry. It was the *way* they said it. They would have killed us.'

'We're OK.' I rub his back as he cries against my sweat-dampened shirt. 'We're going to be fine.'

Are we?

We set up camp off the road but don't light a fire. I try to get Jamie to eat but he barely touches the can of cold soup we open. After he falls asleep next to me, I stay awake listening to him breathing.

I want to be here for him, awake. I remember the nightmares that came after I killed the Fosters. They lasted weeks.

Until I met him.

We're both killers now, and I'm not sure what kind of people that makes us. A gender-bent, post-apocalyptic Bonnie and Clyde, maybe? I want to tell him his reason for killing was much better than mine. Mine was panic in the heat of the moment.

He was saving me. Us.

Jamie lets out a whimper in his sleep and his breathing speeds up. I reach out and grab his hand. In moments his breathing returns to normal and he's asleep again.

Taking one of Cara's detours, we get off the main road, and two days pass without us seeing another person. Each night I stay awake, listening in the darkness for more people from Fort Caroline. Listening to Jamie's cries as he wakes from a nightmare. I reach into the darkness and clasp his hands and he clenches back. I whisper that it's all right. He lies down again and I put my hand on his back.

As much as I want it to be, it's not cute and it's not

romantic. Because he's hurting. And there's nothing I can do to make him feel better.

Day three and we still skirt Cara's main route.

Day four is the same. I tell Jamie about movies but he doesn't laugh. He doesn't smile. I'm trying so hard not to cry because he needs me to be strong, but it's hard. Every time I feel tears burning at my eyes, I tell him I have to pee, then go behind a house or store. Somewhere out of sight so I can cry quietly.

I don't know what else to do.

That afternoon we come to a small, zero-stoplight town. There's a gas station and a diner on the main road and I tell Jamie we should stop. It's still early, maybe four in the afternoon, but the diner looks like it could be a good place to sleep. Also, my leg aches. Rain is coming.

He nods and we march across the gravel parking lot to the diner's unlocked double doors. Setting our packs in a booth by the door, we walk back to the kitchen while Jamie watches the road. Our handgun is still the only weapon with ammo, and he holds it at the ready, his finger on the safety.

There's obviously no electricity but I still flick the light switch on the wall. I don't bother with the walk-ins because if there ever was anything in there, it's rotten now. The pantry has a few food items left, including an unopened industrial-size box of Special K, mouldy, grey bread in plastic bags, and dry noodles. There's also a giant can of peaches in syrup. Everything else has been wiped out.

No protein, but at least we won't starve.

I grab the Special K and peaches. There's a big crank

can opener attached to the side of a steel prep counter. I put the can under it and open it just a bit, then drain half the syrup into an empty sink.

'Andrew!' Jamie's stage whisper from the front makes me jump. I set down the peaches and run back to him. It's gotten darker; the storm clouds are rolling in.

He's behind the lunch counter, crouched with his gun pointed towards the windows. I drop down and join him.

Someone's outside, standing in the middle of the street. It's a girl. I scan the other dusty windows, trying to find movement. Other people. Weapons, cars, something.

But it's only her.

She stands in the middle of the road, wearing a small backpack, her hair tied up in a bun. There's a bicycle on the ground at her feet. She turns slowly, looking around. Looking for something.

Then she faces the diner.

My voice breaks the silence. 'No.'

I move around the counter. Jamie whispers at me to get down, but I want to get a closer look. I want to make sure.

It's her. Even through the dusty window I can see it's Cara. The girl from the motel.

They fucking found us again.

When we met her in Fort Caroline, Cara reminded me of my little sister, her shy, quiet mannerisms and the sardonic way she spoke. Like there was some kind of humour under there that only showed up for the people she trusted to recognise it. She was also a literal outsider, posted at the edge of town where only the motel was. I really thought we could trust her. Of course, she knew the way we were going the whole time.

'What do we do?' I ask Jamie, dropping to the ground behind the counter.

'Grab the rifle.'

'It's empty.'

'They may not know that. Harvey tried to shoot me with it – maybe they don't realise we haven't found ammo yet.'

We should have taken Harvey and Walt's weapons, or at least their ammo, but we were in such a rush we left them.

I pick up the rifle, but even as I do, it feels wrong. I should have the handgun. Jamie is better than me. He killed to protect us – not for food or because he was just scared but to protect me. I know he'll do it again but . . . I don't want him to.

'Wait,' I say. I hold out my hand to him. 'Give me the gun.' He looks down at my hand, then back up at me.

'No, why do—'

'I got us into this. I trusted her and I was wrong. I'm sorry. It should be . . .' I almost say 'my turn' but Je-SUS does that sound awful. I just shake my head. 'Give me the gun. You take the rifle.'

He looks into my eyes like he's trying to find a way to argue with me. Then he gives up.

We trade, then head for the door.

Cara spins as we step outside. Her eyes go wide and her hands go to the sky when she sees we both have our weapons on her. 'Don't. I'm sorry, I'll leave,' she says.

Jamie and I move across the gravel lot, the rocks crunching beneath our worn shoes. 'Where's everyone else?' I ask, trying to make my voice hard.

'I . . . I . . .' Her hands are shaking.

'Answer him,' Jamie says. 'We know you sent Harvey and Walt down one of the routes you mapped out. As soon as we went this way, you show up. And I doubt you'd show up alone. So where's everyone else?'

I can barely hear what she says, so I step forward. Jamie calls out my name in warning, but Cara stammers, 'It . . . it's just me.'

I scan the road in both directions. The high grass on the opposite side of the street. The trees. Thunder rumbles in the distance and the wind picks up, blowing dust in my eyes. I blink quickly, taking a step back, trying to clear my vision.

Jamie is looking around, too. I take a moment to wipe the dust and tears from my eyes and realise they put Cara out front as a distraction.

I spin, looking back at the diner. Expecting to see twenty Fort Caroliners with their guns drawn.

But it's just Jamie with his empty rifle.

A gust of wind blows the trees behind the diner and the leaves flip up, showing their grey-green bellies against the dark sky. Lightning flashes. I turn back to Cara, calling over the wind.

'You're alone?'

She nods. Alone again, just like at the motel.

'Why are you here?'

She mumbles something but a crack of thunder drowns

267

her out. The wind picks up again and the first, fat drops of rain begin pelting the cracked asphalt. She followed the detours she gave us. But if she was trying to stop us, trying to get Fort Caroline to find us, why give us detours? Why give us anything? Why not go right to Sheriff Denton and tell him we were planning to leave?

These are obviously not questions that are going to be answered in this storm.

'Come on.' I can't hear a thing so I reach for Cara's arm. She flinches away but picks up her bike and slowly walks forward.

As she heads towards the diner, Jamie gives me a questioning look. I stop and say to him quietly, 'No one's here. They would have come out by now.'

'We can't trust her,' Jamie says. Cara rounds the corner of the diner, hiding her bike out of the way. Out of sight.

'Why would she provide detours? She knew the roads had been opened by Fort Caroline, so why provide us with detours in case they were blocked or destroyed? Detours we never ended up needing.'

Jamie doesn't seem to get it. The rain is picking up and lightning flashes and thunder quickly follows.

I help him connect the dots. 'It was *her* route.'

Jamie's eyes soften. 'She mapped out her own route.'

'So she could follow us. They weren't detours. It was her route and the places where she could meet up with us. She's been following us. Alone.'

And there's that magic word again: alone. She wasn't with everyone else in the clearing the night we showed up and she didn't go to the final fireworks show the night we left, either. It's possible she went to the first night of fireworks on the third of July, but I highly doubt it.

Jamie looks back at the diner. Cara is already seated at a booth. He lowers the empty rifle and we run inside. And just in time. Pea-size hail begins to patter against the glass windows. Cara's hands are folded on the table in front of her.

Jamie slides into the seat across from her but I remain standing.

'Are you hungry?' I ask over the pelting hail.

She nods and quickly unzips her pack. It's filled with canned food.

'Holy shit.' She flinches. Jamie's eyebrows go up.

'Did you steal all that?'

'It's mine,' she says. 'I've been saving it.'

Jamie and I share a look. She's been planning to leave for a while; it just took us to get her to do it. Maybe she didn't want to be alone. Like Jamie. Like me.

I sit down in the booth across from her, putting my chin in my hand. 'What are we three musketeers all in the mood for?'

In the dim light of the diner, Cara glances at me. And I think I can almost see her smile.

JAMISON

Cara shares her food with us and we eat a dinner that manages to fill all three of us up, though Cara doesn't really eat much to begin with.

'Why did you come after us?' I ask. It's the question Andrew asked me, and I lied, so I'm fully expecting her to lie to me now. I'm not entirely convinced she isn't still working with Fort Caroline.

She shrugs, using her right hand to squeeze the space between her middle and index fingers of her left hand.

'Not good enough,' I say. Cara turns to me and for an instant I see what could be interpreted as annoyance, but it quickly dissipates and she looks back down at her hands.

'Jamie,' Andrew warns.

'No, you left your home – with plenty of food and safety – to come after us. So you can tell us why or you need to go right back.'

'Fort Caroline wasn't my home.' She looks right at me when she says this, briefly, and I see annoyance return in her eyes. Then she's back to staring at her hand, tapping her fingers lightly on the Formica tabletop.

'Where is your home?' Andrew asks.

'Easton. It's in Maryland. On the Eastern Shore.'

Andrew keeps the rhythm of the conversation going. 'How did you get to Fort Caroline?'

Lightning flashes and I can see her eyes are filling with tears. 'I . . . lost everyone.'

Andrew and I share a look. She's alone, like us. It's not a unique trait in post-superflu America, but it's something.

'So did we,' Andrew says.

She shakes her head quickly and I give Andrew a questioning eyebrow.

'Did you go looking for Fort Caroline?'

'No. They found me.'

'How?' I ask. 'They said they only got as far as Virginia.'

'I . . . left.'

'Your house?' Andrew asks. 'Why didn't you stay?'

Again her head shakes. 'It wasn't there any more.'

I can't tell if she means physically or emotionally, but neither of us has the chance to ask. Wiping at her eye, she looks out the window and starts talking faster than I've ever heard her. 'I left and I was trying to go to Houston because my aunt lived in Houston and I liked to visit her there before . . . before . . . And then they found me.' It seems like she jumped over a bit of story to get to the end.

'Fort Caroline.'

She nods once.

'Why were you the only one working the motel?' Andrew asks.

Her voice turns grave and slightly resentful. 'I was out of the way. They didn't want me there at first, but Grover told them to let me stay and help with the motel.'

271

Grover Denton, the sheriff. The one who brought us into town.

'Why did he want you to stay?'

'Because he's nice.'

I barely hold in a scoff. He couldn't be that nice if he associated himself with them – the people who came after us for a few cans of food and threatened to kill Andrew. Fort Caroline is much worse than Howard's group by the cabin.

Andrew points to Cara's bag. 'You'd been planning to leave for a while, hadn't you? That's why you have all this food.'

She doesn't answer for a moment, then nods.

'How come?'

'They can't be trusted.'

'Then why did you wait so long to leave?'

Again she doesn't answer and after twenty seconds of silence, I assume she's not going to.

'Still not good enough.' I reach over and grab the handgun from Andrew, pointing it right at her. She flinches and her hands go up. Tears stream down her face as Andrew screams at me to stop.

My stomach threatens to empty its contents on the table between us, but Harvey's voice echoes in my mind. His threats and his disgusting smile. I refuse to let them hurt Andrew and . . . I will kill her to protect him.

'Where are they?'

'I don't know!' She's trying so hard not to look at me. A thin strand of snot hangs from her nose as tears drip on to the tabletop.

'How can we trust you?' I ask.

'Jamie, stop it!'

I ignore him. 'Fort Caroline sent people to find us because we stole their food. And you're helping them.'

'I'm not.' Her voice is barely audible. She's probably been faking this shy act and is here to get us to drop our guard. They think we'll just let her join up with us because she has food and she's playing nice.

'Put the gun down!' Andrew's hand is on my arm and I realise it's shaking. But no, not yet. I'm not letting this go until I know we're safe. I'll do anything to protect Andrew. I've done it before and I can do it again. I flick the safety off.

Cara flinches, putting her hands up.

'Jamie, no!'

The fear in Andrew's voice is enough so my finger instinctively moves off the trigger. And I have a moment to realise what could have happened. Cara buries her face in her hands as I put the gun down on the table, slowly. Andrew moves around to her side of the booth and tries to comfort her but she moves away, pressing herself to the window.

He gives me a what-the-hell-is-wrong-with-you look and I feel nothing but shame. I don't know what's wrong with me, how I've changed this much. Seven months ago I was terrified of using a gun and now I'm pointing one at an unarmed girl who helped us.

I fold my trembling hands in front of me. Andrew spends a few minutes whispering to Cara, trying to calm her.

For a moment I think that's it, she won't say anything

else. When she finally speaks, her voice is so quiet, so broken, I have to strain to hear it.

'Everyone in my family is dead.'

Andrew looks across the table at me.

'They were killed. Not by the flu. By people like *them*.' She doesn't have to clarify that she means Fort Caroline.

'Then why did you stay there?' I ask.

'Why did you leave?' She looks at me; her eyes are red and glassy but she seems more confident for a moment, like this is something she's thought about for some time. Neither Andrew nor I answer her and when she speaks again that indignation is back. 'You figured it out faster than me. By the time I did, it was too late. So I stayed because I didn't have anywhere else to go. But the two of you didn't stay.'

'We don't know what's waiting for us in the Keys,' Andrew says.

She nods and once again turns her attention back to me. 'That's fine. I didn't know what was waiting for me when I left home, but now I know what I don't want to find. I don't want to meet people like them again. They think they're righteous but they aren't. They're poison, and they spread it to other people who don't know better, and then bad things happen.'

'What makes you think we're any better?' I ask. She doesn't answer, so I tell her what happened before she showed up. 'I killed Harvey Rosewood. And probably his friend Walt.'

She looks at me, her eyes wide with surprise.

Andrew quickly adds, 'They were going to kill us.'

274

Cara's still looking at me as the storm begins to slow. 'They must have sent out groups to find you. Because they were afraid you knew too much, that you'd tell others how to get in and out unnoticed. I'm sorry.'

I turn to Andrew and he looks disappointed. I ask, one last time, 'Did you tell them where to find us?'

'No.' There's something in how simply she says no. She's not lying. Which means I really threatened her for no reason.

'Do you think they'll come after us?'

Cara shrugs. 'They don't like wasting things. But . . . Harvey . . .'

I nod. Rosewood will want revenge, and he might waste whatever he has to in order to get it.

'We should probably get some sleep,' I say. 'Get an early start if we hope to get further from them. I'll take first watch.'

I stand up, taking the gun off the table and tucking it into the back of my shorts. Andrew follows me, out of earshot of Cara.

'Are you OK?'

'I'm fine.'

'You're not. Talk to me.'

'I was scared, all right? Just leave it. Go get some rest, I'll keep first watch. Then I'll wake you up when it's your turn.'

He looks like he's going to argue, but instead he gently grabs my forearm, giving it a squeeze. He goes behind the counter to lie down while Cara lies under a table, as far away from me as she can get.

275

The thunderstorm stops after sundown and the diner windows fog up. After a few hours I wake up Andrew for his watch, but I don't get much sleep.

A little before sunrise, we're on the road again. All three of us.

Cara refuses to leave her bike and brings it along, walking it quietly three steps behind us.

We walk. And walk. The days are hot and Andrew keeps trying to get me to talk, but I don't want to. I keep thinking about Harvey Rosewood and Walt. About what Harvey said and what he was going to do to Andrew. If he was in front of me now, I'd kill him all over again, to protect Andrew, but I wish I knew why I still felt like this. Guilty, but also so sure. So certain that it was horrible, but the right thing to do. Every time I remind myself of that fact, the guilt returns along with Cara's words about Fort Caroline. She said they think they're righteous, but they're really poison.

Maybe that's me now. So poisoned by doing what I *thought* was right, I was willing to pull a gun on Cara and possibly kill her to protect Andrew, too. It feels like some malignant cancer of violence spreading through my thoughts.

I know it's there and there's no cure for it.

We walk.

And walk.

And I keep thinking about Harvey and Walt.

ANDREW

I don't know how to fix Jamie. Having Cara with us doesn't help. She talked enough when she was pleading her case to stay with us, but now she's back to the quiet girl from the motel. There's something so similar about the way they act, and Jamie wasn't like that before. But any time I ask about Cara's family, to break the silence, she shakes her head and doesn't talk. And now Cara's quiet has spread to Jamie the way the bug spread between people. Most of the time it feels as if I'm talking to myself.

I get it, though. We weren't made for a world like this. Before the bug, there were rules and regulations and laws. We had years of moral code ingrained in our minds and now none of it matters. Does anything matter? I feel like all it will take is time and then he'll be Jamie again. But we'll always have the memories of what we did.

I let myself think about the Keys once and only once. Any more and I'll spiral and then it will be both of us moping and Cara is going to be all 'I left my motel for this?' What happens if no one is there? If everyone is dead and all that's left in the world is Fort Caroline, a gay guy, a broken straight boy, a cartography genius with

PTSD and a seventy-year-old woman with a shotgun fighting zoo animals? Plus Howard's crew. Then there's Chris and his brother and sister, but hopefully they're in Chicago by now.

We can launch the first post-apocalyptic sitcom.

I file all this away because it's too dark to joke about right now. Jamie needs to believe that there's going to be something there. He needs to believe we're truly doing this to help someone. I think it's all that will save him.

That will save us.

My foot catches a crack in the asphalt and I trip, crying out, but Jamie's arm is there to grab me before I can stumble any further. 'Thanks.'

'You all right?' he asks. The concern in his voice fills me with warmth. Or is that just embarrassment?

I look at the shoe on my right foot. The rubber sole has completely come loose from the ratty canvas. I wiggle my toes and it looks like my shoe is talking.

'You should get new shoes,' Cara says.

I glance up at her, folding the front of the shoe down so my dirty sock is visible to everyone. 'Amazon's probably still delivering, right?'

She sets her pack down and pulls out the road atlas. As she pages through, looking for Florida, I tempt fate a bit more. 'Did you work for Google Maps before the apocalypse?'

'No.' It's about what I expected from her. Still, I press on.

'So you just like looking at roads then?' Jamie says my name in a warning tone. 'Fine, I'll shut up.' That's a lie though, because I keep talking. 'I'm just trying to learn about our new friend.'

'You're being nosy.'

'Yes! That's how I learn about my new friends. Or have you forgotten?' Jamie actually smiles and it's so fake, but I can't help but love him for trying.

Cara's eyes remain on the road atlas as she scans each page to find our location. I figure she's going to answer but then she surprises me. 'I used to get carsick when I was little.'

I turn to Jamie. 'Oh yeah, that definitely explains it.'

Cara looks up from the road atlas at me. 'Do you want to learn about your new friend or do you want to keep talking?'

Jamie snorts. 'I wouldn't give him the option.'

I stick my tongue out at him and motion for Cara to continue. She goes back to flipping through the road atlas. 'My dad would pick me up from school and without fail I'd be nauseous as soon as we got moving. So to distract me, he would point out street signs as we passed them and say, "Look! Down there is the PetSmart. Now we're passing Madison Street where the library is!" Eventually I started pointing out the streets on my own and it became a game. Then some days he'd make a wrong turn on purpose and ask me for directions.'

She lets a quick sigh out through her nose and focuses on the page in front of her again.

'The carsickness went away as I got older but after I got my licence, I was anxious driving around alone, so I started doing it again. Then it became a habit. It's just . . . soothing.'

I turn to Jamie to see his reaction to this but he's staring at the road, his face completely unreadable. And that's scary. Usually I can tell what he's thinking, but not now. He snaps out of it when Cara speaks again.

'Maybe there's a store in this town.' She points to the small town of Yulee, a few miles north of Jacksonville. 'There's an exit here.'

She puts the road atlas away and we continue down the road, Jamie still quiet. Eventually, through the hazy July air, I can see the exit she spoke of. I do need shoes. And maybe there are a few other stores we can hit up for food. The look on Jamie's face tells me it's up to me.

'You could use a new pair of shoes, too,' I say, pointing at his worn sneakers.

'Can you walk?' he asks. 'Or do you need us to carry you, princess?'

'You mean that's been an option this whole time!'

Before Jamie can say anything, Cara says, 'No.'

Then, barely looking at us, she continues towards the exit.

'Wow,' I say, nudging Jamie. That's the closest Cara has come to telling a joke. I . . . think it was a joke.

Jamie seems to think so as well, because his smile grows into what could almost be considered genuine. Almost.

Yulee, Florida, is quiet and empty. Cara, ever the directional wonder, leads us down a cracked roadway towards a shopping centre. And sure enough, there's a Lowe's, Wendy's, Burlington, a nail salon, drugstore and a place called Sole for Real.

'How do you do this?' I ask, heading for the Sole for Real.

She shrugs. 'I saw the Lowe's sign from the highway. Just thought it made sense they'd have other stores around it.'

Jamie stops outside the store, looking up at the cracked plexiglass sign. 'I don't get the name. Is it a pun?'

'It was an R and B group,' Cara says.

'Oh, sing us one of their songs, Cara!' I try.

'No.'

This time Jamie nudges me and I smile at him. The front windows and door of Sole for Real have already been smashed open. It looks like all the other stores in the shopping centre have been picked over as well.

The glass crunches under our feet as we climb through the front door.

Jamie stops and we listen for signs of life, but there's only silence.

The shelves are mostly empty, the boxes littering the floor with mismatched shoes. Some display shoes are still on top of the shelves above price tags that seem ridiculous now. Jamie flicks on his flashlight and points it at a sign at the front of an aisle that says 'Men's'. I take my own flashlight and hold it out to Cara.

'Here, take mine. You can find yourself some new shoes, too.'

'I'm fine.' She kicks up her feet one by one, grabbing her ankle to check the soles, which aren't nearly as worn as ours.

No, Cara, that was a very subtle hint for you to get lost so I can talk to Jamie. Please take it and go.

'Can you keep an eye on the front, then?' Jamie asks. Oh yeah, that's actually a better idea. She nods, and we head back down the aisle.

'What size are you?' Jamie asks, picking up boxes from the floor.

I keep my voice down. 'Ten and a half. Are you OK?'

'Mm-hmm.' He nudges a box to the side.

'Jamie.'

He sighs and stops looking at the floor to focus on me. 'What do you want me to say?'

'I want you to talk to me.'

'Talking about it won't make me feel any better, Andrew!' His voice breaks and I don't even wait before I pull him into a tight hug. I can feel him trying not to cry.

'It's OK. You don't have to talk, then.' He finally lets loose and buries his face in my shoulder, trying to quiet his sobs. His arm squeezes my shoulders, pulling me tight to him. 'It's OK.'

'No, it's not.' He finally pulls away from me. I turn to one of the benches in the middle of the aisle and motion towards it.

'Come on, sit down.'

He doesn't fight me, just lets his bag fall to the ground and sits. I drop down next to him and keep rubbing his shoulders.

'I couldn't do it before.' Jamie's voice is so quiet I can barely hear him. I think I've heard him wrong, but then he continues. 'I killed them.'

'They were going to hurt us.' We've talked about this.

He's given *me* this pep talk before, when he found out about the Fosters.

'I know they were.'

'So you were protecting us. You did it because it was about survival. Them or us.'

Frustration flares up. 'I know, Andrew!' He puts his palms against his eyes. I turn towards the front of the store and see Cara's silhouette against the open door. She's got her back to us, but I know she probably heard at least that part.

'Before, I . . .' Jamie tries to continue. 'When my mom got sick, she knew what was going to happen. She had seen it so much in the hospital, and she told me. She said she didn't want to die like that.'

My mind moves at a mile a minute. Wondering what she would do. She was a doctor, so maybe she would give herself a lethal dose of the pain meds Jamie had. Or maybe she figured out a different way. I remember my little sister. The bug was painful and drawn out. If I had known a more peaceful way of doing it, I might have done something. I think . . .

'But I couldn't do it. She wanted me to stop her pain and I couldn't.' A fresh round of sobs racks his body.

Meanwhile fury rages in mine. I'm so fucking angry I want to scream. I want to pull the shelves from the walls and burn this entire shopping centre to the ground.

How could she *ask* him to do that? This was the woman who probably saved my life because she raised Jamie to be such a wonderful person. She gave him the notebook that told him how to help me. Why would she ask something so unfathomable of *Jamie*?

Because she was scared.

The fury in my chest starts to dissipate. We were all scared. And fear made us all do incomprehensible things.

'I told her I couldn't,' Jamie continues. 'Then she told me how to administer the drugs so it would kill her. And I told her I would but . . . I couldn't do it. I let her suffer because *I* didn't want to hurt her. I couldn't even hunt when we were at the cabin. My mom taught me, but I was never able to shoot anything.'

Then he met me. That's what he means. Because before he met me, he never would have shot Harvey and Walt. I ruined Jamie.

I kick a shoebox out of the way and crouch down in front of him, pulling his gaze up to meet mine. 'You didn't want to hurt her because you're a good person, Jamie. And that's why I left the cabin and went to Alexandria. Because I wanted to be more . . . good. More like you.'

He sniffs. 'I don't feel like a good person.'

I shrug in the dim light. 'That's what *makes* you good. Despite everything, you don't feel like you've done enough. But there's never an enough, Jamie. There's not some good deed jar we fill up so we get to retire to Florida. I mean, *are* there even good people in Florida?'

He manages to chuckle and wipes his nose with the back of his hand.

'Well, we're in Florida now,' I say. 'So that's at least two.'

'Don't forget Cara.'

'I wasn't. I was counting you and her. I'm a garbage human. I *deserve* Florida.'

I actually get another chuckle out of that and it feels like I'm winning!

'You're not a garbage human,' Jamie says.

I still hold his left hand. His thumb moves slowly across the back of my knuckles, back and forth. My chest tightens.

It's a tiny gesture, one that probably means absolute squat, but it *feels* intimate. More intimate than sharing a bed in Fort Caroline or holding each other in the dark of a flooded tunnel, or even lying on a cabin floor while his hands caressed my leg.

This feels so much different than all that.

I lock eyes with him. Half his face is cast in shadow and there's sadness there, but something else in his eyes. He seems hopeful. Maybe. Is this . . . are we having a moment? Like a *romantic* moment?

'Guys.'

Cara breaks our gaze. She's shuffling up the aisle. I let Jamie's hand go, standing up and pulling away from him. Whatever that was, ew on me for trying to take advantage when Jamie was upset. Ugh, I *do* deserve Florida.

'Someone's coming,' Cara says. 'It's a group. A big one.'

My mouth feels dry. Jamie stands next to me. 'Fort Caroline?' he asks just as I ask, 'How many?'

Cara shakes her head. 'Lots. Maybe twenty? Maybe more.'

'Back of the store.' Jamie's voice is low, serious. If he's scared, he's hiding it well.

'Sorry,' Cara whispers as she passes me.

Sorry for what? She has nothing to be sorry for. We weren't doing anything. Nothing was happening! I follow them to the back of the store and we crouch down behind an endcap.

Two voices shout back and forth from the parking lot. Too far away, indistinct.

'Cara,' Jamie whispers. 'Do they have guns?'

'Yes.'

Shit. I flick the handgun's safety off. I don't know how many bullets we have left, but it's definitely not twenty.

A voice from the front of the store makes me jump. It's a woman. 'One sec! I want to see if I can find JJ a birthday present! I'll meet you in there!'

A voice answers from far away, followed by another.

'Yeah, yeah,' she replies. Glass crunches beneath her feet. She's in the store. Tissue paper and cardboard shuffle across the floor. The woman hums along to herself, breaking in with lyrics. ''Cause you are my love, do you ever dream of . . .' Her voice grows closer.

Jamie taps me on the shoulder and points behind him, away from her. I nod and motion for Cara to follow. We move quietly, stepping carefully.

Or at least Jamie and Cara do. My ratty shoe gets caught on the floor and I trip, falling on to a pile of stacked shoeboxes.

Shit.

I freeze. Jamie and Cara freeze. And the woman's voice stops. Everything is silent and still for a moment.

'Hello?'

What do we do? Answer back? Run? I have no idea if she's armed. Or if anyone else is out there waiting to see her emerge from the shoe store with a birthday present for JJ.

'Who's there?' she asks. Her voice sounds closer. There's a click that sounds like a safety being turned off. Then light flashes up the aisle to the back wall to my left. A flashlight. That's all it was, not a gun safety. I think.

Jamie grabs me from behind, pulling me up by my armpits. The light whips around the corner and there she is. And she does have a gun on us.

She stops. None of us move. I haven't raised my gun but she hasn't lowered hers. Jamie's hands are both on me, so the rifle must be on his shoulder. She's a Black girl who looks to be about our age. Her eyes are wide with fear, her mouth a thin line.

'Wait.' Her hands go up. The gun and the flashlight both to the sky. 'Not gonna shoot you.'

'OK.' But I still haven't put away my gun.

'Are there any more of you?' she asks.

'What if there are?' Jamie says. Of course, because she wants to know if she's going to get ambushed after she kills us.

'Are they in the hardware store where my people are? If so, they might be in trouble.'

Is that a threat or a warning?

'It's just us,' I say. Jamie gives my shoulder a light squeeze and I want to tell him it will be all right. I think it will.

She nods. 'Good.' She tucks her gun in the back of her jeans, still keeping the flashlight up. 'Why did you come here?'

I lift my foot so the broken shoe jaw-flaps at her. 'Need new shoes.'

She looks at me as if she's trying to figure out if I'm joking or not. 'Then get them and go. I think there's a rear exit. Take that out to the alley and follow it to the road that runs along the back of the shopping centre. Turn left towards the highway. I assume that's where you came from?'

I turn to Jamie. Cara is behind him, her eyes wide with horror. Like she's still waiting for this girl to kill us. He finally nods.

'Then you have twenty minutes.' With that, she turns and walks back towards the front of the store.

Jamie whispers to me, 'How do we know she's not just getting the others she came here with?'

Cara steps around us and peeks at the front of the store. 'Because she's waiting at the front.'

I glance around the corner to see her standing by the front door, her back to us.

'Then let's grab some shoes and get out of here.' There's a box of hunter-green low-top sneakers that are ten and a half that I switch to. Jamie finds a pair of dark purple sneakers that fit him perfectly and we head towards the back exit.

I stop as Cara pulls open the door to the stockroom. 'Thanks,' I say loudly. The girl doesn't answer me.

I hope she finds a good gift for JJ.

JAMISON

We put some distance between us and Yulee, trying to get through Jacksonville as quickly as we can, just in case that's the group's central hub. If it is, they aren't as methodical as Fort Caroline. The roads are messy and strewn with litter and cars.

Andrew makes several Blake Bortles references – references I actually get. 'How do you know who Blake Bortles is? He didn't even play for the Jaguars any more when the superflu hit.'

'*The Good Place*, dude.'

And that one I don't know, but out of the corner of my eye I see Cara smirk.

The first night we stop to rest at the burned-down shell of a shopping centre, where no one will think to look. But Cara freaks out, refusing to go near it. She falls into silent tears and shields her eyes from the shopping centre, crouching down in the middle of the parking lot. Her hands are shaking and every time Andrew tries to put a comforting hand on her she bats him away.

'OK,' Andrew whispers to me. 'I'm going to find somewhere else for us to spend the night. Can you just . . . stay with her until she's all right?'

'I'm not letting you go off on your own.' The idea of it racks me with fear and anxiety. Like there's some zombie version of Harvey Rosewood lurking in the shadows of this town waiting for Andrew to drop his guard.

'I'll be fine.' He looks past me to where Cara is crouched down beside a parking lot light pole. 'It's her I'm worried about.'

'So you leave her with the one who pulled a gun on her.'

Andrew's eyes turn serious. 'I don't like that joke.'

My stomach tightens and all the anxiety makes me feel like I'm going to jump out of my skin. Because Andrew's disappointed in me. I try to formulate an apology but his hand gently squeezes my arm.

'She'll be fine, she's just . . . I know it has to do with her family, but she'll never give any specifics. So just stay with her. I'll be back, OK?'

'Yeah.'

Andrew is gone for fifteen minutes before Cara's cries get a little quieter. I grab my water from my pack and sit down next to her. She doesn't flinch or turn away from me, so that's progress. I hold out the water to her.

'You should drink something.'

'I'm fine,' she says in that small voice.

I sigh and put the water bottle on the ground between us. 'When I was six, I cried for almost an hour in the parking lot of the King of Prussia Mall because my mom wouldn't buy me a Godzilla DVD.'

She actually looks up at me. 'What?'

''To be fair, it was *King Kong vs. Godzilla*, the old one. I just thought the cover looked cool. It was only five bucks in the bargain bin. But yeah, almost an hour. And she sat there in silence the whole time until I finally started to calm down. Then you know what she did?'

Cara shakes her head and reaches out for the water. I try not to look at her as she drinks.

'She queues up a song on her phone and hits play. And it's the Rolling Stones. "You Can't Always Get What You Want." I cried for another seven minutes while she sang at the top of her lungs.'

Cara laughs and chokes on the water, covering her mouth as she coughs. I try not to smirk, but it's almost impossible not to find the memory funny.

'But after I calmed down we went back to the mall, and you know what she bought me?'

'The Godzilla DVD?'

'No! Shoes!'

Cara lets out a chuckle and wipes her eyes, drinking more water.

'And school pants.' I shake my head like I still can't believe it. 'Going forward she would always, *always*, play that damn song when something didn't go my way. She'd just be dancing around the house telling me that I can't always get what I want, but if I tried sometimes, I'd get what I need.' Then my eyes start to burn with tears and I let out a sigh. 'I really miss her. So, trust me when I say I get it, crying in a parking lot. Especially when you miss someone.'

Cara holds the water out to me and I thank her and take it.

'My dad used to sing that Talking Heads song about the house and the beautiful wife,' she says, shaking her head. 'He was such a terrible singer.'

Now it's my turn to laugh up water.

A few minutes before sunset, Andrew returns and leads us to an abandoned Holiday Inn Express's lobby to stay the night.

The second night we're in the middle of nowhere, so we get off the highway at a small town and camp out in an empty farm stand parking lot.

We light a fire to boil water from a nearby stream with kindling from dry wood pallets we find behind the peeling farm stand. Andrew finishes telling us about the movie *10 Things I Hate About You* – 'I don't remember the whole poem, but number one is that she doesn't hate him, not even close, not even a little bit, not at all' – and Cara – sitting further back from the fire – wipes a tear from her eye as Andrew stands up.

'BRB, I have to piddle. Figure out which movie we're watching when I get back.'

I smile as he wanders across the gravel lot to the woods. It's windy tonight and the trees sway in the gusts. The only thing louder is the cicadas.

'I like how he tells movies,' Cara says.

'Me too.'

'I've seen *10 Things I Hate About You* and he got all the plot points right.'

I smile again and nod. 'He's gotten a lot better. You should hear how he tells *Miss Congeniality*.'

'Oh, I'd love that, yes.'

'Then that's the one he shall tell.' I nod as I poke the fire.

'You love him.'

I stop, looking up at her. She has her eyes narrowed at me. I don't say anything.

'I can tell,' she continues. 'My sister used to flirt shamelessly with our lawn guy. And then she married him.'

'I don't flirt shamelessly.'

'No. But when he tells movies, you watch him, and if he stands up and gets too close to the fire, you watch his feet and move your arms towards him. And she used to do something similar that you do. When Andrew's telling a story about you both, you tense up a bit because you don't know if it's going to be embarrassing or sweet. But either way you have the same smile on your face at the end of it.'

I don't know how she knows I love him when I don't know it. I know I watch his feet because I don't want him to get too close if he's going to do some physical joke. I certainly don't know what my face looks like when he talks about our journey down here together but yes, sometimes I am worried he'll tell an embarrassing story. And even when he does, I do still like the way he tells it.

'And he loves you,' she says. 'But you don't say it to each other when you go to bed.'

'Wha . . . I . . . No. We don't.'

'Why?'

I kinda want to know where the fuck this all came from.

'Because I . . . I don't know. It's just not something you say to everyone.'

'No. Did you get in a fight?'

'Cara . . . No, I . . . It's more complicated than that.' I spin, looking towards the woods, trying to make sure Andrew isn't coming.

'Why?'

'Because it is. I can't explain months and months of complications to you in the time it takes Andrew to pee.'

'But you don't need to explain to him.'

I imagine Andrew leaning over to me and whispering, 'Bitch got your number there.' Because she does. Andrew's the only person who's been with me this whole time. I've been wishing for someone to talk to about this, but it's been him all along. He's the only one who's left.

Cara seems to take something from my silence. 'I can leave.'

'No. You don't have to leave.'

'I'll get water. You can say what you need to.' She doesn't wait and begins to pack up.

'What if he doesn't . . . like . . . me?'

Cara actually looks at me, locking eyes. But she seems confused. Like she doesn't understand how I could be saying the things I'm saying. 'He does.'

She picks up her water bottle and puts it in her bag.

'Cara.' She turns her attention back to me. There's something that's been nagging at me ever since we saw her in the road outside the diner. 'How long were you really following us?'

She doesn't hesitate or lie. 'Since you left.'

'And you kept your distance. We didn't see you once, but you saw us. You went out in the open and stood in the road so we would finally see you, didn't you?'

When she doesn't answer, I take that as confirmation.

'So why did you finally show yourself outside the diner?'

She watches me for a moment over the small fire. I expect her to say it's because she saw how we were with each other. I expect her to say she knew right away we were safe, that we wouldn't hurt her. But it's more practical than that.

'It was going to rain.' She smirks and turns her attention back to her bag, slinging it over her shoulder. I can't help but laugh. Before she leaves I reach over to Andrew's pack and grab the handgun.

'Here.' I hold it out to her but she doesn't take it. I hold it closer. 'Take it. Andrew will kill me if I let you go off into the woods by yourself without a gun.' I flick the safety off. 'Just point it in the air and shoot. We'll come running.'

Tentatively, she reaches out for the gun and puts it in her pack, using only her forefinger and thumb. 'Good luck.' And with that, she turns and walks off in the opposite direction towards the stream.

I'm alone by the low fire, thinking about what I'm going to say. Cara's right, because I've wanted to say something for a while, but I haven't been able to figure out what. It sounds awful to say that what happened with Harvey made me realise my feelings are real, but it's true. Not the act of killing him – that was awful. That's something I don't ever want to experience again. But protecting Andrew is something I would do in a heartbeat. I would do anything for him.

I hear his footsteps behind me and my stomach tightens. I stare into the tiny fire, trying to figure out where to start.

As his footsteps get closer to me, I pick at the hairs on my leg. I'm so focused on trying to figure out what I'm going to say I don't realise something sounds off with his footsteps until he's a few feet away; and then I hear his muffled yells.

I stand and spin around to find a man holding Andrew's hands behind his back and a gun to his head.

'Don't move,' the man says. Andrew's eyes are wide with fear and there's a shirt or some fabric stuffed in his mouth. Behind him there is a group of four other men, all of them with weapons.

I put my hands up, not that it matters. Cara has the only weapon useful to us now. I gave her the gun so she could shoot it into the air if she needed help, not realising Andrew and I would be the ones needing *her* help.

'Get back down on your knees,' the man says. I do as he tells me, trying to focus my thoughts on Andrew and telepathically tell him everything is going to be OK.

I don't know how, but it will.

One of the men behind him emerges from the shadows and my stomach drops. It's Grover Denton.

He kneels next to me and I can hear plastic straps clicking as he tightens them around each of my wrists, then together.

'Lower the gun, Steve,' Grover says.

Steve, the man holding Andrew captive, kicks the backs of Andrew's knees and he falls in front of me. Instinctively, I try to reach forward, attempting to catch him, and the plastic ties cut into my wrists.

Andrew stumbles on to the gravel, grunting in pain, and fury rages through me, hot and venomous. I wish I had the gun on me so I could make them all pay.

'Goddammit!' Grover shouts. He moves around me, pulling Andrew up by the plastic ties at his wrists. 'You don't have to be such a dick about it, Steve.'

'Fuck you, Denton, they killed Danny's kid.'

Of course they know about Harvey.

Walt. I shot him but he didn't die – he must have found his way back to another search party, or even Fort Caroline. And there he told them what happened. That we killed Harvey Rosewood and tried to kill him. And Fort Caroline set out for retaliation. And somehow found us here.

'Call Rosewood,' Steve shouts back to the men behind him. 'Looks like we got the fuckers.' One of them peels away from the group, walkie-talkie in hand, and begins mumbling into it.

'How did you find us?' I ask Grover Denton. He frowns down at me, not willing to share his secrets. Steve isn't so proud.

'Walt told us where he and Harvey found you,' Steve says. 'We got on the highway and started down from there.'

'Steve, shut up,' Grover warns. But Steve doesn't listen.

'Whole lotta people out looking for just you two, but we saw your fire tonight. Luck just had us stumble on—'

'Steve!' Grover turns to him. 'I said shut. Up.'

Steve makes a face and turns away, walking to the others. Grover reaches down and pulls the gag from Andrew's mouth.

'I'm sorry,' Andrew says. He looks disappointed in himself. Like he should have known we'd be ambushed in the woods by the Fort Caroliners. I didn't. Not this far away.

'You don't have to be sorry.' I look up at Grover Denton, who walks towards the other men out for Harvey Rosewood's revenge. 'I do, though.'

'It's not your fault,' Andrew says, tears in his eyes.

'No, not this. I . . .' My throat gives a subconscious gulp, interrupting what I'm going to say. The others are talking among themselves. They aren't paying attention to us, quietly celebrating their capture. I twist the plastic ties. They aren't the thick white ones that cops used to arrest people when handcuffs weren't available. They're the thinner ties anyone can find in a hardware store.

Andrew looks so disappointed, and I want to reach out to him and tell him it's all right. But it isn't. We're going to be killed. It's all I can see in our future. I move one knee forward, crawling across the gravel, and I lean into him. I put my forehead against his. We probably look like idiots, but it feels wonderful. Andrew looks into my eyes and I look into his. He tries his best to smile.

'I'm sorry because I . . . I wasted so much time,' I say.

'What do you mean?'

My heart's racing and it has nothing to do with the fact

that our hands are bound and we're minutes away from death. 'I have . . . I've . . . It's . . .'

Oh, fuck it, why am I talking?

I kiss him.

He freezes and I nudge forward, trying to tell him it's OK and he can kiss back because I want him to kiss back. He finally does, his mouth opening to mine, and he lets out a held breath through his nose.

Then he pulls away.

'You kissed me,' he says, as if I didn't know what I was doing.

'I did.'

He groans in misery and I'm taken aback. 'You kissed me for the first time and I just spent the last ten minutes with a dirty T-shirt stuck in my mouth.'

'I . . . you . . . what?'

'Screw it, never mind. Can you just . . . do it again?'

'Yes.' The word is barely out of my mouth before his lips are against it.

We kiss and it's difficult because I want to put my hands to his neck and run them through his hair. Which, now that I think about it, needs a cut.

But our kiss has the opposite effect of a fairy tale. When it's over, it isn't happily ever after. We're still in the same predicament.

'Hey,' I say, trying to get Andrew's attention. I'm not going to die like this. We aren't going to die with a shitty goodbye kiss where I couldn't run my fingers through his hair or feel his hands against mine. 'I didn't know what it was at first because it was with you and that's never happened to me before.' I sigh. 'Actually, I don't think anything like this has ever happened before and I want you to know, no matter what . . . It sounds stupid and I hate that I have to say it now, this way.' I'm babbling like a complete idiot, and my heart is racing.

Andrew smiles, attempting to help me through it. 'Are you trying to tell me you love me?'

'Thank you, yes. I am. I love you.' I'm crying now. 'And I will always love you.'

'Dolly Parton or Whitney?' he asks. Tears fall from his eyes and I can't help but laugh and snot flies out of my nose. I groan as he laughs. 'God, you're so attractive.'

I laugh even harder. The tears continue. I know he's just as scared as I am, but it's numbed by our proximity. Our foreheads touching. We're facing the end and it's not OK but it is. It's all OK. The world ended and there's nothing left but shit.

And him.

Us.

So that's all right, then.

'You can use my shirt to wipe your snot,' he says. 'If we're going to die, I'd rather you not kiss me one final time and confess your love to me with snot flying out of your nose.'

I take him up on his offer and rub my face against his shoulder. He laughs.

'This is why I love you,' I say. 'Exactly this. I was so scared before you got here.' I don't clarify, but I mean the cabin. I was lost without him and I would have died, I know that now. I never would have been able to survive another year alone in that cabin. 'You make me feel safe. Like the world hasn't ended and there's nothing left. Because I have you.'

He puts his forehead against mine. 'I may make you feel safe, but you're the one who saves my ass all the time.' His voice breaks and he closes his eyes hard. 'I wish I could do the same now.'

'It's OK.' I kiss him. 'You're here.' I kiss him again, hoping he knows it's enough for me.

'I love you, Jamison.'

Everything is so bleak, but nothing has ever sounded as amazing as hearing him say those words to me. Weeks – no, *months* – of fear and wondering gone in an instant. He loves me. I only wish we could find a way out of this mess so he could retell this whole story to me like it was a Hallmark Channel movie.

I open my mouth to tell him I love him, but a shot rings out in the dark. Both of us collapse to the ground. I try to ask if Andrew is OK, but the men shout over me. Another shot rings out and a cloud of dust bursts from the gravel.

Everyone's shooting now, aiming blindly into the darkness around us. It's Cara, she's out there shooting from the woods. Across from me, Andrew is struggling to get the plastic ties off his wrists.

I twist my own constraints, feeling the plastic digging deep into my skin as I try to find one area of weakness. Then it hits me: Henri's multi-tool. God, I love that woman.

I reach into the back pocket of my shorts and take it, feeling for the knife.

The Fort Caroline men cease firing and listen in the dark. I pause, listening as well. Cara stopped shooting. She only had fifteen bullets to begin with.

But then another shot rings out in the darkness, from the opposite side of the lot this time. Dirt jumps up at Grover Denton's feet, making him dance backwards. The Fort Caroliners spin, all of them shooting now, except for Denton. He's yelling at them to stop wasting bullets, but no one is listening.

I pull the knife open on the multi-tool and nick myself as I try to slide it up against the plastic tie. I gasp and try to cut it, keeping my eye on Grover and the others. They're too busy shooting into the woods.

Christ, I hope Cara's OK.

The tie breaks and I use my hands to push up from the ground. Andrew smiles in the firelight when he sees the multi-tool in my hand. I cut him free.

'We love you, too, Henri,' Andrew says.

'Yes, we do, now let's go,' We're both moving, grabbing our packs. I snatch up the ammo-less rifle and sling it over my shoulder, pulling the bag on as Andrew takes my hand.

We sprint to the treeline. Behind us I hear someone shout, 'Hey!'

I spin to look and Grover Denton is watching us run, his gun pointed down at the ground. A man over his right shoulder is pointing straight at us, his gun raised. Just as we duck into the trees, he starts shooting. I let go of Andrew's hand and a bullet hits the tree that splits us up.

We're running as fast as we can in the dark. A tree branch smacks me in the mouth, bringing blood. There's more shouting behind us.

'Andrew!' I yell.

'Here.' He's to my left and a little further ahead. 'Keep going.'

I do as he says and a bullet whizzes past my ear – way too close for comfort – before it hits a tree to my left.

More gunshots ring out behind us, but they're getting further away. Every time they shoot, they stop moving; it's slowing them down. There's another shot and my foot catches a fallen tree. I don't even have enough time to put my hands out and break the fall. I smack my head on the ground and pain explodes from my side and it feels like I've fallen on to a rock, but I don't have time for the pain.

I'm back up, unsteady for a moment.

'Andrew,' I say quietly. The men's voices are further behind us now.

'Jamie.' His voice is up ahead. I make my way through the woods towards him. My legs are going a little numb but I can make it.

'Andrew,' I say again. He doesn't answer and my heart lurches. Leaves crunch near me and a hand takes my arm.

'Shh, this way,' he says. We move slowly; the voices of the Fort Caroline militia are closer. 'Down here.'

There's a hill. He leads the way and I try to take it sideways but pain shoots up my leg and I collapse, rolling down the hill. I feel woozy. It must be the bump on my head from falling, or the tree branch to the face; I hope I don't have a concussion.

Andrew's calling to me. He sounds so far away but I

don't think I could have fallen that far.

He's next to me, grabbing my arm again. He shakes it and leans close to me, his warm breath in my ear tickling as he asks if I'm OK, and for a moment I'm back. I smile. I open my mouth to say yes, but I can't. The words don't come out.

I'm breathing heavily, each breath bringing a fresh throbbing pain to my side.

'Jamie, talk to me,' Andrew manages to say.

I'm wet. Are we lying in a stream?

I don't even know where the militia are. Andrew's talking quietly but they're bound to hear us if he keeps it up.

'You're hit.' He sounds like he's panicking and he keeps pushing on my side where I fell on the rock.

I try to cry out but the pain brings me crashing back to reality. It hurts so badly and he's making it worse. I try to push his hand away from my side where the pain radiates like fire. But he won't let me move him away and my hands come back wet.

'You're hit.' It's all he says. The pain in my side, it wasn't from a rock.

The baby fawn from the clearing near the cabin flashes to my mind. I never could have shot it, nor its mother. Not if it felt like this.

We never should have left the cabin.

'Jamie,' Andrew whispers. 'Jamie, what do I do? How do I stop the bleeding?'

It's the last thing I hear before his voice fades and all that's left is . . .

ANDREW

'Jamie, you have to help me, OK?' I ask him, but he's still not responsive. He's breathing, but it's in short, sharp inhales.

I press down again. This time he doesn't make that sad hoarse cry like he did before. Like he wanted to scream in pain but knew it would attract the men behind us.

I listen. Jamie's breathing and the voices of the men of Fort Caroline. They're all further off.

I take my hand from the wet spot on Jamie's side and fling off my pack. I reach in, searching for the first aid kit, but my stomach lurches and I feel like I might vomit. Cara has the first aid kit. It's in her pack because Jamie and I took more food to distribute the weight across ours. And I think her bag is back in the clearing. No idea where she is.

That doesn't matter now. I grab two shirts. He's bleeding, a lot. I have to stop that first.

'Jamie?' I try again. No response.

His breathing is slowing.

I put my hand on his stomach again. The blood comes from the right side of his stomach, just above his hip. My eyes are closed, though they don't need to be. It's so dark. Still I touch tentatively, gently, around his side.

There's a hole there.

Oh God. My eyes burn and my heart catches in my chest. Blood pours from the hole in Jamie's side in a steady stream. I take one of the shirts and press it against the wound.

I feel along his side to his back.

Another hole, smaller. They had to have hit him in the back, and the front was his exit wound. I press the second shirt there and reach behind me with a free, sticky, blood-covered hand, and take out a pair of pants.

'Come on,' I say. I pull up his thick torso, slipping one pant leg under him. My arm's covered in warm wetness that I can't see. I re-adjust both T-shirts and tie the pant leg as tight as I can around his stomach. I put my foot against his hip and use it for leverage as I tighten the jeans more, then tie them in a double knot. Jamie groans, still alive but not awake.

'I know,' I said, reaching under the jeans to make sure the T-shirts are still packed against the wound. 'I'm sorry.'

I don't know what else to do. I didn't realise it before, but now I notice the warm wetness on my cheeks. I give in and let out silent sobs as I hold my hand on his stomach.

He's bleeding to death in front of me and there's nothing I can do.

I lean forward and kiss him. His lips are cold and dry.

'What do I do?' I ask him. 'Please tell me what to do.'

He's still breathing, but he says nothing. I can't even think of what could be in the first aid kit that would be helpful, but Cara's bike is in the clearing, too. I could go back for it.

I listen in the darkness for the men from Fort Caroline. I don't hear anything. I look down at the Jamie-shaped shadow in front of me. I know they'll be back in the clearing, waiting for us or searching the woods. That's how they found me when I went to pee. I heard the twig snap before someone sucker punched me. Then there was a group of people on me and before I could scream, they shoved the T-shirt in my mouth.

But if I do nothing, Jamie's dead. I feel along the tied jeans, checking for more blood. I don't *think* there's any more.

Oh God, this is stupid. I lean forward and kiss Jamie's cold forehead. He lets out a shallow breath against my neck.

'I'll be right back.'

I climb up the hill, back the way we came. I don't know how far we ran, and in the dark, I might be totally turned around. But I can't do nothing. I can't sit there while Jamie bleeds to death. And if he does die, I'm ready to kill every last one of those bastards.

It turns out I don't need a mental compass because the men of Fort Caroline can't seem to keep their mouths shut. I follow their voices back towards the clearing. It isn't until I see the dim headlights of a truck in the clearing that I recognise the voice.

It's Danny Rosewood. And he's pissed.

'—and while we're at it, how the frig did you let them get away?'

'I told you, Danny . . .' This is Sheriff Denton. 'Someone else was with them.'

'Well, who the hell was it?'

'I don't know, we haven't found him.' Him? They have to know it was Cara. She left the motel the day after us. So why is Grover Denton acting like he doesn't know who could possibly be with us? Cara's bike is propped up against the back of the farm stand, out of sight. Did none of them even go back to look there?

Cara. She has to be OK. I don't think I'd be able to stand it if they were both shot. If they're both dead.

Fury and grief rise in my chest and I want to run out of the woods screaming. I want to strangle Danny Rosewood to death.

'Get the heck back out there and find them!' Danny Rosewood screams. The men move, but Grover Denton puts out a hand, yelling for them to stop. 'What in God's name do you mean, no, Denton?'

'I mean no, sir. We're not doing this any more.'

'You don't decide what we're doing, I do!' Rosewood takes a large step to Denton, looking up at him and pointing a finger in his face.

'And I'm telling you that we're not doing what you say any more. You're emotional . . .'

'Gosh dern right I'm emotional! They killed my boy! He was strong enough to fight off the flu but those peckerwoods ambushed him like a buncha sneaks and now he's dead.'

Denton is trying to remain calm while still speaking loudly so everyone in the clearing can hear. 'We've wasted enough time and resources on this revenge trip of yours. You wouldn't allow Walt the medicine he needed—'

'Because Walt was a dead man walking. We know exactly where these bums are and you're wasting time jaw-flappin' at me!'

'We're done, Danny! You may be head selectman, but you won't be if you waste all our ammo, food and fuel on this rampage. You need to get your head right.'

Rosewood looks around at the other men. All of them seem to be very interested in the rocks making up the gravel lot.

'Is that what you all think?' Rosewood shouts at them.

Of course they do, you crazy bastard.

One of them actually speaks up. 'It's just . . . We're worried about everyone back home. Half our security is scattered on the road. It leaves Fort Caroline vulnerable.'

Denton jumps on the support. 'We'll figure something else out, Danny. The world's a small place now. We'll put word out to the settlements we know of and get more eyes to help.'

Danny Rosewood spins around and kicks the small fire, sparks and embers flying into the night as he screams in fury. He takes two shaky breaths, then turns back to Denton.

'Fine,' he growls. 'But I think we might need to do a little rethinkin' on our law enforcement when we get home.'

'If you say so, Danny.' Grover Denton turns away, walking back to the trucks parked along the street.

'Pack it in, all of you!' Rosewood pushes past everyone and climbs into a truck. Everyone follows, none of them speaking. The trucks start up and pull out, one by one, into the darkness as their red tail lights disappear on to the ramp to the highway.

It seems too good to be true. Why come all this way to leave us? Unless Grover Denton is actually a lot smarter than Danny Rosewood. He knows everyone's survival depends on what decisions are made.

And judging by what I overheard, they let Walt die. They didn't even try to help him because he was a drain on their resources. But they came all this way. Of course. That's Fort Caroline for you. You don't matter unless you matter to someone in power.

I crouch in the darkness for as long as I can before I move out to the gravel lot. Slowly. I expect the trucks to come roaring back down the street, their headlights turning on as they spin into the farm stand lot.

But no one comes. It's silent. They really did go back.

I move quickly to what's left of the fire.

'Andrew.' Cara's voice makes me jump and I shriek. I spin around to find her right there behind me.

'Jesus Christ, Cara. Sorry, I didn't hear you.'

In the darkness she looks fine.

'Are you OK?' I ask.

She nods and holds out the gun to me like it's a dead rat.

'Thank you. You saved our . . .' Jamie is still in the woods. I have to get back to him. 'Jamie. They got him.' She looks up at me, and I can almost see the fear in her eyes.

'Is he . . . ?'

'He's bleeding badly. I don't know what to do, but . . .
I know we can't do it without some supplies.'

'I'll go.' She doesn't even wait for me to tell her what
to do. She takes the first aid kit from her pack, handing
it over to me along with a few of her T-shirts and pairs
of pants. Then she gets on her bike. 'I'll come back here.
Leave a trail of clothes and I'll follow it to you.'

Cara doesn't wait for me to say anything before pushing
off from the gravel. She flicks on the flashlight and pedals
off into the darkness.

I do as she asks, walking in a straight line and dropping
a shirt every couple hundred paces. I find the hill we slid
down and hang a pair of jeans there for her as a warning
to watch her step.

I stare down at Jamie. I'm scared to touch him. Scared
that he'll be dead, and if that happens I don't know what
I'll do. I crouch next to him and place a hand on his chest.

For a second it doesn't move, and my own chest tightens
with horror and tears burn my eyes. But then he takes a
shallow, shaky breath. I gasp and lie next to him, kissing
his shoulder.

I leave my hand on his chest. It must be four hours
later that I finally fall asleep.

JAMISON

It's hot. I lie with my eyes closed. It hurts to breathe and move and live.

Andrew.

I try to call out to him but the pain in my side shoots out like an explosion across my chest. My muscles flinch and the pain gets worse so I hold my breath and try to let my body relax, then let out the breath, slowly.

I try to force my eyes open, but the eyelids are heavy. I open them enough to look through my eyelashes up at the sky.

The woods. The guns. Fort Caroline.

It all comes back to me. Sun filters through the leaves above me and the sounds of the woods are deceptively calming. But things aren't calm. We aren't safe here.

I'm fully alert now, looking around for Andrew. He's not here. His pack is gone. Fort Caroline must have taken him. They didn't just kill him because they would have left his body here like they left mine.

They thought I was dead because . . .

I look down at the reason for my pain. I've been shot. There's a pair of blood-soaked jeans tied around my stomach.

Good job, Andrew.

He tied them tight and packed the wound to stop the bleeding. And tucked a piece of paper in it. I grab it and recognise it from my mother's notebook.

Getting supplies. Stay put. I love you. A

I smile and let out a shallow sigh of relief. He's OK. I'm not, but he is. He's . . .

'Jamie?'

His hands are on me and I smile, still woozy. When I open my eyes, I can see the sunlight has changed. I feel exhausted, so I certainly didn't fall asleep. I must have passed out.

'Jamie,' he says again. His eyes are wide with worry and relief. He smiles and touches my cheek again. I lean into it. 'Hi.'

'Hi.'

'How are you doing?'

'I hurt.'

'I know. I'm trying to get some supplies for you.'

I let my eyes flit around us. 'Not doing a great job.'

He laughs and rolls his eyes. 'I subcontracted it out.' Cara. Thank God, she's alive – and alive enough to get supplies. 'Just relax and stay still. Is there anything else I should be doing?'

I look again at the jeans around my wound. 'You did great,' I say.

'I had a good teacher.'

I smile and feel his hand in mine. Andrew tries to smile, but he's nervous. He's biting his lower lip and his eyes keep darting around us. It looks as though he's trying to concentrate. To will something to happen.

'What's wrong?'

He jumps, startled, then puts on a fake smile. 'Nothing.'

'You're lying. What is it?'

'It's just getting late. Cara's not back yet and I'm getting worried.'

'We can go look for her.' I try to lean up but the pain bursts again and it feels like I'm on fire. I groan and cry out. Andrew's hands are on me, holding me. The wooziness returns as I lie back.

'Stop. You're not moving any time soon.'

'We can't stay out here for ever. We need to get somewhere safe, somewhere inside.' We have to clean the wound and get someplace warm. We can't be out here when it starts to rain. And then there's the Fort Caroliners – the further we are from them, the better.

'We will, but right now you have to wait here.'

'No,' I say. He's gonna argue with me, I know it, but I also know I'm right, so I talk over him. 'I won't move, but we need to figure out a way to move me. You have to build a stretcher.'

'I can do that. I have pine cones and a sock, it shouldn't be a problem.'

I chuckle but it causes pain. 'Stop trying to make me laugh, it hurts.'

'I'm sorry. How do we make a stretcher?'

He's got me there. But this could be good; he needs something to do. 'Go find some branches around the same length as my body.' As he stands, it's as if he's happy to

314

be busy and not just waiting around. 'Hold on. Put our packs near me. Let me see what we have to work with.'

He unzips them and sets them down next to me.

'Hey,' I say as he stands again. He looks down, determined, on edge. 'Kiss me.'

Just like that, all the fear and worry melts from his face and he smiles. He drops to his knees beside me. His lips are soft, gentle. He leans back and smiles at me.

'I love you.'

'Stop saying it like I'm dying.'

'You have a hole in your stomach.'

'It's only a flesh wound.'

Andrew laughs, mission accomplished. I want him focusing on something else because the chances are extremely high that I really am going to die. I've been shot, we have no supplies, we have no antibiotics, antiseptic, gauze, bandages. We have water, but it's supposed to be for drinking, and once it's gone we have nothing else.

Andrew squeezes my hand once more before he's off.

I want to take a look at my wound to see how bad it is, but I'm terrified to move the jeans and T-shirts packing it. If it's not clotted properly, I could bleed out before I even get a chance to tie it back up.

I'm lucid enough now to be very, very scared. My mom had to take care of gunshot victims when she was doing her ER rotation in Philly. Most of the time the only way a victim survived was luck. They were lucky to get to the hospital fast enough, they were lucky the bullet missed the major arteries and organs, they were lucky they didn't have a rare blood type.

My blood type isn't rare, but there are no hospitals, and there's no way to figure out if the bullet hit an organ until I go septic and die.

I run all the possibilities through my head. I could bleed out when he moves the jeans, I could have a ruptured liver. Then there's secondary infection.

Stop. I need to stop.

Andrew is coming back; I hear his footsteps. I have to be brave and help him. I can't die like this, not so soon after realising he was what I wanted. Everything in the world's gone to shit but he's still here.

I want to be, too.

Andrew comes bounding over to me holding three large sticks bigger than me. 'How are these?' He lays them down next to me; there's one that's much too short but the other two are perfect. He throws the short one aside.

'Perfect. Help me look through the packs. Let's see what we have to make the stretcher out of.' It's only our clothes, but I'm trying to buy time. We can use a sleeping bag, but I don't know how to attach it to two of the sticks so I won't fall off.

'We could cut some shirts into strips and tie them across the sticks like a ladder,' Andrew says.

'Yes. Do that.' He takes out a shirt and holds up the sleeve; he looks like he's about to rip the shirt, but he stops.

'What?'

'I'm thinking . . .' He continues to stare at the shirt, then pushes the sleeve inside out into the torso. 'What about this?'

He does the same for the other one, then puts the end of one of the sticks into the top of the sleeve. He pulls the stick down and out through the bottom of the shirt. Then he repeats the process on the other side and holds the sticks up, pulling the shirt taut. It looks like he's made a little hammock.

'We can put three shirts like this and you lie on them.'

Is it weird that I'm proud of him? 'That's perfect.'

He completes the stretcher and places it next to me. We spend a good fifteen to twenty minutes trying to move me on to it, inch by inch. I don't tell him that I probably shouldn't be moving, and how if I move too much the packing on the wound might loosen and I could bleed out.

I don't want to worry him, but every time I wince in pain, the fear is there on his face.

He takes the end of the stretcher and starts pulling me. At first it feels like I'm going to slide down off the thing. Each bump Andrew hits, each time he adjusts his hands to not lose his grip, is agony. Sharp, searing pain up my side and down my leg.

He keeps asking if I'm OK and I say yes the best I can, but he has to know I'm lying. I feel so useless like this. When the pain gets to be too much and I let out a sharp gasp or whimper, he says he needs to take a break.

He could go on dragging me for ever and he wouldn't complain or stop, no matter how much his muscles burn. He's only stopping for me. We get to a road and Andrew pulls me down the asphalt; it's a little smoother than the woods and I'm able to shut my eyes and rest.

The sun is setting when we reach the farm stand. It's the magic hour and the clouds above us are pink. Andrew sets me down gently and takes a couple of steps towards the end of the treeline, looking for something.

'You have to go,' I say.

'Fuck you.' He doesn't say it meanly; it's more an absent-minded shutdown.

'Andrew, just leave, head south, I'll catch up with you when I can walk properly. I promise.'

He finally glances over at me. He looks like he's going to call my bullshit, but he doesn't. I don't want him to get hurt. 'I'm not leaving you again.'

'You ha—'

'I'm *not* leaving you.' His jaw's tight and his eyes furious.

'You're so fucking stubborn.'

'*I'm* stubborn? You're the one—'

'You're both stubborn and very loud.' It's another voice. Andrew flinches and reaches for his gun but doesn't draw it. He relaxes as he recognises Cara pedalling towards us from the road, her backpack fat and full.

'Sorry,' Andrew says. She drops the kickstand and slides the pack to the ground next to me.

'How is this?' she asks, holding out her haul. Andrew looks to me. There are gauze pads and bandages, a litre of water, a bottle of rubbing alcohol and a few bottles of pills.

'Where did you find all this?' Andrew asks.

'I had to break into houses. Some were empty, some . . . weren't.' I'm pretty sure she means bodies, not living people. 'I wasn't sure what you needed, but I'm sorry it

318

took so long.'

'What are those?' I point to the pills.

She looks in my direction but doesn't answer; instead she hands them to Andrew. He tilts them to try to read them in the dying light.

'Opiates.'

'Fantastic.' I hold out my hands. 'Give me four.'

'*Four?*'

'I got shot, Andrew!'

He looks like he's going to argue with me but then pops out four and hands them over along with the water. I swallow the horse pills all at once.

'Any antibiotics?'

Cara shakes her head.

'We'll have to find some later.' If I make it to later. 'For now we have to clean the wound and change the bandage before it gets dark.' This part is gonna suck.

'What do we do?'

Here it is. I could bleed out in seconds and I don't want to die.

'Untie the jeans. When you do, I might . . . I might pass out from the pain and if I do just keep going. Don't stop, whatever you do. Dump most of the water on the wound, then follow with the alcohol. Put a sterile pad over it and wrap it tightly with the gauze.'

'Wait.' Cara reaches into her bag. 'I did find this.'

A sewing kit. Oh God, that's not gonna be fun. Who the hell knows if I'll even be awake for it? Probably not.

'Great,' I say. 'Dump alcohol on the thread and the needle. Your hands, too. Actually, do all that first. And thread the needle before the sun sets. Cara, can you hold the flashlight when it gets dark?'

She doesn't answer. Instead, she looks at the bloody jeans tied over my stomach and then back at her own pack. She nods.

'OK,' Andrew says. 'Here we go.'

He moves slowly, reaching for the jean legs tied across my middle. I want to hold his alcohol-covered hand but I know I can't. He has to do this if there's going to be any hope for us.

He pulls, but the knot is damp and tight – the jeans have shrunk into it. Every time he tries to untie it more pain shoots up my body. I'm sweating and my mouth has run dry.

The knot is finally coming loose. I'm feeling woozy and sick.

'Andrew,' I manage to say. He looks at me and asks if I'm OK. I don't think I am. I'm so tired and the pain's stopping. I'm getting cold. I think this is what dying feels like. All the jostling must have ruptured something.

He says something else but I don't understand what it is.

'I love you,' I say.

Darkness closes in again.

ANDREW

The storm let up an hour ago, so Cara and I left the library we took shelter in to scout out the town. We're in Delray Beach, Florida, three-quarters of the way down the coast. Because of the bikes we found in Vero Beach, we can cover a lot of ground much quicker than we had been.

Having Cara helps. She checks the map in the morning and her photographic memory map trick has us set for the day.

'There's a pharmacy on the corner in about a mile,' she says to me. She says it carefully, like I'm a bomb and if she says anything too loud or the wrong way, I'll explode. Because apparently that's me now.

I don't want to say what I'm thinking. I've been too negative lately and I feel like it's pissing Cara off. But she would never tell me.

Still, I know what's going to happen. We get to the pharmacy, and it's picked clean. No water, no meds, no food. The grocery stores are all the same. They smell of mould and spoilage from animals and perishable food that was left to rot.

When we get to the pharmacy, I watch the front and let Cara go in.

She comes back empty-handed.

I didn't even have a moment of hope.

'It's fine,' I say. 'Let's head back.'

We mount our bikes and go back the way we came. The streets of Delray Beach are quiet, but I still keep my eyes peeled for anyone peeking from behind curtains in the vacant houses. I watch for movement.

For the last thirty miles or so there have been barely any supplies left in the stores we've checked. Someone is here. Or at least nearby.

Cara insists it can't be Fort Caroline. She hadn't made a route this far for them yet.

We dismount the bikes and stash them behind an overgrown shrub in front of the library.

'I think we should keep moving,' Cara says. She says it tentatively, but it's the most forceful she's been.

'I do, too,' I say.

'I'll hook up the sidecar.'

'Thanks.'

She bends down behind my bike and starts the process of hooking up the wooden cart and making sure it's secure.

I enter the library through the back door. The library is humid but smells dusty and ancient despite the distinctly 1989 pastel fantasy it's serving. The shelves are full and everything looks as though it was barely touched, unlike the rest of the town.

There's a low, hacking cough from the children's section that drives a spike through my heart. I hold my breath and wait for it to continue to a breathless crescendo, but there were only two coughs. That's got to be an improvement.

Right?

Jamie is lying on a foam mat in front of the picture books. His forehead is covered in a layer of sweat. His shaggy hair is wet, and despite his shivering, he's thrown aside the blanket we left him.

I pick up the blanket and pull it over him, becoming the big spoon to his little. It's complicated because he's bigger than me, but he still pulls my arm tight against his chest. I kiss his cheek.

Christ, he's burning up.

'We didn't find anything,' I say. 'We need to keep moving.'

He doesn't answer at first. I say his name and he finally grunts something and tries to sit up. His breathing is fast. It sounds wet.

I help him up and grab the blanket and his pack. I reach into the pack and grab the last two antibiotics from the orange bottle we found in a house on our way here. There weren't many left so we had to spread out the dosages. But what's left isn't doing anything to slow the infection.

When we changed his bandages, Jamie passed out quickly from the pain, or maybe it was blood loss. I stitched him up, and the next morning I thought everything would be fine. I pulled him on the stretcher as Cara rode her bike. We got out of Fort Caroline's approximate search radius and camped for a few days while Jamie rested and Cara and I looked for supplies.

We found a house with a car in the driveway, so – after making sure it was empty of life – Cara and I searched it. I found a bottle of peroxide, gauze pads and four antibiotic pills. Cara found the car keys.

The pills lasted Jamie two days and Cara and I searched for more, but found none. Finally, we loaded Jamie into the backseat and bungeed Cara's bike in the trunk, then drove until we came upon a pile of burned-out cars blocking the southbound lanes on 95 near Vero Beach.

While we were there, I found the other bike and the cart to tow behind it, which we affectionately call Jamie's sidecar. I wish it really was a sidecar. The idea of Jamie sitting in a sidecar with goggles and a helmet is kind of adorable.

Jamie said he was good to travel, so we left.

The infection in his side started two days ago, just outside Jupiter. We checked the hospital, which had been burned down, everything inside it destroyed. We stopped at every pharmacy and house for antibiotics but only found the bottle in my hands. There were nine pills when we started south from Jupiter.

Now there are two.

I hold them out to Jamie, but he shakes his head. 'We should save them.'

'We can't use them if you're dead. Take them. We'll find more.'

But we won't. I know we won't and it's killing me. Just like this infection is killing him.

Reluctantly, he takes the pills from my hand and downs them with water. Cara is ready for us when we go outside. I help Jamie climb into the cart and he cuddles up with our supplies. He slowly pulls his legs to his poisoned chest with a wince.

I look back at him after we've been pedalling for a while and his jaw is hanging open, drool spilling on to the pack under his head. My heart still skips a beat.

He can't die.

'How far to Islamorada?' I ask Cara.

'Three days? Maybe four?' It's been our end goal for so long, I just need to get there. The hope that Henri's daughter is alive and well was all that motivated us before. Now, I'm sorry, Henri, but I need hope for something else. I need there to be anyone alive and well, and with supplies to help Jamie. Then they'd have to be different from the people we've met so far.

'What if we pedal through the night?'

'That wouldn't be a good idea.'

'What if we did it anyway?'

She bites her lips. Top and then bottom. It's something I've noticed she does when she's nervous or uncertain. She bites her top lip with her bottom teeth and then her bottom lip with her top.

'Two days?'

'Cara, he's dying.' She doesn't say anything. 'I'm ready to pedal for forty-eight hours if I need to.'

Top lip, bottom lip.

'We need to find him help.'

'The houses on the way . . .'

'The antibiotics aren't working. We need someone who may have raided a hospital.' There were antibiotics back at the cabin. Why did we even come all this way? It started out as me trying to do the right thing, but for what? So I could feel better about killing two people who also tried to kill me?

Ask me if I feel better.

'There might be hospitals on the way.'

'I'm sure there are, and we'll stop there as well, but we need to get off the road for good so Jamie can really rest. We have to get down there.'

Top lip, bottom lip, repeat. 'What if no one is there?'

'Cara.' There's a warning in my voice.

'We should tape flashlights to the front of the bikes.' So we do just that, and when the sun sets, we continue to pedal through the night.

My legs are burning, my back screams in agony, my butt feels like it's going to fall off. All this and the sun beating down on us. We've stopped three times since sunrise and every time we stop it gets harder to keep going.

Jamie woke up long enough to take a drink of water but he wouldn't get out of the cart to pee or eat and just fell back asleep.

I ask Cara how far we are after we pass through Homestead. On the map it looked close, but she says there's still fifty miles. We're never going to make it.

No. I have to hope. I have to believe the best-case scenario here because anything less will be . . .

I glance back at him. He's still sleeping and the ring of sweat at the neck of his T-shirt is growing. I can't lose him.

I focus on everything Jamie and I have been through instead of the burning agony in my legs and back. I focus on memories of his smile. The way his cheeks dimple when he laughs. The way his hands feel when he holds mine.

'Andrew, look.' Cara snaps me out of my daze. I've been staring right at it, but it takes Cara's voice to make me realise it's there – a large gate severs the road ahead of us. We slow to a stop.

The gate is black steel and ten feet high. It crosses the entire road and connects to a similar-looking fence that goes in both directions on either side; to the left as far as we can see, and to the right until it ends at the ocean.

'Is there another way around?' I ask Cara. She drops her kickstand and goes to the pack at Jamie's feet. She checks the road atlas, turning it and leaning close to the page, moving like a bird as she concentrates. Then the lip bite.

'No. This road leads into Key Largo and down to Islamorada. There's no other way to access it unless we backtrack to SR-905A and try Card Sound Bridge.'

Not an option. This is the end of the line.

I flick my own kickstand to the ground and check on Jamie. He's burning up. I pull the bottom of his shirt up to look at the wound in his side. It's gotten worse.

Before it was just pus and heat. Now it's bright red around the navy thread I used to hastily stitch him up, and the red has spread outward in thin tendrils. Poison looking for his heart and organs. He's going septic, which means he'll be dead in a few hours.

No. He's not dying. I can't lose him.

I run at the gate and pull and push as hard as I can. Shouting at it, screaming until I taste blood. The chains around the gate hold but I kick and kick, trying to . . . I don't know what.

My legs are angry with me for biking through the night and they refuse to hold me up while I abuse them further. I fall to my knees, scraping them against the asphalt. I look back at Jamie in the cart, still sleeping. Still dying.

Cara has her hands clasped over her ears and her back to me.

Shit. The Andrew Bomb has gone off.

'I'm sorry, Cara.'

She doesn't turn. She's probably going to be like this for a while. The last time I screamed in frustration – when we found the burned-out hospital – she didn't move for an hour. Though I think it was more to do with the burnt hospital than my yelling. She responded similarly to the burned-down shopping centre we tried to camp in. But we don't have an hour for her to settle down now.

There has to be something, anything around here. I'll turn back and look through every house in Homestead searching for bolt cutters if I have to. Cara can stay here alone. I'm not going to let Jamie survive the bug only to die from fucking bacteria because a bunch of psycho militiamen shot him.

'Cara, I'm going back to Homestead. You can stay here or you can come with me.' I take my bike handles and start to turn the bike around, but she isn't listening to me. I'm usually patient with her but I'm not now. I can't hide the annoyance in my voice. 'Hey, I'm leaving. Come along or stay here.'

Her eyes are closed, too.

I want to scream at her. I want to shake her and yell at her and . . .

Movement draws my eyes behind her. Beyond the gate.

There's a truck coming.

Now my voice is calm. 'Cara, look. Someone's there.'

Either the thought of someone coming up behind her or the calm worry in my voice brings her back. She opens her eyes; they're wet with tears that threaten to fall and my heart breaks. I'm sorry, but I don't say it. I'll say it later.

If there is a later. I leave my bike and walk towards the gate, my hands held high above my head. I'm unarmed and they need to trust me.

The truck comes to a stop about ten feet before the gate. A man gets out from behind the wheel and walks to the front of the truck. The passenger opens the cab door and stays half in, half out of the truck. He's tall and has brown skin. There's a rifle slung over his shoulder and he keeps his hand on the strap. The driver has his hand at the gun on his hip.

'Can we help you?' asks the driver, a white guy in his fifties.

I don't know what to say. I was so ready to either be shot or to find nothing but more dead bodies and empty stores that my mind blanks. Cara doesn't even say anything, so she must be thinking the same thing. Or she's nervous about a Fort Caroline repeat.

The man with the rifle asks something in Spanish, but I don't understand it with the two years of high school Spanish I've forgotten.

'Uh,' I say. 'Sorry. I . . . We need help. It's my friend.'

The rifle man moves quickly, pointing the rifle at us. I flinch, expecting him to pull the trigger, but he doesn't. 'Is he sick?' His voice sounds panicked now.

'Ye-yes,' I manage. 'But it's not the bug. I swear. He was shot by . . . people who wanted to hurt us.' God, there's so much backstory, but it's not important right now. 'His wound is infected and he might be septic. He's dying. Please help us. You don't have to let us in, just give us any antibiotics you might have that could help.'

The men look at each other. They aren't going to help us. We're useless to them; why would they give any medicine to us? This is just like Walt from Fort Caroline. Jamie shot him and Fort Caroline refused him meds and let the infection kill him.

It's karma, but Jamie doesn't deserve it. Karma has the wrong person. Jamie did nothing but love me and save me and I can't save him.

'Please,' I say. Tears well in my eyes and the world blurs. 'I'll work off whatever it costs, my whole life if I have to. But please help him. I can't lose him, too.' But they aren't going to. They look as if they're about to say, 'Thank you for your application, and while your skills are impressive, we regret to inform you . . .'

'Help him.' Cara's voice surprises me. 'He's not bad. None of us are. You have to help him.'

The man with the rifle hands his gun to the driver and takes a tentative step forward. The driver says, 'Eddie. You sure?'

He shrugs. 'Who is any more, man?'

Then Eddie takes out a set of three keys and uses one to undo the padlock and chain around the gate, then pulls it open.

'Let me see your friend.'

I take him back and show him the wound. Eddie takes a deep breath through his teeth.

'All right, grab your things and help me get him in the back of the truck. Leave the bikes for now, we'll come back for them.'

I do as he says and put my hands under Jamie's armpits. He's burning up. He groans as Eddie lifts his legs and I take his torso.

'Holly's sister's home from the war,' Jamie mutters.

'What's that?' Eddie asks through a grunt as he moves to the truck.

'He's delirious.' Jamie told me about sepsis when the fever started. Fever, rapid heartbeat and breath. Delirium came next, then organ failure and death. 'We need to get him antibiotics fast. Please tell me you have them.' He doesn't answer, which makes me nervous. The driver runs past us and locks the gate back up.

The truck's tailgate is down. Cara sets out the blanket and we put Jamie on it, then Cara and I jump in. The driver does a quick three-point turn and we're speeding back the way he came.

I look down to see Jamie's eyes staring up at me. 'Holly wants us to come home,' he says. 'I miss her.'

'Me too,' I say. I have no idea who Holly is. 'You just have to stay with me and we'll go see her.'

'I want to do that.'

'You'll be OK and we'll go see Holly, right?'

Jamie whimpers something and closes his eyes.

'Jamie!' I shout. I put my hands to his hot neck. I can't feel a pulse because the truck is bouncing too much. 'Jamie, please.'

He doesn't answer me. He doesn't open his eyes.

JAMISON

We never should have left the cabin. It's the only thought I have between dreamless sleeps. By the time I open my eyes, it feels like I've been asleep for years. Fort Caroline caught up with us. But if that were true, they wouldn't be keeping me alive. They should have killed us by now. The early morning sun filters through a window to my right. The lights above me are off. The room smells like alcohol, antiseptic and bleach.

Andrew is there.

He's in a chair to my left, curled up, his knees to his chest and his head lolling to the side. That can't be comfortable. His arm is out towards me, his hand grasping mine. I squeeze lightly and he stirs before turning his head and letting out a snore.

My heart rushes and I let out a shaky breath. I glance around. We're in a hospital room with a drop ceiling and linoleum floor. There's a small bandage taped over the crook of my elbow. I pull down the blanket that's tucked up to my chest. I'm wearing a hospital gown and there's a new bandage where I was shot. I pull it aside and look at the wound. It's pink and puckered and the stitches have been cut out, but the pus and redness have gone away. I prod it with my free hand. There's glue keeping the skin together instead of stitches.

The hospital door creaks open.

Cara.

Her eyes go wide, then she looks away. 'You're awake.'

'I'm *alive*.' It's a surprise to me, so I can only imagine it must be to her. 'Where are we?'

'South of Key Largo.'

Key Largo. Only a little further to Islamorada. What? Thirty, forty minutes? Twenty if there's no traffic. That makes me chuckle.

'How long have we been here?'

'Four days. They gave you broad-spectrum antibiotics and fluids and you started to get better, but the pain meds kept you knocked out. How are you feeling?'

'I'm feeling amazing.' I really am. My side is sore as hell and it feels like I did eighty-five million crunches in three minutes, and I'm *starving*, but I'm alive.

Andrew is still asleep. He can sleep through anything, can't he?

'Cara,' I say. 'Can you help me up?'

'I should get a nurse.'

A *nurse*. I want clarification on that, but I feel claustrophobic in here. The air is dry and hot and I just need to get out of this bed.

'Fine, but help me up first.' I pull my legs out from the tucked-in sheets and hold a pillow against my stomach to brace myself as I lean forward. I kiss Andrew's hand and put it back on the bed.

Cara helps me up to the window and I gasp. There's a

333

beautiful white-sand beach beyond the empty parking lot. How did a hospital get oceanfront views?

'Are these people good?' I ask. But I know the answer. They have to be if they put me in a hospital room. They're also more set up than Fort Caroline if they have broad-spectrum antibiotics they're willing to waste on strangers who have done nothing for them.

'They are.'

'I need you to do me a favour,' I say to Cara. 'Get me down to that beach.'

'Andrew should wake up.'

'No,' I say. I turn to him. He looks so adorable, but he also looks like he hasn't slept in months. 'Let him sleep. And can you get me a robe so my butt isn't hanging out the back of this gown?'

Cara blushes.

The hospital isn't staffed like a normal hospital; we don't even see anyone as we make it out to the parking lot. I can tell by the sun it's morning, but the asphalt is still hot – I feel it through the slippers Cara gave me.

Every step I take pulls at the muscles around my wound, and my gait is short and slow. It takes us fifteen minutes to get to the sand, and by then I'm sweating. Still, the salt breeze from the ocean is worth it. I kick off the slippers and feel the warm sand between my toes.

'I'll leave you be,' Cara says.

'Thanks, Cara.' She leaves me and I take a deep breath of the salt air. I know she's going to go wake up Andrew. I want to hear his voice, but I needed to get out of the hospital. Being in a building after travelling on the road for so long felt off, unnatural. I step into the surf. The waves pull the sand from my feet and I sink slowly. This feels better.

I thought getting here would be a relief, but now I'm not so sure. Yes, it's absolutely a relief I'm not dead. But the emptiness in the hospital reminds me of the one in Fort Caroline, despite these folks being more giving with their supplies. The world has changed – even if people like those in Fort Caroline want so badly for it to go back to what it was. The people here, as well. They might be nicer, but they're still trying to reclaim what was taken from them when the world ended.

The tide is only just starting to come in. I sink lower and lower in the sand as the waves crash against my ankles.

Andrew's arms wrap around me, carefully avoiding my wound, and he puts his head on my shoulders.

'This is the first time I've ever been taller than you,' he whispers in my ear. 'Who's Holly?'

My stomach flips. How does he know about Holly? I try to think back if there was any time I had pointed her out to him at the cabin but can't remember.

'How do you know about Holly?' I ask.

'You were mumbling about her when you were delirious. Saying you missed her. Do I have someone to be jealous of?'

I frown. 'Yes. Holly and I have a special love you could never understand.' I turn back just to see the look on his face. I smile and give him a peck on the side of his mouth. 'Holly is a garden gnome I bought for Mother's Day when

I was ten. She sits in front of the cabin on a little toadstool and has a sheep in her lap. Don't know how you missed her when you *broke in.*'

Andrew laughs, just like I knew he would. 'I didn't know she had a name. I just said "Bye, gnome," when I left.'

'Oh, so goodbye was good enough for Holly, but all I got was a note?' He hugs me again as we turn our attention back to the ocean and stand in silence for a bit. 'What if we shouldn't go any further?' I ask.

'We're already here.'

'But what if she's dead? Amy, I mean. What if we ask around and it turns out she's dead and all this was for nothing. I got shot and—'

'Stop it, Jamie. You're alive. We're here. If she isn't, we go back. We bring Cara with us if she wants, and we go back and we can give Henri some closure. See if she wants to make a slightly shorter trip. Then the four of us hide out in the middle of nowhere and avoid all the mess of the world for as long as we can.'

'This cabin is getting very crowded.'

'It needed an addition and some updating anyway.'

I chuckle, knowing full well I would let them stay even without an addition. 'All right. But what if she's here?'

He doesn't answer at first. 'I think she might be.'

I turn, flinching as the muscles around my stomach stretch. I pull my feet from the sand, standing above him, and turn all the way around.

'What do you mean?'

'While you were knocked out, I asked one of the nurses if she knew of the bookshop Henri's Hideaway, and the woman who owned it.'

'They don't really have a bookshop operating?'

'Course not. Anyway, this settlement goes from Key Largo to Islamorada and down to Key West. There's a lot of people here.'

'So, needle in a Florida-size haystack.' I have to say I'm disappointed. It was always a long shot, but I was kind of hoping we would stumble upon her like we stumbled upon her mother.

'No, Jamie. The settlement is huge, but they have a census. There was some influx of people over the past year, but they know everyone who comes through that gate. Our names are even in it now.'

I hold my breath.

'If it's the right Amy, she's here. Still in Islamorada.'

I'm giddy with excitement. 'Did you go see her?'

He laughs. 'No. I was waiting for you, stupid.' I want to dance, but since I've been shot, I settle for a deep, long kiss.

It's amazing. Up until Andrew says, 'You have really bad hospital breath,' and then I'm mortified. He laughs and kisses me anyway.

They let me leave the hospital two days later, with a week's worth of antibiotics in pill form. We're riding in the back of a guy named Dave's truck for a minute or so before I see someone else. A man on the side of the road with a rifle. He waves to the two men in the front of the truck and they wave back. About half a mile down the road, I see the beach again to our right.

Some houses have solar panels on their roofs. I glance at the beach and see a large structure that looks like a greenhouse that extends out into the water.

Andrew knocks on the back of the truck window. The centre of the window slides back and Andrew points to the beach.

'What's that thing?'

'Desalination house,' the passenger, Eddie, shouts back. 'We dug a little pool so when the tide comes in, it fills it, and we can collect the salt-free water from condensation. There's one every few miles. Not the prettiest things, but they're easy to rebuild if they come down. It's just till the engineers figure out how to restart the water treatment plant and plumbing.'

Engineers. Water treatment plant. Plumbing.

Then there are more people. Kids, teenagers, adults. I start counting and lose track at around sixty as we pass a group of kids between the ages of three and ten in a playground to my left.

I watch them play and my vision turns blurry with tears. I open my mouth to ask when the last infection of the superflu was, but I can't even get the words out. I don't want to know any more. This many people, either they're all immune or the superflu burned itself out.

I finally look away and meet Andrew's gaze. He's as thrilled as I am. There *are* people here. *Different* people. We even see a few who must be close to eighty years old. I lock eyes with an older woman wearing a straw hat as she glances up from a garden. Only it's not a garden; it looks more like a miniature crop farm. She smiles and waves at us. Andrew and I wave back.

Cara just seems to be taking it all in, but her face looks more at ease than I've ever seen it.

This all feels different from Fort Caroline. Everyone we see seems to have an actual purpose. They aren't emptying buildings one by one or doing repetitive busy tasks to show their worth. I don't need to count here.

After a few more miles, and many more people, we come to a stop in front of a large pink beach house. Dave turns around and says through the window, 'Wait here.'

He knocks on the front door of the house and I spin around to look at the community around me. People are coming out of houses and walking down the road to look at us. They don't look scared; maybe nervous or apprehensive. The door to the house opens and the driver speaks in hushed tones to the woman standing there. She has long brown hair past her shoulders. When she looks at us, her face scrunched in puzzlement, my heart leaps in my chest.

'Holy shit,' Andrew says, though it sounds more like a gasp.

It's her. The only picture we saw of Amy was when she was an awkward teen. Now, in her mid-thirties, she looks just like Henri did in her wedding picture.

Andrew stands and hops down from the back of the truck.

'Andrew, wait,' I whisper. I glance around, expecting people to pull guns on him. But no one moves. Amy opens the door a little more.

'You said you know my mother?' she calls out to us.

We nod. She looks uncertain, then glances at the crowd of people that has formed on the other side of the road and frowns. When she looks back to us, she opens the door wider.

'Come on in.'

Andrew, Cara and Eddie help me down from the truck bed. Dave and Eddie get back in the truck, and Amy steps aside as we enter her home. We continue through the archway from the foyer into the kitchen. The windows look out on to a deck, the beach and a dock with a small rowboat.

'Can I get you some water?' she asks.

'That would be great,' Andrew says.

'Yes, thank you,' I say. Cara nods and gives a quiet thank-you, but her eyes are focused more on the windows looking out to the beach.

Amy walks over to the fridge and opens it. The light inside turns on and my eyes go wide. I look over at the electric stove and the microwave above it. Both of them have the time showing in green. As Amy hands us the glasses of water, she follows my gaze to the stove and chuckles.

'You have no idea how excited we all were to get electricity back. The electric comes from solar panels and some wind power. A lot of the people on the Key had it already, but the rest we had brought in from the hardware stores when the power went out.'

I take a sip from my glass; it tastes better than any of the boiled water I've had since we left the cabin.

'So . . .' Andrew says, placing his glass down on the granite island. 'I don't mean to be rude . . .'

'Oh no,' Cara mumbles just as I say his name in a warning tone.

He continues, holding up his hands in defence. 'No, it's just . . . who flipped the switch down here? You guys are pretty well set up and, from our experience so far, fairly . . .' He's trying to find a delicate way to say it, but Amy helps him.

'Progressive?'

'Yeah. I mean, this *is* still Florida, right?'

She smiles and leans against the counter. 'Yes, and there are still some Floridians mixed in, but most of these people are from elsewhere.'

'How did they all come here?' Cara asks.

'Did you try the old SR-905 route here?' Amy asks.

Cara shakes her head. 'We took Route 1. We were about to backtrack to 905 but the men in the truck came.'

Andrew shoots me a look of surprise at how not-shy Cara is being.

'And you would have wasted your time,' Amy tells us. 'There's a bridge there . . .'

'Card Sound,' Cara adds helpfully.

'That's right. Well, I should say there *was* a bridge there. We destroyed it.'

'Why?' Andrew asks.

Cara is back with the assist. 'One road in, one road out.' And Amy nods, smiling.

'We're surrounded on all sides by water. When we demoed the bridge, Route 1 became the only road we would have to protect. Apparently, there were a few other people in the country who thought the same. Guy named Jarrod walked all the way down here from Seattle, picked up about fifty other people along the way. A romance novelist from New Hampshire had a winter house down here, so she came and brought a handful of people. You guys know Daphne De Silva?'

Andrew and I shake our heads, but I see Cara's eyes flicker with recognition. She remains quiet, though.

'Well, anyway,' Amy continues. 'A few others from Texas, California, Illinois. And they all arrived with a small crew they met on the road. There's some old podcast host who's here – he says it's a real thing, when several people have the same idea at once, but who knows if he's making it up. Light bulbs, telephones, record players. Apparently all invented simultaneously by different minds. Multiple discovery? Multiple realisation? Something like that. The point is, every single one of them came here because they thought it'd be safe and secluded.'

The things my mother and I were hoping for when we went to the cabin.

'How many people are here now?' I ask.

'About twenty-five hundred? Give or take. We brought in a few during supply runs.'

Twenty-five hundred people. That's not so secluded. This could be the biggest settlement in America. At least on the Eastern Seaboard, from what Andrew and I have seen.

'So, my mother . . .' She's nervous. She probably thinks Henri's been dead for so long. I wonder if she ever thought about going north to look.

I nod. 'We were travelling through Bethesda and Henri stopped us. She made us dinner and let us stay with her. She told us about you.'

Saying it aloud makes it feel like a dream.

'She asked you to come here?' She looks like she might be about to cry.

Andrew speaks first. 'No, we chose to. We asked her to come with us, but she said she was too old for the trip. Though if you ask me, she was doing pretty damn well for herself.'

Amy lets out a loud laugh and claps her hand over her mouth. Andrew and I smile.

'She helped us and I thought we could repay her by letting you know she's still alive.'

She nods, her hand still covering her mouth.

'Also . . .' I reach into my back pocket and take out the engraved multi-tool. Amy's eyes go wide. 'I wanted to give you this. She said it was your dad's and she didn't have any use for it. But we figured you might want to keep it in the family.'

Tears fall from her eyes and for a moment I think we've done the wrong thing. Maybe it was better when she thought her mom was dead. Now she knows her mom is alive and a thousand miles away. Then she pulls me into a hug and squeezes me. I hold in a groan as pain bursts from my side, but it's only for a moment. She reaches out and grabs Andrew into the hug as well. Cara steps back to avoid being pulled in, too, but I can see a slight smile and her eyes are glassy.

'Thank you,' she manages to whisper. When she lets us go, she laughs and wipes at her eyes, taking the multi-tool from my still-outstretched hands.

She flicks the knife open, then closes it and flicks open the pliers and on down through each feature as she talks.

'My brother, Tommy, and I used to help my dad fix this old truck we had before we moved to Bethesda. My dad had this *huge* toolbox – damn thing had to have weighed eighty pounds – and he'd make Tommy and me carry it out to the garage for him. But he never even used any of the tools in it! He'd just reach into his pocket and take this out instead and then send us into the house for a socket wrench. Like, why wasn't the socket wrench *in* the toolbox? After he died, I looked all over for this thing, but we couldn't find it.'

She wipes away a tear and laughs.

'Sorry. You show up with good news and I cry all over you. You came from Bethesda? That's a really long way.'

I don't correct her that we've come from much further and nod, trying not to cry, but Andrew can't help it. Tears stream down his cheeks in rivers. He laughs and she pulls him into another hug.

A cry echoes from within the house and Andrew pulls away from Amy, startled. She looks through the archway into the foyer, where the steps to the second storey are.

'Oh, damn. She's awake.' She looks at us. 'Would you excuse me real quick? I'll be right back.'

When Amy comes back down the stairs, there's a baby bundled in her arms. She comes over to me, smiling.

'This is the only Henrietta I thought I had left.' Baby Henri looks up at us with the same eyes her mother and her grandmother have.

Andrew steps forward and he looks in awe. 'Hey, Baby Henri.'

She looks like the most amazing thing in the world. I want to hold out my hand to her, but I know you're supposed to wash your hands before, and who knows how clean Eddie and Dave keep the back of their truck.

'Every baby born in the past year or so has been immune to the superflu. They get the sniffles and colds, but nothing too bad. I was so worried I would have the baby only for her to get sick within the first few weeks. But she was fine.' Her voice switches to a high happy note. 'Yes, you're a little trouper, aren't you?'

'She's beautiful,' Andrew says.

Amy smiles. 'Yeah, she is. Now thanks to you she might get to meet her grandmother one day.'

'Think you'll go up to Bethesda?' Andrew asks. 'You guys have a pretty nice set-up here.'

I chime in. 'It might be hard to convince her to travel all this way.'

'Not if she doesn't have to walk here,' Amy says, her smirk growing. She beckons us towards the back door with her head. I open the door for her and she walks out on to the deck, looking west along the beach. She points. 'See that?'

About a half mile down, there's a marina. Six large sailboats are docked at the entrance and another larger ship is anchored further out from the shore.

'We've been sailing up the coast since March for supplies. The furthest north we've gone has only been southern Virginia, though. We've actually been running the Gulf since November of last year. We also have a little trade route with a small community in Cuba.' Anxiety floats alongside the pain in my abdomen. I wonder if they've met Fort Caroline. They seem to be travelling along the same routes, pillaging the same areas. Maybe they will eventually begin trading with them.

'So much for an embargo,' Andrew says, and Amy laughs while Baby Henri fusses in her arms.

'If you want to stick around, maybe we can send you and a few others north to pick up my mom? They're suggesting we wait to go out on extended cruises until after hurricane season ends. But we've been lucky with that this year, too.'

Stay? They invited us in; they gave me antibiotics and let me rest in their hospital. 'How do you know we're safe to have around?'

'Why wouldn't you be?' she asks. 'Have you killed people?'

She means it as a joke, but Andrew and I share a glance that makes her smile drop. Then she nods as if she understands.

'Did you have a reason? No, that's a terrible way to ask that question. I don't know a good way to ask it.'

I look into Andrew's eyes, and I know I would have

killed Harvey a second time if I had to. I don't know what kind of person that makes me. Or what kind of person that makes Andrew for loving me. I don't answer but Andrew does, and he doesn't look away from me when he says it.

'We do what we have to in order to survive.' Something in my chest hurts when he says it because I know he doesn't mean it about the Fosters. He still carries that guilt, even after all this way. Even after completing the mission we set out from Alexandria to accomplish.

I want to pull him close and hold him and tell him I love him. I want to take all that pain from him. If I needed to get shot once a week to take that pain from him, I would.

'Forgive me, but that doesn't give me much confidence,' Amy says.

Out of the corner of my eye I can see Cara getting uncomfortable. It's like she wants to help – she knows we're good – but maybe she also knows we need to tell the truth ourselves.

'We probably don't have a good answer for you,' I say. It's true. There's no right way for Amy to ask the question and there's no right answer for us to give. Everyone is different now because the world is different. 'They were going to hurt us, so we stopped them before they could.'

'One of us still got hurt. And almost died.' Andrew's looking at my arm, which I still hold across my stomach to brace the muscles.

Amy nods once, then looks back down at Henrietta in

her arms. 'Would you say you're happier for it? With those people gone from the world?'

I should be happy because I saved Andrew. They most certainly would have killed both of us, but it didn't change anything. It made things worse, and even after we escaped, we're still dealing with the fallout. It's like something inside me was taken away, taken from both of us.

'No,' I say.

'Then I think you're safe. You came all this way to tell me my mother's still alive. You gain nothing from telling me, yet you did anyway. And not even knowing if I survived. I think if there's one thing the new world needs, it's people like you.' She watches my face, gauging my reaction. 'So what do you say? Want to hang around for a bit, go on a boat trip?'

Andrew speaks for us. 'That actually sounds like a great plan.'

'Fantastic. We'll have to get you guys settled into a house. It might be with a few other people, but it's not like it'll be a frat house. I'll get Dave to come by later. And when you're all settled, we can bring in a couple of the boat crews and talk routes and timelines.'

Cara pipes up, maybe a little too eagerly, 'I can help with that.'

'Perfect. So, it's settled. Right now, though, I must refill the poop machine here.' She nods down to Henri-Two. 'Will you be all right by yourselves a few minutes?'

I look out at the ocean and the sailboats and smile. 'I think we should be OK.'

When she goes inside, I turn towards the blue ocean.

Andrew reaches for my hand and puts his head on my shoulder. I kiss his forehead. Cara gives me a smile over the top of Andrew's head. Small waves crash against the barnacle-covered pilings of the dock ahead of us.

It's not until we've been standing in silence together for almost a minute that I feel something in my chest. Like it's easier to breathe. I take the salty air into my lungs, deeply. It's relief.

We've finally made it; after everything, we're here.

But before I can get too excited, I remember everything that brought us here and my shoulders slump. My eyes sting with tears and suddenly a sob racks my chest. I clamp a hand over my mouth, trying to stifle the sound, and fail. Andrew and Cara both turn to me and for a moment I'm embarrassed. I don't want to explain the mixture of relief, love and sadness I feel all at once.

But when I look at them, I know I don't have to.

Neither has a curious look on their faces. And if anything, they both seem to understand. Andrew reaches up to me, cupping my face with his hands. I close my eyes and let the tears fall, lowering my forehead to his.

'It's OK,' he whispers to me. His voice barely above the sound of the waves. 'We're going to be OK.'

When he kisses me, my chest feels lighter again, like he's taking on some of my sorrow but passing on some of his love. Evenly distributed like the supplies that have been in our packs during this journey. And I remember those first days out from the cabin when he was limping and I carried more. Or when I was injured and he carried everything. That's how we've survived together.

I nod as Andrew pulls away, still holding my face in his hands.

'We're going to be OK,' I repeat to him.

If things get hard again, I'll carry him. And he'll carry me. And we'll be OK.

EPILOGUE

The sun is already setting but he still isn't home. I push open the back door and look out to the ocean. There he is, standing at the end of the dock again. I close the door behind me and start walking out to the beach. I call out his name, but he doesn't hear me over the waves.

He's been doing this a lot lately. Like he's out here trying to savour this moment: the smell of the salt air, the sound of the water against the pilings, the purple clouds in the sky. To memorise it and keep it for ever. Because it might not be our for ever.

It's October 14 now and the hurricane season has stayed mild, so we probably could have left weeks ago. The waters are getting cooler, which some of the weather nerds say means less chance of storms.

We're supposed to leave to get Henri in two weeks or so. Both of us, Cara and a group of four others. They've already taken us out and given us a few sailing lessons. Cara's a natural, aside from the whole seasickness part.

I put my hands around his waist and he startles.

'You're still out here,' I whisper into his ear. Then I kiss behind it. 'You coming in?'

'In a bit.'

I don't let him go and just feel his warm body against mine in the cool autumn wind off the ocean.

'We don't have to come back,' I tell him. We've talked about it a lot in the past few months. We whisper in the bed we share at night. He says it might be better that way. We've both learned that we can survive without this community. And our being here might become an issue sooner rather than later. The world has gotten so small, it's only a matter of time before communication starts between the settlements of survivors that have been popping up. Including Fort Caroline.

We had a good thing going in the cabin. Just us.

It's so much harder to live in this new world. The meek didn't inherit the earth after all. Those people who scramble for power, regardless of who is hurt in the process, are still around. And if nothing else, they're working harder than ever.

Sometimes I think he's right. We should just go north, see that Henri gets on a boat home to her daughter, and leave. There will always be people like Fort Caroline.

But other times . . .

'I know,' he says. He turns and pulls me close. His sweater smells like him and it makes me even warmer. 'I like it here.'

'So do I.' Other times I love the people we've met here. The friends we've made. The safety we feel.

'But after everything . . .' His voice trails off, but he doesn't need to finish his sentence. It's all old hat. This place is much better than Fort Caroline, that's true. We both believe that.

The past few weeks, I've been thinking about the idea of progress. All the progress the world made in the past hundred years or so, gone with a sneeze. Progress halted and possibly reversed. Reversed if people don't fight for it, if we don't remember what we had and hold on to it.

There's a risk to living here. A risk that one day one of the settlements we trade with is going to turn against us. That Fort Caroline is going to expand outwards and find us here. That our own settlement is going to change their minds on who deserves to stay. That the flu will find a way to mutate and return worse than before. There's a lot at stake for everyone.

Sometimes I'm not sure the risk is worth it. Neither is he.

I have moments where my stomach will drop, my chest might tighten, all the dark thoughts cloud my mind. What if Fort Caroline isn't the only settlement with white supremacy on their minds? What if people can't speak out against injustice – or what was considered injustice before all this – because they need help from a community? What if everything continues to spiral downwards and history repeats itself because the people who are here to write it choose how it's written? They know what to put in and what to leave out; what to teach and what to ignore. Suddenly everything feels so hopeless.

But then I look at him; I hear his laugh, I see his smile, and the darkness melts away. Then I do have hope – even just for a little while – because I know that there is something in this world I can fight for. Something I *will* fight for if I have to.

Which always brings us back to the question: do we stay? Knowing that everything could come down on us, and on the people here, do we hope? Do we fight?

Or do we run? Go back to the woods and our home and hide; but know there, away from whatever is rebuilt in civilisation's image, we might be safer? At the cabin we know security isn't an illusion because it's just us. We'll work out whatever we have to with Howard's people and stay on our own.

Does that make us cowards, and do I care? I said I was willing to fight for him, but I want to live for him, too. I want us both to live. If I'm willing to fight for him, it means there are other people out there who have something worth fighting for, too.

I kiss him. 'We still have time to decide.'

'I know.'

I'm scared and I'm angry and those worrisome thoughts return. All the horrible things that could happen to us. But then he puts his arm around me and I feel safe again. We stay like that past the sunset. The tide's coming in now and the stars are coming out. I rub his back and motion with my head for us to go inside. Moving in sync, we turn and walk to the house.

We'll talk about this many more times in the next couple of weeks. But for tonight, it's done.

Tonight, it's just us.

AUTHOR'S NOTE

Why did I write a pandemic book? I know the reason I gave when my editor first offered on the novel you hold in your hands and it hasn't changed (though many other things have): I was tired of not seeing queer representation in post-apocalyptic stories. And that's what this book is.

A post-apocalyptic story.

Editing *All That's Left in the World* over the last two years has been a difficult balancing act. What I originally wrote in 2015 had to be altered because it was reading false. The superflu in this book wasn't meant to be Covid-to-the-extreme. It was its own fictional creature.

When Balzer + Bray in the US and Hachette Children's in the UK decided in March of 2020 to publish this book, I wanted *nothing* about Covid in these pages because we were all living through it together. Why add in real-world pandemic moments when this was always supposed to be escapist fiction? Why even bring up Covid at all?

But the longer Covid went on, the more irresponsible it seemed to try to ignore its impact on our world and not include something about it in the novel. I was torn between making this an alternate reality where Covid never happened and Andrew and Jamie's world never learned the lessons from that, or having it take place in a near-future after Covid, where even the lessons the world learned couldn't protect us from this new deadly virus.

So I came back to the balancing act. How much reality do I put in the fiction? I tweaked this – with the help and understanding of my editorial team – all the way up to the last possible second (Timestamp: 1:57 p.m. on November 8, 2021). While there are brief references to Covid as a part of the characters' histories, the similarities end there.

I've tried to approach the subject with as much sensitivity as possible, but this is a post-apocalyptic novel. It's sad, it's scary, it's thrilling. But hopefully you also laughed, or shook your head and smiled, or even got full-on heart-eyed stomach butterflies.

Like I said, I wrote *All That's Left in the World* as a story of two teens finding hope after surviving a pandemic. I didn't realise by the time it was published the theme would be universal.

Have hope, be safe, and help keep others safe.

ACKNOWLEDGEMENTS

I feel like acknowledgements are for writers and the people that are mentioned in them, but I do hope you'll read about these people who have helped bring this book to your hands as they deserve about as much credit as I do.

First to my wonderful dream agent, Michael Bourret, who plucked me from the slush pile and managed to recite to me – verbatim – my exact thoughts on this book without me having to say it aloud. I can't thank you enough for your wisdom, support, and instincts. Timing, too. And thanks to everyone else at Dystel, Goderich & Bourret including Michaela Whatnall, Lauren Abramo, Andrew Dugan, and Kemi Faderin. Thanks also to Ben Fowler, Anna Carmichael, and Felicity Amor at Abner Stein for representing me overseas.

To my wonderful editors who worked so brilliantly together to help get this messy work into shape. To my US editor Kristen Daly-Rens at Balzer + Bray, in the immortal words of Whitney Houston, 'I have nothing . . . if I don't have you.' From our first call together I was so excited to work on this book with you.

My UK editor Tig Wallace at Hachette Children's, your enthusiasm and support – as well as your comments that made me laugh aloud – mean the world. Don't forget, you owe me cringe stories. I'm keeping track. And thank you also to Amina Youssef at Simon & Schuster Children's.

At Balzer + Bray, I also want to recognize the work of editorial assistant Christian Vega, who I am certain is one of the key reasons deadlines were always met; designer Chris Kwon, who made this book look so much more beautiful than I ever could have imagined; and to illustrator Na Yeon Kim, who brought Andrew and Jamie to life for the absolutely gorgeous US cover! Thank you to the copyediting and managing editorial team including Caitlin Lonning and Alexandra Rakaczki for catching errors in grammar and plot – if there are any errors left, sorry, that's my bad. Allison Brown in production, Michael D'Angelo in marketing, and Mitch Thorpe in publicity. Thank you all!

And an extra special thanks to Alessandra Balzer and Donna Bray for their enthusiasm and support for not only my book, but every book they choose to publish. Balzer + Bray has been putting out amazing, groundbreaking children's books for over a decade and I'm so honored to be a part of this imprint.

At Hachette Children's, I want to thank Michelle Brackenborough for designing the stunning UK cover (and including a very special truck!) and Luke Martin at Suburban Avenger Studios for the beautiful illustration, Laura Pritchard for desk editing, Beth McWilliams in marketing, Lucy Clayton in publicity, Helen Hughes in production, and the entire sales team: Jen Hudson, Nic Goode, Minnie Tindall, Sinead White, and Jemimah James.

You all made this debut author a little less anxious, so thank you so much!

And thank you, kind reader. If you were able to purchase this book, borrow or request it from a library, even if you received it as a gift, you helped support all of the hardworking individuals that I just mentioned.

To the people who read early drafts of this novel and still expressed such enthusiasm: Kieryn Ziegler, Hannah Fergeson, Alexandra Levick, Molly Cusick, Sylvan Creekmore, and Alice Jerman. You all provided so much advice and thoughtful feedback, and you were integral to the development of this book.

Extra special thank you to my favorite beta reader, cheerleader, and wonderful friend, Erika Kincaid, who gave me the best advice in an early draft: 'They kiss too early, don't let it happen until the end.' The slow-burn romance fans thank you greatly.

Amy Ignatow read a semi-final draft and gave such intense and profound feedback that I believe both HarperCollins and Hachette Children's Group should be reaching out to her shortly with a job offer.

Katherine Locke helped whip the query for this novel into shape. They did such an outstanding job you'll find much of it still remains – albeit shorter – as the descriptive copy of this book!

To the Philly Kidlit Group who gave me advice and encouragement and celebrated wins with me. I miss our monthly Low Groggeries and look forward to resuming them in the near and healthy future.

To the good doctors, Dr. Nosheen Jawaid and Dr.

Benjamin Clippinger, who provided the best medical advice to keep Andrew and Jamie alive in the apocalypse. If I got anything wrong, that's on my misunderstanding, and they'll never let me live it down.

Thank you so much to everyone who read and supported this book early on, especially the talented, wonderful authors who agreed to blurb the book.

To my earliest fans and leaders of the Erik J. Brown Fan Club: Naz Kutub (President), Brian Kennedy (Vice President), Susan Lee (American Gladiator), and Anna Gracia (Badass M.C.)

The 22Debuts who have been such an amazing group of supportive authors and, of course, Jason Momoa.

To my wonderful friends who know nothing about publishing, which allowed me to celebrate every milestone of this book when I couldn't talk about it: Brandon McMullin, Kellie Clark, Maureen Belluscio, Bob Gurnett, Brittany Young, Allie Beik, Tim Davis, Nick Biddle, Waleed Yousef, Melissa Marsili, Caddy Herb, Deven Snyder, Kristin Stever, Bob Morgan, and so many others too numerous to name, but absolutely zero thanks to Jon Keller (YOU KNOW WHAT YOU DID.)

To John Brown, Sean, Jamie, Ryan, Ethan, Nolan, and Dylan Brown, Stephanie Sullivan, Sean Mclean, Hunter Brown, Eileen Johnson, Aaron Keels and the rest of my wonderful extended family on all sides for their support and love.

My grammy Margaret Keels. I genuinely can't express how sad I am you never got to read this book, but you told me so many times how proud you were of me. And

I know that you still are.

My mother, Ann Marie Brown, to whom this book is dedicated and the reason I'm a writer. When things didn't go my way when I was little, you used to sing 'You Can't Always Get What You Want' while I cried in the mall parking lot. And you'd emphasise that if I tried sometimes, I'd get what I need. One thing the Rolling Stones don't mention is how important support is in trying to get what we need. You have always supported me and told me that the things I thought impossible were possible. Thank you, and I love you.

Finally, to Michael Miska, the most supportive and loving partner in the world. You never treated my writing as just a hobby. And never once in our relationship did you express any doubt that I could do this, and that's why I will always love you.

And for the record: Dolly Parton.

ALSO AVAILABLE AS AN AUDIOBOOK